FLAMES

The Inferno Series

Emalie Brannigan

Copyright © 2020 by Emalie Brannigan

All rights reserved. This book or any portion thereof may not be reproduced or used in any manner whatsoever without the express written permission of the publisher except for the use of brief quotations in a book review.

Print ISBN: 978-1-09831-484-2

eBook ISBN: 978-1-09831-485-9

Dedicated lovingly to Mom. Without your patience, love, and understanding, this series would have driven me insane. Thank you for everything.

"It is those unafraid of the heat from their flames who become the inferno."

CHAPTER 1

For Peter.

We—Charles Woobi, Eric Stellenzer, David Woobi, and I—took our collective second step away from the Society; the crunch of the green vegetation under my shoes felt wrong, and I twisted back, only to lock eyes with Caleb Woobi, leader of the Society himself. The upturned corner of his mouth rushed cold dread down my spine, and I narrowed my eyes to steady myself against the uneasiness of his gaze.

Peter. I'm leaving Peter.

The paralyzing fear that coursed through my body at the notion must've been noticeable because Caleb's sinister smile grew larger. Memories of my brother—now forced to be Caleb's prisoner—almost caused me to sprint back into the warm familiarity of the Society, but a loud fizzing sound reverberating around the trees stopped me before I could move. I hesitantly looked up toward the sky to see the boundary of the Society—a beige, electromagnetic field that would cause instantaneous disintegration if touched—forming around what I had once considered my home. I didn't stop glaring at Caleb's figure until the boundary sizzled with the grass, and the entirety of the Society was distorted from view once again, signaling the distinct separation between everything I had ever known, and me.

Mr. Woobi insisted we continue moving forward and began maneuvering through the trees, the three of us falling into step right behind him. A sudden gust of wind forced goosebumps to erupt along my arms, and I became acutely aware of the horrendous state of my clothes, tattered and ripped from the blade I used to cut a sling for my injured shoulder and splattered with blood, blood from people I had once loved.

I watched as Nelly's eyes rolled back into her skull and she slumped down to the cement. Dead. Another gunshot. Alvin hit the ground, blood trickling out from the side of his head. Another gunshot. Anna toppled over, her once bright, shining eyes now drained of life. Another gunshot. Another coworker. Then another. Then another. Then another.

My coworkers were all dead, and their blood stained my flesh. How badly I wanted to rip it off to avoid feeling the sting of their goodbyes.

But I couldn't afford to think that way, not when I had an older man, an infuriatingly unaware ex-Uniform, and an unstable best friend to look after.

I returned to reality when I heard Dave hiss in pain and saw his hands twitch. I latched onto his upper arm to stop him from going any farther and asked, "Are you hurt?"

"Not badly," he assured, but I didn't believe him.

There was another thing I couldn't believe: David *Woobi*. Just the thought of it was revolting. He was the son of the man who had tried to kill his grandfather, the grandson of the man who had sent my brother away to gather seemingly useless information on his broken family. *A Woobi.* I desperately wanted to finally ease Dave's searching and tell him the truth about his family, but Mr. Woobi's warning was still fresh in my mind:

"He'll be lost, confused, unhappy—everything I know you know he is not."

The idea of losing the Dave I knew then—positive, uplifting, enthusiastic Dave—was so terrifying that I kept my mouth tightly sewn shut, if not for his sake, then for mine.

"Zelda, David, come here," Eric commanded, breaking my chain of thoughts.

I saw that he and Mr. Woobi had stopped, and upon advancing closer, I too glanced down to view a ten-foot drop down to rushing, dangerous water with pointy, caramel brown rocks jutting out of its depths and splitting the water into foam. The mist the water produced covered the gorge, but I could still see the land on the other side. The thought of being enclosed shook me more than anything else. "Is there any way around it?" I asked no one in particular.

"No," Mr. Woobi exclaimed, pointing to a certain point in the water where the current seemed strongest. "See how the water gushes like that?" We all nodded, and he continued, "That's a pipe feeding this river. This is all man-made to keep us in, and the others out. It wraps around the Society completely, all 360 degrees of it. Caleb built it as a precaution. It's controlled by Caleb."

It was difficult to imagine that there were, in fact, other people beyond the Society, but I chose to ignore that, instead opting to turn my attention to Eric, who had freely sprawled out onto the grass and played with a blade of it between his fingers. "So, we're stuck here until we can find a way out," he restated with his nose scrunched up in displeasure. "Because the water would sweep us up if we tried to swim across it, and those rocks would kill us for sure."

"Looks that way," Mr. Woobi answered, but I refused to believe it.

"I will not allow us to be stopped by water. We just need to come up with a plan to stop it from killing us," I said.

"And how do you propose we do that, Zelda Ellyn?" Mr. Woobi snapped. "There's nothing we can use to block the pipe, and even if there was, the water pressure would overcome any barricade we might conjure up. Our best bet is to wait it out."

"Wait it out?" Eric repeated, sounding incredulous. "You think Leader Caleb is just going to let us go like that?"

"It's what he wants," I announced, thinking back to my last conversation with Caleb Woobi:

"I suppose now it is time for you to learn. Leave. Go. And if you do come back as you say you will, you will understand what I am talking about. They want a war, Zelda Jadestone. They've been desperately searching for that spark to ignite their fire, and unfortunately for the both of us, with your words and your passion and your spirit, I'm afraid they're about to find it."

"Caleb *wanted* me to leave the Society. He wouldn't completely stop me now."

"He wants us to beg," Mr. Woobi elaborated. "There's no food on this side, and I'm not convinced that the water is safe to drink. He'll let us go once we're begging for mercy."

As if on cue, my stomach growled, and I became acutely aware of how dry and pasty my mouth tasted.

"If I had known there wasn't going to be any food, I would *not* have left," Eric groaned, and it was difficult to tell if he was joking or not.

"There must be something," Dave argued, his rounded, blond eyebrows knitted in distress. "If there was an emergency evacuation, the citizens would all die out here. It would be stupid to not have anything to eat, or at least to survive on."

"You really think Leader Caleb is that smart?" retorted Eric, and no one had the energy to protest.

Silence ate away the minutes we stood there beside the trees, wondering how we were supposed to survive this new reality. No one dared to move, let alone speak, and by the time I started to get antsy, the grass had developed a golden tint to it that twinkled like little sparks ready to catch ablaze. The sky had changed from the color of Mr. Woobi's eyes—an icy, medium blue—to a radiant, bold orange, with twinges of reds, yellows, and pinks intermingling with the fluffy, gray clouds. The sun's perimeter bled a fiery orange into the sky, but the middle shone white, as if the heat had burned all the colors away.

"It's beautiful," I whispered, unable to tear my eyes away from the sight of the sun lowering itself onto the horizon.

Mr. Woobi wobbled over until he was within distance to place a comforting hand on my shoulder. "I haven't seen this view in over fourteen years," remarked Mr. Woobi, and the thickness behind his voice did not go unnoticed.

Mr. Woobi, Dave, and I chose to sit near Eric then, content with watching the sun's light bounce off the bark of the trees and gleam from the shivering leaves. I scooted closer to Dave and laid my head on his shoulder as he placed his head on mine, and Mr. Woobi fell back to look directly above at the colors. The sharp red intensified, curling itself around the clouds like a snake does its prey, and it drenched the four of us in spectacular technicolor, rendering us as mere shadows passing through this forest we were now supposed to call home.

No one dared disrupt the silence, and it wasn't until indigo blue crept its way into the sky that Dave whispered, "Goodnight, sun," under his breath.

I smiled softly at the suggestion. "Goodnight, sun," I mouthed to myself, and for the rest of the time, we sat and watched the world turn from red to black.

It was once we were all swathed in darkness and silence that I really began to process everything that had transpired. "We left the Society," I stated, my eyes wide in disbelief and a hint of fear.

"Yes," assured Eric.

"I left my brother." *He never got to hear me say I loved him back.*

It took the group a bit longer to affirm that, and even a reluctant Dave ultimately had to agree.

"And…" The horrific images forming in my mind made me wince. "And we killed people." There was no "yes" to that, but there didn't have to be; I already knew the truth. Behind the shield of my eyelids, I saw first Nelly, then Alvin, then Anna, then the rest of my coworkers kneel to the bullets that struck their heads. I saw innocent civilians of the Society collapse to the concrete, grasping their wounds while their faces twisted in agony before becoming nothing more than flesh, muscles, and bones. I saw one Uniform after another pummel the ground as Blake Yandle fired away inside my workplace.

Noises accompanied these visions. I heard Leader Caleb chuckling at my suffering with a chilling, evil laugh. I heard crying, sobbing, and shrieking that always seemed to precede death. But above the cacophony of noise, I heard my name. It rang around and around and around my head, engulfing it like flames. The crowd chanted it. The Uniforms spat it out. Peter yelled it.

Zelda. They run after me, clawing their way up my skin until they stab my heart.

Zelda. They taunt me with my name, making sure I know what I have done to them.

Zelda. He tries to reach me; his voice echoes in my mind, trying to get to me, but somehow, I know it never will.

I hadn't realized my screeching until I opened my eyes to meet Dave's electric-blue ones, our noses pressed together. "You're okay," he kept on telling me, moving his hands up to cup my face. Shivers ran up my spine and into my neck, but I didn't know if they were caused by Dave's touch, the coldness of the air, or the images and sounds that ran rampant in my head. All three, perhaps. My hands had become cold and somewhat clammy as I shook violently and started to calm down. Looking around at everyone's expressions—Mr. Woobi's understanding, Dave's fear, Eric's concern—I apologized, but they all insisted there was nothing for which to apologize. They were right, in a sense; I shouldn't apologize to them, but instead to everyone who died in my name.

But you can't, hissed the voice inside my head, and that was what caused the ache building inside my chest.

Mr. Woobi suggested we get some sleep for the night, and the boys agreed, but I knew I wouldn't be able to sleep. Instead, I lay down on the soft grass and gazed up at the specks of light that littered the dark night sky, watching the way they winked with a new kind of terror. What would we eat, come tomorrow? My stomach rumbled so loudly, it hurt. When would I have something to drink? The temptation to fall into the river just for a sip of water was almost overpowering, but knowing Caleb had control over the river was enough to steer me away. Would my coworkers be given a proper cremation ceremony, or would Caleb sweep their ashes away like they were leftover food scraps? A memory struck me then, one of the twelve of us wrapped in a hug, collectively mourning Jack's assassination, and I stupidly wished on the stars for them to be here with me, able to witness something as spectacular as the colors of a sunset, or as simple as saying goodnight to the sun.

I stood back up and walked over to the edge of the gorge, allowing my legs to dangle over the rushing water. Sprays of river water caught onto the hair on my shins and gave me goosebumps, but I couldn't bring myself to move. Memories slammed into me in waves, memories of Nelly hooking her arm around mine; of Ruth braiding Jack's hair and giggling when he would sashay around the office; of Alvin speaking loudly at the lunch table and grinning with pride when the rest of us would erupt into laughter. Memories I'd never get to relive.

I ripped some grass out by its roots and tossed blades of grass into the river, each one representing a coworker and what I wished I could tell them if they were sitting next to me now.

Nelly. I wished for her to never lose that bubbly, vivacious personality or that wonderfully loud belly-laugh that could make just about anybody smile. I wished for her to understand that she was the closest thing to a best friend that I had, save for Eric. I wished for her to know that I loved her, even if I didn't show it.

Alvin. I wished he would keep the confidence I knew he earned. I wished for him to know how brave he was, and, I added with a trace of a smile, I wished for him to know how much Anna admired him.

Anna. I wished for her to know how loud her kindness was, even if her words were not.

Irene. I wished for her to know how motherly she was, from helping us with organizing our equipment to being a shoulder for Nelly to cry on when Eric respectfully declined Nelly's invitation to have dinner with her. I wished for her to know that she didn't need to hide her crooked teeth when she smiled because her smile could've brightened the entire laboratory.

Gabriel. I wished for him to know how endearing I found his blond, curly hair, or how smart I thought he was. I wished for him to know that

I'll miss his chirpy good mornings and I'll miss his solemn goodbyes until forever ends.

Agatha. I wished for her to know how helpful she was because I remembered the way she lit up whenever someone appreciated her good work. I wished for her to know that her generosity inspired all of us to care for each other like a family.

Jeremy. I wished for him to understand that strength radiated from him, even in his last breath. Strength shows in shielding your friends' bodies when a bullet strikes your lungs, and strength shows in handing your coworker half your sandwich when hers goes missing in the cafeteria on a random day in May.

Ruth. I wished for her to know that her gift in the visual arts was astounding, and I wished for her to feel the pride that swelled in our chests every time she would show us a new doodle at lunch. I wished for her to know her talent never went unnoticed.

José. I wished for him to know the kind of joy he brought to our group, sometimes by just being there.

Elizabeth. I wished for her to know that although we would groan at her snapping at us for "getting off task," we appreciated her for keeping us in line and focused. I wished for her to keep that power she had.

Joseph. I wished for him to know that he had a home with us, even if he had no one to go back to when the workday ended. When Peter left, he and I bonded over that, and I wished for him to know how he could feel accepted when he was with us.

Jack. I wished for him to know that he was the stupidest, most aggravating, most frustrating, most generous, happiest, *bravest* soul I had ever encountered, and I wished his death wouldn't define him because there was so much more to him than his end.

By the time I had said my goodbyes to all my coworkers, there was a single blade of grass left in my grip, and as the wind whipped my hair into a tangled brown mess, I thought of Peter. My little brother. The last person left in my family. And as I dropped that last spade of grass into the river, I wished for him to know that I love him, that I'm sorry for having left him, and that I would return to him at any cost.

"They're called stars," said Dave as he came over to sit beside me, startling me so much I almost fell into the river. "Charles told me that the lights in the sky are stars."

I closed my eyes and strained not to think about my coworkers-turned-family, murdered at Caleb's instructions; about Peter, all alone in that Society; about the innocent civilians who fought against the Uniforms when my speech to save Mr. Woobi ignited them; but that was impossible. Dave lay down, and I followed suit. "Stars, you say?" I asked to try and distract myself.

Zelda. It was a soft calling I fought hard to ignore.

"Yep," chirped Dave in his usual happy voice. "I bet there're over a million up there. What do you think?"

Zelda. The whisper had turned into a shout that I tried to swallow down.

"Oh, I think there are more than that," I croaked, shutting my eyes to block the sound filling my ears, the images clouding my brain, and the mental pain splitting me apart. Dave placed his hands up and underneath his head like a barrier between it and the ground; I took it as an opportunity to place my elbows out in the same fashion but with my hands covering my ears in an attempt to stop the voices, but that only intensified them into screams.

Zelda! Zelda! Zelda!

"Do you think anyone has ever touched one?" He wondered aloud in a dreamy voice, but it sounded so far away, the chanting and the yelling and the screaming overpowering every sense of mine until I drowned in my own name. *Zelda!* I curled up into Dave's figure, pressing my face firmly against his side so he couldn't hear me scream or see me cry. *Zelda!* He took one of my hands—both clenched tightly into fists on top of his chest—began to knead it until it opened, and massaged my palm, planting kisses to it from time to time. Dave's actions relaxed me a little, but the pulsating sensation that had exploded behind my eyeballs ruined the effect. *Zelda!* It wasn't until I accidentally bit his side in an effort to keep my shrieks at bay that he turned my face to look at his. I saw Dave's eyes go from contentment to concern as he took in my tear-stained cheeks and the haunted look in my dark eyes. I didn't have to explain; he knew.

Before I could really protest, he turned on his side and wrapped his large, strong arms around my fragile frame to stop the shudders going up and down my body. "Everything will be fine," he whispered against my hair, but I could make no other sound but a moan in response.

"I… I l-left him," I choked out between sobs. "How could I do that? He's my brother, and I abandoned him because I was too scared to die! People in the crowd died chanting *my* name, Dave! I killed my friends! It's all my fault!" I pounded my fists against his broad chest, but he restrained my wrists before I could do any real damage.

"It was not your fault," he declared. "None of this is your fault. Peter chose to leave. It was the mob's idea to storm that stage and get into fights with the Uniforms. It was Leader Caleb who killed your coworkers, Zelda. Don't blame yourself for things out of your control."

"But they were in my control," I told him, not wanting to elaborate.

Dave chose to not argue with me, just kissed my head one last time before helping me stand up. "Are you okay now?"

"Just a bit cold," I admitted sheepishly. The voices had reduced to dull whispers, and I was scared for the silence to return. They always seemed to return or grow louder in the silence.

Dave smiled and gave a short-lived chuckle. "Here, you can have my jacket." I averted my gaze while he was taking it off, but I couldn't help but peek through my fingers when he laughed out loud. "You don't have to cover your eyes while I'm taking off a jacket, silly," he teased.

I felt my face grow hot in embarrassment before turning around sharply as Dave opened the jacket up for me to shrug into. "I didn't know if you had a shirt on underneath," I mumbled, crossing my arms and not looking at him when he had walked around my body to face me.

"It's not like you wouldn't see anything you don't like," he joked further, throwing a wink my direction for good measure.

"You're not funny," I snapped at him, but to my surprise, I had to fight the grin that wanted to form on my face.

"Would you two shut up?!" Eric shouted, but I could hear the smile in his voice. "I'm trying to sleep over here."

Dave rolled his eyes, yelled back, "Yes, sir!" and winked at me once more. "That's our cue," he whispered in my ear before kissing it sloppily.

"Ew! David!" I wiped my ear with the back of my hand, and he shot me one more quick look over his shoulder before walking away to lay down relatively close to Mr. Woobi.

I didn't bother trying to sleep, so I found myself once again sitting on the precipice of the river, playing with the container of red pills I had stolen from the Society right before we escaped. I knew the blinding pain the pills caused as they eradicated memories from one's brain. I was nervous that if Eric, Dave, or especially Mr. Woobi found them, he would get the wrong impression. I wasn't going to use them on myself or anyone in our little troop; I had taken them in order to save everyone else in the Society from enduring the mind-altering drugs. If Caleb had found the capsules in my old office after investigating it, which I knew he would, he would have mass-produced them and given them out to the entire Society in order to forget what I had done in the Main Square to save Mr. Woobi. Without much consideration, I swung my arm and happily watched as the container drowned in the raging waters.

After several minutes of sitting by the river and listening to the constant slap of the waves against the rocks below, I walked back to stand over Eric's body, wrapping my arms around my midsection as the drone of those voices in my head began once again.

Zelda. Zelda. Zelda.

"Can't sleep, Zelda?" Eric murmured when I wasn't necessarily looking at his perfectly chiseled face, and I jumped at the sudden sound.

"No," I grunted like a child.

Eric rolled onto his stomach to push off from the ground, and before I could ask what he was doing, he asked me to follow him to the base of a nearby tree. We nestled between two of the tree's large, sturdy roots, sitting so close our sides clicked perfectly against each other. He wrapped one arm around my shoulder protectively, and I snuggled slightly into his embrace, immediately feeling that warm tingling that started in my chest and fizzed out to the tips of my toes. "I've got you," he whispered once we were settled against the tree's trunk, and I somehow knew that would always be true.

Just as I had feared, the crowd, the Uniforms, my coworkers, and Peter all made a reappearance the moment my eyelids closed. *Zel—No!* "Eric?"

He shifted around to the sound of my voice. "Yeah?"

"My friends died today."

Eric sighed a defeated, heavy sigh. "Yeah."

"They're haunting me," I confessed. *Zelda. Zeld—No!*

"Me too."

"We left the Society today." The wind threatened to whisk my words away before Eric could hear them. "I'm scared of Caleb and what he can do to us, and to Peter."

Eric tilted his face to look at me directly. "I'm going to tell you what we're going to do, okay?" Once I had nodded, he proclaimed, "We're going to find a way to cross this stupid river, and we're going to eat to rebuild our strength. Then, we're going to find a way back into the Society, free Peter, and live happily ever after. How does that sound?"

"It sounds too good to be true," I answered honestly, dropping my head down to rest against his shoulder.

"You know, sometimes the truth needs to be just a little too good, so we have something to strive for."

I nodded in response, and there was a fleeting moment when I thought he had fallen asleep before he whispered, "I know you're thinking about our friends, Zelda."

Zelda. Zelda. Zel—No! I hadn't noticed I had flinched until Eric squeezed his arm in reassurance around my shoulders.

"This is going to be difficult for the both of us." Eric finished his next thought with a shudder: "I'm scared of myself and what I can do to other people without really thinking about it."

"I'm not scared of you, Eric," I told him as I tilted my face up to try and look into his eyes, but he shied away from my gaze.

There was an awkward, lengthy pause before he finally spoke again. "You were, though, in that room. I saw your face when you looked at me. You... you were horrified at the man I am capable of becoming, and so am I, even if it was an accident. I'm sorry."

The crack of the first bullet leaving Eric's weapon caused me to jump back, and I helplessly watched as it sliced the air and struck an unsuspecting Uniform in the chest... I could only watch Eric as he stared at his hands, which were trembling incredibly, and whispered to himself: "What have I done?"

The memory terrified me, but not as much as the lifelessness in the Uniform's eyes even before Eric accidentally pulled the trigger. "Don't apologize," I spoke to him in the soft voice I saved for intimate moments like these. "We both killed people today."

"You didn't kill our friends, Zelda."

"And you didn't kill that Uniform, Eric. He was dead long before your finger slipped. But we still *feel* like it was our fault, and I think that's a burden we're both going to have to carry from now on."

"Maybe we can carry it together."

Inwardly, I smiled at the sweet way his sleep-riddled voice uttered the suggestion, but I didn't say anything until I was sure his soft snores told me he had fallen into exhaustion. I snuggled closer to his tall frame, exhaled contently, and couldn't stop myself from whispering, "Yeah, maybe we can carry this together," before allowing the tiredness to seep into my bones and claim me for the night.

CHAPTER 2

I see her fall to the ground. I see her eyes widen in terror before the life drains out of them. I see her face blanch when a bullet contacts her flesh.. I hear bullets flying from their guns before cracking against men. I hear yells that transform into screams that transform into cries for help. I hear my name, sometimes soft like a prayer, other times loud and screechy like a newborn baby, most times pleading and desperate like a prisoner crying out for his sanity. I feel Peter's hands around one ankle, Nelly clinging to the other, both of them trying to drag me down into a world unknown. I feel my hands tremble as I hold my hands out for Eric to grab onto so he can pull me away from the people I left behind, but the more he tries to reach me, the farther we seem to get from each other. I feel Mr. Woobi's scream—a man lost in his own world—vibrate inside my ears, making me want to scream, too, but I can make no sound; Dave's hand covers my mouth and nose, trapping me in my own mind.

I woke with an unexpected jolt, and the sudden action caused Eric to stir beside me; I carefully wiggled out from under his arm so as to not wake him. My back protested at the small movement, and it took several minutes of cracking my vertebrae and stretching my muscles before I was even capable of sitting upright. My stomach grumbled loudly at the lack of food, and I bent over to try and appease the piercing sensation in my abdomen. My mouth felt like sandpaper, and little knives pierced the back of my throat from dryness as I attempted to swallow my saliva. My gunshot wound from the day before itched at the newly healed edges from the cream Blake Yandle had applied, but my arms were too short to reach up and alleviate the sensation.

I inhaled the crisp, cool morning air as a strong longing for my comfortable bed, perfectly cooked, preplanned meal, and easy access to water washed over me. I hated that I wished for my old life in the Society, but luckily Eric groaned before I could dwell on it any further. I turned just in time to see him cracking open his eyelids and wincing at the brightness of the morning sun.

"Wow, okay, so not the best sleep I've ever had," Eric muttered to himself, and I snorted in weak laughter.

I was about to retort when Mr. Woobi coughed wildly from his sleeping spot on the ground, sending Eric and me to spring up and rush over to see if we could help in any way. Dave immediately scrambled awake and ran over to aid as well, but Mr. Woobi waved his hand dismissively and coughed a few more times before looking at us with an apology already in his eyes.

"Well," Eric sliced the uncomfortable silence. "This sucks."

We all shared a collective breath of laughter before the bleakness of our situation became apparent once more. I could see worry written on everyone's faces as the sun illuminated us more with each passing moment, and I was thankful when Dave finally asked the question we were probably all thinking: "What now?"

"We wait," answered Mr. Woobi. "There is nothing left to do." The elder's cool blue eyes swept over the three of us, pity forming in the wrinkles on his face, and it was then that I truly noticed his change in appearance since his re-arrest four months previous. The Societan emblem—two rings surrounding an "S"—was carved into his face, the top curve of the "S" sitting against the bridge of his now-crooked nose. His hair, once a salty gray, looked like a muddy Uniform jacket with its dirty whiteness. I felt sympathy for him, but the resentment bubbling underneath my skin when I thought about how he knew the reason behind Peter's abandonment four years before overpowered any pity I had managed to muster.

"I'm sorry," Mr. Woobi articulated, almost as if reading my thoughts. "You three are too young for any of this."

"I'm twenty," argued Eric. "I wouldn't call myself 'too young.'"

"I'm eighteen," I added.

"I'm eighteen, and I've dealt with worse things that just a little hunger," chimed Dave.

Mr. Woobi's stiff posture allayed at our responses. I saw how his gaze stayed on Dave, and for a second, I couldn't seem to catch my breath at the blatant love that radiated from his stare. "I know you were robbed of your childhoods," Mr. Woobi corrected himself. "But even if it's just for a day, you should know what fun feels like." At that, he got to his feet, waddled over to me, patted the top of my head, and yelled, "You're it!" before attempting to run away from me, walking cane in hand.

Dave, Eric, and I exchanged confused looks before Mr. Woobi, now a good ten yards away, shouted, "Zelda's it! We have to run before she catches us and *we're* it!"

Eric burst into laughter before he shrugged, rocketed to his feet, and sprinted away with Dave hot on his heels. At my stunned expression, Eric yelled, "C'mon, Zelda! Try to catch us!"

For a few moments, I was dumbfounded, watching with my mouth slightly agape at the way Dave and Eric purposefully crashed into each other, slapping one another on the back and throwing their heads back in loud laughter. Before I could really register what I was doing, I got up and dashed toward Dave, giggling when his face transformed into one of fear and he took off running away from me.

"Run, David!" Mr. Woobi bellowed, but I was faster than the ex-Uniform, and I was soon slapping Dave on the shoulder as we both came screeching to a halt.

He grinned when we paused for a split second, but the moment didn't last long; I stuck my tongue out at him playfully and challenged him to catch me before bolting in the opposite direction. I tried my best to avoid tree roots and ditches as I raced toward Eric, who vehemently advised against the two of us clumping together. We slammed into each other; Eric instinctually wrapped his arms around my abdomen to keep me from losing balance, and we both squealed when Dave charged in our direction and pushed Eric a good few feet away from me.

"*Try* to catch me, Stellenzer," Dave teased, already taking large strides away from the other boy.

"You're on, 125," retorted Eric, and the two of them took off again, chasing each other in circles.

I was panting and completely out-of-breath by then, so I took my little moment of rest to watch Mr. Woobi as he observed the way his grandson moved. Dave wasn't graceful in the slightest; he stumbled over exposed roots or his own feet every few steps, and his arms flopped loosely at his sides, almost as if he didn't know what to do with them. His goofy, lopsided grin accentuated the youth in his eyes, and I watched as Mr. Woobi's gaze never left the ex-Uniform as he laughed alongside Eric.

"I'm sorry he never got a childhood like this," Mr. Woobi attempted to say as evenly as he could, but the thickness in his voice alerted me to the tears cradled in the elder's eyes. "David. You. Eric. Peter. I'm sorry none of you got to live like real children."

Unbridled anger ripped through me at Peter's name on Mr. Woobi's tongue, but I kept myself in check long enough to say, "Yeah, well, his father took that away from him."

Mr. Woobi shook his head. "No. His father didn't have a choice."

The two of us turned our gazes away from Dave to look at each other, and even though the boys were quite out of earshot, I couldn't stop myself from lowering my voice to ask, "What happened, Mr. Woobi?" Again, Mr. Woobi shook his head, but I relentlessly demanded he explain, arguing that Dave was too far away to hear us and after declaring that *he,* my father figure, was the reason my little brother left me four years previous, I deserved answers. "You owe me an explanation," I proclaimed, and finally, Mr. Woobi relented.

He led me over to the base of a tree, where he sat down and leaned against the trunk. I joined him on the ground, and once we got comfortable, the older man brushed his wispy, wild hair away from his forehead, took a deep breath, and began:

"Caleb was an introverted child growing up: quiet, kept to himself, didn't enjoy socializing much at all, but my son was brilliant, so much so that I think he isolated himself. Your father, Owen Jadestone, was his first and only friend in school, and those two boys were absolutely inseparable. Owen's natural enthusiasm to talk made it easy for Caleb to slip into his shadow, I think, and Caleb, as far as I'm aware, was fine with that. During their childhoods, the war was brewing, and as one of the generals for the

Republic, I often brought work home with me, which I think sparked an interest in politics for both Owen and my son. Owen introduced Caleb to his debate class in junior high, and it was in high school debate class where Caleb met Juniper Monsella."

Monsella.

David Monsella. Juniper Monsella. Dave's mother.

The mental image of Caleb Woobi meeting Dave's future mother in such a normal, natural way almost made me laugh at its absurdity, but I composed myself for Mr. Woobi's sake, not wishing to interrupt.

"Caleb has never, and as far as I know, will never love anyone as deeply as he loved… *loves* Juniper Monsella," Mr. Woobi stated. "The two of them met when he was seventeen years old, got engaged six months later, wed when he was eighteen, and a month after, Juniper announced she was pregnant with David. Married and pregnant after a single year of knowing each other, and I had only met her once before." Mr. Woobi huffed, gray eyebrows knitted harshly in frustration. "At least your parents were childhood friends growing up, so their wedding was only a matter of time."

"Why the urgency?" I asked.

Mr. Woobi inhaled sharply, like my question had speared him. "The war, Zelda Ellyn, was practically at our doorstep. Bombs, gunfire, soldiers were just a daily routine, and Caleb despised it more than he hated anything else. Before Juniper, he had opinions about the war, about which side he favored, but after they met, his opinions were washed away. He just wanted the conflict to *end,* and he didn't care which side won, despite my position as a general. It became all about Juniper and the baby, Juniper and the baby, Juniper and the baby. Caleb was unhealthily obsessed with her, and—"

"I won!" Eric yelled triumphantly, and Mr. Woobi and I snapped back to reality to find Eric and Dave walking toward us with gigantic grins across each of their faces.

"In your dreams, Stellenzer. You're lucky I'm too tired to move right now," Dave retorted, coming over to sit on the grass beside me, but he winced in pain and hissed through his teeth the second he sat down. At everyone's questioning stares, he turned red and refused to acknowledge the pain he clearly suffered.

"I'm starving," Dave announced to the group.

We all nodded in agreement, and it was in that silence that I heard it again: *Zelda. Zelda. Zelda.*

The pain from my losses simmered under my skin, and I felt dirty, like an infection had crawled its way into every pore on my body. *How unfair it is,* I thought, *that I am alive, and they are either trapped, alone, or dead.* Dave's once-pristine Uniform jacket wrapped around my shoulders felt like a betrayal, but the warmth was too comforting to lose. I briefly wondered if Peter felt that way every time he dressed in the same uniform every morning.

Dave and Mr. Woobi, the former desperate for some semblance of nutrition, decided to at least try and search for food, leaving Eric and me to sit beside each other on the grass. It wasn't until Dave was completely out of earshot that Eric asked, "Can I talk to you?" in a hushed, urgent tone.

"Aren't you talking to me right now?"

Eric shot me an exasperated glance, and I offered a satisfied smirk in response. "Not funny, Zelda."

I shrugged. "Debatable."

The tips of Eric's ears turned an adorable shade of sunset pink, and he rubbed the back of his neck anxiously. "Do you like him?" he blurted.

I narrowed my eyes in confusion at the question. "Who?" I tilted my head in Dave's direction. "Dave?"

Eric nodded wordlessly, and I looked down to see him cracking the knuckles on his fingers nervously, his posture rigid and tense.

"Of course, I like him," I answered. "What kind of question is that?"

"I'm sorry, I—"

"It's kind of impossible not to."

"I guess," Eric sighed. "But—"

"Why?"

"I just—"

My eyes widened, and at my expression, Eric sat up straighter, raising his eyebrows in fear. "Do *you* not like Dave?" I asked.

Eric blinked once in shock, but he quickly recovered and shook his head vigorously. "No! What? No. Of course, I do. He's a great dude. I just… I… I don't know."

My palms began to sweat, and suddenly, anxiety swept over me, a different kind of anxiety with which I wasn't necessarily familiar. The nervous sincerity in Eric's forest-green eyes scared me more than it should've, and I felt that pull toward him again, the way a magnet attracts metal. My stomach flipped at how his face softened when we locked eyes, and I fought down the urge to run my fingers through his deep brown, soft hair. I flexed my fingers and discretely wiped the sweat on the front of my pants before stammering, "Why… why do you ask then?"

He held my gaze for a beat, then two, then three, and just as I was about to say *anything* to fill the silence, Eric lifted his mouth into a soft smile and muttered, "I just want you to be happy, Zelda."

"He makes me laugh," I proclaimed like it was some kind of pathetic explanation.

Eric indulged me by forcing a stuttered laugh, and my heart shuddered at the sound. "Me too," he said, and with that, he stood up, stretched his arms above his head, and feigned a yawn. "I'm exhausted."

"Me too," I answered.

Eric glanced down at me, and our eye contact felt new, like I was looking into his muted green eyes for the first time. When I visibly quivered from the sudden goosebumps, Eric arched a perfect, dark eyebrow. "You're cold, and you're wearing a Uniform jacket?"

A part of me wanted him to know *he* caused the shiver, that *his* gaze raised goosebumps down to my toes, but the words died in my throat. "Eric—"

"Yes?"

We collectively held our breath, watching each other's movements: the way his lips perked up in a reassuring-yet-reserved smile, the twitching of his hands, the tapping of his foot against the hard earth, the way I couldn't seem to stop fidgeting, the wind picking up my hair and tossing it around, the steady rise and fall of my chest. We stayed that way, studying one another, until Dave and Mr. Woobi came stumbling back over toward us, grumbling about the lack of food, and just like that, the moment was lost.

Hunger gnawed at the insides of my stomach when Mr. Woobi mentioned the noticeable lack of edible vegetation, but the sharpness of the pain from before had transformed into a pulsing ache. The overwhelming want to drink the river water dizzied me, and my head fought back against the current of exhaustion. My tiredness and conversation with Eric left me almost gasping for air, like I was chasing oxygen just for a taste of it. *Inhale. Exhale. Repeat.* The mantra strengthened me to focus on breathing, but even an act as simple as that made my bones quake in fatigue.

The roar of the river drew me once again to stand by the edge, but instead of watching the water swirl, my gaze traveled down to the other side, where people could've possibly been lurking, just out of reach. Caleb Woobi crossed my mind, and I lingered on the idea of him being a devoted father, infuriatingly dedicated to his little family to the point where neither the war mattered, nor the people who fought in it. The mental image of Caleb in love with anyone other than himself was as murky as the water below me, and I almost wanted to laugh at how foreign it seemed.

Dave clearing his throat made me turn around, and I scrutinized him for any similarity to his father. They both had golden blond hair, but Dave's was thicker, chopped short into a military-style cut from being a Uniform, whereas Caleb's was thin and greasy. Dave's electric-blue eyes contrasted with Caleb's deep brown; the former held an innocence unmatched to anything I had ever experienced before meeting him. Although Caleb still towered over Dave, the latter was much broader and more built.

I was so entranced in trying to work out how Caleb Woobi's son could've turned out to be the boy standing in front of me that I missed Dave's lips quirk up in a shy smirk, and I only broke out of my haze when he asked, "What?"

I shook my head. "What?"

"I asked you first."

I rolled my eyes. "You're insufferable."

Dave hummed, rocking back and forth on the heels of his striking red Uniform boots. "Am I insufferably cute, at least?"

"Unfortunately," I quipped, biting the inside of my cheek to keep from giggling.

Dave shrugged. "I can live with that."

"You just seem so much more...human, than the rest of the Uniforms." I wrinkled my nose at my confession, and I heard him chuckle beside me.

"You look disgusted by that," he commented.

"I can't make up my mind on whether or not that's a good thing."

"Let me know when you've decided," he joked, and that drew a rueful smile out of me.

The memory felt fake, like the girl who talked to Uniform number 125 that day wasn't me but someone else, someone who didn't know what his lips tasted like, someone who didn't know she would live long enough to find out.

Dave clicked his tongue against the roof of his mouth in mock-disapproval. "Still daydreaming about me?"

"Oh, please." My wobbly, high-pitched voice and the red heat spreading to my face betrayed me.

"Hm." His wicked grin threatened to tear his face in half. "Nice try, sweetheart, but I know when you're lying."

I took notice of the way the broad Uniform began bouncing on the balls of his feet, and I pointed it out, saying, "Do I make you nervous, Dave?"

"No." It was his turn to blush—something that rarely, if ever, happened—and he swiftly looked down at the ground. "Well… yeah. Kind of." He lifted his gaze then to lock eyes with me as he announced, "I just really want to kiss you right now, but I'm not sure how to… approach it."

I actually laughed out loud at how insanely endearing and ridiculous his statement sounded. "It's not like you haven't done it before," I countered.

He resumed bouncing in place, and the sheepish smile that crept onto his face reminded me of the first day we met. "Those were different, Zelda. We were sad, crazy, thinking we were going to die…" He shook his head and furrowed his blond eyebrows as if the memories stung his brain. "It's just different. I'm not sure how to approach you this time, when we're both sane, and conscious, and not thinking about our dead parents, or forgotten identity, or saving people, or—"

"Then forget those other times, Dave. Treat it like it was our first."

And he did. Coming close to me, he stopped just before we touched, brought his hands up to cup my face, and dropped his head so his forehead touched mine. The air that separated our lips was charged with the same electricity I felt the first time we had kissed, so long ago in that database back in the Society.

One second. Two seconds. Three. One heartbeat. Two heartbeats. Three. Inhale. Exhale. Repeat. I was beginning to wonder if Dave would ever work up the courage to kiss me before his lips were on mine, sweet and gentle and everything I knew Dave to be. I softly pressed back against his lips, content with letting my eyelids flutter closed.

"Take cover!"

Mr. Woobi's shrill warning caused Dave and me to jump apart just as a wave of explosions ripped through the dirt around us. Reds, oranges, and yellows nothing like the sunset swallowed my entire line of vision, battling each other in a raging display of violence. Dave pounced onto me, using himself as a human shield as he forced us to the ground. His sudden weight on me crushed my organs, and my vision started to go black. I heard a crack underneath me, like rock splitting against rock, and I started to scream about how we needed to move immediately. Still, Dave did not budge, muttering incoherent words into the grass below.

He didn't understand, and it was too late to explain it. The ground shattered like glass from beneath us, and we went tumbling headfirst into the river.

CHAPTER 3

My body slapped the freezing cold water with incredible force, but I didn't have time to process the pain of it; my mouth and nose had filled with water, and it blocked my vision with its swirling white waves. My instant thought was to swim over to the riverbank and crawl out, but that was going to be near impossible with the strength behind the current. My lungs burned at the lack of oxygen from being underwater. *Inhale.* Mouthful of water. *Exhale.* Nothing. *Repeat.* I could feel my organs starving for air that I couldn't supply them. Screaming wouldn't help. Looking for a way out wouldn't help. Waiting for someone to come and drag me out wouldn't help. I was alone.

The river tossed me like I was nothing but a blade of grass as I flipped over repeatedly, twirling with the time of the current, turning against my will. My right arm slammed into an unseen rock, and I tried screaming out in pain, only to feel bubbles rising out of my throat. Bubbles fizzed inside my own blood as I struggled to break free from my watery prison. *Why does it feel like fire if I'm underwater?* I remember thinking as everything in me started to burn, from my insides to the skin that covered them.

My left leg caught onto a different rock, but because of the vigorous tug of the waves, I escaped that with just a gash down my thigh. I tucked my knees up to my abdomen, and from there, I wrapped my arms around my legs, forming a strange human ball that allowed the river to take me as it pleased. *I am going to die,* I thought just as I started to feel sleepy, my body so starved for oxygen that it teetered on the verge of shutting down.

Finally, a breakthrough. My face pierced through the surface of the water, and I swallowed the air that allowed me to keep fighting. Immediately, my limbs sprang back open and began flailing wildly, but as soon as I thought I had a chance, the river dragged me back down again, my face once again covered in water. More swirling, more turning, more flipping. With all the movement, I was beginning to become extremely nauseated, and I almost couldn't believe I was still capable of feeling such a feeble thing.

I convinced myself that there was nothing else I could do, but just as I settled into that ball position again and accepted defeat, a voice—a memory—came to me: *Eric moved toward me but stopped when I shuffled away from him again, a defeated look in his eyes and an empty look in mine. "May I propose that you fight whatever has gotten into you? Don't let them snuff you out. You're alive. You're human, and I don't want them to ever take that away from you. Don't let them."*

I'm powerful. I'm human. I'm still alive.

And there was no way I'd let Caleb kill me now.

I kicked up with my remaining good leg to break free, and my efforts were rewarded; I was able to inhale not water, but air, and for the tiniest of seconds, I was able to quickly scan my surroundings. I was in the dead center of the river, so swimming to the sides wasn't an option, considering its width and the strength with which the waves pulled me. But I did notice two large rocks that were rapidly coming up on either side of me, and I formulated a plan of action.

I planted my legs on either side of the rocks and semi-stood so that only my knees were being pulled by the rushing, frantic water, and I bent over by the waist in order to firmly grip the pointy tips of the rocks with my hands, steadying myself as I fought against the pulling river. I yelled in an effort to extinguish the pain that emanated from every inch of my body. My legs shook ferociously from the amount of strain they felt from holding me up, and I yelled a second time to distract myself from the pain. All too soon, my legs gave out, leaving me to support myself with my arms alone. The one that had been struck by the rock earlier caved to the pressure almost instantly, and it left me with just one arm desperately clinging to the sharp end of a rock while the entire lower half of my body was on the brink of succumbing to the grip of the rapids.

Although the water was freezing, sweat had broken out along my hairline from the exertion. Now instead of my lungs burning, it was my muscles, stretched out and ready to snap at any given moment. My bottom lip quivered at the almost unbearable pain once I realized my fingers had lost feeling. But no physical stress could've prepared me for the emotional drain at the sight of Dave's unmoving form as he rushed past me, carried by the river like he weighed nothing.

It was a reflex to jump from the rock and go after him. I used the current as a friend rather than an enemy to propel myself through the water, and I kicked as hard as my injuries allowed to try and catch him. I was too far behind him to see if his face was above water or not, but I desperately hoped it was. Kicking faster still, I began moving my burning, overworked arms in a desperate attempt to reach him faster, but the current circled me as if intentionally attempting to discourage my efforts.

Nothing worked. No matter how hard I kicked or how much effort I put into reaching him, the current was faster, and I couldn't get to him. It was a living nightmare; the white water soon became too overpowering, and I lost track of him. I suddenly became hyper-aware of my heart pumping until it was thumping loudly in my ears, in my veins, in my head, like it wanted to alert me of when it was taking its leave, like it was pushing against my skin to go where Dave went, like it wanted to remind me of how close it was to death. Drifting on my back now since the river had calmed down substantially, I proceeded to think of a way to escape this nightmare until I felt something squishy touch my ankle.

My initial reaction was to scream in horror at anything other than water touching any part of me before I realized what, or who, it was. I grasped his cold, limp hand in mine and proceeded to pull him so that his mouth and nose could take in air instead of water. I dragged the both of us—mainly him, but all strength had left my body as well—up the side of the riverbank, and patiently waited for Dave to regain consciousness. Except he didn't.

I whispered his name into his ear, but when that didn't work, I slapped him hard across the face, because surely if he could feel pain, he was alive.

Nothing.

But I was undeterred. I screamed at him to wake up, to move, to give me any sort of sign that he could hear me.

Nothing.

I told him every good thing I remembered him doing for me. When he let me go from going to the Jail the day we met. When he made me laugh with his boyish charm in order to calm my nerves. When he held me after I had finished seeing Peter without knowing what had upset me so greatly. I told him that I remembered that time we laid on my province's sculpture and made that deal to continue our friendship in secret, our first deal, the only deal that truly mattered to me. There were smaller things that I whispered to him as well, like the way he always kissed the crown of my head in an effort to soothe me, how he smiled at his own jokes because I think he knew how much I loved it when he smiled, and how he always made sure I was comfortable before he was. I then told him every good thing I remembered him doing for other people, too. When he saved Mr. Woobi from being physically abused just because he couldn't stand the thought of another human being getting hurt. When he accepted Peter and Eric and protected them because he somehow knew that I wouldn't be able to live without them. When he shielded Mr. Woobi from the attacking Uniforms' bullets and comforted the older man while he experienced one of his psychological episodes.

Nothing.

I love you, I wanted to whisper, but I was terrified that the words wouldn't matter, that he wouldn't understand, that I didn't mean them completely.

I couldn't tell David Monsella I loved him, but could I tell David Woobi? It didn't matter, because at that very moment, Dave's eyelids began to flutter. The moment he opened those incredible blue eyes of his, he groaned multiple times. "Hi," he croaked once his moans subsided, squinting his eyes in discomfort as he tried to lighten the mood, but upon seeing my lips trembling, he frowned and asked, "What, is it something I said?"

I rocked back on my haunches to squat beside him, eyes blown wide, ears ringing from overstimulation, body paralyzed. I shivered as teardrops of river water ran down my spine, and I wrapped my one good arm around my wet Uniform jacket for some semblance of warmth. My right arm hung loosely at my side, throbbing and utterly useless. A stinging sensation coursed through my body from my left leg, which prompted me to look down to see my gray Societan sweatpants torn almost all the way up and a gigantic, rapidly bleeding gash running up my thigh. The blood stained my pants a dark red color, one that eerily reminded me of my coworkers' blood on the cement Societan streets.

Caleb tried to kill me, I thought bitterly, and that alone set off a chain of explosions inside my brain.

Dave almost died. I almost died.

Mr. Woobi? Eric? Where are you?

My friends are dead. Random civilians are dead. Uniforms are dead.

I abandoned Peter.

Zelda. Zelda. Zelda.

I wanted to cry. I wanted to cling to Dave as I sobbed embarrassingly into his chest. I wanted to complain about being hungry, complain about being tired, complain about almost dying, losing my friends, abandoning my brother, misplacing Mr. Woobi and Eric, and just wanting my simple life back. I wanted to express how truly terrified I was of *everything*. But I could only muster the strength to give Dave a glassy-eyed look through my eyelashes and demand, "Make a deal with me that you won't leave me, Dave."

The ex-Uniform looked stunned, but nonetheless, he nodded. "Deal."

"And that we'll find Eric and Mr. Woobi."

"Deal," he said immediately.

"And promise me we'll live long enough to forget what this kind of pain feels like."

Dave bit his lip at that one, but eventually, he proclaimed, "I promise, Zelda."

I nodded once, choosing to believe Dave's assurances held some meaning in this unforgiving universe, and attempted to stand. My bad leg buckled underneath me almost instantly. I tried again, and again, and again to stand, each time crashing back down with a mighty thud, and I was just beginning to rise again when Dave muttered, "Zelda, stop."

I whipped around to glower at him, finally able to stand on shaky feet. "What, Dave? We can't stay here forever. We need to get moving."

"Sweetheart, your leg—"

"What about it?"

"It looks bad. Worse than bad. It looks really, really horrible."

"Thanks," I muttered sarcastically. "If we're comparing pain, what happened to your back? You've been in pain since we left the Society."

Dave promptly closed his mouth, shook his head like a child, and refused to meet my eyes.

"Dave," I coaxed, much gentler this time around. "What happened to you?"

He glanced at me once, as if to make sure I wouldn't run away, and then began peeling away his white Uniform shirt that had clung to him from the water earlier. I looked away to give him some privacy, but Dave insisted that I wouldn't be able to see the injury if I kept doing that, so I gathered my courage and turned to face him fully.

His abs were toned just enough to see the subtle definition of muscle underneath, and I fought a small smile from forming on my face when I noticed how his hair had changed to a light brown from our plunge. Beads of water dripped down his forehead and collected on the tip of his nose, and it was so cute I had to restrain from kissing it. It wasn't until he coughed loudly that I visibly jumped and broke my stare.

He laughed at my bashfulness, and now I could see the way his broad chest moved when he did so. "So much for modesty," he teased, and I felt heat rush to my face.

"Turn around so I can see your back, David," I commanded, but it was difficult to keep the smile out of my voice.

I patiently waited for him to turn around, but when his stiff posture didn't ease, I walked around his body myself, only to gasp in horror at what I found.

A flaming red, permanent "S" with two rings surrounding it—the Society's signature emblem—had been seared directly into David Woobi's flesh. The vicious burn covered the entirety of his back, and the marking looked so painful that I had to bite back a sob or a scream or a mixture of both, but something like a whisper escaped past my lips anyway.

"I guess they really do own me now," he meant as a joke, but there was no humor behind his voice, and I certainly didn't find it funny.

"When did you get this?" I didn't mean to whisper, but my voice was faint as I took in the sight of his branding.

"That day they arrested us, I think. They said something along the lines of how important I was, how I had *earned* this, but I don't…" Dave stole a glance at me and sharply looked down at his feet. "I don't really remember."

I thought back to that day. I had been taken to the interrogation room—the same room I had seen Peter in—and given three red pills to take in an attempt to make me forget all the knowledge I had recently acquired in the database: the war, my parents, the meaning of love. They threatened to torture Dave—and did, clearly—if I didn't take the medication, and ultimately, it was his terrified yelp of pain that forced them down my throat. The side effects were brutal that night, but it was crucial I endure that pain; I discovered the true evil behavior Caleb was capable of exhibiting. I vowed never to be under his control again.

"Why can't you remember?" I asked Dave, but he meshed his lips together and refused to speak until I asked a different question: "Why didn't you tell me earlier?"

Again, he didn't seem to want to answer, but eventually mumbled, "I didn't want you to think I was weak."

I wrinkled my nose, and without much thought, lifted a section of my wet hair to reveal the scar that ran from the middle of my head, along my hairline, and down to my right ear. "I got this the same day you got that burn," I declared, my hoarse voice replaced with one hard and impactful. Dave opened his mouth to rebut, but I interrupted him: "Do you think I don't hate it? Because you're wrong if you think I don't. I hate it with everything in me, but that doesn't mean I don't respect it. I fought for this scar, not against it. If anything, I earned it for the amount of pain I put myself through that night. It reminds me that I was strong enough to overpower what I battled. You look in the mirror and see an imperfection, but all I see in front of me now is a man who fought to free himself and ended up with scars in the process. Wounds may be a sign you've been hurt, but scars are a sign you are healing."

I continued, "We are all bound to the Society in some way or another. I have this scar. You have your tattoo on your arm and their symbol burned into your skin. Mr. Woobi has that same figure branded on his face. Caleb does that to try and own you, but Dave, you're *not* the Society, I promise. You are not weak."

Dave took a few minutes to process my impromptu speech, and when he finally met my gaze, his blue eyes cradled pools of profound sadness. "Thank you," he murmured, and I couldn't help myself from closing the distance and pressing a gentle kiss to his lips in an attempt to soothe him.

He kissed back just as sweetly, bringing his large, calloused hands to cup my face and taking a step closer to me. Our lips broke apart, but we stayed wrapped in an embrace for several more seconds, relishing each other's warmth until Dave shyly suggested he redress. Flustered, I agreed, and I politely turned myself around to give Dave some semblance of privacy, which made him chuckle.

Freezing, famished, and exhausted, it took every ounce of strength left in my body to announce that we should look for Eric and Mr. Woobi, to which Dave heartily agreed. We tried calling their names, but the desperate cries bounced pathetically around the trees. No answer. We yelled several more times, but by the end, my voice grew hoarse and cracked, like broken glass. Although the heavy bleeding had since stopped, my left leg trembled so much I could barely stand. My right arm throbbed so badly, a part of me wished to chop it off, but I restrained from complaining; surely, if Dave could deal with a permanent burn on his back, I could handle my arm.

"Zelda," Dave started, but I shushed him, closing my eyes to try and fight the current now swirling inside my body. I fought to keep myself from swaying.

"Eric and Charles, they're not, I mean, they can't be—"

"They're not dead, Dave. I would know if they were."

Dave smartly chose not to comment.

The ground below me moved as I battled the sudden dizziness, and again, I found myself wishing to be back in the Society, swaddled under my blankets, warm, fed, and relatively safe. I had never experienced exhaustion to this degree before, where both my mind and my body wanted to simply *stop*. I stole a glance at Dave, and one quick look at his slouched posture and drooping eyelids told me that we were going nowhere. I took the initiative to announce that I, truthfully, had no idea what to do next, and Dave heaved a heavy sigh. "Peter mentioned people outside of the Society, right?" he asked, and when I had nodded, he said, "Then our best chance is to look for those people. They can help us look for Eric and Charles."

"Or hurt us," I countered. "No one has ever escaped the Society before. They could see us as the enemy."

"Zelda, we look horrible and defenseless. I'm sure we'll be fine. Our best option is to look for other people and hope to find some food along the way. Can you walk?"

I nodded despite the shooting pain in my leg, and we wobbled onward, fingers intertwined for support. I leaned heavily on Dave as we walked, and although he at first tried to make the journey enjoyable with small jokes, those eventually dissipated until we were trudging along in silence. Eventually, the sound of the river faded into a symphony of various birds chirping, and judging by the movement of the sun, it must've been hours later when we stumbled upon a red berry bush. It took Dave and me a few moments to process if what we were seeing wasn't a mirage, but once it had sunk in, he and I attacked the bush with feverish intensity, shoving so many berries into our mouths at once that more than a few bounced onto the dirt below.

My overwhelmed taste buds tingled at the tenderness of the berries, and juice dribbled down my chin as I chomped them down and swallowed them in a single gulp. Once the humble bush had been stripped clean, we collected the berries that had fallen at our feet and ate those, too, uncaring of the dirt that coated their exteriors. I didn't stop until my hands were completely covered in berry juice and my stomach could physically hold no more.

Dave wiped his mouth with the back of his hand, apparently just as messy of an eater as I was. "That," he said, "was amazing."

I sighed, and as much as I would've benefitted from lying down, taking a nap, and letting my arm, leg, and mind heal, I was too determined to find help to stop then. We once again began trekking through the forest, not even stopping to say goodnight to the sun as it set for the night. We only decided to rest when we genuinely couldn't see our feet in front of us any longer. Dave chose to lay down where he had been standing, and I followed suit, immediately cuddling into his side for warmth as a cool breeze swept over us. Dave threw his arm over my torso—allowing my injured arm to dangle over his—and snuggled closer, burying his face into the back of my neck and falling asleep almost instantly.

My arm ached like a bruise on bone, and the muscles had grown so stiff that I could barely move without excruciating pain. My leg still stung considerably, and I marveled at the fact that I had been lying in my bed in the Society awaiting Mr. Woobi's execution only forty-eight hours beforehand. I tried to envision Peter, Eric, and Mr. Woobi all safe, but sleep claimed me before I could begin to conjure an image.

Nelly and Peter smile at me from behind a pane of glass, and I take a second to capture the warmth behind their gazes, choosing to ignore Uniform number 545537, Blake Yandle, as he comes into view. He, too, smiles at me, but there's something colder about the way he's looking at me. I don't notice the gun he's pulled from behind his back until he's aiming at Peter's skull, and even then, I can't seem to move when he fires a bullet right between my little brother's eyes.

I kicked Dave's heavy, hot body off mine, wailing about a nightmare. Dave reassured me whatever I saw wasn't real, but it still took me several minutes to calm down. In the meantime, Dave had collected berries from a nearby bush, and eventually, I was able to eat some before starting our aimless journey once again. My mind kept wandering back to the mirthless smirk Blake had on his face in my nightmare, and how eerily it mirrored his demeanor in my real memories.

"Dave," I asked in a rush, "do you know a Uniform named Blake Yandle?"

Dave tripped over an exposed tree root the moment I asked; I yanked him upright from our interlocked hands, and when he had readjusted, I saw how red his face had become. "Ye... yeah," he answered. He cleared his throat rather loudly. "Yeah, I do. We're friends. How… how do you know him? Why do you ask?"

I proceeded to tell Dave about my encounter with Blake from a few days previous, from him killing the rest of his Uniform squadron when they had threatened me, to him promising to take care of Peter until I returned. "He said you guys met during Uniform Academy, and I don't know, you both are so different, and he gives me this strange feeling. He killed *nine* people, Dave." Saying those words out loud unsettled me. "How can I trust him to look after Peter?"

The ex-Uniform scrunched up his nose. "He's not a murderer, Zelda. That must've been self-defense. I've known him for a long time. Other than you, he's the only person who knows about my memory impairment." Dave gave me a soft, reassuring smile and quickly squeezed my fingers. "I promise, I trust him with my life."

Dave's assurance put me at ease, and I nodded in agreement before he swiftly changed the subject to something much more lighthearted, though eventually, the conversation ebbed into silence when water fell on us from the rapidly graying sky. We stopped walking and opened our mouths to drink the water from above, but the droplets were too unsubstantial to really quench my thirst. The water pelted the earth in blinding sheets, splashing mud onto my shins and soaking Dave and me down to our bones. I felt Dave's body shaking when he wrapped his arms around me to shield me from the rain, and I hadn't noticed I was doing the same until he gently kissed my temple and told me so.

We stood there, desperately clutching each other for warmth, as water assaulted us from above until my skin began to burn. I could almost hear Caleb's mechanical laugh through the roaring noise of the rain slapping our skin, taunting me, calling me weak, calling me ignorant for ever leaving the Society in the first place. I almost believed him.

The rain subsided almost as quickly as it had arrived, but moisture still clung to the air to the point where it felt as though I was inhaling water vapor. We continued to walk through the day, only stopping to eat berries we found along the way or drink from the puddles the rain had left. My body had adapted to the physical pain to where I could barely feel my achy arm or sliced leg, but as mud continued to cake around my ankles and slow me down, every pore screamed for warmth. My clothes felt crusty and cold on my skin, and I doubted Dave felt any better. A part of me wanted to give in to the pure exhaustion.

But that was until I heard the voices.

My hope rose as I idiotically began to sprint before tripping over my injured leg and forced to crawl closer to the sound. I could just about make it out: a bunch of raised voices in synchronization to a certain rhythm that I found enthralling. I discovered I was slightly swaying to the beat while Dave seemed to be floating toward it.

A clearing between the trees allowed us to see exactly who was making the wondrous noises: not Eric and Mr. Woobi, but children, about thirty or so, all standing on a wooden platform with a crowd of adults watching them with rapt attention. It was as though Dave and I were drawn in by the sound of their voices as we unconsciously inched closer into the clearing. I didn't wish to disturb them, but a little girl with long, shiny auburn hair caught sight of us and promptly closed her mouth. Her eyes squinted curiously at us, the dirty fugitives with no place to go.

I'm not sure what Dave did, but whatever it was, the action caused the girl to break out into a huge smile and wave her small hand in our direction. This caught the attention of the other children on the platform, and, following her lead, each one closed their mouths, ending their brilliant sound to gaze at us inquisitively. My heart pounded against my chest as the adults, curious as to what their children were looking at, turned to face us one-by-one, some eyes widening in fear while others squinted, just like their children, to get a better look at Dave and me. I noticed how most of them were eyeing my jacket, which had the Society symbol on its left side, and I quickly unzipped the front, took it off, and tied it around my waist as my silent peace offering.

The tension in the air was almost as thick as the humidity post-rain shower, and it seemed to only be getting worse as time ticked on and each side did nothing but stare. I stayed frozen to my spot, watching helplessly as these foreign people, adults and children alike, analyzed Dave and me with curious fear. The prospect of turning and running the other direction was tempting, but I knew I wouldn't get far with my leg injury, and if they had weapons underneath those modest, baggy clothes, I would be dead in less than a minute.

The crowd rippled suddenly as someone I could not see made their way toward us. It wasn't until the figure was three rows of people away from us that I saw who it was: a short, older woman with shoulder-length, peppery white hair, a petite frame, and a nose with its tip curved upward slightly, just like Dave's.

She stopped right in front of us, her head turned upward so that she could get a good, close inspection of our filthy faces. Dave took the opportunity to intertwine our fingers together, and I clenched his fingers until he gasped a little. The older woman noticed our woven fingers and stared at them for a while, studying them with such an intense, unreadable glare that I began to sweat. She stepped closer to me until our bodies almost touched, and she stood on her toes so her eyes could examine every detail about my face. I could feel her penetrating gaze drift over my features, scrutinizing every part of me until I almost backed away from her. "Zelda?" she asked quietly, so quietly that I wasn't even sure if Dave heard her, but I most certainly did. "Are you Zelda?"

How this unfamiliar, strange woman knew me, I didn't know, but I nodded my head nonetheless.

She sucked in a breath before she moved onto Dave, and admittedly, I saw beauty in the way she admired his every blink, his every breath, his every flutter of movement. "David?" The woman exhaled the question disbelievingly.

At the sound of his name, Dave gulped, but ultimately, he nodded, too. "Yes."

The older woman stepped back from the two of us, and I had never seen a brighter, more joyous smile on anyone's face before when she whispered, "You're home."

CHAPTER 4

The woman broke up our hands—mine, sweaty and his, so steady against all the confusion—in order to place herself in between us and lead us over to the stage the children had been standing on. The children scattered, running back to the parents fearfully as the two filthy runaways hobbled up the steps. Upon getting situated at the front of the platform and facing the crowd, the older woman raised our joined hands toward the navy sky. "Sisters and brothers," she began, and just that statement alone made me yearn to see Peter. "Mothers and fathers. Friends and family. I present to you…" She paused, but our configuration made it difficult for me to see if she paused for effect or out of emotion. "Alina and Owen Jadestone's daughter, Zelda."

The crowd rustled with confusion, and I heard my name being repeated like a forbidden whisper that reminded me of another crowd back in the Society.

Zelda, the crowd chants like it's the only thing anchoring them to sanity as they storm the stage to free an older man from the shackles of death.

Zelda, a leader growls with venom in his tone as he watches his power slip away from him, a glittering promise to kill laced through the name he utters.

Zelda, this group of strangers murmur like it's a foreign taste in their mouths, not unpleasant but too unfamiliar to be any good.

I did not like the sound of my name in other people's mouths. I bristled at their voices, and my face involuntarily hardened into a frown.

"And the boy?" someone in the pack called out.

I could hear the smile in the older woman's voice when she answered, "My grandson."

She's a Woobi. A strangled gasp flew out of my mouth, and I helplessly watched Dave's Adam's apple bob up and down, struggling to swallow the news, his blue eyes wide in shock. He reached out toward the woman but quickly retracted his hands, as if afraid his touch might break her. Dave took just the smallest step closer to her and straightened his spine, towering over the small woman; I would've considered him intimidating had his voice not cracked when he whispered, "Grandson?"

He was shaking hard when she turned her back to the crowd in order to look at him face-to-face. "My baby," she croaked, her deep brown eyes welling up with thick tears.

Dave brought his trembling hands up to his mouth to hide either a sob or a smile, and he gulped before he removed his hands and chirped, "Hi."

The woman chuckled thickly and repeated a soft "hi" back to him, finally daring to bring her hands up and cup his face, running her calloused thumbs across his cheeks tenderly. "Look at you, all grown up," she joked, and Dave chortled, covering the top of her hand with his.

He looked so happy. So deeply happy that I was confident there was nothing more perfect than seeing him so content, and the world would be cruel to ruin this moment, *his* moment. And yet, Mr. Woobi's warning still rang inside my head—*because it will ruin him*—and panic struck me violently. David could not know he was a Woobi. It would change him—torment him, even—and I needed him to keep me grounded. I couldn't afford to give him the chance to change.

I lurched forward, grabbed the microphone at the front of the stage, and said, "We need help, please. We have friends out there. We need a search party. They could be hurt."

Dave looked disoriented, as though someone had shaken him awake from a pleasant dream, and he took several steps away from his grandmother to stand next to me. The crowd hummed with confused energy again, exchanging perplexed looks and murmuring things I couldn't hear, and they only settled down when the Woobi woman stepped forward, stretched her arms out, and shushed them.

"This is an unexpected turn of events," the woman joked as she took control of the microphone, and there were a few pity laughs heard amongst the crowd. "We have here from the Northeastern Society Zelda Jadestone, my grandson, David, and apparently a few others in the forest. Entrance and exit from the Society is reportedly impossible. I'm curious to hear how you managed to escape." She turned from addressing the crowd to looking at me, and I noticed how the crowd had focused their attention on me as well. Adults and children alike held little screens in their hands that they had trained to my face, recording my movements.

I shot the Woobi woman a confused, startled look, and she politely ushered toward the microphone and cleared her throat. Dave put his hand on the small of my back and pushed me forward, and I tripped over my own feet when he pushed just the tiniest bit harder. "Hello," I awkwardly said into the gray metal mesh, and the sound seemed to carry much more weight than when I had yelled about Eric and Mr. Woobi. I snuck a quick glance at Dave, who offered me a tight-lipped smile in response. "We escaped the Society almost three days ago and have been wandering the trees since, trying to look for civilization." A small giggle erupted from the pit of my stomach, and an overpowering sense of relief bubbled through my bloodstream. "We're really relieved we found you."

This seemed to comfort the crowd immensely, and a few people in the front even smiled up at me sympathetically when I had visibly exhaled in exhaustion. "How?" asked a man, perhaps in his late thirties. "How'd you escape?"

"What's it like in there?" asked another man closer to the back of the group.

"Why is there blood all over your shirt?" a younger girl asked.

"What happened to your friends?" asked a child clutching his mom's leg.

"What happened to your leg?" asked another.

"What changed inside the Society that made you leave?" asked yet another.

"Zelda," called someone.

"Zelda?" asked another.

"Zelda!" they shouted, but they sounded like static compared to the voices chanting inside my head.

I was tempted to cover my ears to protect myself from the assault of their yelling, but I chose to copy the Woobi woman's approach instead: hands outstretched, shushing them quietly until they calmed down. The crowd seemed to gravitate closer toward the stage when I opened my mouth to answer their questions. I began by telling them about Mr. Woobi's execution, excluding his identity, and how Caleb had threatened to kill me. I walked them through the ambush that separated Dave and me from the rest of our party, and I explained to them the difficulties we faced from aimlessly walking through the forest for two days. Words poured out of me so quickly, I almost couldn't keep up with my own sentences as I exposed my story for the crowd to digest.

When a woman said, "So you saved your family," I could do nothing but lower my gaze and try to swallow my guilt. The crowd's silence as they waited for my response pierced my mind, and all I could picture were my dead coworkers' corpses lying at my feet, my little brother's retreating form as he went to open the boundary, Mr. Woobi's vacant gaze as he stared into the eyes of death at his almost-execution.

"I tried," I settled on saying, but suddenly, tears sprung into my eyes, my throat tightened, and my words strained. I reached behind me in search of Dave's hand, and I released my breath when I felt his pinky finger curl around mine. "It was more realizing the bubble I lived in and coming to terms that anyone could pop that bubble so long as they're willing to try. I guess I was the first to try."

The Woobi woman took over for me then, and I was more than happy to step back and stand next to Dave as she reclaimed her place at the front of the stage. She only glanced back at the pair of us once, and her face portrayed such sorrow that I couldn't begin to understand before she addressed the crowd: "I'm sure we are all aware of the effects, both positive and negative, that David and Zelda's unexpected arrival may have on our village. There are bound to be risks involved with taking them in. I am open to a discussion of pros and cons before we take a deciding vote."

"They need medical attention, Eve," a woman said, and I clung to that name. *Eve Woobi.* "We can't let them go."

"She's a liability," countered a male voice, though his comment attracted many groans in protest. "No, hear me out. She's the first person to escape a Society ever. Their leader clearly isn't happy with that and may want to make an example of her. She knows too much. She's a ticking bomb with this target on her back."

A few people grumbled their agreement, and panic gripped my body once again at the thought of being cast out. A woman, faceless in the sea of bodies draped in darkness now that the sun had set, stomped her foot forcefully and said, "No! Who would we be if we didn't care for these people? They're refugees, not fugitives. I mean, look at them: they're disgusting."

"Flattering," I muttered under my breath, and I heard Dave squeak trying to cover up his snicker. The sound made my lips perk up, and we quickly traded amused looks before focusing on the crowd once more.

"And there are more out there!" the woman continued. "You're right. Zelda did the impossible. Don't we owe it to her and to her parents to welcome her back home?"

"I just have to say it," spoke the same man from earlier. "What if she didn't escape, but was sent? What if she's a Societan spy? Didn't you see the jacket she was wearing when she arrived?"

The man's proposal elicited the pack to voice their opinions at once. "Oh, that's ridiculous—"

"Insane!"

"It's possible—"

"Absolutely moronic—"

"Maybe..."

"Enough!" I shouted, storming my way back to the microphone. "We don't want to put anyone in any danger. I can promise you I'm not a spy. I'm *hurt*." The adrenaline that had been coursing through my body finally wore off, and my exhaustion caught up with me then, making my shoulders slump and my eyelids heavy. My arm ached like a fresh punch to the gut, the gash in my leg throbbed as if it had its own pulse, and I wanted these village people to *feel* it, to make them understand my pain. "I lost my family, the only home I've ever known, *everything,* but if we're not welcome here, then I will not stay. I'd rather die free than live with my life dictated for me. I won't let that happen again."

Inhale. The congregation absorbed my words, looking either at me or the stars above them.

Exhale. "Let's take a vote," declared Eve solemnly, and I walked back over to Dave and took his hand in mine, completely this time.

Repeat. "Raise your hand for denying David and Zelda permanent residence in our village. After immediate medical attention, I will accompany them to the city and delegate my duties to my council while I am away."

Inhale. My eyes scanned the crowd, but the darkness prevented me from seeing anything but a few scattered shadows.

Exhale. "Raise your hand for accepting David and Zelda into our village and providing them shelter, food, medical attention, and a search party to look for the rest of the escapees."

Inhale. No one dared to move, and the world held its breath until a little girl, the same one who had spotted Dave and me first, shouted in a small, young voice: "Let them stay!"

Exhale. "Let them stay!" the little girl shouted again, and again, and again, until the chant carried weight, until others around her began shouting it with her, until it reverberated around the trees when hundreds of voices came together in unison to shout, "Let them stay! Let them stay! Let them stay!"

Repeat. A unanimous vote.

Eve Woobi grinned into her words when she turned to face us and said, "Welcome home, David and Zelda."

I slumped against Dave as relief knocked me off my feet, and he quickly caught me as the crowd surged onto the stage, now all yelling incoherent things as they yearned to see me up close, to touch me, to assure themselves I was real. They fired questions at us about our time in the Society, about the escape, about what living in the forest felt like, but their words bounced off me. I could only hear Dave as he murmured, "You did it, sweetheart," repeatedly. He cupped my face and kissed my forehead roughly, as if his lips on my skin tethered him to Earth.

Despite my fatigue, I could only think of the next step ahead, of finding Eric and Mr. Woobi, of freeing Peter, and I broke out of Dave's embrace to stand and look for Eve Woobi among the mob. We spotted each other at the same time, and I stumbled over to her to grip her forearms and say, "The other people out there in the forest, they're—"

"We can't do anything now, Zelda," Eve told me. "I'll send people to search tomorrow morning."

I dug my fingernails into her arm forcefully and shook my head violently, suddenly desperate to get her to understand. "No, listen, it's Eric Stellenzer—"

Eve tried to break the hold I had on her. "Zelda, please—"

"And Charles Woobi," I finished.

Her smooth façade shattered the moment I said her husband's name: her eyes pooled with tears; her features softened; her hardened frown went slack. "Charlie?" she said, disbelief so heavy in her voice that it made my heart shudder.

I nodded. "He's the man that was almost executed."

Eve furrowed her brow in confusion. "Executed? But Caleb—"

"Zelda Jadestone! We need to escort you to the hospital immediately," someone called out, but I ignored her.

"I know it's complicated, but Dave can't know he's a Woobi," I implored her, gripping her so hard I was slightly fearful I might break her. "You can't tell him who you are."

Eve looked past me to catch a glimpse of the ex-Uniform in question. "He doesn't know?"

I shook my head, suddenly finding myself unable to speak another word at the anguish behind her penetrating gaze.

"I must tell him," Eve said, determination replacing the pain I had seen just moments ago.

"You can't!" I ordered, but at that moment, someone grabbed my wrist and tried dragging me away, saying something about an immediate medical procedure. I wrestled out of the person's grasp long enough to say, "Eve. You can't. Trust me," but then the grip on my wrist returned, tugging me farther from the older woman. "Hey," I called out to her, trying to get her to look at me and not her scuffed shoes. "Trust me."

Eve finally caught my gaze, but the distrust that lined her pupils was new, as was her sudden commanding tone when she said, "Doctor Cortiana, sedate her."

"Yes, ma'am," said the woman holding me.

I didn't even get a chance to voice my betrayal. Dr. Cortiana jabbed a needle-like contraption through my neck, and I plunged into tranquil darkness.

CHAPTER 5

My eyelids snapped open, and I attempted to sit up, but the action made me so dizzy and lightheaded that I was forced to stay down. Balls of color bounced through my line of vision, and I cradled my head and groaned at the tenderness of my skull. My sudden movements startled a nurse who had been graciously setting down a tray of food by the small bedside table, and I cringed at her frightened expression. "Sorry," I said to the frozen nurse, and my apology seemed to put her at ease.

"Don't sweat it, baby doll," she said, and her voice was so sweet it was almost sickening. "I startle easily, and you're a little intimidating."

I didn't know whether I should take that as a compliment or an insult, but when she patted me on the shoulder and handed me a cup of water, I feigned a smile and chose to take it as the former. "What happened to me? Where's Dave? Where's Eve?" I asked her, and it was then that I noticed a needle stuck inside one of the veins in the crook of my elbow, feeding my blood clear fluid from a bag that hung from a metal "J" beside my bed. I reached to pluck it out, but the nurse quickly stopped me, insisting that the liquid was only saline solution to rehydrate me. I chose to believe her.

Although the bright white, florescent lights strained my eyes, my gaze traveled around the expansive room as I finally became alert enough to survey my surroundings. The room was massive, with bed after bed filling the space, little metal tables on the left side of each one. In the farthest corner of the room stood a pair of double swinging doors with small slats for windows, and as I inhaled, the stinging stench of rubbing alcohol burned my nostrils. I recognized that smell from my days as a doctor well, and it reminded me strongly of my coworkers. The mental image of their smiling faces wedged the knife of their deaths deeper into my soul. I cringed and clenched my fists to alleviate some of the pressure building inside my bones.

"Why am I in a laboratory? Where is Dave? Where's Eve?" I asked the nurse again, more insistently this time. Saying Eve's name out loud reminded me of her betrayal, and I involuntarily bit my tongue at the memory. "What happened to me? Is there a search party out looking for the other members of my group?"

"You're not in a laboratory, honey, you're in a hospital," answered the nurse. "David's injuries were less severe, so he was discharged before you. We fixed your broken arm and cut leg. Take a look."

I lifted the covers to find the gash that had been on my leg now nothing but a pink scar, and I rotated both my arms to be met with zero pain. "Wow, thank you," I said, and the nurse nodded like it was no big deal. "But where is Eve? And what about that search party?"

"Ms. Redding is giving David a tour of the village, and she ordered a search party early this morning."

I wrinkled my nose. "I'm sorry, who?"

The nurse shot me a look that made me feel insane. "Ms. Redding? Eve Redding?"

Before I could articulate a response, the woman in question burst through the double swinging doors with an excited, peppy gait to her walk, clapping her hands excitedly and shouting, "Good morning," to the nurse and me. I tensed at the sound of her voice—gruff and a little raspy, as though she had spent her life screaming—and visibly flinched when I saw Dave politely push one door open, hands stuffed inside his new, brown pant pockets. I scanned his face for any insight as to what Eve might have revealed to him, but he was, perhaps for the first time, unreadable.

By the time Eve reached the foot of my bed, I had forced a smile to appear on my face for Dave's sake. "Why look at you, Zelda!" Eve said a little too enthusiastically. "Healthier by the minute. How are you feeling post-surgery?"

I barely heard her. My focus stayed on Dave, and I extended the arm not tethered by a needle toward him. "How are *you*?" I asked him, and nothing felt sweeter than the touch of his warm, rough hand wrapping around my own.

"Like a new person. I can't wait to give you a tour," he answered, and Eve gasped at his words like she had a sudden epiphany.

"Oh, what a great idea, David! Want to grab our tour guide from this morning quickly so we can give Zelda a proper introduction?" she asked, but the subtle tilt of her head and commanding hilt to her voice told me she wasn't asking.

Dave brightened at her suggestion, and he practically slid down the aisle and through the doors to collect this "tour guide."

The second those doors swung shut, I whipped around to interrogate Eve, but she held up a hand to stop me. "I didn't tell him," she said, and I sagged in relief. She sat at the foot of my bed before saying, "I know I don't understand you yet, Zelda, just as you don't understand me, but you trust *me* now, not the other way around. I'm giving you this one chance because I can tell you and my grandson share a strong bond, but he is *my* grandson. This is *my* family. I have waited almost fifteen years for David, Caleb, and Charlie to come back home." She leaned in close then, so close that I could see the ferocity shining through her dark eyes. "I did not work this hard to have my family denied from me, you understand?" When I didn't immediately nod, she moved her head so I had no choice but to look at her and raised her graying eyebrows expectantly. "Zelda, are we clear?"

Eve Woobi fascinated me. The intensity with which she stared at me, eyes narrowed almost into slits, reminded me of her son, Caleb, and the force behind his gaze. The two of them radiated a kind of power that seemed to simmer through the ridges of their brains, and yet, somehow, I remained unafraid of them; something about them made me want to dissect them, pick them apart until their power faltered. So I couldn't stop myself from saying, "We're clear, Mrs. *Redding,* but in those fourteen years, Mr. Woobi became like a father to me, Dave and I grew close, and Caleb committed awful, *unspeakable* crimes. Mr. Woobi and Dave are my family, too. I know what's best for them."

Eve pursed her lips, closed her eyes, and took a deep breath to collect herself. "I love you, Zelda," she said, and I wrinkled my nose. "I loved your parents, too. Don't make me forget that."

"Wouldn't dream of it," I retorted.

Eve looked like she wanted to say more, but the doors swung open to reveal Dave and the little girl who had first spotted us the day before, his entire hand enveloping her little one as they hurriedly walked toward me. Her head only came up to his hips, forcing him to lean down slightly on her side, and the image was so endearing that I had to let out a small giggle.

The little girl, her curly red hair bouncing behind her, stopped right in front of me, stuck her hand out, and declared, "I'm Sharlee Davidson, and I'm here to take you on your tour," like it was the most obvious thing in the world.

I stole a quick glance at Dave, who was grinning. "Hi, Sharlee Davidson. I'm Zelda Jadestone," I told her.

"I know who you are," replied Sharlee smoothly, already turning around and walking back outside.

My squeak of surprise made Dave choke on his laughter before he hurried to catch up with her.

Just as I was pushing the door open, Eve called out to me: "'Redding' is my maiden name. I am still a Woobi, Zelda, as is David, no matter how many lies you concoct."

I turned around to say, "I understand, ma'am. Oh, one more thing."

She looked up from her lap. "Yes?"

"It's Dave, not David." And I slammed the door shut behind me.

Sharlee led Dave and me around the village's perimeter first, telling us what she called "fun facts." According to her, the village was the only civilization for many miles. Most of the surrounding land belonged to either the Society or had been destroyed in the Second American Civil War. Before the war, the village was considered a town, but bombs—presumably, the bombs that killed my parents—reduced it to ash. The village now was a fraction of what it once was. She emphasized how the village mainly focused on conservation efforts, and most of the forest trees Dave and I walked through had been a part of its ongoing regeneration program.

Dave asked many questions, and I could tell it wasn't just to amuse Sharlee. From his questions, we learned that the capital city of the state—a metropolis called Neweryork—was one hundred miles or so from the village, over an hour's drive. We learned that places like the village weren't too uncommon, as many people after the war escaped the city to evade the destruction bombs had caused. The villagers grew most of their food in a specific laboratory in the hospital, and they imported their water from the city. No one ever went near the river surrounding the Society. Sharlee told us that right after the Society's formation, Eve had taken charge of the major reconstruction project, and people were so impressed with her efficiency that they elected her unofficial leader of the village. They hadn't bothered to elect anyone else since. People respected Eve, and from what Sharlee explained, seemed to trust her. Something about that reminded me a little too much of the trust Societan citizens had in Caleb, but I decided not to draw too many similarities.

Sharlee started her official tour of the village where Dave and I had first entered as filthy, broken fugitives to give us a better sense of direction. The village was built up in an "L" shape in the middle of the forest, with the inside of the "L" being free to use for large social gatherings or events. At the head of the village stood a stage, and in the dead center of the open space was a fire pit that Sharlee said was only for special celebrations.

The main buildings covered the length of the village, and there we found the three-story hospital—where we would be kept for the time being—and the school. As we walked past the hospital, Sharlee informed us that it was the most important building the village had; the first floor was for medical work, the second dedicated to food production, and the third reserved for regeneration research of the surrounding area.

Perpendicular to the main buildings were these househut-looking structures, though these were much larger, sometimes sporting a second story. One in particular caught my eye; its aged, charred-looking brick didn't match the stucco, modern exterior of the other buildings, and although it stood tall on the top of a hill, seemingly looking over the rest of the village, it seemed abandoned, untouched, as if nature was just about ready to swallow it whole. "Houses," Sharlee explained when Dave had asked her what the buildings were.

"Which one is yours?" asked Dave.

The little girl squinted into the distance but eventually shrugged when she didn't spot it. "You can't see it from here, but it's in the middle."

"And the brick one?" I spoke up, eyeing it curiously.

"Oh," Sharlee squealed. "That's the haunted house."

"Haunted?" Dave laughed. "What makes it haunted?"

Sharlee shrugged. "I don't really know. Ms. Redding said we can't go there because that's where the war died. Kids at my school say ghosts of dead soldiers are inside."

Dave and I chose not to push the subject any further, so Sharlee led us back over to the hospital, where Eve was waiting in the main lobby. She seemed pleased when Dave complimented her on the village's fantastic leadership and organization, and despite my uneasiness toward the woman, I couldn't help but agree with him.

"Sharlee even pointed out the 'haunted house' on the top of the hill," said Dave. "She was a great tour guide." The comment made the little girl grin, but Eve dropped her smile, and her gaze quickly flickered over to me with the slightest trace of sympathy.

"Maybe I should give Zelda a more intimate tour," Eve suggested, and both Dave and I gave her puzzled looks.

"I don't think that's necessary," I said.

"Actually," said Dave, shifting from foot to foot, "I was thinking maybe you and I could talk. You're my grandmother, and I don't even know you."

Eve froze from Dave's words, and I sucked in a breath when she said, "Maybe later, David. I have something I have to show Zelda."

And without so much as a second glance at him, Eve grabbed my forearm and began leading me out of the hospital toward the houses.

It was like a maze, each house laid on its own plot of land in no particular pattern, all leading up to the hill where the burnt one sat waiting. We climbed to the top in silence, and my fingers instinctively reached out to touch the charred brick. Its windows had old-looking, yellow fabric covering the inside so I couldn't look in, and no light illuminated the interior. It reeked of abandonment. "What is this place?" I asked Eve, still exploring the exterior with my fingertips.

She inhaled deeply, and it took a while, but at my pleading gaze, she finally whispered, "The Jadestone residence."

My heart leapt into my throat as I retreated backward. "M... may I have a minute alone, please?" I asked shakily, and Eve nodded, twisting the doorknob and pushing the large wooden door open to let me in.

I was in a trance as I took in the sight of my old home, my feet barely touching the smooth wooden floors beneath me as I floated in and saw a sofa with two chairs, between them a table with a wooden chessboard, its pawns still waiting to be played. The house was dauntingly dark, but luckily, enough sunlight streamed through the tattered fabric to allow me to see everything without having to really squint. The stench of mold and mildew slapped my nose the minute Eve closed the door behind me, and I wrinkled my nose in disgust.

I moved from the entryway over to take a left, walking down a hallway littered with wall paintings of small, miscellaneous, vibrantly colored handprints. As I walked down farther, two doors appeared on either side of me. I turned right and found a small kitchen, equipped with a wooden table and four wooden chairs to the left, and cabinets, a refrigerator, and a sink to the right. I felt numb as I surveyed the room with dishes still in the sink, ready to be washed, crayons littering the floor with paper still waiting to be drawn on, cabinet doors on hinges still waiting to be cracked open again.

I couldn't stay in there any longer, so I moved onto the next room, crossing the hall and entering what looked to be a bedroom. The walls were a beautiful, pastel green color that were slightly covered by large flower paintings that hung from them, a darker green rug on the floor complementing the walls perfectly. The bed had a dark iron bedpost that twisted and swirled in delicate, intricate patterns with white sheets and what looked to be an overly-played-with handmade doll tucked into them. I took a step closer to investigate the little doll, and in the process stepped on another toy that squeaked from the weight of my shoe. I lifted my foot to see multiple different dolls, plush animals, and little figurines; I stumbled out of my room gagging, rushing down to the other side of the house and tripping into the door on my left.

An unmade bed. Two tall glasses with calcified rims. Shoes peeking out of the closet door. The room that belonged to people who were supposed to be alive. I creaked open a door that led to a bathroom. Used, frizzy toothbrushes near the sink. Water droplets still falling from the leaky shower head. The toilet seat up. I couldn't take it anymore and ran out of the room, but not before noticing the open eyeglass case on the nightstand to the right side of the bed. How simple was that morning? Did they know it would be their last? How could they? Death is so unfair like that, I suppose; you never know when it will claim you. *But why them?* I screamed in my head. *Why did it have to be them?*

Inhale. Exhale. Repeat.

I sprinted into the last room across the hall, slamming the door shut behind me as if that would help me escape this hell I was trapped in. The blue walls seemed to close in around me; I lost my balance and fell onto the matching blue rug, landing on a brown, furry thing I later recognized as a teddy bear. The bed was also unmade, with small, sloppy, toddler-like drawings of things like the forest behind our house and stick figures of what I guessed to be the four Jadestones sticking very loosely to the walls. A rocking chair hovered over me, staring me down as I willed myself not to cry. I clung to the bear, hugging it tightly against my chest, willing for it to be what would fill this hole in my heart, this ever-present feeling of emptiness, this consuming loneliness.

I had to get out.

But I couldn't. Just as I was about to run out of the house and outside, where I could finally breathe, another door at the end of the hallway sparked my curiosity. I turned the doorknob, and the room behind it was much different than the others I had come across. This one had no windows. The only furniture in the room was one large circular table.

I shakily typed "Jadestone" before I could stop myself.

I was met with only one image. It was of four people, two men and two women, huddled over a table with papers scattered all over it. All four of them looked incredibly familiar, but only one of the women resembled me with her small chin, long, cascading, dark-brown hair, and large, dark-brown eyes scanning the papers intensely. The man standing beside her had dark hair and eyes as well—the Jadestone trademark—and glasses that seemed to be slipping down his long, pointy nose, a nose that matched mine almost exactly.

Mom. Dad. My parents. My family.

This was the room where that photo I had found in the Society's database was taken. This was the room in which my parents fought and lost a war. As I thought back to the image, I recognized another person standing at that table in this room as Caleb Woobi, side-by-side with my parents, pretending to be their ally.

All oxygen had been sucked out of my lungs, and I stumbled back to the living room to let myself out before something shiny caught my eye.

There, surrounded by a cream-colored, polished ceramic frame, was a family portrait of the four of us. My father looked so handsome in a black suit and tie that complemented his dark hair well, smiling lovingly at my mother who, just like him, looked so radiantly gorgeous in her deep blue dress that flattered her dark hair and eyes remarkably. I seemed to have been in the middle of laughter, my eyes squinted shut and my mouth open, a light pink ribbon woven into my braided hair that matched my little pink dress perfectly. Peter was sitting on Mom's lap, a goofy, baby grin making him seem so happy as he posed in his baby blue outfit for the picture. *Our last picture.*

I grabbed the photo frame and held it against my chest next to the bear, close to my heart, as the darkness and the musty smell and the frozen time of the house I once inhabited all became too much. I collapsed onto the floor of the living room and screamed when memories from my earlier years, before the Society, tried to force themselves into the forefront of my consciousness after being buried for so long. Memories of my father holding me tightly against his chest as my mother sang a gentle lullaby. Memories of my mother cooking in the kitchen while my father attempted to feed my baby brother. Memories of teaching two-year-old Peter how to paint while my parents locked themselves in the other room, the two of us trying to ignore their raised voices. My eyes stung from the tears that so desperately wanted to fall, and finally, I let them, sobbing for all I had lost in a matter of one fateful morning that I couldn't remember.

I cried for the loss of my mother. I missed her velvety, soft voice that I remember eased my pain, whether it be a small scrape on my knee or an emotional scar from seeing the sky light up with explosions at night. I missed the way she combed her fingers through my hair whenever I placed my head in her lap, allowing myself to succumb to the rhythmic way her fingers wove into my hair. I missed her gently rocking me to sleep every night and how the warmth of her body made me feel so safe, so loved. I wanted her here with me as I grew up, to help me with everything that came with the pressures and joys of growing older. I wanted her to be there when I fell in love, guiding me through such a crazy thing as love in the way only a mother can. I wanted her holding my children, bouncing them on her knees and telling them embarrassing stories of me as a child. I needed her to hold me on the days when I wasn't strong enough to hold myself. I needed her to tell me everything was okay, that she was so proud of me and what I had accomplished. I needed her love. I needed my mommy.

I cried for the loss of my father. I missed his deep laugh that eased my worries in a way nothing else could. I missed the fantastical fictional stories he would make up to distract me from the realities of the world I was growing up in. I missed his big, steady arms that kept me safe from the darkness that was our world. I wanted him to walk me down the aisle at my wedding, whenever that would be. I wanted him to help me with and provide advice for any career I might have wanted to pursue. I wanted him to make me feel safe, held, loved. I needed him to guide me through all the tribulations life brings. I needed him to chase away any ex-boyfriends I might have had. I needed him to make me a confident, independent, strong woman with his encouragement and pride. I needed my daddy.

And I cried for the loss of my brother. I missed seeing him with me every day. I missed the laughter and jokes and overall silliness that only my sibling brought out of me. I missed holding him in my arms, safely guarding him as he slept in our househut. I wanted him with me at all times, so I could keep him safe from anything that might hurt him. I wanted him to grow up to be what he wanted, not what was assigned to him. I wanted him to understand the world and all it had to offer him: the good, bad, and everything in between. I needed him with me, to hold me up in my times of weakness. I needed him to make me laugh when I couldn't muster a smile on my own. But most of all, I needed him to know that I loved him, more than anything or anyone else in the world. I needed my brother.

I cried for all these things, because even throughout everything, I still needed my family.

It was Dave who found me, weak and tear-stained, on the floor hours later, unwilling and unable to move from my position, my trembling hands still clutching the teddy bear and the portrait. Multiple attempts on his part were made to reach me, but I think both he and I knew that wouldn't work. He tried to pick me up from the floor to hold me, but I pushed him off. He attempted to take the picture from my hands in order to help me forget, but I didn't want to forget, so I glared at him so fiercely that he had to drop it out of pure fright. "Why does it hurt so much now?" I whimpered softly to Dave after a few minutes of him just sitting on the floor next to me. "I've known they were dead for months, so after all this time, why now?"

"Sometimes, we're so accustomed to pain that we don't realize we still have it with us," he said just as gently, touching my hand to bring it away from my face so he could erase my tears with the pad of his thumb. "I'm so sorry you have to deal with this, but hey, you got me, and Eric, and Charles, and now Eve and her village people, right?"

Eric. Mr. Woobi. Peter. Three people I was certain I loved. I yearned for them.

"They'll be okay," Dave assured as if he had been reading my thoughts, kissing my temple lightly. "You'll see, sweetheart. They'll all be okay."

I clung to him like I did that day I was taken in for questioning, when I was so terrified for my life and could think of nothing else but holding onto him so they couldn't take me. He was my anchor then, and he was my anchor at this moment, too. "Promise?" I asked.

"I promise."

Only then did I allow him to help me out of the house to drop off the teddy bear and family portrait at my bed in the hospital.

Sharlee discovered us about an hour later huddled up with my head on his shoulder and his hand on my bouncing knee, sitting on the hospital's front steps and absorbing the reality in which we found ourselves. She noticed the solemn look on both of our faces and asked what was wrong in the blunt, obvious way that most small children do, and Dave had to explain that we were missing our friends and family. Her little red eyebrows scrunched up in a rather adorable fashion that reminded me of when Dave did it, and she asked us if we wanted to return to the Society.

"Yes," I answered her before Dave could. "I do."

The little girl looked incredibly confused. "But why? The bad people live there, don't they?"

Dave picked her up, placed her comfortably on his lap, and kissed the top of her head. "It's complicated, Sharlee. We've grown up there our entire lives, so it's what we're used to. Zelda's little brother is still there, too. She doesn't want to leave her brother there all by himself. It makes her sad, and when she's sad, I'm sad. But can I tell you a little secret?"

She nodded, and Dave leaned in to make it appear as though he was sharing confidential information with her. "We'll find our friends out in the forest, and we're going back for Zelda's brother, so he won't be lonely. Isn't that nice?"

Sharlee glanced over to me; I tried to smile reassuringly at the little girl, but she wrapped her small arms tightly around Dave's neck in fright. "That's scary," she announced. "Zelda's little brother must be scared of the mean people, huh?"

Dave and I exchanged a look over her head before I replied, "Peter isn't scared of anything, Sharlee. He's a big boy and can handle all the mean people. He's stronger than anyone else I know."

"I would be scared, Dave. Really, really scared," Sharlee said. She stuck her thumb in her mouth reflexively and clung to him just a bit tighter.

Dave pressed another kiss onto her head, but he lingered there just a bit longer than usual. "You don't have to worry, sweetheart. You're safe here, in the village, with your family and friends. And I'll always be here to protect you against any mean people, I promise."

"You're sad still," Sharlee stated abruptly, staring directly at me.

"It takes a while to become…uh… un-sad about your family not being around anymore," I tried to explain to her without wanting to cry again; I distracted myself by cracking my fingers and looking anywhere else but into her eyes.

"We're having a festival because of you," she told me, reaching her hand out and patting my cheek rather roughly. "Will that make you un-sad?"

"What's a festival?" I asked instead of answering her question, holding her hand as she hopped down from Dave's lap and landed with a thud onto the ground.

"Like a party," was her elaboration, her focus clearly not on us but on wiping the dirt and dust from her pants. "With dancing and music and singing and food and stuff like that."

Dave and I once again exchanged glances when she wasn't necessarily looking at us. "Dancing. Singing. Music. Party. I don't know any of that," he said with a hint of melancholy in his voice that I instantly wished would go away.

She lifted her eyes to us, and the look on her face was one of confusion and borderline disgust. "Well, you'll learn soon. All the grownups are getting it ready now." Her name was called out in the distance then, and she looked at us one more time before taking off in the direction of the sound.

Dave grinned at her tiny retreating figure, and I cuddled closer to him as we watched the sun disappear from the sky in the form of a brilliant sunset, its rich, magnificent colors captivating me as they always did. Just as the last of the sun dripped away and the Earth turned that blue-black color, thousands of soft, golden yellow lights illuminated around the center of the village, the little lights enclosed in glass jars and hanging from ropes that were strung through the trees. Some lined the ground, brightening up the grass and casting their glow around the village in a way that transfixed me. The fire pit had been lit in the very center of the village, and it provided warmth on this chilly night as well as true lighting. I felt my lips curl up into a soft smile at the warm feeling of the lights and fire.

Nothing compared to what I heard. Just like when we had first arrived, the children were all congregated onto the stage, their mouths opening and closing as they vocalized words in synchronization. Some of their voices were high while others were low, but that only created an interesting sound that completely thrilled me. They kept going, always repeating the same sentence after a few different sentences, for a few minutes, and it wasn't until Eve walked up the stairs and straight to the microphone that they stopped. "Thank you, children, for your beautiful song. Now I wish to invite my grandson, David... David, and our beloved Zelda Jadestone to the front of the stage, please."

I let out a breath of air I had been sucking in at the mention of Dave's name, but all my fears flew away the moment he stood up, offered me his arm just like he did on the first day we met, and guided me to the front of the stage. The older woman smiled at us, and out of the corner of my eye, I could just make out Sharlee's hand waving to us from her place with the other children.

"You two have battled and won against impossible odds to be with us here tonight," Eve said. "Your efforts and triumphs deserve to be greatly commemorated, and this celebration is just one way of showing our respect for you two heroes. Accept these necklaces woven from flowers by the hands of the children as a gift for you." Two people brought us the necklaces adorned with beautiful, blooming flowers; Dave turned to place his around my neck, and I did the same for him with mine. I usually hated attention, especially when called something as ridiculous as a hero, but having them welcome me with their open arms made me feel like I was a part of something whole, something good, something permanent.

"We begin this festival remembering what you've done to escape the Society," continued Eve. "We respect you. We honor you. But above all, we welcome you." Eve lifted the cup that was in her hand and shouted, "To Zelda and David!"

"To Zelda and David!" the rest of the village echoed, and at that moment, I couldn't remember a time when I had felt so utterly loved before.

We were directed toward a teenage girl at the front of the stage who was holding a strange wooden thing with strings attached to it. She connected the stick in her hand to the strings, eliciting wonderful sounds that I didn't know existed before then. Fast-paced and high-pitched, I couldn't take my eyes away from the teenage girl producing mesmerizing sounds from such a strange, slender wooden object and skinny stick. An electronic-like sound was added to hers to create an amazing backbeat for her, the two sounds intermingling perfectly. "It's called a violin," Dave said from behind me to grab my attention. "Someone told me it's called a violin, and it's creating what Sharlee said before: music. The children were singing earlier as well."

Violin. Music. Singing. "It's beautiful." I committed it all to memory—the sound of it, the look of it, the *feel* of it—and grinned as the girl, with her violin tucked under her chin, developed a small, proud smile on her face at my comment. "What about dancing? Didn't Sharlee say something about dancing?"

Dave chuckled, gripped my shoulders loosely, and spun me around gently so I could see the entire village from where I was standing. Everywhere there was light, there were people moving together. The children hopped up and down, their giggles of pure delight tickling my eardrums. The adults clapped in time with the music's beat produced by the violin and unseen computer, moving their limbs in a floppy-yet-organized fashion. Everyone's smiles and hearty laughs brightened the village much more than the lights or the fire ever could.

I laughed along with them when someone tugged at my hand and pulled Dave and me into the circle they had created around the fire pit, everyone connected to someone by their interwoven hands. It took a few tries, but I eventually learned to kick up my left or right leg at the same moment as the rest of them, to clap my hands together when they did, to spin around in circles whenever they decided it was the right time to do so in perfect synchronization. The warmth from the fire felt so nice on my body.

The young girl at the front of the stage never played the same song twice, presenting new melodies each time. We shouted, we laughed, we cheered. Kicked, clapped, and spun. Sang. Danced. Talked. And with that, with the new feeling that I *belonged,* all the anxieties, all the stress, all the pressure I had felt melted away. I allowed myself to get lost in the dance, in the music, in the people. I felt alive in the way my bones hummed with the vibrations from everyone's stomps and claps. I felt electrified by Dave's touch as we danced hand-in-hand. I felt such a surge of warmth that I was sure I would burn.

One song was slow, nothing like the other ones we had danced to before. Dave and I watched as everyone grabbed a partner, held them close, and spun in slow circles, looking content in each other's embrace. I smiled sweetly at the image, but that smile grew quickly into a grin when I felt Dave tap my shoulder lightly, a bundle of freshly picked wildflowers and even some from his necklace in his hand. He dipped into a bow, that boyish grin of his standing out against his reddened cheeks, and he asked in a regal manner: "Zelda Jadestone, would you do me the great pleasure of dancing with me tonight?"

I graciously accepted the bouquet of flowers and stuck out my other hand for him to take. "I'd be honored."

He swept me up into his arms and held me close to him as we mimicked the rest of the people in their movements, spinning slowly in a circle. I sprinkled the flowers into his hair when I didn't know what to do with them; I couldn't help but laugh at the way they tumbled into his eyes and how happily annoyed he looked when he had to blow them away from his face. "Think that's funny?!" he playfully shouted, to which I nodded fiercely, nearly doubled over. Dave developed that devilish smirk I knew well, and before I knew it, I was twirling in his arms before he dipped me low to the ground, his face hovering just a few inches from mine.

"Dave!" I teasingly scolded, my breath coming out in small pants from the rush of the dive.

"Don't worry, I've got you," he said lovingly before planting a short kiss on my nose. "I'll always catch you."

I could do nothing else but close to distance between us and press our lips together, but my sudden rush of affection caused Dave to falter, and we both ended up on the floor. "So much for always catching me," I joked, smacking him playfully on the shoulder.

"You didn't let me finish my sentence, sweetheart," he responded in defense, his grin almost reaching his ears and threatening to split his face in two. "I'll always catch you, *and* I'll always fall when you do."

Dave picked us up from the ground, and we resumed twirling around, laughing, and absorbing as we much as could about one another. I didn't leave his arms for the rest of the night as we became lost in our own little world, one full of music, dancing, and us, just us. I looked around my surroundings: the people trying not to peek at the two of us, the children running around without a care in the world, the lights and the fire, and I knew when I crawled into bed that night that I could call the village my home, and its people, my family.

CHAPTER 6

I woke up in a panic from a nightmare I couldn't remember. My arms flailed and my legs kicked out to try and balance myself from falling off my small bed, but I ended up on the cold tile floor regardless of my frantic movements. I searched for Dave to make sure he was safe and found him asleep with his mouth half-open in a bed about five cots down from mine. Not wishing to wake him up but needing some fresh air, I gathered the teddy bear and family portrait, crept slowly through the maze of small beds, pushed the swinging door open quietly so it didn't squeak, and padded on my toes down the main hall of the hospital and out the door. The sun had not yet risen, so everything was still covered in the darkness of an early morning, the lights and fire long burnt out, but I didn't need light where I wanted to go.

From the small amount of light that the moon provided me, I navigated through the village until I reached a tree along the outskirts. I safely tucked the teddy bear underneath my arm and the portrait into the waistband of the front of my pants before climbing the tree, grasping branches and pulling myself up, much like what I used to do back in the Society with my province's sculpture. I didn't stop climbing until I reached a good place to sit down and think, maybe eight or so feet above the grass.

I leaned my head back against the trunk, my torso parallel to the tree, and I let my mind wander to distract myself from my nightmare. I placed the picture on my lap and traced Peter's baby face with my forefinger, trying to imagine myself running my fingers through his real hair instead of the glass. "I miss you," I whispered to his image; to all of them, really. I missed my mom, my dad, and my younger brother. A realization hit me that I would never get to say the three words that meant everything to my parents who fought so hard for love to be present in everyone's lives, to my brother who put himself in danger for my safety alone. So up in that tree eight feet from the ground, I carved those three, simple words into the wood, just to hold the Earth accountable for taking them away from me, if only for a moment.

The air is much colder and much more unforgiving when there's no one around, and I suddenly missed the feel of Dave's—now mine—Uniform jacket around my shoulders. I panicked for just a second when I realized for the first time that during the operation on my leg and shoulder, the doctor must've changed my clothes. I was wearing a brown shirt now, the same cut as the mandatory gray one the Society made me wear, and rather bulky pants that, unlike the ones I had to slash, reached my ankles. I was grateful for the change in wardrobe, although I sincerely hoped they didn't destroy that jacket; regardless of the emblem on the side and the five, glittering red stars, I had taken a liking to it.

I left the Society. If I closed my eyes tightly enough, I could try to convince myself that this was all a particularly awful nightmare, but the images were too vivid to be considered anything but reality. I could still see the blood trickling out of Alvin's head as a Uniform sent a bullet flying through my coworker's skull. Caleb's chilling sendoff still echoed in my ears. Mr. Woobi's almost-execution and my reaction stained my mind permanently, and knowing I could do nothing about these things made them that much more painful. Except one. One I was determined to change.

Peter. How could I have left him alone in a Society determined to take him hostage? From the way Caleb had grinned when I left, I knew he knew that I had abandoned Peter to be under his jurisdiction. I kept repeating to myself that I would free Peter, but realistically, *how*? I had no power. No great master plan of action. No idea how to pop the boundary surrounding the Society. I was nothing but an eighteen-year-old girl who ran away from the only place she remembered, from the only piece of her family left standing.

The orange sun started to kiss the horizon good morning, and as I gazed at the colors that come with sunrise, I thought of the night before and how much Eric would have enjoyed himself. He loved silly little movements like that, and his natural charisma around people would've made him instantly popular among the villagers. I grabbed the teddy bear a little more tightly when the thought of the search party *still* not finding him or Mr. Woobi crossed my mind. Eric had to be alive. I didn't know a time when there was a Zelda without an Eric, and I liked it that way. I liked that we knew everything about each other, that he could read my emotions better than I could understand them, that his presence alone was enough to fill me with peace. He couldn't be dead. The search party would find him and Mr. Woobi alive and well because I was certain that if Eric Stellenzer ever left Earth, Zelda Jadestone would, too.

Despite their irreconcilable differences from a past falling out over four years ago, I knew Eric cared deeply for Mr. Woobi, the man who practically raised him from the time he was six years old, and that Eric would take good care of him out there in the wilderness. A part of me continued to resent the elder man for intentionally sending Peter away, but a much larger part loved him deeply, the way a daughter loves her father.

I was so wrapped up in my thoughts that I barely heard a clicking sound close by, and I turned my head sharply when I heard an unfamiliar female voice say, "Oh, that's perfect!"

The words were so sudden that I fell out of the tree with a shriek of surprise, still holding both the bear and the family portrait while landing right on my arm with a loud thud. I groaned and shut my eyes for a few seconds before feeling someone grasp the arm I didn't fall on and pull me to my feet. I had to blink a few times before my eyes adjusted to see a woman, her long, platinum blonde hair pulled back in a tight elastic, her brown eyes twinkling at me in a mischievous way as I tried to regain my senses from the impact of the fall. "Hi," I said, rubbing my sore arm. "Sorry, I didn't see you. I was up in the, uh, tree."

"I know," said the woman brightly. "You fell out."

I chuckled awkwardly and waited for her to say something more, but when the silence continued for too long for comfort, I finally asked, "Um, can I help you?"

She took my question as an invitation to stick out her hand, soft and perfectly manicured, and introduce herself as Allyson Killians, age twenty-nine, from Neweryork, an alum from some professional media communications school, the name of which I couldn't be bothered to remember. None of that interested me, so I was about to bid her a good morning and be done with it when she said, "And you're Zelda Jadestone."

"Yeah," I said with my eyebrow raised. "I am."

"We've heard all about you." I was just about to ask who "we" were and how they could have possibly known me when someone stepped out of Allyson's shadow.

"Hi," she greeted brightly. Her hair was red, much like Sharlee's except perhaps a shade or two browner, and her eyes were a rather stunning green color that I thought complemented her hair nicely. She was much shorter than I was, with a larger build, and when she stuck out her hand for me to shake, I noticed freckles traveled up the length of her forearm. "I'm Marlena Heist. Call me Marley." Her eyes got wide. "I mean, if you want. You can call me Marley. It's really up to you. I'm seventeen. I'm interning under Allyson for my gap year from school." Marley turned a bright shade of red. "You probably don't care. Sorry. I talk when I get nervous."

Her rambling made me smile, so I said, "Of course, I care," which made the girl turn away quickly, although I could still hear her squeak into the sleeve of her brightly patterned shirt.

"Wow," she squealed. "I can't believe we're really, actually meeting you. This is crazy. I mean, you're not crazy, this whole thing is... I... just... I... wow."

Allyson raised one side of her lip up in disgust at her comrade. "Sorry about her," she apologized. "She's a big fan."

"Of me?!" I exclaimed, shocked when I saw the pair of them nod. "Why? How?" The sun had bid the horizon a good day by then, rising steadily into the sky, and I squinted at the sudden brightness.

Allyson squealed and clapped excitedly, and I had to bite the inside of my cheek to make sure I wasn't delusional from the fall. "Oh, you're so humble. We're here for the interview," said the blonde, kneeling now as she began to pull items like two foldable chairs and fancier cameras from the large bag on the ground. "This is a good place," she spoke again, except this time, not to me. "The sun in the back will make for a good backdrop."

"Agreed," Marley responded, proceeding to place the cameras in specific places around where Allyson had set up the chairs.

"Whoa, whoa, whoa," I interrupted, putting up my hands, one of them still holding Peter's teddy bear. I quickly put that hand behind my back to hide the bear from their view. "What interview?"

"We spoke to Eve Redding yesterday after the video of you speaking went viral," Allyson told me nonchalantly. "Now sit. We have much to discuss."

The commanding undertone to Allyson's voice convinced me that I didn't really have any other option, so I took a seat in the makeshift chair across from her, arranging Peter's teddy bear so it sat neatly on my lap. I tucked the family portrait in between the bear and my torso to hide it from view, but I knew it wasn't entirely concealed.

Marley stood behind the camera that faced me, its black emptiness making me anxious and twitchy, but I had no time to think about my discomfort. Allyson's face cracked into a huge fake smile, and she half-sang, "Good morning, Neweryork, from me, Allyson Killians, and the rest of the crew at NewerNews! I hope everyone is having a fantastic morning. I know I am. I'm reporting from the village closest to the Northeastern Society, where I'm joined here today with the girl we have all quickly grown to love: Zelda Jadestone!"

Marley gave me an enthusiastic thumbs up accompanied by a reassuring smile, and I forced a smile full of confusion onto my face as I waved half-heartedly to the camera. A red light blinked at me every few seconds, and it made me uncomfortable.

"Now Zelda," spoke Allyson, directing my attention back to her. "You are the first person to ever escape the boundary successfully. How'd you do it?"

"I, uh…" The lens got closer to my face, focusing in on my facial expressions, and I broke out into a sweat as I tried to swallow the lump that had formed in my throat. "Um… I was chased out. I had no choice but to leave the Society."

She nodded understandingly. Except she didn't understand; she couldn't possibly. "Why were you chased, Zelda?"

Zelda. Mr. Woobi's gruff voice uttering my name through a smile. How could I have lived with myself if he had died under my gaze?

Zelda. Caleb's harsh reprimand, reminding me that I was still only a child that he had to discipline.

Zelda. My friends' joyous yelps when they saved me from death, right before meeting death themselves.

The camera lens felt intruding, like a stranger's gaze on my naked body. I shut my eyes in an effort to hide.

"You can tell us when you're ready, Zelda," Allyson said in a soft tone of voice that tricked me into thinking she cared.

"I made a speech to stop the death of Charles Woobi," I said tentatively, clasping the soft teddy bear closer to my stomach. "Caleb had him strapped to a chair, tied down with metal restraints. And he was going to electrocute him. I didn't know what else to do, I—"

"You're so brave, Zelda," Allyson interrupted, reaching out to pat my arm.

I recoiled away from her touch. "I'm not brave."

"Of course, you are," she argued. "You are the only person to ever escape alive."

"It wasn't just me. I didn't do it alone," I heard myself say before I could stop the words from tumbling out of my mouth. I instantly regretted them when I saw Allyson's eyes sparkle at my confession.

"Elaborate, please." The "please" felt like an afterthought.

"My little brother, Peter, he popped the boundary long enough for Dave, Mr. Woobi, Eric, and me to escape." This admission filled me with such blinding shame that I couldn't help but rush to say, "But I'm going back to save Peter." I sat up straighter in my chair, no longer caring about the camera trained to capture my every movement. Heat sparked in me, and I felt it spreading outward from my chest, undulating in waves until I felt like my body had turned into a furnace. "There is no other option. I *will* go back."

"I believe you," she said, and the sincerity behind her voice seemed too real to be false. "I bet that's who this little plush belongs to, am I correct?"

I nodded. The bear had a calming presence, just sitting on my lap, and I patted the top of its fuzzy head. "I'm going to return it to him when I see him again," I said.

Allyson smiled sweetly. "Zelda, you and Peter are the children of Owen and Alina Jadestone, two people this state considers heroes for their sacrifices during the Second American Civil War. I think I even see a photo of them on your lap. Can you show me what photo you're holding?"

Gently, I unveiled my family portrait, and Allyson immediately placed a hand over her heart. "Oh, how precious," she cooed. "Look at how adorable your family was." Allyson glanced me over in pity. "You must miss them so much, Zelda."

I wished I knew how to properly miss Alina and Owen Jadestone. Since walking through my old home, I remembered a few scattered memories, but the memories were more feelings than anything concrete. I missed my mother, my father, my family unit, but when Caleb erased my memory upon entering the Society, he robbed me of ever getting to know my parents as anything more than my caregivers. I didn't remember what my mother's favorite things were, what angered my father most, stories from when they were my age. I didn't remember anything other than warm, fuzzy comfortability, the familiar feeling of coziness and safety. A distinct boundary separated my parents and me, and I hated that this boundary was one I knew I could never destroy.

"Caleb erased our memories when we entered the Society," I told Allyson as I secured the family portrait between Peter's teddy bear and my body once more. "I don't remember my parents, or my time outside the boundary. It's all a blur."

"Leader Caleb wiped everyone's memories from their time before the Society?" Allyson audibly gasped after I confirmed her statement. "That's terrible! They don't remember their families."

I shook my head. "Trying to find out any information resulted in extreme punishment, most likely execution. No one wants their memories badly enough to risk death."

"How dangerous was escaping the Society then, Zelda?" asked Allyson.

"Very," I croaked. "Innocent people died."

"How many people?"

I couldn't hold her penetrating gaze any longer. "More than a hundred."

"And who killed them, Zelda?"

Me, I wanted to whisper, but she wouldn't understand that answer, so I whispered the first name that instantly popped into my mind: "Caleb."

"Can you repeat what you said? The microphones didn't pick that up."

I lifted my head to lock eyes with her, raising my voice so she could hear me clearly this time: "Caleb Woobi killed them. Caleb Woobi killed my friends. And Caleb Woobi has my brother."

Allyson grinned like she had discovered some great fortune, glanced at Marley, and said eagerly into the camera's lens: "Thank you for watching this segment. More on this story later." And the red light stopped blinking.

"You were perfect!" chirped Marley from behind the camera. "Thank you!"

I wasn't about to say, "You're welcome," but I nodded nonetheless.

"We sent the footage to production, so it'll air on the eight o'clock morning news in about fifteen minutes. You can watch it on any screen then," said Allyson, and I nodded again, despite having absolutely no desire to watch myself.

As Allyson and Marley started to pack up their things, Eve and Dave came walking out of the hospital to meet us; the sight of familiar faces made me instantly relax, and I waved Dave over to stand beside me. Eve and Allyson shook hands and exchanged pleasantries like they had been friends for years; despite Dave asking me questions about what had happened, I couldn't take my attention away from the two women. From the way their heads bowed together and the hushed nature of their voices, I figured something deeper was brewing, but before I had the chance to confront them, I heard voices calling to us from the forest.

I turned to see a large party of around thirty people walking toward us, waving their hands excitedly and yelling words I was too far away to hear. Dave turned to see what I was looking at, and we both squinted to try and get a better look before it clicked. There would only be one reason a group that large would be emerging from the trees, and my suspicions were confirmed when a familiar, deep, male voice shouted, "Zelda!"

I didn't have to see his dark hair, slender build, or green eyes to know who said my name that way, and I took off running toward him just as I saw him take his place at the front of the group.

Eric Stellenzer and I met halfway, and I launched myself into his arms before we had a chance to slow down. He took it in stride and caught me, twirling us around as we both laughed deliriously. "You're alive!" we said simultaneously, and I wrapped my arms around his neck until he turned purple from the lack of oxygen.

He gently put me down, but we still stood impossibly close, shooting random questions at each other without really expecting any answers. We looked up when we both heard a mighty "Eric!" to witness Dave sprint toward us, only to slam into Eric with a ferocious hug. "It's so good to see you," Dave said.

"You too, man," Eric said just as sincerely, and they clapped each other on the back once before eyeing me and opening their arms for me to join them. The three of us hugged each other for several seconds; having Eric near me again made my heart want to burst from the intense surge of affection.

Eric placed his hands on his hips, sighed heavily, and joked, "Wow, what a great reunion. I hope you guys greet the old man over there"—he jabbed his thumb in the general direction of the search party—"with as much enthusiasm. He might get jealous."

Mr. Woobi. I whipped around to catch a glimpse of him, Dave quickly following my gaze. I scrambled to distract the ex-Uniform long enough for him not to notice Eve and Mr. Woobi's reunion, but I didn't move quickly enough; the older man's icy eyes found Eve's immediately, and the pull between the two was as undeniable as gravity itself.

The two lost spouses took several steps toward each other, the magnetism between them seemingly yanking their souls closer together, and they stopped just a few feet away. I could tell by the way his astonished stare never once left her that Charles Woobi could only see Eve Redding. Eric swooned a little when we watched the older man's hands reach out to touch her, only to unsteadily retreat. Mr. Woobi's whole body trembled like a leaf when the wind blows, and he kept blinking as if trying to wake up from a dream. He looked younger, too: not the wise elder who told Peter and me stories from the past; not the broken old man who barely flinched at his execution; not the scarred, older, crazy man who was haunted by his memories; but a man who lost his heart years ago and had finally found it again. His face, mutilated by the Societan emblem etched in his skin, softened and glowed, like all the suffering he endured during his time in the Society had melted off his body. At the sight of Eve Redding, Charles Woobi transformed into a wounded, bleeding heart just beginning to scab over.

Eve attempted to observe her husband stoically, the way she had with Dave and me, but the glassy look in her dark brown eyes gave her away. She, too, quivered in longing, but seemed afraid to touch him. "Charlie" left her lips in just above a whisper, yet the air carried it away so quickly that I wondered if I had imagined it. The older woman's gaze traveled from his toes to the top of his head, analyzing every part of him. Once she seemed certain that his chest rose and fell in time with his breaths, she cracked a minuscule smirk and said, "Just in time for breakfast, Charlie."

The grin that bloomed on Mr. Woobi's face lit up the entire village. "I wouldn't miss it for the world, my love," he replied smoothly. "I know how you feel about me skipping meals."

Eve didn't get a chance to respond, because Mr. Woobi closed the remaining distance between them, throwing his arms around her and bringing his hands to clutch her hair. She stood perhaps an inch taller than him, giving him the opportunity to bury his face into the crook of her neck and mumble words only she could hear. Eve immediately reciprocated the affection, quickly pulling him closer to her until I was sure that their two souls clicked together. Although there were many words I couldn't overhear, I did catch her disbelievingly asking, "How did you not forget me?"

Mr. Woobi placed a leathery kiss to her cheek, lingering there long enough to say directly into her ear: "I could never forget you, my love. Not when you have given me so much to remember."

She laughed through a pool of thick tears, and as they tightened their embrace, I knew that they had found their way home.

I had temporarily forgotten Dave had been standing next to me until he exclaimed, "Wait, *what*?"

Everyone—Eve, Mr. Woobi, Eric, Allyson, Marley, the search group, and I—turned to look at the ex-Uniform absorb the news. Dave clenched his fists and opened them again, alternating between a blooming flower and a wilting one, as if he couldn't choose which to be. Redness crept up his face from the back of his neck when he spat at Mr. Woobi: "*You?*" A disbelieving crackle of a laugh flew out his mouth. "No. No, that's impossible."

Dave twisted to look at me with wide, glassy eyes that screamed for reassurance, but I could barely muster, "Dave, let's go somewhere and talk, okay?"

He took a clumsy step away from me and shook his head. "Wait, wait, hold on. Zelda, you *knew*?"

Words stumbled to escape my mouth. "Dave, I—"

Dave took another step backward and lifted his head so I could see the fury that raged behind his bright eyes, fury directed at *me*. His eyebrows were knitted so intensely against his eyes that they cast a dark shadow in his eye sockets, and for a singular moment, I thought I saw Caleb in Dave's angular facial structure. "You knew!" He roared so loudly, my eardrums vibrated. "You knew about my *family*. Even in the Society, you knew."

"Dave—"

"NO!" His throat must've rubbed raw from the fierceness behind his yell. "To think, I trusted you. Blake told me months ago that you'd get me killed, but this"—he gestured to our surroundings, but I wasn't sure if he was referring to the village, to Mr. Woobi and Eve, or to the forest around us—"*this* is so much worse. Did you know this whole time?" When

I struggled to answer him, Dave narrowed his eyes and yelled, "What, can't talk anymore, Zelda?"

"David, don't blame Zelda Ellyn."

The ex-Uniform whipped around to glare at Mr. Woobi then, storming up until he loomed over the elder's hunched form. "And you," he said with so much malice laced through his voice that I could barely tell it was Dave speaking. "I arrested you. You let me *arrest* you to be *tortured*. And you're my... my..."

Mr. Woobi stretched his hand toward Dave in a pathetic attempt to make a connection. "David, I couldn't tell you. Caleb and I made a deal—"

Dave paled at the name. "Caleb? As in Leader Caleb?" When no response greeted him, he shook his head viciously. "No. No way. No! That's not possible. That can't be possible. Leader Caleb is—"

"My son," Mr. Woobi interrupted.

"A murderer!" finished Dave, his voice cracking halfway through as anguish slowly replaced his anger. He lifted his hands up to his eye level and stared at them in absolute repulsion.

"David," Eric spoke softly, a stark contrast to the other boy. "Why don't we go somewhere to cool off, huh?"

Dave turned his gaze to Eric then, and despite the wrath Dave attempted to bury him in, Eric remained undeterred. "Did you know, too, Stellenzer?"

Eric put his hands up in surrender and said, "Hey, dude, this is just as much of a surprise to me as it is to you."

Dave looked Eric up and down, his breathing erratic. "How can I trust you?"

"Like I'd let you live down having *Woobi* as a last name?" Eric raised an eyebrow and smirked. "C'mon. Let's take a walk."

Dave's jaw muscles twitched, and he eyed everyone surrounding him with distrust before he said, "I'd like to be alone."

Eric faltered. "I-I don't think that's a good idea, bud. I'll go with—"

"Zelda!" Sharlee's high-pitched squeal got everyone's attention, and we all watched her run up to me with a small screen in her hand. "Look, you're on tv!"

Eric, Dave, Mr. Woobi, Eve, Marley, Allyson, and I gathered around Sharlee's screen to view what she meant.

One man sat at a desk, back rigid as he stared directly at us through the screen and said, "Viral sensation Zelda Jadestone, the first person to escape the boundary alive, has spoken out about the trauma she experienced during her time under Caleb Woobi's dictatorship. Allyson Killians, head reporter at NewerNews and owner of Newer Media, sat down with Zelda Jadestone in an exclusive interview earlier today."

The photo Marley had captured of me in the tree materialized on screen, but I barely recognized myself. My body bathed in shadows, with just my outline highlighted by the spectacular, fiery orange of the rising sun. The tips of fuzz on Peter's teddy bear glowed yellow, like the sun had just begun to set it aflame, and despite the low lighting, you could see my head tilted down toward the bear, my forehead just about to graze its own. Although the picture only stayed on the screen for a few seconds, I knew from Allyson's breathy, "Wow," that it had resonated with those watching, wherever they might've been.

The program cut to the actual interview Allyson and I had done, beginning with Allyson asking how I had escaped the Society. I closed my eyes and cringed, expecting to hear the stutters and clumsy wording that I had uttered earlier, but instead, I heard a confident voice—*my* voice—say, "I had no choice but to leave the Society."

I wrinkled my nose in confusion and opened my eyes again, watching more intently as interviewer-Allyson nodded and asked, "Why were you chased, Zelda?"

Again, I waited for the awkward pause that had followed as a result of my cracking composure, but that never came. Interviewee-Zelda tugged the teddy bear closer to her stomach and answered, "I made a speech to stop the death of Charles Woobi. Caleb had him strapped to a chair, tied down with metal restraints, and he was going to electrocute him." My words flowed easily on the screen, completely unlike the way they tripped out of my mouth earlier. I didn't know whether to feel relieved or appalled.

The man at the desk flashed back onto the screen, interrupting the interview to say, "Zelda Jadestone explained most of her story in the now-viral video of her when she arrived at Eve Redding's village."

The program showed a clip of me in the village the night Dave and I arrived, but I didn't recognize that girl on the stage, either. This Zelda had her dark hair tangled behind her, skin covered in dirt, and pain written so clearly on her body when she croaked, "I lost my family, the only home I've ever known, *everything.*" But there was something else as well, something smoldering about the way she spat her words, something burning behind this Zelda's irises that made it impossible to look away when she announced, "I'd rather die free than live with my life dictated for me. I won't let that happen again."

The man at the desk returned, saying, "When asked about her parents, local war heroes Alina and Owen Jadestone, Zelda Jadestone claimed Leader Caleb Woobi of the Northeastern Society erased his citizens' memories upon entering his Society."

The program cut back to the interview to show me revealing my family portrait and saying, "I don't remember my parents, or my time outside the boundary. It's all a blur. Caleb erased our memories when we entered the Society."

I watched interviewer-Allyson exclaim, "That's terrible! They don't remember their families."

"Trying to find out any information resulted in extreme punishment, most likely execution," I heard myself explain, but I didn't recall having that much raw anger in my voice. This Zelda had much more conviction in her tone than I remembered. "No one wants their memories badly enough to risk death."

The man behind the desk appeared once again to say, "Zelda Jadestone also revealed how she managed to escape, citing her brother, Peter Jadestone, as her savior."

There I was again, declaring, "My little brother, Peter, he popped the boundary long enough for Dave, Mr. Woobi, Eric, and me to escape."

Interviewer-Allyson asked, "I bet that's who this little plush belongs to, am I correct?"

Interviewee-Zelda nodded, and again, I took notice of how the editors of the interview rearranged certain segments or cut entire portions out. I involuntarily leaned closer to the screen to absorb every moment.

"How dangerous was what you did, Zelda?" Allyson had asked.

"Innocent people died. More than a hundred."

"And who killed them, Zelda?"

I watched as interviewee-Zelda stared at Allyson with seething intensity, enough anger in her eyes to take out an entire Society of her own, and I held my breath when she growled, "Caleb Woobi killed them. Caleb Woobi killed my friends. Caleb Woobi has my brother. But I'm going back to save Peter. There is no other option. I *will* go back."

"Why was the interview edited out of order like that?" I blurted, but no one listened to me.

Eric, Dave, Mr. Woobi, Eve, Marley, and Allyson watched as the man behind the desk wrapped up the news segment, but I was too baffled to care. Once Sharlee stepped away from the group and slipped her screen into her pant pocket, they all turned to stare at me, emotions on their faces ranging from shock to amazement, from anger to awe, from pride to disbelief. The weight of their eyes made me want to fold into myself.

"That," declared Marley, "was—"

"Exactly what we needed," finished Allyson, and Marley nodded enthusiastically in agreement.

"What are you talking about? I doubt anyone watched it, anyway. It's just me," I said, crossing my arms in front of my chest.

Loud shouts interrupted Allyson's rebuttal, and we all turned to see a hoard of people storming out of their houses and marching to the center of the village. It started as twenty or so individuals, but the longer we watched, the more people exited their homes to congregate around the fire pit until I was sure the entire village surrounded it. Older people, parents, adolescents, and children alike gathered to yell in unison, and even from the outskirts, I could see the rage building inside their bodies.

"Oh no," muttered Eric under his breath, taking a step closer to me as we watched the scene unfold.

The crowd of thousands surged like a tidal wave, acting not as individuals but as a collective, singular body. They raised their fists together, stomped their feet together, and ultimately, chanted together, each person raising his or her voice until one thought rang around the trees: "Kill Caleb Woobi." They recited the mantra like a prayer, screaming it until I'm sure Caleb Woobi himself heard. I watched the way those words lit them up, watched the way the people ignited at the taste of his name on their tongues, and I trembled at their power, at what their sudden lust for blood meant, at what *my* words made them do.

Mr. Woobi's voice held a hint of disbelief when he proclaimed, "Zelda Ellyn, I think you may have started a war."

CHAPTER 7

I chose to sit on one of the benches surrounding the fire pit with Eric once everything simmered down and we had all gone our separate ways. Allyson and Marley went back to Neweryork after filming the riot in the village, thanking me profusely for the "incredible work" I had done. Mr. Woobi, Eve, Eric, and I tried speaking with Dave, but he couldn't bring himself to look at any of us, so the older couple chose to take a walk around the village while Eric and I went to sit by ourselves.

Eric and I traded stories about our time spent apart to get our minds off what had just transpired. I learned that for the three days he and I were separated, Eric and Mr. Woobi stayed on the Societan side of the river, and thankfully, Caleb's explosions hadn't significantly hurt them: only a few minor burns on their legs. Eric had gone to chase after me when Dave and I had fallen into the river, but the water current whisked us away faster than he could run. In those three days, they didn't eat a morsel of food, but eventually, halfway through the second day, Eric caved and drank the river water.

Once I had finished rehashing my last three days and we had fallen into a comfortable lull, Eric quipped, "So, 125 is a Woobi, huh? How long have you known?"

My chest tightened at the memory of Dave's anguished gaze. "The day we left," I answered. "You?"

Eric sighed and crossed his legs. "Charles and I, we didn't just sit in silence all three days, you know?" He pursed his lips before saying, "I feel awful. David doesn't deserve to have Caleb Woobi as a father."

The thought made me queasy, and I locked my hand around Eric's for comfort, which he took as an invitation to wrap his arm around my shoulder and pull me closer. His touch provided peace, and I rested my head into the crook of his neck. "Dave's so *angry*," I whispered. "The way he looked at me, I—"

"You were furious when you found out about Charles persuading Peter to become a Uniform," interjected Eric, but before I could respond, he shifted in his seat and said, "Speaking of, actually, I've been meaning to tell you something for a while now. That falling out Charles and I had years ago, it wasn't random."

"I figured."

"No." Eric drew a shuddered breath, and I felt him clasp my hand tighter as he surveyed the surrounding area with wide eyes. "Had it not been Peter, it would've been me. I just realized his tricks sooner."

I sat up straighter. "What are you talking about?"

"Charles spent years telling me these stories about what life was like before the Society until I became obsessed with it, like we all did. I would've done almost anything to know more about my old life, but a year or so before Peter left, Charles changed, somehow. The fun stories he would tell became stories of his missing family members, war, my own parents' disappearance, you name it. And then, Uniforms got involved; he would talk about this database with all the information that would cure my curiosity, but only Uniforms have access to it, and all this other stuff. I don't know, Zelda, it was weird. When I finally asked him if he wanted me to spy for him after Peter's eleventh birthday dinner, he said yes, and when I said I wouldn't do that, wouldn't just *leave* you and Peter like that, he wanted nothing to do with me. And then, a few months later—"

"Peter leaves," I said.

"To become a Uniform," Eric finished, casting his gaze down to the floor and scuffing his shoes against the dirt. "Zelda, I'm so sorry, I should've told you that I had a suspicion about why Peter left sooner, but I didn't know how to bring it up, and—"

I shook my head fiercely. "No, it needed to come from him. I needed to hear that he stole my brother from him, not you. I am so tired of his secrets."

I caught sight of Mr. Woobi approaching in the distance, and hot, blinding rage coursed through my body, capable of incinerating any rational thought. I rose from my seated position to meet the elder man halfway, my muscles taut and tense from unchecked fury. My old neighbor had one hand raised in greeting when I drew my fist back and almost socked Charles Woobi in the mouth before thinking better of it and punching the closest tree trunk instead, my knuckles throbbing in protest the moment I clumsily connected with the sturdy bark. I tried to shake the pain out of my hand as I shouted, "How dare you? How *dare* you convince me to keep your dirty secret about Dave? How dare you use Peter? How dare you try to use Eric? I…" Words couldn't even begin to express the boiling anger I felt eating away at my skin, so I whirled my other hand up, fully prepared to inflict another blow, but Mr. Woobi caught my fist before I had the chance to punch the tree again.

"I wouldn't do that again if I were you, Zelda Ellyn," he said in a slow, low tone, and I only stepped out of his grasp after blood trickled down the back of my hand from my knuckles.

"Don't act like you're not complicit," Mr. Woobi stated. "What stopped you from telling David about his lineage those three days you two roamed the woods together? What stopped you from exposing the truth then, hm, Zelda Ellyn? What gave you pause?"

I floundered for an answer. "I—"

Mr. Woobi brought a handkerchief out of his pocket to wrap my injured hand. "You knew I was correct when I said the information would destroy him. You were scared David would view you differently. Your fears about David were mine about you knowing the truth behind Peter's disappearance. Do you see that? I was afraid you'd see me differently if you knew the information I had kept from you for your own protection, just as you have done with David." The elder took several steps closer to me and studied me intently. "I feel as though it would be unfair to ask for David's forgiveness if you cannot even bring yourself to forgive me, don't you think, Zelda Ellyn?"

I glared down at him defiantly, refusing to admit my defeat. Impulsively, I spat at him, my saliva dripping down his cheek slowly, just as his did on Dave's boot all those months ago.

Mr. Woobi wiped my spit off with the back of his hand calmly, grinned, and declared, "Apology accepted, then. Now, Zelda, we need to discuss the implications of your viral interview today."

The mental image of the villagers screaming for Caleb's blood made me cringe, and I wiped my palms on the front of my pants nervously before wrapping my arms around my body. "I don't really want to talk about it," I said.

"But you will," barked Eve, stepping next to Mr. Woobi and placing a hand on his shoulder. Despite our height difference, the power Eve exuded in that moment made me want to shrivel under her gaze. "Zelda, you saw how that crowd responded to you, and that wasn't even live footage."

I internally groaned and shook my head. "Yeah, but that was spontaneous. It was nothing, really."

Eve took a screen out from her pocket, motioning for Eric to join us as she played NewerNews' live reporting stream. The headline under the video read MORE RIOTS ENSUE AFTER JADESTONE INTERVIEW, and we watched as hundreds, if not thousands, more people were shown gathered in the streets of the city, carrying various signs and screaming to invade the Society, kill Caleb, and free the Societan citizens. Scenes of violence flashed across the screen, clashes between law enforcement and the protestors, and it reminded me strongly of the fight between the Uniforms and the citizens the day of Mr. Woobi's execution. "Still think it was 'nothing,' Zelda?" said Eve after sliding the screen back into her pocket, and I thought I detected the hint of a smile in her voice.

"But I never said any of that. I never said anything about killing Caleb, or invading anything," I protested, but as the villagers' shouts rang through my ears, I could feel my resolve slipping away from me. "I don't get it." I looked to Mr. Woobi to provide answers, but he seemed to have difficulty meeting my eyes.

"Let's see," said Eve, pretending to think as she cocked her head to the side. "'Caleb Woobi killed them. There is no other option; I will go back.' Oh, and let's not forget my personal favorite: 'I would rather die free than live with my life dictated for me. I won't let that happen *again*.' Does any of this ring a bell, Zelda?"

"I said that, yeah, but..." Panic rose into my chest, and despite being outside, I felt cement walls closing in around my body, keeping me prisoner.

"But I don't want a war," I said in a rush, as if my words would stop the walls from crushing me. "I don't want to free any Society or kill any leader. I just want Peter away from anything that might hurt him, and that just so happens to be Caleb, and Caleb just so happens to be the leader of the Society."

"How naïve can you be?" yelled Eve, and I felt Eric tense beside me. "You are not the only one who has a Peter inside that boundary. Almost everyone in this village has at least one loved one in the Society, and the people in the city aren't any exception. No one cares about Peter. No one really cares about you either. You are only a representation of what they want, Zelda."

"And what do they want?" asked Eric.

"To free the family they've lived too long without," answered Mr. Woobi.

"In that viral video of you when you first arrived here and in the interview today, you became them, Zelda," elaborated Eve. "Your voice is theirs, but louder. Your body is their thoughts personified. You are the person they've been needing for fourteen years, and you're perfect. Perfect backstory, perfect personality, perfect words. You're authentic, approachable, but powerful. You speak directly to their souls. We couldn't have found anyone better."

"You can't possibly approve of this," I said, incredulous. "I can't inspire these people to start a war. The people who would die…" I thought of Nelly, Alvin, Anna, and the rest of my coworkers who had died for me, and I almost dry heaved. "No." I turned my gaze to Mr. Woobi, and he seemed unable to look away when I whispered, "I can't."

Mr. Woobi inhaled deeply before saying, "I love you, dear girl. Please believe me when I say that. But unlike the last one, this war must be fought. I must free my son from this prison he's built around himself. You must free Peter from my son's control. Everyone deserves a chance at freedom, and that includes the people imprisoned inside that Society. You could start a movement, Zelda."

"I'm not starting anything," I retorted. "I'm saving Peter. That is all."

"Zelda—"

"I said *no*."

"Don't be selfish."

"Don't be stupid!" I shouted. "Think of everyone who would die. No."

"You really think you can save your brother without our help? You need our technology to pop the boundary surrounding the Society. You need our manpower to fight off the Societan soldiers long enough to grab your brother and run. You need us to provide safety for you and your loved ones"—she gestured toward Eric, who immediately lowered his stare to the grass—"and to go through all that for one little boy is pointless. There are people here, in the village and in the city, that are hurting just as much as you are, Zelda. Isn't it our duty to help them when we are granted that opportunity?" Eve raised her eyebrow up challengingly, daring me to object to her argument.

I tried clenching my fists again, but the knuckles on my left hand ached from when I had punched the tree, so my hands hung loosely at my sides. "Peter isn't just some 'little boy,'" I barked. "He's the only reason your husband, grandson, Eric, and I are still alive. Without him, you'd have nothing but your village left. I convinced myself that leaving him behind was the best—the only—option, but that was the biggest mistake of my life. I won't let myself get convinced again. I'm no freer here than I was in the Society." I leaned in close enough to Eve to where our noses almost touched and asserted, "No."

Eve pointed to my face and announced, "Look at that. It's that passion that I want to direct into this war. Can't you just see the masses of people that will rally behind her words? I've witnessed it happen before, not just on the television or my phone, but in person."

Mr. Woobi looked at me almost sympathetically and murmured, "I have, too." As he and Eve turned to leave, he said, "I know the burden in front of you is one you think you may not have the strength to carry, but the weight of inaction is always heavier, Zelda Ellyn. If you wish to save Peter, this is your only option." And they walked away, leaving Eric and me to ponder what they had said.

The instant the older couple stepped out of earshot, the severity of my situation slapped me in the face, and I fisted my hands into my hair, swaying back and forth on my feet. I bit my bottom lip until I tasted the metallic flavor of blood, but that didn't stop me from running my teeth over the wound, grazing it over again as my heart began to pound.

Zelda. My coworkers' voices warn me against it, auditory reminders of the consequences of violence.

Zelda. Caleb taunts me, sneering at my weakness and indecision.

Zelda. Peter sounds so afraid, so lonely, and so scared, and war doesn't seem so awful if it means he can be free. But what kind of person does that make me to think such things?

I squatted down to my knees and held my head in my hands, gripping my skull to try and squeeze the voices out of my mind.

Eric crouched down beside me and placed a comforting hand on my back, and I curled into him until we were entangled in each other, my arms wrapped around his neck and his around my torso, our legs a jumbled mess. "How can I even *think* about entertaining the idea of being Eve's, or Allyson's, or whoever's puppet for *war*?" I croaked into Eric's neck, and he held me tighter in response. "What kind of person does that?"

"A person faced with an impossible situation," said Eric as he brought a hand up to cradle the back of my head.

"I'm a bad person," I mumbled.

"You are *not* a bad person, Zelda," Eric declared. "You are not evil for wanting to protect your brother."

"Aren't I?" I retorted. "I saw those photos from the Second Civil War in that database. It looked so *painful*. But I'd give anything to get Peter out." I clung to Eric's neck tighter as panic drove itself further into my heart.

"I'll support any decision you make," announced Eric suddenly, and before I had the chance to refute, he said, "because any decision you make will save someone's life, either Peter's or a stranger's. Besides, you know how things are; those crowds might be wanting a war today, but tomorrow, they might forget all about you."

I contemplated his words, but the fury I saw in the village crowd's eyes convinced me nothing I said would be forgotten any time soon. "Would you start a war?" I asked.

It took him a while to answer, but after many long moments, he whispered, "It depends," into my hair.

"Depends on what?"

"Who I'm fighting for."

I loosened my hold on Eric to gaze into his forest-green eyes. I saw only sincerity in his irises, and it frightened me to think that one day, I could look into his eyes and see disgust because of my poor choices. "You can't hate me, Eric," I said suddenly, grasping his biceps to make him understand.

He let out a low chuckle. "I wouldn't worry about that."

"Why not?"

Eric tilted his head and gave me a lopsided smile. "Because you're the person I'd fight a war for."

The look in his eyes had shifted from sincerity to something else, something more unnerving, and suddenly, I became acutely aware of the way his breath tickled my face, of the way his fingers had been unconsciously drawing circles on my skin, of the way I could've easily leaned in just a few inches and connected my lips to his. My sudden awareness made my heart race, and heat surged through my body when Eric inched closer until our noses touched and murmured, "Zelda—"

I shot up onto my feet and watched as Eric did the same, both of our faces bright red and neither of us able to look the other in the eyes. "I'm going to go look for Dave," I stated.

Eric nodded enthusiastically and rubbed the back of his reddened neck. "Yes! Yes, great idea. He needs you. Yeah." He clapped his hands together. "Yup, okay, I'll... go back, somewhere. Go find David. I'll, um, see you later." He smiled at me, but it seemed forced. The sincerity I had seen so clearly in his irises before had vanished, replaced by something unidentifiable.

I returned the gesture, and although my legs wobbled and my knees were on the verge of buckling, I headed in the direction I thought Dave had gone.

He wasn't anywhere in the village, and I genuinely feared he had run off—perhaps back toward the Society—before someone told me that she had seen him walking up the hill near my old house. It took a bit of searching before I found Dave's hunched figure on my old back patio, the sounds of frustrated grumbles and a strange scratching noise filling the air around him. "C'mon," he grunted to himself. "Why won't it..."

"Hey," I said softly so as not to startle him.

No response, only that weird scratching sound.

"Crazy day, huh?"

Again, no response, but I did see his back muscles tense through his shirt. I took that as a sign of progress.

"I *am* sorry for not telling you earlier," I confessed. "Mr. Woobi warned me about the consequences, and I guess I didn't think about what you would want, and…" I sighed when he still hadn't said anything, and I crossed my arms in front of me in annoyance. "Eve thinks I can start a war against the Society because of what I said today, but I don't want a war. I don't even know how my words could spark something like that. I just want Peter back. I don't want people getting hurt because of me."

"Wouldn't be the first time," Dave muttered under his breath, and the sharpness of his words amplified by that same scraping noise convinced me to grab his shoulders and turn him around.

Blood covered the entirety of his left forearm, oozing from wounds inflicted by a stray brick that he was aggressively rubbing against his flesh, desperately trying to erase the Uniform number tattoo that permanently inked his skin.

"Dave, what are you doing?!" I gasped in horror at the state of his arm. Those wounds would leave scars.

"Trying to get it off me," he replied curtly, his full attention on trying to get the number out of his skin. "It won't… It's not… ARGH!" He pressed the brick against his arm harder, and the sound of scraping flesh, the sight of his blood, and the stench of the charred exterior of my old home made me sick to my stomach.

"Dave, stop. You don't have to do that. Stop. David! STOP!" I had no choice but to yank the blood-stained brick out of his hands and hold it behind my back. As much as I tried to hide it, I gagged at the way his blood ran between my fingers.

His eyes looked wild as he finally turned to face me. "No. Give that back," he begged me, reaching out his right hand in a feeble attempt to grab the brick. "I need that. I need to get it off me. I need…" A tear escaped him when he grabbed another brick that laid at his feet, gently cradled it against his chest, and leaned forward so that his elbows rested against his knees. I sat down beside him and tugged the second brick out of his hands; he didn't protest, too weak from his sobs to fight me. "I'm Leader Caleb's *son*. I am his son, and he burned his symbol into my back, and scarred my arm, and almost *killed* his father. He abandoned me, took my memories, and, what? Forced me to become a Uniform? He tortured Charles, he tortured me, he tortured you, and I'm *related* to him?" Dave was reduced to a beautiful mess, weeping freely into his bloody hands. "I'm not Uniform number 125, I'm not Dave Monsella, and I am *not* Dave Woobi. So who am I, then?"

I hated the way his shoulders slumped forward as if the weight of this newfound information was too heavy to carry. I hated how broken he sounded when he spoke. But I especially hated the distance between us, both physically and emotionally, and I was terrified that I would lose the person I trusted to help me escape my own terrors. "Maybe I can—"

"Do nothing," he cut me off, turning away from me so I couldn't see his tortured face. "For once, you can do nothing. I want to be alone. Please, Zelda. Go."

"I know who you are," I proclaimed. "You're Dave. Not Woobi, not Monsella, not number 125. Just Dave. You smile a lot but only while looking down at your shoes because you think you look goofy when you smile. You laugh at your own jokes not to make me laugh, but because no one has really made you laugh before, and you like to laugh. You put other people's needs before your own because you're selfless and good, even if your father tried to erase that. The number on your arm never defined who you were, who you are, or who you will be, and neither does your lineage, because you were never a Uniform or a Woobi to me. You're just Dave."

I tried placing my hand on his shoulder, but he scooted away from me before I had the chance to touch him. "And who are you?" he responded, his voice hollow. "Not the Zelda I met when taking Charles Woobi to the Jail. Not the Zelda who would sneak out of her househut after curfew to talk to me. And not the Zelda I thought I knew. Actually, I don't think you're just 'Zelda' at all anymore. I'm not sure you ever were. I guess you've always been Zelda Jadestone, the potential war hero. And I'm not sure I trust Zelda Jadestone."

"I'm not a war hero, Dave."

"You sure about that, sweetheart? I watched that interview, and I was there when you spoke to the people here and when you saved Charles from execution. I think you know who you are and what you can do." He stood up then, and the hill made him seem significantly taller than me, a first given our similar statures. "For what it's worth, I think I've figured out the Zelda I trust. I trust the Zelda who does whatever it takes to save her brother. That's the true Zelda."

It took quite a while for me to get up and follow him back to the village, my mind still stuck on how I could possibly help Peter escape without inciting any violence, my body heavy with the burden of guilt, and my heart heaving from Dave's harsh words. *Why couldn't they see what I could?* I asked myself, lying down on the cool grass.

Surely, judging by what had happened to the people outside the Society in the past, they could judge the amount of destruction and overall death this new war would cause. I could not be blamed for the devastation that would certainly follow; it wouldn't just destroy those immediately affected, but me as well. How would I live with myself if I looked in the mirror every day and saw the reflection of a murderer? How would I be able to stand there, up on a stage, and lead people blindly to their deaths? How would I be able to withstand the pressure of the guilt that would crush me every time I saw Peter, but some mother wouldn't get to see her baby, or some child wouldn't get to see his or her parent, or some wife wouldn't get to see her husband? I wouldn't. I couldn't. *I won't.* Yet somewhere, deep inside my heart, I knew that I would do whatever it took to get to Peter because I had made a promise to return to him, and I was not planning on ever breaking that promise.

But would you fight a war for him? I hated my immediate answer, and I hated myself for continuing to pretend as if I didn't know.

Finally, I decided to trudge back down toward the center of the village after the eerie feeling of being watched wouldn't leave me alone. I didn't see anyone outside when I got back, which was a rarity for the village, usually buzzing with people socializing on the benches that surrounded the fire pit. Upon closer inspection, I noticed all the hospital lights on the first floor had been turned off, but the houses glowed with light, so I walked through the maze of homes until I spotted Mr. Woobi's gray hair through one of the windows. After opening the front door, I saw the Woobis and Eric sitting on either the couch or the floor and watching the monitor intently; all four of them visibly flinched and Dave let out a small screech when I accidentally knocked over a ceramic bowl of assorted fruit. My mouth opened, ready to stream out a string of apologies, but when I saw that their eyes focused on the screen once more, I floated into the living room, plopped down beside the older man, and watched it with them.

Caleb Woobi, cloaked in darkness, streamed live onto this screen, his voice computerized just as I remembered it. He was in the middle of his speech, but I had arrived in time to hear the rest of it. "—power is dangerous. Are all of you prepared for this war you preach? Are you prepared for the consequences that will follow? Are you prepared to die, fools?" He sneered, and I could make out the glint in his dark eyes. "I bet you think you are. I bet you think you can kill me, free my Society with minimal resistance, restore what you perceive to be freedom. You blindly follow a young girl with a knack for destruction and the poisonous talent of persuasion without thinking of the cost. I can assure you the death you will see if you choose to follow Zelda Jadestone will severely outweigh any benefit challenging me would bring."

I saw his lips stretch up into a proper smile, and he leaned in closer before saying, "This is now directed only to you, Zelda Jadestone. I have watched you long enough to know who you are and who you will become. You are a girl frantic to reach her little brother, you are a girl who reacts without thinking, but you are especially a girl who underestimates herself. The words you spew are meaningless to you now, barely blips in your consciousness, but you are inspiring people to kill for you, Zelda Jadestone. Better yet, you are inspiring people to kill *me* for you, and that never seems to work out, does it?"

I thought I saw a flash of bodies, my *friends'* bodies, but I barely had time to blink before the image vanished.

"Come now, Zelda Jadestone. You know better than that. You are smart enough to know by now I cannot be touched. I will always win. But you know what? I give you permission to try and destroy me. Gather an army. Invade my Society. Start this war. By the end of it, it won't be me who's destroyed. Oh no, no. By the end of it, I think the person left buried in ashes will be you, Zelda Jadestone. I want you to remember I warned you when you watch your war snuff out, just like the people you incite."

The screen flickered to a faded image of a younger boy with clouded, Jadestone brown, bloodshot eyes holding unshed tears, surrounded by dark black-and-blue circles. His hair was buzzed down to his scalp, and his skin looked drained of any color, almost translucent in the harsh white light. His mouth hung open like he was just about to let out a scream. But it wasn't a scream; it was a whisper, a plea, a secret cry for help: *"Zelda."*

Then the monitor flashed the Societan emblem and went black, taking with it the image of my broken brother.

CHAPTER 8

The three Woobis and Eric found me crouched outside the hospital building, emptying myself of the contents that had resided in my stomach all over the once-green grass. Nausea slammed me in waves; despite having vomited everything substantial from my system, I continued gagging a disgusting mixture of bile and saliva. Air caught in my throat, forcing me to cough until my lungs burned; I hadn't realized how intensely I was shaking until I felt Eric reassuringly glide a hand up my back. Dave shuffled from one foot to another, unable to look at me, but eventually followed Eric's lead when the latter knelt to comfort me.

"He's going to kill Peter," I gasped through my overbearing sobs. Eve and Mr. Woobi attempted to convince me that Caleb wouldn't kill his best friends' son, but I remained unconvinced. If he could abandon his son, almost murder his father, and torture me in this way, what stopped him from killing my brother as my ultimate punishment for disrupting his utopia? No one in the Society—save for Blake Yandle, but even he couldn't be fully trusted—could stop Caleb from killing Peter. As the leader, he possessed the freedom to do as he pleased.

No. I couldn't allow him to kill my brother. I couldn't allow him to get away with the crimes he had already committed. And as long as I was alive, I wouldn't.

The moment I regained the strength to speak, I pleaded with the older couple to let me go into the city of Neweryork, agreeing to strike a deal with the person in power to give us the resources we needed to go back to the Society in exchange for whatever they asked for within reason. Mr. Woobi and Eve rejoiced in my decision, enveloping me in hugs and telling me how much they admired my bravery, how proud they were of my actions, and what a good thing I was doing not just for Peter, but for the world. I tuned all that nonsense out.

"He looked awful," I whined through my hands to Eric, covering my face to conceal my shame as we waited for Eve and Mr. Woobi to get transportation and such settled.

"Well, I don't think he'd appreciate that comment very much."

I peeked through my fingers to glare at him. "Eric."

Eric withered under my pointed look. "Sorry. You're right, he didn't look his best, but Leader Caleb loves special effects, right? He easily could've changed Peter's appearance to make him look worse than he actually does to scare you. That whole video was clearly a scare tactic."

I sat upright, running my fingers through my long, dark hair to preoccupy myself. "I don't understand him, and that's killing me. Why would he entice me to start this war? What could he hope to gain from that? What am I not getting?"

Eric leaned toward me until our shoulders bumped. "He's trying to intimidate us, that's all. He challenged you to make it seem like he's stronger than us, but he's not. We will get Peter back, Zelda, don't worry."

Just as I opened my mouth to respond, Eve called to me to signal our departure. Eric and I stood up from the front steps of the hospital together, and the two of us stood there awkwardly for a few moments before he asked, "You sure you don't want me to come with you?"

I nodded my head in affirmation. "I'm sure. I need someone I trust to watch over Dave while I'm away."

We both stole glances at the man in question, standing over by the fire pit with his left forearm wrapped in gauze from his self-inflicted injury earlier.

"Don't worry about him," assured Eric. "I got it covered." He gave me a smile, one that didn't show his teeth and definitely didn't reach his eyes.

I wrapped my arms around his torso and gave him a quick squeeze before stepping back. "I should probably go talk to him," I sighed, and Eric agreed, making me promise to be careful in the city before I reluctantly walked in Dave's general direction.

I stopped with a few feet of space between the ex-Uniform and me, the two of us unable to look at the other directly. "I'm leaving," I stated when the tension became unbearable.

"I heard."

"We can figure this out when I get back."

"Figure what out, Zelda?" he snapped. "I think I already figured out that you lied to me about my own family. What else is there to figure out?"

His words lashed at me, and I took a step back before crossing my arms. "You're not the only one suffering. Peter is trapped inside the Society, possibly being tortured."

"Yeah, well, at least he knows who he is."

My head snapped up, and I stared at Dave in surprise, opening and closing my mouth like a fool as I tried to see past my hurt and utter an adequate response. Upon realizing the severity of his statement, Dave tried to backtrack, but before he could even begin to apologize, I ran to the awaiting vehicle, slammed its door shut behind me, and didn't look back once it started to roll away.

"Boy trouble?" remarked Mr. Woobi jokingly in a sad attempt to lighten the mood.

I slumped further into the plush red seat. "Something like that," I muttered.

"Give him time, Zelda. He'll come around," advised Eve, and I grunted in response.

The scenery outside rolled by at a remarkable speed, to the extent that I got a headache watching the ever-changing setting and had to rest my head against the cool glass of the luxuriously large window. The fiery red velvet benches in the back compartment of the vehicle made it extremely difficult to resist my growing exhaustion, but I refrained from sleeping, knowing the moment I drifted off, nightmares would ensue. To distract myself, I tried to listen to Eve explain the computer-satellite technology that guided us to our destination, but eventually, I couldn't bear to pretend to care any longer, and Eve quieted down. Luckily, speakers in the roof of the car softly played music that floated through our compartment, and as I tuned into the sound, I recognized the melody as the song the schoolchildren were singing when Dave and I first arrived at the village.

"I stand here tonight.
So afraid. So alone.
But you're there, in the light.
You won't leave me on my own.
It's so dark. It's so dark.

The whole world has turned black.
But you, you've made your mark.
Please tell me you'll be back.
Hold me tight tonight.
Right before you go,
Tell me everything will be alright.
We never did fit the status quo.
Tell me you'll miss me.
Tell me you need me.
Tell me you love me so.
I know I'll miss you.
I know I need you.
I know I love you so.
I know you love me.
I know I love you.
Tell me…
What I already know."

Throughout the duration of the song, I noticed how close Eve had gotten to Mr. Woobi, how age melted off the pair of them when they took refuge in each other's embrace, how effortlessly they portrayed love, and I found myself wanting to ask them so many questions. How had they survived fourteen years without each other? Did Eve ever doubt she'd see him again, and vise versa? What happened to Caleb? Why was he brimming with hatred for his father, so much so that Caleb was willing to execute him publicly? Despite my overwhelming curiosity, I chose to leave the two alone for the time being, content with pretending not to watch the way they found complete peace in one another's presence.

When I saw more vehicles beginning to accumulate on the pavement to the sides of ours, I lifted my head from the windowsill and watched them zoom past our vehicle. Houses, both big and small, started to pop up in the green fields on either side; I tried not to think about the robbery of my own childhood as I observed the blurs of children running in the greenery.

Huge, blinding lights in every color imaginable illuminated the roads into the city, and screens fixed on the buildings flashed bold, loud symbols, images, and words at us as we drove closer to the center. Although at first, I deemed it all ostentatious and unnecessary, it soon became apparent that the screens were needed to provide light to the streets. The buildings—skyscrapers, as Mr. Woobi called them, which I found to be an incredibly accurate name—were so tall, they didn't allow any natural sunlight to reach the cement below. Some buildings were composed of glass, others metal, but most were made of the same cement substance that created the sidewalks. People littered the streets in long, flowy dresses, brightly patterned dress shirts, or colorful business suits. The whole scene was very heterogeneous; not one person dressed the same or seemed to be going in the same direction. My eyes didn't know where to focus.

The vehicle came to a smooth stop in front of one skyscraper made entirely of shiny, silver steel, save for the large glass windows, and as I stepped out of the vehicle, I noticed myself on one of the larger screens on a building a few doors down. The screen projected the image of me immersed in the sunrise's shadows, cradling Peter's teddy bear, with the words, "I'd rather die free than live with my life dictated for me," running underneath the photo. A strange, foreign anger overwhelmed me at seeing myself up on the television, those being my words but not how I had intended them. Who thought they had authority over my face, my body, my words, my *thoughts*? How could anyone possibly interpret what I believed was only mine? I could almost feel my autonomy slowly being ripped from my grasp, but then I thought of Peter and his own prison, and I quickly shut out any negative thoughts regarding my situation. This was for Peter. I would gladly give my freedoms to these people if it meant Peter could be safe.

I had been so focused on myself on the monitor that I neglected to notice the people gathering around me in a circle, staring at me in awe, and whispering my name like one would softly pray to a deity. It wasn't until the screen switched from the sunrise photograph to real-time with me standing there in fascination that I realized just how many people were looking at me: random onlookers, camera crews, small children. Mr. Woobi and Eve jumped into action before I could make a bigger fool of myself, pushing me forward and leading me to large brass doors that we stepped through together.

The receptionist at the front desk eyed me with antipathy when we entered the building's lobby, and as strange as it sounds, I felt relieved not to see a look of adoration on her face. "May I help you?" she asked in a clipped, slightly bored tone.

Mr. Woobi pointed to the television that still had my face from thirty seconds before displayed on it, the bolded headline ZELDA JADESTONE RETURNS! now running below the image. "That is her." He moved his finger to point to me. "We need an immediate appointment with the president."

She leaned back into her chair and blew a breath out of her purple-tinted lips. "Well, you sure are making a statement." She nodded her neatly cut blonde bob over to the locked doors, where people with huge cameras were pressing to enter. "Everything you do seems to make some kind of statement, huh?"

I ground my teeth together and muttered, "I hate that," under my breath.

My comment stopped her perfectly manicured, long nails—painted a hideous, neon green color—from reaching the phone. "You must've known your 'escape,' or whatever they're calling it now, would attract some media coverage. People would kill to be in the spotlight you're in now, you know."

I wanted to tell her that in actuality, I possessed no power in the slightest, that I most definitely wouldn't be standing in front of her if I had any power at all, that I practically acted as Caleb's personal puppet for as long as he had my brother. But I refrained, instead opting to shrug and say, "It would appear that way."

The receptionist looked like she wanted to refute, but Eve insisted on the urgency of the matter of our arrival, so she settled on scanning my body with disdain before picking up the phone and instructing us to wait for "President Dassian" in the lobby chairs. As we sat down, Eve jokingly commented on the receptionist's judgmental glare, and I giggled alongside her despite myself.

Mr. Woobi was the only one out of the three of us who didn't appear the least bit amused by Eve's remark. When I asked him what was wrong, he pursed his lips and answered, "I didn't know Cody Dassian was elected into office while I was away."

"Away" made his fourteen years stuck inside the Society sound like a short vacation, but I didn't draw attention to it. "What does that matter?" I asked.

Mr. Woobi furrowed his brow. "I don't know how he will react to your demands, Zelda Ellyn. He's a bit of a character, to say the very least."

This struck me as worrisome, but before I could react, a shorter, wide man with whitish-gray hair and thick, black glasses that barely stayed on his round nose burst from the elevator doors, a huge grin on his pudgy, red face. "Charlie!" he exclaimed, rushing over to Mr. Woobi with open arms before he made eye contact with me. "You must be Zelda Jadestone," he proclaimed after diverting his path from Mr. Woobi to me and kissing both of my cheeks sloppily. "They just won't shut up about you, darling! Practically every news station in the state is rambling about you! And may I say, you are more radiant in person than you are on tv! Why have you come all this way, honey? Not just to see me, I hope!" He laughed loudly at his own dare-I-call-it-a-joke, his mouth wide open and his soft brown eyes aglow as he clapped Mr. Woobi awkwardly on the back.

The two Woobis and I exchanged equally concerned looks before I explained to President Dassian the business we needed to discuss. He led me excitedly over to the elevator, chirping the entire way up to the 200th floor about how grateful he felt that I had dropped by and how happy he felt to see me alive after escaping the Society. The golden doors of the elevator opened to reveal a spacious office equipped with a glorious view of the entire city of Neweryork through floor-to-ceiling windows, a gigantic desk running practically the entire length of the room, and strange little knickknacks scattered around. I made myself comfortable by sitting at one end of the desk, and President Dassian scurried to sit beside me. His vivacious grin slid off his face the moment I announced that I hadn't intended to stay long.

"We certainly aren't staying in this office long!" he laughed again, but it seemed forced this time, like he was almost coughing on his laughter. "I have to give you a tour of our gorgeous city. After being held prisoner in that dump for so long, this must be so—"

"I'm going back to the Society," I announced before he could drag on any further.

President Dassian clapped his hands together, and some strange-sounding squeak left his mouth. "Yes, of course you are, darling." He took off his glasses, stood up with a flourish, spun on his heels, and pointed to a map on the wall scattered with varying multicolored dots, predominantly red. I was just about to ask what those dots signified when he explained, "These pins are where violent pro-war demonstrations have taken place. The blue ones, in the past year. The green, in the past six months. The yellow, the past three. And red? Those are the riots that have happened ever since your face appeared in that viral video of you in Eve Redding's village three days ago."

I stared in disgusted horror at the map and the violence I had unintentionally elicited. "I'm so sorry," I mumbled when I couldn't find the right words to say.

The president wagged his finger at me. "Never apologize for inciting change, Zelda. The public has been wanting a war for a long time now. They just needed an extra push to get them angry enough to start one, and you happen to be the person to motivate their anger."

"I don't want a war," I clarified as I watched him pace around the table.

President Dassian laughed again, the sound bouncing off the walls of the room. "And do you think I do?" he asked. "Do you think I want to spend millions of my taxpayers' dollars on military equipment to free a Society the size of my office? Do you really think I want to go to war when it would last not even two days? No, darling. A war is not my wish."

I breathed a sigh of relief to know I finally found an ally holding a position of power. "Mr. President, I—"

"But the people want a war," he interrupted, and I scrunched up my nose. "They're begging for it. They're desperate for that violence they think will bring back their loved ones, and I can see that desperation every time my assistant adds new pins into the map on my wall." He stopped pacing, spread his arms out wide, and grinned, and I saw the crazed look his eyes carried when he declared, "Who am I to deprive them of their dreams, Zelda?"

"I plan to go back to the Society for Peter before Leader Caleb Woobi decides to kill him, but I have no intention of lighting a fuse for any kind of revolution." I crossed my arms in front of me. "Peter is my only priority."

President Dassian bit the nail of his thumb. "If your brother really is your first priority, then you must be willing to face the consequences of freeing him, Zelda. Freeing your brother means freeing everyone else. You must understand how unfair it will look in the public's eye if only Peter gets to walk out of that Society. They're going to want their own loved ones as well. Something has to be in it for them."

"I don't care how it looks in the public's eye. I just want my brother back," I retorted. "I don't know these people who scream for war; why should I care what they want?"

The president's cheery demeanor finally slipped off his body like one would shed a heavy jacket, his short body holding so much tension I feared he might pop. "Now, that's a little selfish, isn't it? Those people admire you. Those people have been wanting to invade the Society for quite some time now, but they had no one to rally behind, no one to root for, and no one to make them feel invincible—which is exactly the kind of people you need to start any sort of conflict—until you came along. Zelda Jadestone, you arrived, and everyone fell in love with your perfect story: parents dead in the last war, brother now trapped in a bubble that you escaped, and now here you are, ready to go back in to save him and the rest of the people. It's beautiful how quickly they have gravitated toward you. You owe those people what they want."

I shook my head in confusion. "Mr. President, I don't owe anyone in this city anything. I only owe my brother the opportunity to live after abandoning him to be tortured."

President Dassian angrily pointed to the spectacular view of the city and said, "You gave those people down there in 'this city' hope again, Zelda Jadestone. You owe it to them to follow through after giving them such a powerful gift."

"You are their leader," I countered, my voice raising with each word I spoke. "Tell them that you do not wish to pursue any war."

The president threw his head back and laughed cynically, his cackle holding zero amusement. "It doesn't matter if I'm their leader, darling. It doesn't matter what I want or what I think is best. I am the public's servant.

If I agree with your current public agenda to invade the Northeastern Society, then I will be fueling the fire for this war. If I disagree, I'll be hated and impeached out of office for not honoring the people's demands. We can't have me thrown out of power. I will gladly sit on the sidelines for this one, Zelda Jadestone."

My eyes narrowed in anger, and I rocketed out of my seat, leaning over my hands perched on the table as I shouted, "Sit on the sidelines?!" What kind of president just 'sits on the sidelines' and watches his state unravel like that?"

"One who doesn't want to lose his job."

"Being a leader isn't a job, sir. It's a duty."

"I can't have thousands of people murdering each other in the streets!" yelled President Dassian while combing his fingers through his wispy, white hair. "We have to give them what they want, or they will just keep murdering each other. This is my state, Zelda Jadestone. My sovereignty. I won't have innocent people slaughtered because they want their loved ones back with them."

I ceased leaning on my hands and stood to my full height, crossing my arms in front of my chest and saying, "I am here for one thing, and one thing only, and that is for my brother. But I am just one person, Mr. President. I don't know how to pop that electric bubble or go in unnoticed. I don't know where to find Peter, or how to get him out without dying. I don't entirely know why everyone holds me to such high regard because of one interview edited to misconstrue my words. But I do know this: I will *not* put other people's lives in danger for me. Here I am, just an eighteen-year-old woman with the weight of my brother's life on my shoulders, and what I am asking is for you to give me some options. Give me something to help me figure out how to rescue my little brother. I can do the rest alone."

President Dassian vigorously rubbed at the skin on his forehead as he said, "This is more than just helping out your little brother now. This is politics, millions of dollars in expenses, and possibly the death of hard-working soldiers. Did you realistically think I'd go through all that just to help you save one boy out of the goodness of my heart? Allow me to teach you an extremely valuable lesson: no one ever does anything out of the kindness of their heart. No one ever has. The sooner you understand that, the easier it will be when your ridiculous, childish demands are rejected. You are asking for more than you realize: manpower, technology, information on your brother back in the Society. You, darling, now have a decision to make. In order to save Peter, you must save everyone else with him. It is simply the way it must be. I am willing to grant you access to the supplies you need, but you must agree to my demands. You must earn the right to my help, Zelda Jadestone. Nothing in this life is ever free."

"So, what exactly do you want me to do?" I asked cautiously.

The president grinned and said, "I want you to be the person who sparks this war against the Northeastern Society. I want you to not hold back anymore: no smiles, no little waves, no avoiding the cameras' eyes at every opportunity. We all saw Caleb Woobi's message to you earlier today; you're angry—furious, even. You're determined. You're chomping at the bit to extract revenge on that man for hurting your family. Let the public inside your passionate mind. All the fire that's up there"—he tapped his temple—"the people should feel from the words you choose. You make sure you fuel every negative emotion you feel about your separation from your brother, Caleb Woobi's torture, your parents' death, whatever it may be, into speech after speech after speech. You do whatever you can to inspire as many people as possible."

President Dassian threw his arms up in the air and gave a breathy, almost wild-sounding laugh. "Let the people see all the hatred that burns through you, Zelda Jadestone. Spit. Punch. Shout. When that stupid electric boundary comes crashing down, you're right there, urging them on. When whatever Caleb uses for law enforcement comes running at them, bullets flying, you will tell them that it's okay, that in the end, this will all be worth it. When you reunite with your sweet little brother, let that be a symbol for all that victory is near."

"Just to make it clear, you will provide me with professional-grade troops, technology to pop the electromagnetic boundary, and information on Peter's present state, and I will…?"

The man smiled widely once again and came back around to my side of the table to stick out his hand for me to shake. "You will inspire a nation."

I wanted to tell him I couldn't. I wanted to tell him that I had no clue how to begin the process of inspiring people to die for a cause I didn't believe in. I wanted to run back to the familiar safety of the Society before Peter ever left to become a Uniform, a time spent in simplicity with Eric, Peter, and Mr. Woobi: no impending wars, no leaders lusting for revenge, no complex political games I didn't yet understand. But the mental image of Peter's face, twisted in agony, promptly sewed my mouth shut from voicing any of these things. Peter's pain taunted me; the shakiness in his scared, small voice as he whispered my name shackled me to his freedom and my pressing desire to obtain it.

"I promise, Peter. I'll come back for you," I had whispered as I watched him crawl out our househut window, and I had no intention of breaking that promise, not then, and certainly not now.

I grabbed President Dassian's hand and shook it firmly, trying desperately to tune out the wails of my coworkers in their final moments, pretending not to have seen the blood spilled on the streets after the riot, ignoring the image of Caleb Woobi smiling as he watches me solidify my death with a single handshake.

No. This is for Peter.

Zelda, my friends cry.

No. I'm sorry, no. Peter must be saved.

Zelda, the crowd chants after the almost-execution.

No. I don't know you. I shouldn't care. Peter deserves to be freed.

Zelda, grins Caleb. And I can hear his next thought, too, because it matches my own:

What have you done?

The sound of the president's rumbling, obnoxiously loud laughter stayed with me even after I had stepped back into the lobby and stumbled over toward Eve and Mr. Woobi, who stood up to greet me the second they heard my feet on the marble floors. Selfishly, I wanted for the older man to cradle me tightly in his arms and tell me that this was all one long, horrible nightmare, but he only returned my embrace for a moment before he whispered, "Be strong, you're still on camera," and proceeded to lead me outside the doors, where hundreds of people with and without cameras were shoving one another to talk to me.

I recalled Dassian's words, *"No smiles, no little waves, no avoiding the camera's eyes at every opportunity,"* and with a quick glance over my shoulder to make sure the camera people were following me, I confidently strode over to a girl with bright, almost sickening pink hair in what looked to be her mid-twenties. She held up a sign that read in big, bold letters: I STAND WITH ZELDA JADESTONE, and I asked her why.

My presence made her nervous, I could tell, but she still answered with a proud grin: "Because it's the right thing to do."

"Why is it the right thing to do?" I questioned.

Her eyes, dyed pink to match her hideous hair color, narrowed at me confusingly. "Because… because it is. I can't explain it. We have to help all those people. It's just the right thing to do for them. They need us."

"Do you know anyone in the Society?"

She shook her head. "No, but my best friend's brother's friend knows someone in there."

"So then why? Why stand out here when you don't know anyone personally? Why do you want to fight a war?"

She lowered her gaze for just a moment, thinking about her response, before she lifted her head and answered, "Same reason you do, I guess. Why do *you* want to go back and start this war?"

Because my brother needs me, and I need him. Because if I don't, Caleb will kill him. Because I'm afraid to live without him. I didn't say any of these things. Instead, I gave her a small, what I hoped to be sweet smile that I made sure the cameras picked up on, took her hands—cold from waiting outside all this time—in my hot ones, and declared, "Because it's the right thing to do."

CHAPTER 9

I dropped my head into my hands the instant the vehicle doors closed behind us. I tried to lean against Mr. Woobi for support, and he allowed it for a total of five seconds before shifting around so he could whisper, "They're following us," discreetly in my ear. *For Peter. For Peter. For Peter*, I had to keep telling myself just to pick my head up and look out the window at the masses of people hollering and shouting at me as they chased the vehicle down the street.

Every now and again, I would get out of the vehicle and speak with them, but only a few people stood out in my mind, like a woman with her four older children, protesting in the street for her husband and the father of her kids to come home to them. Or a man sitting alone amongst the huge group of people, waiting for his entire family to be freed from the Society. Or what seemed to be an entire population of teenagers wanting war even though they had no real ties to anyone directly involved in the Society. It both fascinated and terrified me.

Mr. Woobi, Eve, and I stayed in Neweryork for an entire month after my meeting with President Dassian to film my interactions with the protestors, participate in interviews, and in one instance, have my photo taken for the front of an extremely popular magazine. I told the protestors stories of what life consisted of in the Society, such as what my old job as a doctor entailed, the standard of living inside a househut, or how everyone inside held no memories of the outside world. The cameras captured it all, of course, and my face was plastered on every possible screen—big or small, personal or not—in the city and beyond. Almost all the interviews consisted of the same regurgitated nonsense: questions about my final day in the Society, about Caleb's dictatorship techniques, about Peter's predicament and my attachment to him. I answered all their generic questions to the best of my ability, and usually, they weren't anything I hadn't experienced before with Allyson. Except for one.

The magazine insisted on conducting an interview before the scheduled photo shoot to pair with the pictures, and Eve confirmed the interview before I had a chance to voice my discontent. The setup seemed relatively normal when we arrived—two chairs for the interviewer and me and a few cameras to capture every angle possible—but right as I bid the Woobi couple farewell for the day, I noticed the entourage of people behind the cameras, way more than had ever been present for an interview before. I shook hands with my interviewer—a man named Vincent with the sides of his head cleanly shaven, his platinum blond hair gelled into three spikes on the top of his skull—and took a seat, but not before skeptically eyeing the team of people staring at me. "Who are all those people?" I finally asked.

"Your costume, makeup, and hair teams," Vincent answered like my question confused him.

His perplexed gaze made me feel moronic for asking my next question: "What do I need those for?"

Vincent laughed and cupped his own face. "You're so adorable!" he exclaimed. "Did you really think we'd let you on the cover looking like *that*?" He looked me over, clearly judging my appearance, and I twisted the base of my brown shirt awkwardly, suddenly self-conscious. Although almost everyone in the city wore gaudy, outlandish outfits with wildly colorful designs, I stuck to the same outfit the village had provided me the day I arrived: a basic, brown t-shirt with long, brown cargo pants. Luckily, Eve had the forethought to pack a few extra pairs before we left, but the general concept remained the same. I chose not to comment on the slight insult, instead choosing to say, "So, the interview?"

"Right! Now, for Knew Magazine…" Vincent paused and flailed his hands around. "I just think that name is so creative, don't you? Like instead of 'New' for Neweryork, it's Knew, like 'oh, I *knew* that already because I read it in Knew Magazine'? Ugh, it's just glorious. That's why this is my dream job. I love keeping it fresh. Don't you agree?"

My mouth fell slightly open from my immediate surprise, but I composed myself enough to respond, "Yes, very creative. But what does that have to do with—"

"Because here at Knew Mag, we crave creativity. That's why I won't ask you about how you escaped, or what Leader Whoever—"

"Leader Caleb."

"Leader *Whoever*," Vincent repeated sternly as if I ruined a perfectly good joke, "was doing to you for fourteen years, or what convinced you to leave. Who cares? Been there, done that. Old news. The people want to know who you really are."

"Oh," I squeaked when I couldn't think of anything else to say. My fingers twisted around the bottom of my brown shirt even tighter.

"So, let's start easy." Vincent motioned for the cameras to begin rolling. "Who is the blond stud who was with you when you first came to the village?"

"My boyfriend," I said, already feeling antsy. I hadn't anticipated this turn, and talking about anything other than the Society, Caleb, and to an extent, Peter, made me uncomfortable.

"'Boyfriend' as in friend-who-is-a-boy, or as in boy-you-sleep-with?"

My eyes widened, and I felt heat quickly rising into my face. "Um…"

Vincent held up a hand to stop me. "Don't answer that. Viewers and readers will like the mystery. What's his name?"

"David."

"No," Vincent declared, holding a hand up to his heart and jaw hanging open. "Shut up. David as in David Woobi? Like the son of Caleb Woobi? Wait a minute, aren't you also tied to Charles and Eve Woobi somehow? Describe that relationship."

To describe my relationship with the Woobi family proved impossible. Mr. Woobi's actions angered me beyond belief when I thought of his exploitation of Peter, attempted corruption of Eric, and lies to Dave, yet I loved him; that, I knew. I recalled times from my childhood, simple memories of him telling us jovial stories or staying with us as we fell asleep, and I knew I could never hate him.

I'm snuggled into Mr. Woobi's side, Eric and Peter next to me as we listen to the elder explain what the sun used to feel like on his skin. He describes the changing seasons in amazing detail, and I'm envious that I don't remember the way a summer breeze feels on my face, the way the orange leaves crunch under my feet, the way snow blankets the world, or the way the birds chirp in delight as the flowers bloom. The Society's temperature is set to a consistent 74 degrees Fahrenheit all year round, and the only sky we see is a beige one created by the boundary. Six-year-old Peter lays his head on my lap right as my envy reaches its boiling point, and suddenly, my perspective shifts. I don't need to feel the sun's summer warmth or understand the heat a hearth brings inside a home during a blizzard. Not when I can find the same feeling right here, with my family.

"He's the father I never had," I finally proclaimed.

Vincent visibly swooned. "That's so beautiful. And what about this David Woobi; can you describe your relationship with him? Remember to keep it vague, though. We don't need the dirty details."

Dave and I proved complicated as well. No one had captured my attention as quickly as he had. His laugh made me feel lighter, and looking into his electric-blue eyes felt like staring at the stars. Our instantaneous connection scared me in the moments when my heart surged just from watching him smile, because it seemed irrational to care so much for someone I had known for such a short amount of time—half a year at the most.

It's our one month knowing each other, our third weekly Wednesday visit, yet I still get a fluttering in my stomach when I hear Dave's soft knock at my househut window. I practically skip to my door, and it slides open to reveal Dave leaning against the exterior of my househut casually. I can't help but grin as I breathlessly exhale a hello.

He stands to his full height, not much taller than me, and wiggles his eyebrows playfully. "Did you miss me?"

I don't give him the satisfaction of knowing my answer, instead opting to take his large, calloused hand in mine and lead him over to Province One's sculpture, a place we had made ours. We quickly climb the sculpture and lie side-by-side comfortably, as per usual. I don't give Dave a second of rest before poking his side and asking, "So, are you ready to tell me where the database is?"

Dave smirks at the excited tone of my voice but ultimately shakes his head. "It's too dangerous still, Zelda. Not yet."

"I'll tickle it out of you if I must," I threaten.

"Oh yeah?" Dave challenges, sitting up and leaning on his elbow. "I'd like to see you try."

Before I can strike, Dave's fingers drift across my stomach, causing me to reflexively curl into him and squeal in laughter into his shoulder. He shushes me gently through his own chuckles, a poignant reminder of who we are and what we're doing, and I stop, but not before watching the crinkles that form around his brilliantly blue eyes as he quietly laughs alongside me.

I knew my lies had hurt the ex-Uniform badly, if not permanently. The rage I saw burning behind his eyes before I left for Neweryork scared me into thinking he'd stay angry forever, which influenced my decision not to contact the village during my time away. Although I didn't enjoy being in the city, I dreaded going back and facing Dave's fury once again. A part of me didn't think I could withstand his accusatory glare. I had blindly trusted that I could never truly anger him, but now that our connection wavered, I didn't know how to approach him. Yet despite this, my feelings for him stayed the same.

"I care about him very much," I told Vincent sincerely when I could think of no other adequate response. "He inspires me to do good. He makes me a better person."

The interviewer accepted my answer with an excited squeal. "So precious. I wonder how your relationships with these Woobis affect your perception of Leader Caleb Woobi."

I squirmed in my seat and suddenly found it difficult to look at Vincent directly. "Uh…"

"Like, do you secretly care about Leader Caleb's wellbeing because of his connection with the closest people in your life?"

"Oh, no, I—"

"He *is* the father of your greatest love. That must mean something. You might even have a soft spot for the dictator." Vincent gasped at his own words. "Oh, how scandalous!"

"No, he—"

"This is truly a family affair," Vincent said with a mischievous twinkle in his dyed-white eyes. "I'm living for this drama. You, our very own Zelda Jadestone, madly in love with the dictator's son, willing to do anything to protect the old Woobi man and your cute little brother. But, a twist! You can't hate Leader Caleb because of your loyalty to the Woobi family. You—"

"I hate him," I declared fiercely. Heat bloomed inside my chest, and I held on tightly to the warmth that anger sparked in me. "Did you get that?" I turned my face to the nearest camera, stared straight into its lens, and reiterated, "I *hate* him. He abandoned his son, almost murdered his father, killed my friends, and is now torturing my brother to hurt me, not to mention the atrocities he's committed against his own citizens in the Society. He's a criminal in the worst sense of the word."

"You were right," I rasped from my spot on the floor right before he exited the room, and he crouched down low to hear me. "You aren't human."

Leader Caleb smiled at me before brushing my hair away from my face. "Zelda Jadestone, today is the day you have learned that I am always right. I look forward to watching your progress."

"I despise Caleb Woobi," I proclaimed louder when the memory of the leader of the Society's arrogance kindled even greater rage. "I greatly look forward to the day he burns."

Vincent grinned, leaned back in his chair, and crossed his legs. "Brilliant. You don't love Caleb after all. You want to kill him for what he's done to your family. Now *that* is what I call a story. It's a wrap."

The cameras shut off; the studio lights dimmed; Vincent walked out; and I was left with pangs in my stomach that burned as the makeup, hair, and costume teams got to work on my appearance for the photoshoot. Based on Vincent's comments from earlier, I expected them to embellish me somehow, but they chose to do the exact opposite. The costume designer on set dressed me in filthy-looking, tattered rags, practically just torn strips of gray cloth loosely sewn together that reminded me greatly of my mandatory Societan attire. The makeup department splattered mud against the exposed areas of my skin and streaked dirt across my face, applying a thin layer of sticky gloss to my lips as a final touch. The hair team only tussled my brown locks slightly.

The set consisted of a room as dark as midnight, and as I stood in front of a black backdrop, still grappling with my fury, the photographer instructed me to stare directly into the barrel of the camera. I was about to ask about the lighting when small, individual flames lit up in a semi-circle in front of my face, but still out of range for the camera, just enough to illuminate my features.

I tried a few poses, but they all felt unnatural and strange, which must've been evident, since the photographer quickly peered around the camera to say through a giggle: "Just relax, gorgeous. I need to feel your passion. Channel your emotions into your face."

Leader Caleb shouted, "See how that crowd chants your name and the consequences at doing so? Death, all caused by you, the idiot girl with a smart mouth. Look at the destruction you've produced all to save a man who will end up killing everything you hold dear. You snuck into that database to look up war, so now here you go, child: this is your war. This is your death. This is your destruction. This is your pure chaos. Revel in it while you can, Zelda Jadestone. I will not continue to make the mistake of keeping you alive."

The core of my very being ignited with hatred for this monster who called himself a leader. I thought of Jack Garrole and the rest of my coworkers, of Mr. Woobi, of Dave, of Peter, and I ached for the day when this inferno would swallow Caleb Woobi whole. I wanted Caleb to burn alive from the flames I set ablaze. I wanted to watch Caleb rendered as nothing more than ash I could crush underneath my shoe. I hated him. I had to hate him. He deserved for me to hate him.

The camera clicked, and I felt jarred, like someone had rattled me awake from a particularly deep sleep. The photographer clapped her hands in delight and informed me that she had captured the perfect frame, and the magazine would publish my article, along with this photo, in approximately a week or so. A pre-destined vehicle took me back to the building in which the Woobi couple and I were staying, and as I entered our shared hotel suite, I took a moment to collect myself before joining them at the dining table.

Eve eyed my outfit and dirty appearance with amusement. "How'd everything go today?" she asked with a trace of sarcasm, but I certainly wasn't in the mood for her pleasantries and surface-level conversations.

"I think it's time you tell me everything," I announced. "What happened to Caleb? How could *he* have a son? Why does he hate you so much, Mr. Woobi? Why wasn't Eve put in the Society with us? Why did he abandon Dave like that? If he was such good friends with my parents, how could he hurt Peter like this? How—"

Mr. Woobi clasped Eve's hand underneath his and interrupted, "You're right, Zelda Ellyn. You deserve answers. But please understand that there are some answers I cannot give you. There is so much even I cannot fully comprehend."

"You've had fourteen years to figure it out," I snapped.

"Fourteen years caring for you, your brother, and Eric," he refuted just as swiftly. "I didn't think of much else."

I chose to ignore his comment. "So, Caleb marries a woman named Juniper, has a baby, and then what? Becomes a tyrant?"

Eve glanced at Mr. Woobi fearfully. "How much does she know?"

"Clearly not enough!" I shouted. "Not nearly enough to explain his erratic behavior. Why does he want to kill you, Mr. Woobi? What could make a son want to kill his father?"

"He blames me," Mr. Woobi answered as he knitted his eyebrows.

"Charlie," warned Eve. "I really don't think Zelda should know yet. It's too soon."

"With all due respect," I countered, turning in my seat to glare at her. "Eve, your son has kicked me out of my Society, killed my friends, tortured my brother, abandoned your grandson, left me to suffer, and almost executed your husband. I think I had the right to know why a long time ago."

Eve looked to Mr. Woobi for support, but he couldn't seem to tear his proud-yet-sorrowful gaze away from me. His eyes roamed my face as I openly pleaded with him to tell me, and ultimately, Mr. Woobi said, "Caleb blames me for the deaths of Juniper Monsella and—"

"Charlie," Eve hissed. "Don't."

"And...?" I pressed.

"And your parents, Zelda Ellyn," Mr. Woobi sighed defeatedly after a moment of consideration. "Alina and Owen Jadestone. Caleb blames me for killing his wife and best friends."

His words knocked the breath out of my lungs, and it took several moments for me to recover enough air to gasp, "What? Why would he think that? You told me my parents died in an explosion during the Second American Civil War."

"I think that's quite enough for tonight," stated Eve loudly.

"No." I shot up from my seat at the dining table and crossed my arms. "What are you talking about? Why would Caleb blame you for something you clearly couldn't control?"

My stare never once left Mr. Woobi's mutilated face, scrunched and riddled with wrinkles from anxiety, as I tried to analyze him for the answers I wished to hear him speak. I wanted to read the words dancing around his brain, wanted to scrutinize the knowledge he possessed and dissect it until I could piece together the truth about the past Caleb robbed me from remembering. I wanted to know. Yet the longer I studied the elder's facial expressions, the more certain I became that Mr. Woobi would never willingly tell me everything he knew. I'd have to fight for my right to his information. The two of us played our own game of "tag," except this time, he manipulated the game so I could never win, forcing me to relentlessly chase after his answers he knew I could never reach. I despised that.

"Caleb believed I controlled everything that occurred in that village during the war," Mr. Woobi answered after our lengthy silent assessment of each other. "I was elected mayor, and I acted as general of the squadron assigned to protect the town back when that village had much more infrastructure than it does now. When the opposing forces occupied the perimeter around the town, I tried my hardest to reach some sort of peace agreement. I couldn't have anticipated the massacre that followed months after they invaded. How could I have predicted that they'd blow up an entire village of innocent men, women, and children? It was unfathomable."

Mr. Woobi's breathing changed to becoming irregular, and he shut his eyes tightly to block whatever images were playing out in his mind. Eve flipped her hand up to intertwine their fingers and reached across the table to place her other hand on top of his, so that she sandwiched his hand with hers. She soothingly rubbed her thumb along his, and her actions smoothed some of the harsh lines around Mr. Woobi's closed eyes. "Caleb and Eve had taken David, Peter, and you into the forest to play while Owen, Alina, and Juniper stayed with me to draft one last potential peace plan. But then it exploded. Everything exploded." Mr. Woobi sucked in a shaky, pained breath, as though his lungs were still filled with ash, and Eve squeezed his hand in support.

"Caleb never got to say goodbye," Mr. Woobi rasped between ragged breaths. "He never got to bury the bodies because there was nothing left to bury. He left four people behind, and only one stood to face him. But I wasn't the person he wanted to see still standing."

"Charlie…" Eve cooed, swinging her body so she could sit in the chair next to him and easily rake her fingers through his wispy, crazy hair.

Mr. Woobi's body began to vibrate, and a feral look overtook his eyes. Eve leaned in and kissed his temple; her touch seemed to be the only thing that could calm him. "We fought," the elder croaked. "I didn't approve of Juniper or the baby. I couldn't. They had only known each other a year beforehand. I could never approve of such impulsive behavior. Caleb hated me for my disapproval, and after David's birth, Caleb hated me for what he called 'perpetuating the war.' After Juniper, Owen, and Alina died, he reached his breaking point. He believed I conspired to kill them, that because only I survived, then I must be to blame. He has despised me ever since, Zelda Ellyn. He left Eve outside the Society so she couldn't see the way he tortured me. I believe Caleb would stop at nothing to kill me in the same manner he believes I killed his wife and closest friends."

"You don't mean that," chastised Eve. "Surely, Caleb wouldn't kill. Not our baby." Her voice cracked in the middle of the last word, and tears leaked from her dark eyes, tears she quickly wiped away.

Mr. Woobi tilted his head to rest against Eve's forehead. "I'm afraid we've made a monster, my love," the older man whispered, a single tear dripping down his cheek like a raindrop.

"No," Eve rebutted, bringing her hand out from Mr. Woobi's hair to wipe his tear. "Not Caleb. He's broken, Charlie. He lost his love, and then they used him."

"Who?" I asked. "Who used him?"

"The Federation," answered Mr. Woobi. "The same people who killed his extended family. They loved his story—the son of the general who had just supposedly killed the mother of his child—and transformed him into a poster child for their cause. They trained him in the art of public speaking, and after years of attending debate class with Owen, Caleb had already developed the talent of persuasion. He mobilized an army. Caleb is the reason they won; without him, they would've lost their momentum. As a show of gratitude, the Federation elected him Leader of the Society, and the rest is, as they say, history. I never saw my son, Caleb Woobi, again. Only Leader Caleb remains now, the man they sculpted him to be."

"That is not true," argued Eve as she cupped the side of her husband's face. "We'll bring our baby back home, Charlie. We must bring our son home."

Mr. Woobi hunched into Eve's embrace, their foreheads now plastered against each other, and I watched as pain seemed to emerge from their bodies while they whispered consoling words to one another. Suddenly, I felt like an intruder, so I walked out of the hotel suite to stand on the street corner and get some air. The city buzzed around me, flurries of activity, lights, sounds, and people, but for once, I wanted nothing but silence. I wanted the Earth to stop spinning, if only for a moment, and acknowledge what it had stolen from the couple upstairs. I wanted the Earth to cry for its failures, to pelt me with its tears that fall from the sky, but no rain came. Just noise, bright, flashing light, and hundreds of people pushing past me on their way toward nothing.

"I will gladly make sure there is not one trace of Charles Woobi left. He has to pay for what he's done."

"What has he ever done to you?!"

"More than you know," Leader Caleb snapped.

This memory ran rampant in my mind as I went back up and settled into the couch for the night. Although I tried to dream of my joy when I meet Caleb in a coffin, I instead dreamt of a man—blond hair, slim, tall frame, and deep brown eyes—bouncing a blue-eyed baby boy on his knee, a wife looking down lovingly at the scene, a family blissfully unaware of the tragedy soon to strike.

The following week, Knew Magazine published my article in their newest issue, my face displayed on their front cover, but I hardly recognized myself. Shadows swathed the young woman in this photo, the dirt streaked across her face alluding to scratches and scars. With her eyebrows knitted tightly together, she looked furious, boiling over with hatred, but one look into her impossibly dark eyes, and the little flames the magazine had used for lighting flickering inside her irises illuminated her inner pain, desperation, and longing. A stunningly beautiful photo that made me feel like a fraud. "I Hate Him," read the headline. "Zelda Jadestone Speaks Out on Her Relationship with Caleb Woobi." I ripped up the magazine before Mr. Woobi, Eve, or even I could open its pages.

President Dassian called on the night before our departure to praise my efforts and inform me that the public's persistent push for war had been amplified by my actions. The thought made me want to run, but I had nowhere to go.

On our way back to the village, I barely looked out the window to watch the swarm of people screaming my name until we drove past a smaller cluster gathered on the side of the street that looked significantly different than the others I had seen. As I stepped out of the vehicle, I instantly noticed why they had captured my attention; there were twelve total—a relatively small group compared to the mobs I had encountered before—and out of those twelve, four of them used wheelchairs, two had crutches, three were in slings of some kind, one's face was burnt almost completely, and the rest had yellowing bandages placed in miscellaneous areas of their bodies. They didn't smile or squeal or stare at me in absolute awe when they noticed me approaching; they held their heads high, unafraid to meet my gaze.

Everything came to a standstill when one of the men in a wheelchair, with a scraggly beard but no hair on the top of his head, came rolling over to me, picked up my hand in his trembling one, and kissed the top of it gently. Rendered speechless for a moment, I was just beginning to articulate my gratitude when I glanced down, only to find both of his legs missing from the mid-thigh downward. I suppose my emotions played on my face because the man chuckled and explained, "From the war, years ago."

"Why do you want to fight then?" I asked in a loud whisper, unable to look away from the nothingness that was the space where his legs should have been. "Why do any of you want to fight another war?"

"These are just physical wounds," said the burn victim whom I had turned to finally face at the sound of his broken voice. It was difficult to completely understand him from the way his lips were configured, but I tried my best to grasp the gist of it. "There are people in that Society that are hurting much more than we are, emotionally, mentally, maybe even physically. It's our duty to help them."

I looked around and saw the same determined look on all their faces. "But why is it your duty?" I inquired, still immensely confused. It was evident they had suffered at the hands of war, ruined forever both physically and mentally, so why then were they so eager to fight again? They even considered it their responsibility to help the citizens stuck in the Society, but where was their personal gain, their trophy at the finish line, their satisfying conclusion? I only saw death, anger, and vast grief when I thought of the war's conclusion. How was it that I could only see what I thought to make sense when everyone else saw things so much differently?

The man in the wheelchair answered, "Because soldiers never leave each other behind."

"You aren't soldiers anymore," I retorted quite forcibly, hating the mere idea of that statement. "That war has ended."

"Oh, yes we are, Miss Jadestone," he replied calmly. "We will always be soldiers. Whether or not the visible war has ended is irrelevant to us now. The real war, the mental one, we will always be soldiers in. Those people in the Society are soldiers to their leader just as we are to our own minds, and you are to this war and to the younger people who are looking to you to guide them through it. We must all help each other to not just survive, but to live." His expression softened considerably, and he continued, "We know you're frightened of what is to come with every good reason to be, but what you will come to learn is that fear will always bow to bravery. Sometimes, the most beautiful things come after the most destructive disasters."

A woman, perhaps in her early forties and missing her right arm, came up and unfolded her hand to reveal a single gold bullet with a sharp rose gold tip at the end of it. "Don't let this get the better of you, Miss Jadestone," she told me as she placed it into my open palm and wrapped my fingers around it for me. "Just one can kill you."

"Just one bullet?" I asked.

She shook her head. "Just one person."

I dropped my gaze and bit my lip hard enough to open a fresh wound, the taste of blood making my eyes water. The whole way back to the village, the two Woobis and I barely said a word, leaving me to play with the bullet by twirling it around in my hands and weaving it in and out of my fingers. I chose to call that group of people the Twelve Soldiers because they were the only people who made me truly think about leading this war not just for Peter, but for the rest of the people in the Society as well. I slipped the bullet into my pocket silently when that thought became too loud in my head.

The village teemed with people when we finally returned, all packed closely to the ashy fire pit and murmuring amongst each other when I stepped out of the vehicle compartment. I joined those gathered around the pit, hoping for some explanation, but the crowd fell silent the closer I got until silence descended on the whole crowd. No one dared to break the electric energy running through the air until one older woman waddled over to me, took my hand in hers, said, "My son. My son is in there. Thank you. Thank you," and wrapped her frail arms around my midsection in a tight hug.

This lady triggered the rest of them to rush over to me in waves, squeezing my hands or hugging me in some way, whether that be around my legs, around my middle, or around my neck. I listened to their stories about their family members, sat with weeping parents to try and console them, hugged them back with an equal amount of force. It all made me slightly uncomfortable, but the pure joy behind their smiles made it worthwhile, and I slowly began to enjoy bringing some hope to their faces when I heard a familiar, deep voice rumble, "Finally come to mingle with the commoners, Zelda?"

A wide grin stretched across my face at the sound of the voice I knew all too well. *Eric.*

His name was the only incentive I needed to go sprinting into his arms. He opened them wide enough for me to jump into his embrace, our bodies colliding as my arms wrapped around his neck. I nestled my face into his shoulder to hide the blush that bloomed across my cheeks when the crowd burst into applause at our reunion. I wished I possessed the ability to articulate how comforting his arms around me felt, but I could only pathetically utter, "It's only been a month, but you look older somehow. More mature."

Eric guffawed, turned his head slightly, and caught sight of something that made him break into a grin. "Yeah, well, a month ages a man after spending it with that guy over there." He nodded his head to the right, and I glanced to see Dave standing off to the side of the crowd, anxiously twirling a fresh bouquet of wildflowers in his hand and glancing at me sheepishly. My eyes drifted down to his left arm, and I saw vicious scabs covering his Uniform tattoo.

I withdrew from Eric's embrace to walk over to the ex-Uniform, the crowd parting to let us draw nearer to each other, but not quite close enough to be face-to-face. Dave didn't look up from the ground as he thrust the flowers in my direction. "I picked these this morning," he muttered. "Here, they're for you."

I raised the corners of my lips slightly and closed the distance between us to accept the bouquet. "Thank you."

The crowd swooned at the gesture, and again, my face burned red from their reaction. Dave nervously glanced over in Eric's direction, and I followed the ex-Uniform's gaze to see Eric giving him a supportive thumbs up. The slight smile on Eric's lips juxtaposed the way his eyebrows furrowed in the way they would when the sun shines too brightly and it hurts to see.

"Zelda?" asked Dave quietly.

"Yeah?"

"Can we go somewhere to talk?" He glanced around at the crowd enthralled by our interaction and added, "Privately?"

I nodded, and after Dave took my hand in his, we set off toward the direction of the hospital, weaving our way through the crowd until we had gone inside and sat on beds facing each other. Stiff silence prevented me from saying anything, but thankfully, Dave spoke first: "So, how did everything go? Eric and I watched you on the television, but I bet it was so different being there in person."

Dave's questions brought my mind back to the meaningless crowds I had swum through, to the Twelve Soldiers, to Dassian and his poisonous words, to Peter himself, and I physically cringed at the memories. "I don't want to talk about that," I demanded, although I softened my expression when I saw the flash of hurt across Dave's face. "Sorry, but I—"

Dave waved dismissively and shook his head. "No, I get it. Too overwhelming right now."

I nodded, and he smiled sympathetically at me. An anxious shiver shot up my spine, and I said, "Dave—"

"Zelda—" started Dave simultaneously, and we shared a breath of awkward laughter before he said, "I'm so sorry for what I said about Peter. I crossed a line, and—"

"No," I interrupted, wanting to cross the distance and take his hand, but too afraid to act upon it. "Forget about that. I'm sorry for not telling you about Mr. Woobi and Caleb sooner."

Dave dipped his head before looking at me through hooded lashes. "So why didn't you?"

I opened and closed my mouth several times, swallowing the words I felt trying to escape my throat, only to regurgitate the same excuses every time I tried to speak again. I knew I could spit out the half-truth that Mr. Woobi had coerced me into hiding Dave's family lineage, but I knew Dave deserved the truth, regardless of how bitter it tasted inside my mouth. There were so many things I wanted to tell him, so many things I knew he deserved to hear, but I eventually settled on saying, "I was afraid."

"Afraid of what?"

"Losing you."

Dave huffed from his nostrils in a poor attempt at laughing, and I noticed how his lips carried a small smirk from my words. "It's funny, Eric said the same thing," he responded. "He said the only reason you would hide this from me is because you were scared I would get hurt."

I raised my eyebrows at the statement. "Eric said that?"

Dave shrugged. "Yeah. We talked about you a lot, among other things. He's cool. I like Eric a lot."

I smiled at Dave's words and nodded. "Yeah, me too. Eric's right; the only reason I kept this from you was to protect you. I didn't want you to feel any pain because of me."

"Did you ever consider that keeping the fact that I am a Woobi from me would hurt me more than just being honest, Zelda?"

I lowered my gaze at his question. "No."

"I don't know if I can forgive you," proclaimed Dave, and I bit my bottom lip hard at his declaration, dropping my gaze down to my shoes until I felt the bed dip beside me and looked up to see Dave sitting next to me, his forehead bent toward mine. "But then again, I don't know if you can forgive me for killing Jack Garrole."

"I-673637," proclaimed Peter to both the Uniform and the congregation. "You have broken the universal Uniform oath of chastity by engaging in a relationship with Mister Jack Garrole. Such a crime holds the punishment of immediate death."

"And you, Jack Garrole," spoke Dave with the slightest wobble to his voice one would only notice if one knew him well enough. "You are punished by death for being in a relationship with a Uniform. Both I-673637 and Jack Garrole get a final sentence before their execution."

Both Jack and the Uniform uttered the same sentence simultaneously: "All I did, I did for you."

Dave and Peter stepped to the side to let the other Uniforms do their jobs, and the look on their faces confirmed what I knew was coming next. I willed my feet to go faster as I sped through the crowd, pushing my way through to try and reach the stage. I could vaguely hear Eric calling my name as he, too, raced after me, but I didn't care enough to look back. "No!" I screamed, hoping that someone would hear my voice over the whistles of applause and thirst for death. "Stop! Peter, Dave, stop them! Stop!"

The pair of them heard me; I knew by the way they both turned their heads to look at where the sound could've possibly come from, unimaginable sadness in both of their eyes when Leader Caleb ordered, "Kill them. Now."

"No!"

But I was too late.

The memory slammed into me so hard that I gasped and clutched the tops of my knees to stabilize myself. "Dave..."

"Don't deny it. You can never forgive me for killing your friend, even if you wanted to. Your mind won't allow it because I am in the memory of his death, just like you're in my memory of finding out Caleb Woobi is my father." Dave scooted closer to gently place a hand on top of mine, and I clasped my knee harder at his sudden touch. "So, let's have our sins cancel each other out. We're even."

I wrinkled my nose. "Even?"

"Even," Dave purred, inching closer and closer until his forehead grazed my temple.

I turned my head to rebut, but Dave captured my lips with his before I had the chance to utter a word. I reciprocated eagerly, elated to feel his affection again, but I could sense that the Dave I was kissing now was not the same boy I had kissed after dancing the day the village threw us a welcome celebration. This boy acted much more aggressively, pushing his lips harder against my own than he ever had before, angling his body so I had no choice but to lie down beneath him. He clutched my face between his hands suddenly, and I hissed against his mouth from the unexpected tightness of his grip. "Sorry," he mumbled against my lips, and it was only then that he eased his tempo. "I missed you," he whispered as he ghosted kisses along my jaw, and had I possessed any breath left in my lungs, I would've shared his sentiment.

Dave and I were so engrossed in each other that we failed to notice someone walking through the hospital doors until we heard a metal table clang loudly against the floor, followed by a resounding, "Ow, dammit, ugh." The pair of us sat up to see Eric's body bent over, his hands grasping his shin, his head picked up to look at us fearfully. "Hi," he greeted awkwardly, his body still contorted in the strangest position. "Sorry, um, I didn't mean to interrupt your... uh... reunion. I accidentally bumped into this stupid table." At our perplexed looks, Eric shook his head in regret and announced, "You know what, I'll come back later. Sorry. I—"

Dave laughed, and the sound filled me with a surge of joy after not hearing it for so long. "No worries, man, you didn't interrupt anything," he assured, and despite my intense embarrassment, I smiled in reassurance as well.

"Hi, Eric," I squeaked, wanting nothing more than to hide my face into Dave's shirt to conceal how red my cheeks glowed.

"Hi, Zelda," he responded politely, rubbing the back of his neck and cracking an amused smile. "Hi, Dave. I really didn't mean to barge in on your... session."

I groaned from the sheer humiliation, grabbed the pillow next to me, and smashed my face into the plush square, much to Dave and Eric's enjoyment; the boys rumbled with teasing laughter at my reaction, and despite my complete mortification, I couldn't help but giggle into my pillow at the sound of their delight.

"So, what's up, Stellenzer?" asked Dave through his chuckles after we had settled down somewhat.

"The Woobis…" Eric stalled and eyed Dave, a humorous glint in his eyes. "Present company excluded—"

Dave rolled his eyes, and Eric burst into laughter again, expertly dodging the pillow Dave threw at him. "Oh, shut up," Dave announced, but the mocking hilt to his voice undermined his serious exterior.

Eric grinned in amusement. "Sorry, bud, I couldn't pass up that perfect opportunity. But yeah, the Woobis invited the three of us to dinner at their house tonight. I was thinking we could all walk there together… unless you two are otherwise occupied, of course." He wiggled his eyebrows suggestively, but again, his playful actions didn't match his body language; he stuffed his hands deep inside his pant pockets, and he rocked back and forth on his heels nervously, as if waiting for the moment he could dash away. I tried to catch his eyes to see if I could rationalize his behavior through his gaze, but Eric refused to glance my way for very long.

Dave agreed to walking to dinner as a group, so the three of us set off from the hospital through the maze of homes toward the Woobi residence. Dave insisted he had the route memorized, so Eric and I allowed him to lead the way, the two of us content with loosely following behind him.

"You know, for a Uniform, he's not half-bad," Eric stated as we walked, gesturing toward Dave's back.

I would've laughed had it not been for the memory of Dave scrapping his inked skin with a charred brick the month before. "He's not a Uniform, Eric," I corrected, lowering my voice so only Eric could hear. "Not anymore."

Eric shrugged. "Well, whatever he is, I enjoyed babysitting him this month. He's not nearly as obnoxious as he looks."

"Heard that!" yelled Dave from in front of us, and we cracked smiles at his expense.

"I'm so relieved you get along well," I mentioned to Eric.

"And I'm relieved to see everyone's favorite couple back together again, it seems," he responded, although I thought I detected a trace of bitterness in his voice as he said so. "How are things on that front?"

"Um, we're fine. I think we worked things out." I shoved him playfully and added, "Thanks to you, actually. I think you helped Dave understand my rationale."

Eric hummed from the back of his throat. "Hm. Happy to be of service."

Again, I thought I heard sarcasm laced through his tone, but I chose to ignore it, happy to spend the rest of the walk talking about nonsense. Dave successfully led us to the Woobis' home for our scheduled dinner, and although it proved slightly awkward with all five of our vastly different personalities around a single table, we ultimately thoroughly enjoyed each other's company. Dave and Eric shared stories of their adventures while we were in Neweryork, demonstrating a choreographed dance the schoolchildren had taught them, regaling stories of their exploration of the nearby surrounding forestry, and showing off their intricate new "secret handshake" that consisted of kicks, spins, and hops in the air.

As the boys talked, I took notice of the way they comfortably interacted with each other, with their shared, private jokes that one would mention to make the other uproar in laughter, and their playful, natural behavior, acting as if they had known each other for more than just a month or so. Although I hadn't realized it before, I could sleep easier knowing Eric not only approved, but welcomed Dave's relatively new presence in our lives.

After Mr. Woobi, Eve, and I had relayed our stories from our experience in Neweryork, we decided to stay at the Woobi residence overnight, with the two boys sleeping on the floor and myself claiming the couch. Dave fell asleep quickly, but I didn't possess that talent; instead, I lay awake on my back, staring into the darkness of the living room, listening to Dave and Eric's steady breaths.

"Hey, Eric?" My voice pierced the still silence, but I knew from the way Eric breathed that he had not succumbed to slumber just yet.

Sure enough, I heard Eric stir from his place below the couch. "Yeah?"

"I missed you."

Although the darkness prevented me from seeing his reaction, I could hear the smile in his voice when he replied, "I missed you, too. Hey, Zelda?"

"Yeah?"

"Let's agree not to get separated again, okay?"

This time, it was my turn to smile into my response: "Okay."

And I allowed myself to give in to the alluring, warm feeling of peace, if only for a singular night.

CHAPTER 10

I tried to recall that warmth when I woke up to someone hitting my feet and loudly whispering for me to awaken. After finally sleeping through a whole night without horrific nightmares, I pressed my face deeper into the couch and instructed the person to promptly leave me to catch up on my rest.

"Zelda, it's Peter," announced Mr. Woobi, who I finally identified as the man shaking me awake. I hurriedly scrambled off the couch at the mention of my brother and proceeded to follow the older man toward the direction of my old home, wondering along the way just how long I had slept, given the sun's relatively high position in the sky. A pinching sensation on my thigh caught my attention, and I searched my pockets to find the golden bullet one of the Twelve Soldiers had gifted me the day before. I stuffed the bullet back inside my pocket so as not to lose it.

Mr. Woobi led me into my old family home without a word, and despite my perplexed look, he refused to talk to me until we had entered the room at the end of the hall: the "war room," I had labeled it. We walked in to find Eve, Dave, Eric, Allyson, and Marley gathered around the sole table in the room, projecting what looked to be a map of some kind and talking in low, hushed voices. "What's going on?" I meant to say in an even, calm tone, but my natural morning voice combined with my worry for Peter made my voice break halfway through.

"NewerNews received another transmission from Leader Caleb Woobi," answered Allyson. "We came here as quickly as we could."

Marley smiled to try and alleviate the tension. "Hi, sleepyhead. Good to see you're finally awake."

"A transmission from the Society?" I questioned, suddenly panicked. "Is it Peter? Is he okay?"

Instead of answering my question, Marley pressed a button on her personal screen. At first, nothing happened, but then the projection on the table flickered. The coward himself, Caleb Woobi, appeared in his usual fashion: wrapped in the darkness that brought him comfort, voice mechanized by the computer's audio software, sporting the coy smile that haunted my dreams. Caleb started out by addressing what a great little actress I made, how truly impressed he was at how easily I could captivate a whole state, but sadly how he would have to eliminate my followers for their incompetence.

Then, just as he did last time, Caleb directed his speech to me. "Zelda Jadestone," he began, his voice making my skin crawl in perceived hatred. "You and I both know I am not an evil man. I cannot and will not kill anything that lives, which is why I have not killed your brother just yet."

Caleb took this opportunity to pause and grin. "Your little brother, Peter Adrian Jadestone. The last piece of your ripped-apart family. The one person you're willing to fight this meaningless war for. The little boy you thought abandoned you, but how does it feel to know that it is you who became the abandoner?"

I swallowed bile, and a sudden onset of dizziness threatened to bring me down to my knees.

Caleb clicked his tongue against the roof of his mouth. "Poor, poor Zelda Jadestone. You are truly trapped in the perfect paradox, aren't you? But do you know what traps you inside this paradox, this seemingly impossible situation, Zelda Jadestone? Your own selfishness. People will die because of you: children without their parents, spouses without their other halves, friends without their friends. You kill one person, you shatter another. And all for what? I ask. For your precious Peter's supposed safety, away from everything he knows, away from *me*? How do you know I won't kill him the instant you try to retaliate against my Society? How can you guarantee Peter Jadestone is any safer with you out there than he is in here with me; judging from your previous track record, people end up dead when they get close to you, don't they, Zelda Jadestone? Jack Garrole, the rest of your foolish peers, almost Charles himself: all dead because of you."

My mind conjured images of Jack's lifeless body, still twitching from the aftershocks of his electrocution; of my coworkers' blood on my gray Societan shirt; of Mr. Woobi's defeated eyes right before I gathered the courage to save him. I wanted to scream from the pictures flickering inside my brain.

"You cannot possibly predict what I can do, what I might do, what I *will* do once you choose to destroy my life's work," rambled Caleb. "Zelda Jadestone, you may think you have all the power in the world right at this moment, with your words intoxicating your followers and those airheaded, empty shells they call leaders spilling poison in your ear, but do not be fooled. I have the secret for solving your impossible situation, and it is the same solution I offered you six months ago when you foolishly chose to interfere with Charles Woobi's arrest: let Peter go." Abandon your brother the way he abandoned you: in honor of the greater good. Why risk the lives of millions for the slim chance of 'saving' one? Why risk Peter's life for the slight possibility of a pathetic, unobtainable reunion? Why gamble with God, Zelda Jadestone? You know how to save yourself. You know how to save the thousands that follow you blindly. You even know how to truly save Peter."

Caleb leaned dangerously close to the camera in front of him, so close that I could see the individual blond eyebrow strands above his impossibly dark, impossibly honest eyes, the peaks of his upper lips, the sweat dripping from his slicked-back hairline. "Give up," Caleb commanded. "Surrender. Do not fight, because you cannot win. I am greater than you, greater than that moron in charge, Cody Dassian, greater than any celestial power at play in our little scenario. If you continue, I will kill you, Zelda Jadestone. Slowly, painfully, publicly, I will kill you. I will kill not your body, but your soul. I will show you what true horror looks like, what true agony feels like, what true terror tastes like. I will rejoice when you surrender, relish when you beg for mercy, and I will savor the moment you can no longer stand. I will kill you, Zelda Jadestone. And if you continue, I may just kill your brother, too."

Peter's pleading whisper of my name then invasively infiltrated the stale air around us, the sound lingering long after the screen went black.

"We must retaliate," announced someone in the room, but I didn't care to listen. My mind focused solely on Peter, trying to figure out what Caleb would do to him if I continued with what I had agreed to do in my deal with President Dassian. What if everything I had done only inched Peter closer to his death? Every speech, every action, every movement I made seemed to push Caleb to a point of no return. I intimidated the leader of the Society, so much so that he was practically holding my brother at gunpoint, and I was terrified to make another move in fear of him pulling the trigger.

I tried to analyze Caleb's motives in my head by stripping everything down to the basics. He wants me dead. He doesn't want a war. He wants to keep his position of power. I said these three things under my breath until they stuck in my mind. Okay. He is using Peter as bait. He hates his father. He doesn't know how to feel about his son. My eyes shut from the headache that suddenly pounced into my head. Okay. I scare him. He scares me. War scares the both of us. Okay. I could feel myself falling... *No, no, no...*

"Zelda?"

I couldn't respond. Everything spun around me at a rapid pace, faster and faster and faster until I was sure my head was set to explode. *Inhale. Exhale. Inhale. Exhale. Inhale. Inhale. Inhale.* Twirling. Spinning. Whirling. *Zelda, get a grip.* Peter. Peter. Peter. *Zelda, stop.* "I can't." I was dizzy. Was I spinning? I didn't know. *Exhale. Inhale. Repeat.* Death. *My fault.* War. War. War. *No. Yes!* I didn't know. *Zelda. Zelda. Zelda.* My coworkers pulling at my ankles, grasping my wrists, holding onto my waist. *What?*

Eric dashed across the room to hold me against his chest protectively. "Everybody let her have a moment to herself," he instructed. "Hey Dave, you okay there, bud?"

I lifted my head to see Dave shaking tremendously, his electric-blue eyes cradling thick, foggy tears. "That's my *father*," Dave spat, and that was all he had to utter to have Mr. Woobi and Eve turn their attention away from me and place it on him instead.

Eric pressed his face against the top of my head and held me tightly against him as I whispered, "He... Peter... He's going to hurt P-Peter, Eric."

"No, he won't, Zelda," Eric assured. "We won't let him."

"What do I do?" I cried out. "I don't know what to do anymore. I just want Peter back, but I don't want him killed... he can't die, Eric! But then what's my next move? How do I free him? What do I do?!"

"You make sure no one gets the better of you, okay? Not Caleb, not the people who look up to you, not Charles, Eve, Dave, or even me. You listen to *yourself*."

"I don't know how to do that," I answered honestly.

"Something has to be done today," Allyson interrupted in an annoyed tone, which made everyone look up and stare at her in disbelief. "It's obvious Leader Caleb's words hold weight, and his words could make some people wary of the war. If people start to doubt, that'll set us back not days, not months, but *years*. Zelda must make this official; we need to fight a battle."

The chatter in the room came to a standstill as we all let her words sink in. "What are you proposing I do?" I asked, instinctively reaching for the bullet in my pocket to occupy my mind.

"You were flawless this past month," Allyson stated, turning our attention to the projection on the table, now playing an edited compilation of me in the city. There I stood, stepping out of the vehicle with determination blazing behind my eyes. There I stood, talking to the pink-haired girl, my voice suddenly booming, "Because it's the right thing to do," through the speakers. There I stood, accepting the golden bullet from the woman without her arm and conversing with all the others who had been injured.

Then the screen changed, and unexpectedly, I saw myself back in the Society, projecting my voice to the crowd of Societan citizens as I saved Mr. Woobi's life and watching them react to my words. I saw myself face-to-face with Caleb as I leaned forward in my seat and declared, "I don't want you to *give* the options to me, I want to create them myself." I saw myself pick myself up from the ground, smile almost evilly at Caleb, and proclaim, "The only twisted politics are in here, where you keep people ignorant for the sake of power, where you erase their memories so they can't feel anything, where you filter out love and thinking from their lives until they're nothing but your personal machines. Doesn't matter when, but I *am* coming back, and you won't be ready when I do." The program then flashed the words GIVE THEM THE FREEDOM TO CHOOSE. STAND WITH ZELDA JADESTONE before going black for the final time.

My voice quivered in fear and disgust as I growled, "Where did you get those clips of me in the Society?"

"Hacked into their surveillance video," answered Marley with a proud smile, but I wasn't impressed in the slightest.

"That's pretty impressive propaganda," praised Dave. "It really shows all sides of what a leader should be: kind, brave, outspoken, strong, smart, fearless. It really highlights who Zelda is and why she's such a perfect role model and leader. Beautifully done."

"But I'm not a perfect leader," I argued. No one listened to me.

"So, this is what I'm suggesting we do," said Allyson. "After Zelda's propaganda video goes live in about an hour, Caleb will be vulnerable. He'll be sitting in a nice, comfortable office chair as he yells at his advisors to write more speeches so he can create a retaliation video. He won't have eyes on the outside because he believes we are only concerned with cyber warfare. This is our time to coordinate an attack. Zelda, today you will call for eligible men and women to travel to this village to fight. We will supply them with the current technology we have at the moment to try and pop the boundary around the Society, as well as military-grade trucks to bring them there. Camera crews will accompany them to get footage to use in future propaganda. Zelda will be sent back to Neweryork where she'll lift the morale of the people whose loved ones are out on the front, attend press conferences, and so forth. This'll get the ball rolling. This is what we need to propel us into war."

A strange, uncomfortable feeling came over me then, like there was information I was missing, so I asked cautiously, "These men and women, they're soldiers, right? They know how to fight? They can live?"

No one answered me.

"How long do they have to prepare, then?"

Again, no one answered me.

"If someone doesn't speak up this instant, I will walk out of here," I warned.

"No, Zelda," stated Allyson. "They're volunteers, and they would leave tonight."

My eyes widened in complete revulsion and horror as I shouted, "Without proper training, they'll walk in blind! It'll be a mass suicide mission. I cannot authorize that!"

"You have no choice!" screeched Allyson right back at me. "You're not in charge around here, Zelda Jadestone. You might think you are only because the public is made to believe you are, but wake up, honey. You won't be making any executive decisions anymore. You *will* go out there, and you *will* make that speech, because that is what you have been ordered to do."

"I'm not saying a word for you," I growled. "Not one word out of my mouth will be pro-war if this is how it will be done. I can't condone that."

Allyson rolled her glowing, angry eyes. "Well then, you can kiss Peter goodbye," she stated, smiling when she saw my ice façade crumble from the unbearable pain behind those words. "He'll be destroyed, damaged, most definitely dead by the time you can figure out how to get into the Society on your own. You need us much more than we need you, Zelda. So, go ahead and quit. We'll all be here, ready to mourn, when you bring Peter back in a little-brother-sized coffin."

I closed my eyes in concentration as I weighed my heavy options. As much as I hated to admit it, I knew Allyson's words rang true in a sick, twisted way; I wouldn't be able to save Peter alone, and although I knew I had at least Dave and Eric by my side, I couldn't keep them safe at all times, protection I knew Eve and her village could offer. But all those people I would be calling to fight trusted me, looked up to me, admired me. How could I lead them to what could be their deaths like that? Who was I to control life and death that way? How would they still call me a hero after that?

But I needed Peter. I knew I wouldn't be able to survive, much less *live*, if I consciously knew of his imprisonment in the Society. I had promised myself that I would come back to him. He never truly abandoned me, not even when he was faced with meeting certain death. And I knew I would never abandon him, regardless of the obstacles stacked against me. So, I agreed, to all of it. *I'm here for you, Peter,* I told him in my head as the leaders in the room began to celebrate all around me. The only thing that kept me sane was the thought that soon, he would be able to hear me say those words to him in person.

After Allyson got approval from President Dassian regarding this decision, they ushered me over to the stage and told the villagers to get back to their homes as quickly as they could. Marley had set up the camera to stare at me point-blank in the face, the way the barrel of a gun would. Mr. Woobi, over to the left of the camera, gave me a weak, tight-lipped smile, and as I returned his gesture, I couldn't help but marvel at how our positions had switched so quickly. I wished I could hate him for it, blame him for my misfortune somehow, but every time I remembered the way he'd kiss my forehead goodnight when I was younger, I couldn't bring myself to hold him accountable.

"Now, Zelda, we knew that this would be difficult for you, so I pre-wrote your speech for you. The words will appear in the lens for your convenience, but don't worry, they won't show up on the broadcast. This is all pre-recorded anyway, so take your time," said Allyson, and I nodded in appreciation.

Marley gave me one of her signature thumbs ups, silently signaling at me to start, but as I opened my mouth to speak, a rush of cold guilt swept through my entire body and made me shiver. *We will win,* flashed inside the lens, and my stomach clenched at the blatant lie I was expected to regurgitate to those who admired me most. "I can't say this," I declared to my small congregation. I could feel something within me dying, receding quietly from my cognitive grasp into a darkness I dared not venture.

Allyson sighed and released some of the tension in her shoulders. "This isn't about you, Zelda. This is for Peter," she reminded.

I heard Peter's pleas for help from where I stood on this stage, desperate calls for freedom only I could provide him. I saw the gauntly nature of his malnourished, beaten, adolescent body, every pore oozing unimaginable pain. I could almost feel him reaching out for me from his cell in the Jail, begging for me to save him from Caleb. *This is for Peter,* Allyson had said, and her words sparked the embers inside me.

Allyson was right; this was for Peter.

And as I fixed my gaze once again on the dark, imposing lens, I remained determined to remember that fact, channeling every ounce of my fury into my words, ignoring the scripted ones Allyson provided.

"Hello to all citizens of Neweryork and its surrounding towns, villages, and suburbs," I began. "I am Zelda Jadestone, humbly coming to you today to ask for your collaboration as we begin to fight Leader Caleb Woobi of the Society. As we are aware by now, Caleb Woobi has engaged in cyber-terrorism against me, against you, and against the leaders of this great state. He has threatened my life, my little brother's life, and the lives of the millions who live outside the Society. He believes in us surrendering to his whim, as if he holds any power over us, but Caleb Woobi severely underestimates the strength we hold together. I have had enough of Caleb's threats, accusations, and torture. I say we end this cyber warfare and retaliate not with words, but with firepower, to show Caleb Woobi that his reign over our loved ones will not be tolerated any longer."

I didn't give myself a chance to think before announcing, "I am calling for willing, eligible, healthy individuals over the age of sixteen to gather in the center of Eve Redding's village by tonight, 7 pm sharp, to get prepped for the fight we will bring straight to Caleb Woobi's door. I am counting on the people of this society—this free, democratic society—to embody justice and fight for the freedom to choose. The people inside the Society, they need us to fight for them. My little brother, Peter, he needs us to fight to free him. And we will not abandon them. Thank you."

The red light blinked off, signaling my freedom to leave, but I stood perfectly still, so preoccupied with the weight of what I had just done that I failed to notice someone walking up to me until I heard Eve say, "Zelda, you are everything we could've asked for and more. That speech was stunning." She lifted my face with her two cold, clammy hands and shook my head rather roughly. "You are perfect, fiery girl. Do you hear me?"

My body burned so hotly, I momentarily thought I would implode, cave inward from the weight inside my core. "I did something bad. People might get hurt," I rasped, coughing on my words. I wanted to wiggle my face from Eve's hands, but I didn't have the strength to move.

"No, baby. You just saved so many innocent people," Eve argued. "Including your brother. Including my son. Thank you." She gave my head one final shake before dropping her grip, and I wanted to collapse onto the stage from the sudden lack of support.

I refused to move until Mr. Woobi helped me walk to the hospital, allowing me to use him as a crutch up the steps and into my bed. He observed me for a moment—sheets pulled up to my chin, dark eyes shiny with tears, body feverish and shuddering—and smiled sweetly. "You looked this way when you were afraid of the dark," he told me. "Caleb never provided nightlights inside those househuts, so you would ask me to stay with you until you fell asleep to protect you from the darkness." The elder man unsteadily leaned forward to kiss my hairline, and my eyelids fluttered shut at the childhood familiarity of the action. "I am so proud of you, Zelda Ellyn," he whispered in my ear right before pushing himself back into a full standing position. "Rest now. I will come to wake you at seven so you can send the troops off."

I didn't leave my hospital bed for the remainder of the day, although I did not rest. I knew my speech had aired once I heard the entire village descend into an uproar, hollering their approval and chanting my name triumphantly. The villagers' shouts made me draw my knees up to my chin and stay in that curled position for hours.

Zelda, the villagers yell in celebration, my name tasting as sweet as the rum on their tongues.

Zelda, cries Peter, and I want to cry, too, I want to cry with him, holding him, together with him.

Zelda, Caleb reprimands, a scoff at my disobedience. I wish I wasn't so afraid of the truth hiding behind his words.

Zelda Jadestone.

Zelda Ellyn.

Zelda. Zelda. Zelda.

All different interpretations of the same girl. A poster child, an older sister, a threat. A daughter figure, a mechanism for change, a girl unable to recognize herself in the mirror. What else would this job, this duty to serve the public's interests, strip from me? They chained me to the idea of freedom, snatched my identity, forced me to comply with their demands; what else could they possibly want from me? What more could I give? What more was I *willing* to give? I wished to shower, but the mere idea of leaving this bed pained me, so I stayed still.

It wasn't until I heard Dave's distinct, smooth voice yelling at somebody that I finally abandoned my sterile white bed. I found Dave red-faced, his fists clenched but down at his sides as he shouted at his grandparents. I didn't wish to interrupt, so I crept down beside the swinging entrance doors to the patient section of the hospital, content with letting the words filter through the crack between the two doors.

"You don't know me!" Dave shouted ferociously. "You don't know me, so you wouldn't understand. I have to go with them. I have to go back into the Society as soon as possible." The raw urgency in his voice did not go unnoticed, and I visualized him tapping his foot impatiently.

I heard Mr. Woobi sigh from the other side of the door before he said, "David, we already lost your mother. We don't want to lose you, too. We love you. We're just trying to protect you, my boy."

"I don't remember my mother," Dave stated, his voice breaking halfway through. "I don't remember what she looks... looked like, what her voice sounded like, what she used to do for fun." All my memories, the only memories I will have ever had of her, were erased. It was so easy to blame someone I didn't know, but now that I know it was my father, my own *father*, who took someone that precious away from me... it's like I lost a piece of myself. A piece of me I might find if I talk to him myself, face-to-face. Once the Society is opened again, I'm going to go talk to him. I'm going to convince him that what he is doing is wrong, and I'll finally have a father, a real one."

I could imagine Mr. Woobi and Eve opening their mouths to interject before Dave continued, "And Zelda's brother is in the Jail, which is supposed to be impossible. Blake promised Zelda that he wouldn't let anything happen to Peter; he swore on his life. Blake would never break a promise like that purposely. My father must've done something to him, something bad, maybe even something worse than what he's currently doing to Peter.

I have to go back and help him." Dave sounded frantic now, desperation creeping into his voice as he said, "Blake might not even know I left. I have to go back and make sure he's okay. He was my first friend, my first everything, really. I have to know if he's safe and save him if he's not."

Mr. Woobi inhaled slowly, and I could hear him dragging out his breath as though savoring it. "David, this Blake is one Uniform out of thousands. He would be impossible to find."

"No," argued Dave, his voice sharp and pained. "No. I can find him."

"How can you be so sure?" asked the elder man.

"Because I always could before," answered the ex-Uniform plainly.

A tense period of silence followed, and I feared Dave's grandparents might actually allow him to join the others in going to the Society until Eve declared, "We cannot let you go just yet, baby. No one understands Caleb anymore; no one knows if he's able to be convinced that his actions are wrong, even if his own son tells him. And I will simply not allow you to put yourself in harm's way for some boy you once called a friend. I'm sure he's fine."

I could feel Dave's frustration rippling through the stifling air when he barked, "Blake is not someone I called a friend once or twice. He's my family. Present tense."

"*We* are your family, David," reminded Eve.

"Since when?" Dave bit back. "Since you accidentally revealed we're related?" He scoffed. "No. Blake was the only person I cared about for years, and the only person I knew cared about me, too, until Zelda and I met. He's family to me. Charles, you, Zelda, Eric: you all came after him. Let me go and make sure he's safe. Please."

"David—"

"I'll run away," stated Dave abruptly. "If I have to, I'll run away. I am so sick of other people making decisions for me. It's about time I start taking control of my own life."

Mr. Woobi's shoes scuffed the tile flooring loudly, an indication of his scurried movements before he said, "I admire your bravery, David, but we simply cannot afford to lose you. I'll call Doctor Cortiana over to secure you in a safe location."

Dave let out an exasperated yell and shouted, "This is so unfair! You don't treat Eric like this."

"That's because we don't care about Eric the way we love you!" retorted Eve forcefully, quickly followed by the squeaking sound of the main hospital doors opening.

"Oh, that was nice," Eric remarked, refusing to give Eve an opportunity to apologize before he swiftly asked, "Where's Zelda?"

"Baby, I'm so sorry—"

"Nope, no, don't worry about it," dismissed Eric, but I could detect the strain in his voice. "Do you know where Zelda is?"

"Asleep," answered Mr. Woobi.

"Right here," I announced, standing on my feet and pushing the swinging door open, unable to stand the disconnect between the rest of the group and me any longer. My presence froze everyone else in place, their surprised expressions reflecting a fear I did not recognize. I instinctually stuffed my hands into my pant pockets and twirled the golden bullet around my fingers to distract myself. "What's going on?" I asked.

"I was just going to wake you," said Mr. Woobi.

"I was never asleep," I corrected, still eyeing them all with skepticism. "Why—"

"Eric!" called Allyson, suddenly bursting through the main hospital doors and barging in our conversation. "It's time to go, sweetie."

Eric visibly flinched at Allyson's words, and I narrowed my eyes in confusion when he responded, "Okay, just let me say goodbye."

"Say goodbye?" I repeated. I scanned Eric's body, searching for some explanation, and it was then that I saw the words "squadron 343" marked on his forearm.

CHAPTER 11

I vaguely heard Dave instructing everyone congregated in the lobby to give Eric and me some privacy, but my attention wasn't on them. I scanned Eric's face for some semblance of laughter, something that would tell me this was all a cruel joke the boys had planned, but when Eric refused to lift his head to meet my gaze, I knew our situation was anything but.

"I volunteered," Eric announced suddenly, as if that offered any explanation.

"Yeah, I see that," I retorted, crossing my arms and trying to appear angry, although the quake in my voice gave my fear away. "Why?"

Eric rewarded my question by lifting his head to look at me fully. "You didn't think I'd leave Peter with Caleb, did you? I'm going back for him. Besides, I don't think anyone here will miss me too much." I strongly shook my head in opposition and opened my mouth to retaliate, but he raised a hand to quiet me. "I know what you're going to say, Zelda, but Charles has Eve, and Eve has Dave, and Dave has you. You're not going to change my mind."

"They say I'm pretty convincing," I deadpanned.

Eric huffed in laughter. "So I've heard. But they also say I'm pretty stubborn." He grew serious and said, "I've got to do this, Zelda. You know I do."

I wished to articulate so much—how fiercely everyone he met loved him, how desperately I needed his presence in my life, how destroyed I'd be if he left—but the terror I felt when I thought of him going to fight inhibited my ability to coherently string words together. I noticed Eric often possessed the ability to steal my words when I most needed them. "Where are you going?" I heard myself ask, and I cringed at how poorly I could speak.

"It's a secret surveillance mission. Caleb has no idea we're coming. We're going to pop the boundary, sneak around for information on where Caleb might be hiding weapons, an army, and Peter, and come right back." I saw that he could also hear how shaky his voice sounded, so he rushed to assure, "I'll be back, okay? I'm coming back," but it sounded more like he was trying to convince himself rather than me.

"Why are you leaving?"

Eric sighed, and I could tell from the way he rubbed the back of his neck that he was growing agitated. "You already know why. I'm going back for Peter."

I shook my head. "No, not why are you going. Why are you *leaving*, Eric?"

The question clearly caught Eric off guard; he stood still for a few moments, mouth slightly agape, before he promptly closed his mouth, stiffened his posture, and looked at me so intensely, I feared he'd drill a hole into the back of my skull. "The worst feeling in the world is knowing you're second-best," he announced suddenly, shoving his hands into the pockets of his stiff, green pants.

Eric had done it again: stolen my words and stashed them away somewhere I could not reach. It infuriated me, the effortless way he robbed me of my proper articulation when words usually flowed through me so easily. I could be moments away from confessing the weightlessness of my heart whenever he drew near, the technicolor he brought to my life, yet one look into his forest-green eyes rendered me speechless. How foolish I was that I could convince an entire state to riot against a leader they did not know, but could not convince Eric Stellenzer to stay. "Eric?" I started to ask, but my question terrified me so badly, I didn't dare utter it aloud in fear of prophesying it. *Are you not coming back?*

"Zelda?" Eric mimicked in a poor attempt at humor, but neither of us even smiled.

"Eric…" I hated myself. I hated myself for allowing Eric's simple proximity to scramble my brain, hated myself for not even wanting to overcome the nervous feelings he elicited from me. I could only say, "If you don't come back, I'll kill you," and pray he understood what I meant.

Eric cocked his head and gave me his signature lopsided, easy smile, the one that made my stomach twist into knots. "What did I promise you, huh?" He opened his arms wide. "Come here." I hurried into his open arms and buried my face into his chest, and as I listened to the steady thump of his heartbeat, I focused on committing the sound to memory. "I promised you forever," he said, his voice much lower now.

"I'm scared you're saying goodbye," I finally voiced, uncaring for a moment if the universe decided to take my words and use them against me. I needed Eric to feel my fear, needed him to understand how wrecked I would be if I lost him forever, needed him to *stay*, just stay with me, forever if possible, but right now sufficed, too.

"You're insane if you think I'd ever say goodbye to you," he tried to joke, but when I only clung to him tighter, he said, "It's there and back. I promise." I had run out of things to say, so we stood there for a few moments, soaking in the other's presence, until Eric stuttered, "I, um, I actually do have one request before I go."

"Anything," I responded.

"Tell me you love me," he murmured so quietly, I could barely hear him above the commotion ramping up outside the hospital doors. "Please."

I drew my head back to look him in the face, and there I saw the hopeless desperation glimmering in his muted green eyes, a longing unlike anything I had ever encountered before. His expression—lips parted, ready to utter an apology, eyes shimmering a silent final goodbye—extracted the words from my mouth before I even had the chance to consider their implication. "I love you," I exhaled.

Eric dropped his head, pressed his forehead against mine, and released a shuddered breath. "Thank you," he whispered, and his lips were so close to mine, I thought I could feel them feathering against my own when he spoke. My own face glowed red at our close proximity, but I didn't dare move away. I watched his eyelids flutter closed, and my heart thundered inside my chest when a tear dripped down his face. He chuckled thickly to himself and said, "You know, when we were kids, I used to dream you'd say something like that to me, even though I didn't know the word love existed."

"Did you picture it like this?" I asked, choosing to indulge in his fantasy for a moment, maybe two, however long it took to convince ourselves that maybe our reality was nothing but a dream, too.

My question caused Eric to grow solemn, and another tear fell from his closed eyes. "No. Not even close." He held his breath, paused for a second, and then asked, "Do you mind saying it again? Just one more time."

I love you. I'd say it again, three times, a thousand times over if it convinced him to stay with me. I'd sing him those words from the hospital rooftop; I'd shout them from the top of President Dassian's skyscraper; I'd broadcast them for the entire Neweryork population to hear if he asked. None of it mattered. I knew my declaration wouldn't change his mind, either; nothing would. But I couldn't let him go fight to free my brother alone, not after we had just agreed not to separate the night before, so all at once, I knew what I had to do. "I love you," I proclaimed to Eric, louder this time, loud enough for him to know I meant it, and I would prove my sincerity to him.

He smiled, but the moment didn't last long; Allyson harshly knocked on the hospital doors, reminding Eric that time had run out, and he must board the last truck headed out immediately. Eric stepped back, loosely swinging my hands in his a few times before giving them a squeeze and letting them drop to my sides. He took another step backward but refused to move another inch, intent on gazing at my face for as long as the universe allowed.

"You better come back," I said before quickly adding, "Alive. You better come back alive, Eric Stellenzer."

"You got it, Zelda," he quipped. "I promise." He started to turn around before he stopped himself to look at me and say, "And for what it's worth, I love you, too." He stuffed his hands in his pockets and added, "Always have, and probably always will."

His declaration caused my heart to stutter inside my chest, a trip in my circuit, and I gasped loudly enough for him to hear. "I'll walk you out," I stammered, and Eric nodded in agreement. We walked out of the hospital together, pushing the doors open to reveal the three Woobis standing at the bottom of the steps, patiently awaiting their turn to say goodbye. I chose to stand off to the side to give them their space.

Eve stepped forward first, roughly grabbing Eric into a hug that didn't last long. "You brave boy," she announced before motioning for Eric to lean down so she could kiss his cheek. "I am sorry you overheard what I said earlier. I *do* care, Eric, I—"

Eric shook his head and stood upright to hug her one more time, saying, "No, I get it. Family first, right?"

Mr. Woobi stepped up next, eyeing Eric with pride as he declared, "Eric, I am so proud to have been there to watch you become the courageous man in front of me now. I hope one day you can find it within yourself to forgive me for my wrongdoings of the past."

Eric stiffened, and it took him several seconds before he responded, "I want to hear you say it."

"Say what, son?"

"Say you used me," declared Eric, his voice slightly wobbly, but his anger unwavering. "Say you groomed me since childhood to become a Uniform to spy on your son and your grandson." He quickly peered over at Dave and added, "No offense, man," to which Dave replied with a curt shake of his head. "Say you did the same to Peter, and maybe even to Zelda, too: whoever would listen and fall for it first. Say you take responsibility for getting us into this mess in the first place by convincing Peter to become a Uniform. Say you wanted to use me to feed you information from the inside, and when I said no, say you wanted to throw me into the incinerator and forget I ever existed because I was just that dead to you."

Mr. Woobi unsteadily stepped back, his icy blue eyes wide and his posture extremely rigid. "I—"

"But," continued Eric, "say you loved, or at the very least, cared about me. Say I meant something to you. Say you saw me as a grandson, too, maybe. Say my childhood wasn't a complete lie. Say it. Say *something*. Please." He tried to look stern by crossing his arms in front of his chest, but from the way his body twitched, I could tell Eric felt torn up, vulnerable, chewed up and hollowed out, and I hated it.

"You cannot imagine how proud you make me every single day," Mr. Woobi settled on saying after struggling to respond for a few moments. "I never had any intention of hurting you, dear boy."

I watched Eric deflate: his shoulders dropped, his arms swinging heavily by his sides, his chest flattened from his exhale. "Okay," Eric sighed defeatedly, sticking out his hand for Mr. Woobi to shake. "I guess that's settled." The elder took his hand and shook it firmly, the man refusing to let Eric go until Eric forcibly tore his hand out of Mr. Woobi's grasp.

Dave didn't give Eric any time to recover from his latest encounter before squashing him in a ferocious hug, mumbling incoherent words into his ear that made him crack a smile and ultimately, laugh out loud. "I'm sorry I can't come with you," Dave said after breaking the hug, motioning to his grandparents standing a few feet away. "Right after this, they're locking me up somewhere, so I can't escape and follow you."

"You know I'd love to have you by my side, bud," replied Eric as he clapped Dave on the shoulder. "But your family needs you. Remember what I said?"

Dave nodded. "I'm lucky to know them."

Eric shook Dave's shoulder playfully and released him with a light shove. "So lucky, man, you don't even know how lucky. Take care of them for me, would you?" Eric gestured his head in my general direction. "Especially Zelda, yeah? You take great care of her."

"I think she's the one taking care of me," Dave joked.

Eric laughed. "Isn't that the truth. But seriously, please—"

"Don't worry, Stellenzer," Dave said, nodding understandingly. "I will."

Eric's expression softened, and he gazed at Dave fondly before saying, "While you're at it, take care of yourself too, huh, Woobi? Think you can handle two-in-the-morning-breakdowns without me?"

Dave chortled. "I think I can manage for the next couple days."

"Let's make it so you can manage without me for longer than a couple of days, huh?" Eric replied nervously, not giving Dave a chance to respond before lowering his voice to say, "Remember what we talked about. You are more than a Woobi, yeah? You are more than just a Uniform. I want to hear who you are. Who are you?"

"Dave," Dave answered shyly.

"Sorry, I didn't catch that. Who are you?"

"Dave," Dave answered louder, smiling widely through his answer.

"And who is Dave?"

"More than a Woobi, and more than a Uniform."

"And…?"

Dave shook his head in humorous disbelief as he said, "Eric Stellenzer's best friend."

It was Eric's turn to grin. "Damn right."

The boys briefly hugged once more, parting only after Eric promised Dave he'd search for Blake during his short visit into the Society. Dave stepped closer to me and curled his arm around my abdomen after thanking Eric profusely, and Eric stared at us all—Dave and me wrapped up in a comforting embrace, Mr. Woobi and Eve in a similar position—one last time, smiling sadly before turning and walking toward the trucks. My body ached at the sight of him walking away from me, and I reached out to touch him, perhaps yank him back, but he had already faded into dusk's shadows.

Mr. Woobi and Eve wasted no time in roughly grabbing Dave and shackling his hands together with a pair of thick metal handcuffs, excusing the action by claiming locking Dave away would be the key to his safety over the course of the next few hours. I knew Dave would've tried to stop me from following Eric to the Society—or worse, attempt to join me—so although I didn't approve of their dramatic decision to shackle his wrists, I felt grateful to the Woobis for imprisoning him, if only for the time being. I cited preparing for my trip to the city as an excuse to leave, and Dave innocently bought it, pressing his face into mine for a quick kiss before bidding farewell and reminding me to visit him in his "cell"—really, just the spare bedroom in the Woobi residence—before I took my leave. I wordlessly nodded in agreement, trying to wipe the sweat from my palms onto the front of my pants discreetly as I did so. I caught Eve and Mr. Woobi staring at me suspiciously, eyes narrowed and focused as though trying to read my thoughts, and I made the mistake of trying to smile to appease whatever distrust they had.

Mr. Woobi dropped his embrace around Eve to cross his arms. "Where are you going, Zelda Ellyn?"

"To the city, as Allyson instructed," I responded, my voice an octave too high, the twinge of a challenge in my tone. I cleared my throat rather loudly.

Eve raised an eyebrow. "Is that so?"

I fidgeted from the intensity of their stares. "Yes."

Mr. Woobi and Eve exchanged disbelieving looks before the former said, "Take care of yourself, understood?"

"Understood. Take care of Dave while I'm away."

The couple nodded in agreement, and we stood still for a second, assessing each other's validity, before I bid them farewell, observed the quaint little village one more time, and set off toward the trucks, toward the civilians posing as soldiers, and most importantly, toward Eric.

"Zelda, wait."

Eve's forceful voice stopped me in my tracks, and I turned around to see her trying to catch up to me. "Yes?" Again, my voice sounded much higher than normal, and I cringed.

She waited to say anything until she stood about a foot away from me. "You're not going to the city," she declared. "You may have fooled Charlie, but you have certainly not convinced me."

I raised my eyebrows in surprise. "Excuse me?"

"I know where you're going," she said, "and I'm telling you now to be careful. Bring Eric and yourself back alive. My grandson would be devastated if you didn't."

"Would you, Eve?" I countered before I could stop myself, crossing my arms in front of me and raising my chin. "Would you be devastated if I didn't come back alive?"

Eve closed the distance between us and lifted her hand to tenderly caress the scar along my upper forehead, an incredibly maternal action I found soothing. "I swear, Zelda, sometimes..." She sighed. "Sometimes, you remind me so much of him."

"Who?" I asked.

"Caleb."

The comparison shocked me, and I took a large step backward. "What?"

"I love my son, Zelda," Eve proclaimed. "And I love you, too. Be careful and return home to us, okay?"

"I'm not going anywhere dangerous, Eve. I'm going to the city."

She smiled sadly, and the action softened the wrinkles around her eyes. "Honesty wasn't one of his best traits growing up, either. So defiant, you two are. So alike in so many ways. It's okay, Zelda. I won't tell David or Charlie where you went. Just promise you'll come back with Eric alive."

I knew there was no sense in continuing to lie, so I promised her I would, and she observed me one last time before turning to follow Dave and Mr. Woobi back to the Woobi house.

Thankfully, the vehicles that would take everyone over to the Society were still parked when I arrived, and I managed to climb into a cargo truck filled to its maximum with weaponry right before someone gave the signal for them to start their journey. I crept down low in the right corner of the truck, staying in that position for about an hour as we cruised through the forest at a relatively slow, quiet pace.

With only the guns to keep me company, I found my mind racing with thoughts that did nothing to cure my raging anxiety the closer we drew to the Society. *What are we doing?* I couldn't help but think. This entire mission felt so spontaneous and ill-planned that I found it difficult to compute its success. I wanted to believe Eric—that we were to surveil the Society for information and quickly return—but my instincts told me there must be more to this if just under a thousand people volunteered and were accepted to participate. Why would numbers matter for intelligence gathering?

The entire premise uneased me, especially as I sat among the weapons that could take life so easily. I had seen it happen firsthand, and I couldn't see it again. I *couldn't*. Especially not to these innocent, brave, naïve people. I couldn't watch them take lives, and I most definitely couldn't watch their lives be taken. The thought of throwing all the guns off the truck crossed my mind more than once, but I withheld myself in favor of trusting the people in power here.

Cody Dassian, president of Neweryork, and Allyson Killians, owner of Newer Media, wouldn't endanger such innocent lives this way; I was sure of it. The president wouldn't dare risk his precious reputation for information alone, and what real power did Allyson's news station have, anyway? I found it difficult to believe that the media would influence the president's decisions, especially decisions regarding human lives. These thoughts helped ease my nerves a bit because certainly, the president of a state and the head of the largest network in the area would not want innocent blood staining their hands.

"All clear!"

I scrunched up my nose in confusion as the trucks rolled to a stop, presumably outside the Society. How could that be? I hadn't heard the rushing sound of the river as we floated over its gorge. I didn't have time to dwell on my confusion; knowing that people would come to collect their weapons soon, I jumped out of the vehicle and rolled underneath, watching shortly after as men and women alike came to claim their weapons without hesitation.

I listened from underneath the truck as those in charge relayed the plan of action; everyone would shoot the boundary until it eventually popped, and from there, different squadrons would investigate specific sections of the Society for clues on where Caleb might be hiding, where the Jail was located, where Caleb stored his weapons, and where the Uniforms might be. We had parked fairly close to the boundary, maybe fifty yards or so, and I peeked around the hood of the truck to find everyone inching closer to the electromagnetic bubble on their tiptoes, their guns aimed and ready to fire when instructed. I tried searching for Eric, but in the dark of night, the back of every man's head looked about the same.

I climbed onto the truck until I was squatting on its roof to get a better look at what was happening. No sound permeated the air except for the squishing of the grass underneath the people's feet until they were ordered to stop about ten or fifteen feet away from the bubble.

"Ready!" yelled a general, and the troops moved together in unison to hoist their heavy guns up from their places at their sides. I clenched my fists until the tension made my forearms ache.

"Aim!" yelled a general, and the people aimed the barrels of their weapons at the shimmering, beige, electromagnetic boundary. I held my breath.

But before any general could declare the order to shoot, a bullet accidentally left a woman's gun and struck the boundary, only to bounce right off and whizz over the troops' heads. At the lack of movement from the boundary, everyone began mumbling to each other in confusion, wondering what to do if the bullets could not penetrate the boundary. As they argued over what the next course of action should be, the leaves on the trees suddenly rustled despite the lack of wind, and I hesitantly looked up to see something shiny flash in the pitch-black sky before it vanished. A feeling of cold dread spread across my entire body, temporarily paralyzing me in terror when I realized we were not alone.

"I warned you."

Whatever had flown above our heads broadcasted Caleb Woobi's unnerving, mechanical voice for everyone to hear, and it quickly silenced the troops as they assessed the danger in which they had suddenly found themselves.

"Kill them," ordered Caleb, and at his command, hundreds of Uniforms emerged from the river's dried, silent gorge, weapons trained at the unsuspecting people in front of them.

I barely had time to blink before a Uniform shot first.

The troops were sent into a frenzy the moment the Uniforms began firing away, bullets striking the innocent men and women who had gathered so naïvely to fight. The camera crews filmed the slaughter from the safety of their luxurious vehicles, their mouths forming perfect "o" shapes at the sight of people dying. The impromptu soldiers tripped over their own people, their screeches of terror and shock filling the once-still night air. Chaos. Chaos everywhere.

I watched as the Uniforms shot the people's legs, arms, abdomens with amazing precision, and as I watched these people bleed, I took notice of the way the Uniforms never aimed at their hearts or their heads. *I don't take pleasure in killing things that are alive,* Caleb had told me once, and as I witnessed the improvised soldiers grasp at their wounds, stumbling for someone to end their pain, I knew what he meant. Caleb wanted to make sure they were long dead before he killed them.

I scrambled off the roof of the truck, my mind still reeling from what I had just witnessed, and I began yelling Eric's name, taking cover behind vehicles and trees when necessary. I had forgotten how recognizable my voice was—somewhat deep and scratchy from my screaming—until people began crawling toward it, moaning, whimpering, and reaching out to touch me as if I could heal them. I kneeled by one girl, no older than me, the desperation in her voice too much to ignore, and she grasped my hand in her bloody one. She seemed to be glowing in pride, a pained yet strangely beautiful smile on her cracked lips as she mouthed things I couldn't decipher. I held her tightly against my chest and told her I was sorry, so sorry, her face pale as she croaked out her final word: "Zelda." I felt her hand go limp in mine and didn't need to see the light leaving her face to know she had died.

Everything went in slow motion now. More and more people began to recognize me, their groans of agony turning into grumbled moans of joy as they all started to crowd around me, pressing in until I was suffocating in the stench of the almost dead. They called out my name a couple times, many times, several times, until it seemed like the entire battlefield was chanting my name. Cameras caught sight of me and zoomed in, capturing the way they flocked to me like moths to a light. But with this new wave of admiration and strength from my face came Caleb noticing I was here. As I heard the rustling of the leaves once more and Caleb's voice boom, "Zelda

Jadestone is among them; find her!" I bolted away from the crowd, my mind focusing once again on finding Eric and keeping the two of us alive.

The sky lit up when the Uniforms chucked explosives in our direction, their intent no longer to kill the soldiers slowly but to annihilate anyone left standing. I tripped over body after body, some dead, others still calling out to me in a desperate attempt at hope, but I wasn't listening to them anymore. I *couldn't* listen to them anymore, unless I wanted to end up next to them, dead.

Except a few did catch my attention: a teenage boy hiding behind the bullet-riddled trunk of a tree, his hands clawing at his face as he shrieked in horror, kicking into the air to get away from nothing but his mind; an older woman, her hair singed off at the tips, a small-but-steady stream of blood exiting her mouth; a girl around my age on her knees, her face streaked with red and black, her voice almost gone as she used it to scream at her companion, the girl who had died in my arms, to rise again. I tried to force myself to keep pushing, shoving, fighting to find Eric, but my feet felt frozen, my mouth went slack, and my ears rang with the sounds of gunfire and explosions and screaming and crying and death.

I grew lightheaded, and I couldn't seem to place my feet correctly as everything swirled together—the boy by the tree, the girls in their last embrace, the woman too petrified to move, the people calling my name as they died at my feet, the Uniforms shooting like machines, Caleb watching it all unfold, Peter imprisoned in a Society I could not reach, Eric quite possibly dead—*c'mon, Zelda.* I pushed myself to ignore the chaos, at least for now, and to move, stumbling my way through the bloodbath until I caught sight of a tall, slender, dark-haired man kneeling over a body and screaming at her to stand, to no avail.

"Eric!" I shrieked, and the man looked up at the sound of his name, his green eyes locking with mine, widening when he recognized me.

"Zelda?" Eric yelled in return right before a bomb exploded in the space between us, sending me flying backward onto a bleeding body and causing him to let out an ear-crushing scream of pain.

I jumped back onto my feet, ignoring the burns across my collarbone from the explosion, and ran over to his side to be met with him hissing through clenched teeth and grasping at his leg, the blood from his wound quickly staining his pants. "We have to get out of here," I told him sternly as I applied some pressure to his injury with my bare hands. My name—whispered, yelled, moaned—grew louder, but I wasn't sure if the sounds were real or not.

"H-h-how a-are y-you here?" he stumbled over his words, looking up at me in pure shock. "Am I d-dead?"

I shook my head and attempted to lift him up before quickly discovering that I did not possess the upper body strength to carry him. "You're not dead," I stated forcefully, biting off a chunk of my shirt so I could wrap it around his leg to keep the pressure there. "Not yet. Now c'mon. I need you to stand up so I can get you into a vehicle and drive back to the village. They can help you there."

We soon discovered that any weight on his injured leg was unbearable, so Eric unsteadily leaned on me and hopped on one foot through the mess of the bodies and the blood. We eventually reached the nearest news broadcasting vehicle, completely ignoring the stunned camera crew in the back as I used my last remaining strength to dump his body into a seat. But before I climbed in myself, I heard it again: "Zelda."

Zelda. The innocent people dying practically at my feet moan my name, begging me to save them.

Zelda. My coworkers call out to me, whispering my name into my ear, reminders of those whom I had failed to save.

Zelda. Peter chastises gently, disappointment heavy in his tone. Peter, my little brother, the boy I used to justify these deaths, the boy I knew I couldn't look in the eyes again if I didn't at least try.

I ordered Eric to stay, and I ran back into the heart of the massacre, determined to save those I could.

I swerved around the trees and jumped over bodies, somehow narrowly dodging bullets and sidestepping explosions that bit at my ankles before coming across the boy I had seen earlier, pulling him up sharply by the elbow and dragging him toward the vehicle. He didn't protest; in fact, he didn't resist me at all, still too stunned to fully process his surroundings. I haphazardly threw him into the vehicle, letting the camera people deal with him as I rushed back to gather the older woman, gripping her hand as I led her over to the vehicle. The last one, the girl, was much more difficult to collect, her punches and kicks and screams reminding me painfully of myself as she tried to reach for her deceased friend. Eventually, she gave up, slumping against me as I shoved her face into my injured collarbone to hide the horrors from her before stuffing the two of us into the car and slamming the door.

I harshly ordered the camera crew—two girls, perhaps in their late twenties—to set the coordinates of the village into the vehicle's global positioning system. They rushed to obey, wasting no time in setting the vehicle at its highest possible speed and guiding it toward our directed destination. As soon as the car sped off, I glanced out the window, catching one last glimpse at the Society and the people outside it whom I had so miserably failed.

Eric's loud groan caught my attention, and I turned to see him writhing in his seat with his eyes shut tightly, his head lazily moving side-to-side as if mentally wrestling with his pain. Blood oozed from the wound in his leg, and I could do nothing but stand there uselessly, watching as he gasped for breath and willing him not to die, not yet, not until I had the chance to die first, because I knew I couldn't stay in a world Eric didn't live in. I did not have any memory of a life without him in it, but any life without Eric would be a life not worth remembering anyway.

Mr. Woobi knocks on our househut door, and I scamper to answer it, sliding the door open to reveal the elder man and a small, shy, dark-haired boy hiding behind our old neighbor's legs as he always did, subtly beautiful green eyes never once leaving my little face.

"Hi, Mr. Woobi. Hi, Eric," I greet happily as I usher them in. Peter sits up from his hunched position over his homework at the kitchen table and waves excitedly, his enthusiasm matched by Eric's when the older boy waves back.

Mr. Woobi hurries over to Peter's side to help him with his work, promptly leaving Eric and me standing beside each other by the door. Eric fidgets, sways on his feet for a few moments, and brushes his dark hair out of his eyes, a nervous habit he's picked up ever since he started growing his hair out. I make a mental note to remind Mr. Woobi to cut Eric's hair; the longer length makes him look juvenile, and with his thirteenth birthday rapidly approaching, I don't think the look suits him anymore. I reach out and pinch a stand of his hair, lightly pulling on the strand as I say, "You have to cut this, you know," with a teasing hilt to my voice.

Eric flushes an amusing red color and pulls his head back until I'm forced to let his hair go. "I know," he mumbles, silent for a second before he adds, "Does it look ugly?"

I giggle and respond, "No, not ugly." I tilt my head as my gaze travels all over his face, scrutinizing his features: his delicate-yet-long nose, the curve of his lips, the kindness of his eyes. I smile. "You can never be ugly, I think."

Eric straightens his posture and smiles toothily, the same smile that always seems to warm my insides. "Really?"

I nod. "Really."

I observed Eric's hair now, much shorter and coated in sweat, blood, and dirt, his features scrunched up in excruciating pain, and I hated myself for what I had done to him, for putting him through such agony, for the extent to which I had ruined him. I had never before considered the possibility of Eric's death, but as I watched him slowly start to lose consciousness, my body buzzed in shock as static filled my ears. The thought of experiencing the rest of my life without Eric blinded me with terror, and the ringing in my ears grew louder, so loud that I barely heard the older woman in the car with us say, "I'm a doctor, please, get out of my way. I can help."

It took a second for her words to process, but once they did, I scrambled out of her way and watched as she unslung a large, boxy bag from her shoulder and began working furiously on Eric. Her larger build prevented me from seeing anything, but I felt grateful for the fact that I couldn't see what his injury really looked like.

I took the opportunity to study the others in the car with us. The boy looked so much younger now that real light bathed his skinny body. His stick-straight blond hair was barely blond from all the dirt encrusted in the strands, and that same dirt covered his small, shaky hands. His olive-green shirt and pant combination did nothing to conceal any grass stains, and I noticed a large rip in his pants by his knees, revealing a nasty-looking scrape on his kneecap. His entire body vibrated either in fear, shock, or a mixture of both, and his bouncing leg shook the entire car. I wished I could do more to help him, but my own shock prevented me from moving.

The girl, on the other hand, presented a stark contrast to the young boy. She was stoic, a silent storm personified. Her dark eyes stared straight ahead of her, never wavering, only blinking when absolutely necessary. Sometime during our journey to the village, she had tied her big, black hair back in a low bun, exposing her neck for me to see the scratches, gashes, and wounds that probably covered her entire body. A particularly deep gash ran across her entire forehead, and blood from the gash had dried onto her dark skin. Unlike the skinny boy, this girl seemed to be made of muscle, and strength radiated from her admittedly short frame. I wished to console her, but she did not look to be in the mood to receive help.

Eric yelped and openly sobbed into the plush red of the bench as the older woman stitched his wound back together the old-fashioned way, and his agonizing sounds alerted me to the reality of our situation. Blood caked my hair, hands, and clothing; my face was smeared in black soot from the ashes of the bombs, and my eyes watered from the putrid stench of rotting flesh and fresh blood. Despite my best efforts to avoid it, I leaned over and vomited onto the floor, which I saw made the stoic girl cringe as she watched it dribble down my chin.

I was ready to usher an apology when the strong odor of something burning singed the words off my tongue, and I looked out the window to see a column of orange-red flames and smoke quickly rising into the night sky.

My stomach clenched, and although I could hear the camera crew in the front of the vehicle speaking to me, I didn't absorb a single word they said, only finding enough strength to order them to stop the car. The moment the vehicle came screeching to a halt, I threw open the door, hopped down from the compartment, and went sprinting through the trees over to what should have been the village.

In its place stood a blazing fire, engulfing everything from the homes to the school, its heat radiating over to me as I stood and watched the only home I had ever known burn to the ground.

CHAPTER 12

I ran. Away from the village. Away from the truck. Away from what the ashes really signified. *It's gone. The village is gone. The people are dead.* I couldn't stop the flow of thoughts in my head as I sprinted into the dense forest of trees, stumbling over exposed roots and tripping over my own feet. Adrenaline kicked in until I practically drowned in it, legs burning from the speed at which I galloped through the forest. The trees, the stars, the faces of the people I had lost all blurred together until it all exploded in the back of my head, their ashes trickling into my eyesight in the form of swimming black dots and causing me to crash into the ground headfirst.

Faces of the villagers flashed in my head, but I could do nothing to stop it, nothing to save them, nothing to quench the fire that had burned them. I couldn't cry. I couldn't scream. I couldn't move. Every muscle, every cell, every atom inside me ignited with excruciating pain. The weight of their deaths crushed me, consumed me until I succumbed to the fire behind my own eyelids.

Dave. He was so innocent when we had first met in the Society; what had my selfishness done to him? I never should have taken his deal to become friends illegally. I unknowingly condemned him to be nothing but fallout from my toxic destruction that day, and I should've known better than to go against my instincts. Yet his entrance into my life was so natural, like the universe knew we were meant to know each other, so who was I to interrupt fate? How could I have let him walk away? With his breathtakingly beautiful blue eyes and dazzling smile, Dave had wormed his way into my life and ultimately, into my heart. He was my sunset, my exhale after a long day, my promise that there would always be a tomorrow, and I didn't know if I could stand to see the sunrise if he wasn't here to experience the day sunrise brings with me.

Mr. Woobi. I found it ironic that my impulsive decision to save his life the day of his execution led us here. My good intentions only seemed to make things exponentially worse. The older man was far from perfect, but then again, so was I. We complemented each other nicely that way. I wished for his arms around me in this moment, cradling me like he used to when I had trouble falling asleep. I wished for him to tell me that this was just a story, just one of his silly stories, and the hell I was living in was nothing but my imagination. I wished I could tell him I loved him just one more time, if only to feel the peace it brought me when he said it back. I hoped he could feel my adoration from his newfound place amongst the stars.

Eve. She was right. Caleb and I shared an uncanny ability to inevitably scorch the ones we held closest. I wondered if that's what she meant when she had caressed my face; that despite our lists of sins, she loved us anyway. She loved us regardless of our actions. I wondered if she knew I had grown to love her regardless, too, despite her sometimes questionable decisions. I wondered if she knew how much I truly admired her loyalty to her family, and how much I wanted to possess half as much strength as she did.

Something—no, *someone*—pressed against my throat, stopping the flow of oxygen from reaching my lungs and leaving me gasping for air. The figure was faceless, its form changing from Dave to Mr. Woobi to Eve to Allyson to Marley to Sharlee, then to the villagers who had danced with me, and to the people whom I had seen die by the Society. My mind screamed at me to run, but I lay frozen on the floor.

Zelda. A calling to join him. A soft plea to take his warm hand and follow him into a world unknown, someplace where the air didn't smell of smoke, where the world didn't burn, where my head could finally rest.

Zelda. A harsher tone, no longer Dave's. A sinister voice that had spoken of consequences and ashes. The leader who continued to win.

Zelda! Their shouts of terror, of hope, of faith that I could help them.

But I couldn't. There was absolutely nothing I could do. No home. No food. No power. Just a scared eighteen-year-old girl on the run, always on the run. Where was I to go? What pieces of me remained after tonight? Who had the pressure forced me to become? Certainly not the strong, brave young woman Allyson had led people to believe. Not the fearless warrior who vehemently despised oppression and fought back with brutality. Not the compassionate older sister who sparked a movement to rescue family members trapped inside a bubble. Only the voices knew who I really was, and they screamed it out to me. *Zelda! Zelda! Zelda!*

They were right. I was Zelda Ellyn Jadestone, and I was terribly afraid.

I knew I wouldn't survive wandering the forest alone, but how could I walk back and face those waiting for me in the vehicle? Where they expected a leader only stood a girl desperate for her little brother. *Peter.* My desperation to reach him sparked these flames, I knew, but still, I could not be angry with him. Only myself. How had I allowed this to happen? Where had my judgment failed me? What had led me here, to the ashes of loved ones, as my brother sat prisoner in a place I could not reach? *I'm sorry. I'm sorry. I'm so, so sorry,* I told them all: Dave, Mr. Woobi, and Eve. Sharlee, Peter, and Eric. Allyson, Marley, and the innocent people who followed me so blindly. But they didn't want to hear my pathetic apologies, so they screamed my name. Over and over and over again.

Memories of Dave, of Mr. Woobi, of everyone else I had lost intensified my agony, and I slammed my hands into the place right above my heart, making a yanking motion to try and tear the aching organ out of my body, but that only created a few pathetic nail marks on my chest. Emotional, mental, and physical pain all blurred together into one cohesive ache that enveloped my entire body. I could almost hear Caleb's voice—his real one, not the computerized version—as he sneered at my current state: shivering from the cold and the amount of pressure I felt building up behind my eyeballs. I attempted countless times to rise from my spot on the earth and run back to the truck, but I would crack from the weight on my chest and fall back down, where my efforts were rewarded with mouthfuls of dirt. It was hopeless. There was no human way to heal this pain.

Terror ripped through my body when I felt a cold hand on my shoulder and a soft, feminine voice telling me to stand. When I exclaimed that I couldn't move, the woman shushed me gently, dropping down to her knees to pick up my fragile form, place me on her lap, and rock me back and forth.

This moment of weakness was one I would allow. I curled into the person and sobbed into the pocket where her neck met her shoulder. Shivers ran their way up and down my spine as the wind blew itself into me, whipping my hair around and causing some strands to stick to my streak of tears. "All gone," I kept mumbling into her neck, my bottom lip quivering. In an attempt to soothe me, the woman brought up her hand to take the stands of hair away from my face and muttered that she knew, she knew. Except she didn't know. How could she possibly have known what I felt? Fire and ice. Screaming voices and silence. Unimaginable pain and indescribable numbness. All at once. There wasn't a way she could know what I was feeling, what I was thinking, who I had become. Nor did I want her to.

She commanded me to stand once again, but I couldn't; my legs would not work. I was glued to the ground as punishment for the murder of everyone in the village and beyond. Every part of me, inside and out, ached. But as I told her these things, tried to explain my inability, the woman shook her head and said, "You can always find the strength to stand."

I tilted my head up to see her fully, observing her hard, defined chin, her high cheekbones, her long, wiry, salty black hair, the wrinkles around her mouth and eyes, and I finally recognized her as the older woman I had grabbed back by the Society. She informed me that the others in the vehicle were waiting for us, waiting for *me,* and she'd help me go to them if I could just stand. "They need you," she said. "C'mon now. Take care of who you have left."

Take care of who you have left. I understood that sentence. And it was then that I allowed the woman to help me to my feet, using her as a crutch to walk as she led the way to the vehicle.

Everyone's heads snapped up when the woman and I opened the car's compartment door, yet no one dared to speak until we had all gotten settled: the older woman, Eric, and I on one side of the car, and the others facing us on the other bench. Once the silence got unbearable, one of the girls from the camera crew slowly asked, "What happened?"

The woman who had helped me answered, "It's gone. Caleb Woobi burned the village down with everyone in it. There's nothing left."

Eric rasped from his spot next to me: "Nothing?"

She only shook her head, I suppose not trusting herself to say the words out loud.

The shocked silence that followed didn't last long, as the younger boy squeaked, "So, that's it? It's just us now?"

Just us. But who were we, really? Seven lost souls with nowhere to call home? Misguided fools on the run? Survivors who wished they weren't? I couldn't answer—I didn't know—so we stayed quiet until the younger boy again disrupted our silence by stating, "My name is Will."

The girl I had rescued along with Will scoffed and crossed her arms. "Really?" she ridiculed. "Thousands of people just died, and you want to play the name game?"

Will cowered in his seat at her words, eyes suddenly shiny with tears, and Eric shot her a glare before saying, "No, Will, I think that's a great idea." He managed a weak, tight-lipped smile and reached out to shake the younger boy's hand. "I'm Eric."

The older woman spoke next: "I'm Jannet Wineslowe."

The camera crew girls introduced themselves after Jannet. The first one, Lucy Catray, had her relatively short, curly, mousy brown hair in a low ponytail, her hazel eyes almost bulging out of her narrow skull. Her frail, small body made her almost disappear into the red bench, and the paleness of her skin reminded me of bright moonlight. The other one, Harmony Holland, sat tall in her seat, and judging from the length of her legs, she probably stood only an inch or two shorter than Eric. Her long, straight black hair framed her sharp jawline perfectly, and her narrow, angular eyes pierced right through me. The two gave each other rather dumb rubs on the back as the other spoke, looking to one another when they caught themselves beginning to cry. I was glad they had each other, at the very least.

I raised my hand in greeting. "I'm Zelda," I tried to say evenly, but my voice shook as badly as my body did. I subtly sat on my hands so no one could see them shaking.

The girl who had yet to introduce herself rolled her eyes. "I can't believe *you* are the 'great and powerful' Zelda Jadestone." She eyed me up and down and curled her lip up in disgust. "What a waste."

"And you are?" I asked defensively.

"Sasha Brooks," she declared like it was obvious.

"Sasha," I repeated, and my mind flashed back to an image of her holding a lifeless body and screaming in repulsion. The memory made me grimace. "I'm so sorry for your fr—"

"Don't," growled Sasha. "Don't apologize for Melanie when she means nothing to you." Sasha motioned her hands around the entire car as she said, "None of us really mean anything to you, do we, Jadestone?" When I failed to find an answer in time, Sasha lifted her arms up victoriously. "That's what I thought. That little stunt you pulled where you 'saved' us, that was all orchestrated for good publicity. You don't care if any of us live or die."

The weight pressing against my chest grew heavier with each lashing word Sasha uttered, and I floundered to speak through my quickly closing throat. "No, I—"

"I never admired you," Sasha proceeded to rant. "I watched that first viral video of you and some blond dude after you left the Society, and I remember thinking, 'wow, this girl is so full of shit.' And then I watched you on television because you were everywhere, and you were so full of shit then, too. You're such a fraud. Do you even *have* a brother? Or is that another lie to get people invested in your pathetic story?"

With each breath I took, I felt a fire ignite in my lungs that forced me to cough as an exhale, and I gripped my throat to indicate my difficulty breathing. "I—"

"You should've left me to die out there," proclaimed Sasha, but it was then that her voice finally cracked a little, just enough for me to hear her hesitation before she quickly cleared her throat and continued: "You never should've taken me away. Now I'm who-knows-where with a bunch of strangers, and I can see it in your eyes, Jadestone; you have no idea what you're doing. For once, you don't have a plan to get us all killed. I'd say I'm surprised if I weren't so disappointed."

"Okay," Eric interrupted, clearly irritated. "That's enough. Zelda, are you okay?"

His voice sounded muffled and far away, drowned out by the sounds of gunfire, screaming, and *Zelda, Zelda, Zelda.* I covered my ears to try and block out the noise, but it rang in my head so loudly, I was sure my eardrums bled. I rubbed my eyes awkwardly and straightened up only after Eric's worried voice sliced through the other noise. "She's right," I confirmed. "I don't know what to do next."

"Say it louder for the kids in the back," Sasha exclaimed.

"However," I continued, much to Sasha's dismay, "that does *not* mean I don't care. You wouldn't be sitting in this car if I didn't care."

"So, what, everyone else out there tonight, you didn't care enough about them to save them, too?" Sasha rebutted.

A million thoughts raced through my head, so many words I wished to tell them, specifically Sasha, but as I looked around, I knew no amount of words would heal what I had done. Eric, the same boy who could cure any problem with one of his jokes, looked unrecognizable as he knitted his eyebrows in pain and wiped the last of his tears from his filthy face with a blood-stained, trembling hand. Will, clearly the youngest in our little group, had such clear fear written on his face that I wished I could eliminate. Jannet kept her composure and guard up relatively well, but any time she tilted her head to crack her neck and shuffled in her seat, I saw the glint of fresh tears as they rolled down her aged face. Lucy and Harmony looked shocked, as though somehow trapped inside a particularly bad nightmare, and Sasha clearly experienced a great deal of pain, which was not something I could fault her for in the slightest. And as I looked at them, at these six people I had managed to ruin, I found the only words I felt sufficed: "I'm sorry."

"You're going to have to do a lot more than that," snapped Sasha.

"It's okay," said Will.

"You're doing fine, sweetie," assured Lucy.

"Apology accepted," stated Harmony.

"Don't apologize," commanded Jannet and Eric simultaneously.

I said nothing else, for there was nothing else to say, so one-by-one, we all settled into our seats to try and fall into a restless slumber for the remainder of the night. Unsurprisingly, Harmony and Lucy were the first to succumb to slumber after disabling the vehicle's inside lights, quickly followed by Jannet, then Eric. I watched from my slumped position in the corner as Sasha tried hard to keep her eyelids from drooping, but eventually, she nodded off as well. I thought Will had fallen asleep when perhaps Eric had, but right as I went to close my eyes to at least give myself a chance to sleep, I heard his unmistakable small voice squeak my name questioningly.

"What is it?" I rasped rather unkindly in response.

"I'm scared," Will whispered in the dark. I heard the distinctive sound of sniffling, and the sound reminded me painfully of Peter when he used to wake up in the middle of the night, crying about his night terrors.

"Me too," I answered honestly, my tone much softer now. I opened my arms widely as an invitation for Will to crawl onto my lap, which he took gladly.

Will waited to speak again until he comfortably settled on my lap, his arms wrapped securely around my neck and his face pressed into my burnt collarbone. I rocked him back and forth, just as Jannet had done with me earlier, as he said, "I never thought of Zelda Jadestone as someone who would be afraid of the dark."

"Hm, well, I'm not invincible," I mused as I lightly combed my fingers through his ashy blond hair, trying to take the little knots and tangles out of his soft tuft.

Will stopped sniffling long enough to shift his face up to look at me. "I thought you were when I saw you on tv."

I combed his hair back and out of his eyes. "No one is invincible. Not really."

"Not even you?" he asked in awe.

"Not even me," I repeated.

Will sighed peacefully from the ministrations to his hair. "My real name is William, by the way, but everyone calls me Will," he blurted. "Dad would sometimes call me William when he got mad, though. He'd say something like, 'William Finnley, get back here right now!' if I ran off to do something without asking him first, which was a lot. I don't know. I like to go on adventures and enjoy the world my way if only for, like, an hour or two. Benji, my best friend, would join me sometimes, but usually, I like doing that sort of thing alone. A few months ago, on my fifteenth birthday, Mom and Dad chased me around the village for an hour because I had snuck out right before dinner to take a walk." He giggled into my collarbone at the memory, but quickly stopped when he noticed me gazing down at him endearingly.

"Sounds cute," I told him.

He shrugged, the tips of his ears pink. "The average fifteen-year-old boy doesn't like his words being called 'cute,' just so you know."

"Sounds... loveable, then," I corrected myself.

Will scrunched up his face in displeasure. "That isn't much better."

My lips perked up ever so slightly at his words, but I didn't have a chance to respond before Will said, "That's kind of how I ended up volunteering. I just get these urges to *do* things, stupid things, because I get so bored at home. So, I lied about my age, volunteered, got accepted, and now here I am, wishing I was back home, bored again." He paused for a moment, contemplating his next words: "My home is gone. And my mom, and my dad, they're dead, aren't they? My parents are dead." He inhaled sharply. "They're all dead, I guess. Zelda, I don't want them to be dead."

I hugged him closer to me and buried my face into his hair to kiss it once, twice, three times over to try and disguise the tears building up at the back of my eyes. "You lost your family today, just like I did, and I… I don't know what to do anymore. I don't think I ever knew what I was doing. I'm sorry, Will. I'm so, so sorry." I brought my hand up to wipe first my tears, and then the ones off his face.

We were quiet for a long time after until Will sleepily stated, "You know, if I close my eyes and don't think about it too hard, I can almost pretend like I'm back home."

I gently placed him across from me in his original spot on the other bench, where he automatically leaned his head against the windowsill. "Then close your eyes," I said softly. "Try to sleep. You're safe with me."

"Promise?" he muttered. His eyelids began to droop, but he sprung them back open in a last effort to stay awake.

I nodded and leaned down to lightly kiss his forehead. "Yeah, buddy. I promise."

My assurance made Will smile, and after just a few minutes, his soft snores filled the compartment. Eric shifted in his sleep when I attempted to get comfortable in my own spot on this little bench, and I envied his ability to sleep. A crawling, itchy feeling traveled along my skin, making it prickly and uncomfortable, as the sounds of gunfire, screaming, and the crackle of the raging fire that destroyed my home raged inside my head. I shut my eyes, and behind my eyelids I saw blood red. Fatigue hit me in waves, but it was never enough to put me to sleep; I wondered if I would ever be able to sleep peacefully again.

It was well past two in the morning—I could tell from the clock blinking above Sasha's form—when I began to think about any survivors either back by the Society or in the village. I didn't think of Caleb as careless, so I doubted there would be any survivors after the massacre by the Society, but did anyone in the village somehow anticipate Caleb's fire? Did Caleb drop bombs, or did he somehow set the village on fire from the inside? Was there any chance Dave, Mr. Woobi, Eve, *anyone* could be alive? I desperately wished for that to be true; it almost seemed incomputable that they could be dead. Surely, the stars would misalign, the cosmos would shift, the world would permanently tilt off its axis if Dave or Mr. Woobi left Earth. I would know it. I would *feel* it. Or so I told myself to keep my sanity in check.

What was I to do now? I had no place to rest, nowhere I could call home, any longer. No plan of action. No motivation even if I did have a plan of action. But I did have six injured souls to care for, people with no place to go, people who looked to me in some way to guide them. But guide them toward what? Where would we go? Where *could* we go? Once Caleb rummaged through the mess of bodies outside his Society and didn't find me among them, his fury would fuel maybe another attack to kill me. How many more people had to die before Caleb reached me? Or, more accurately, how many more people had to die before I reached him? I couldn't make a single move without fear of Caleb's retaliation, and somehow, I knew he felt the same. We danced to each other's rhythms, synchronized in our destruction, and I despised being so tethered to a man I was supposed to hate.

And President Dassian: what was he thinking now that his approved plan had backfired so miserably? What did he plan to do with me and the mess I had created? I wondered if he would search for me out in these woods. And what if he did? Was I prepared to live in the city, a place I had come to dislike for all its noise and activity, and face the president I had failed? Not just the president, either; how could I face the people who had cheered for me, only now to know I had failed, to know I killed their own? I didn't think I possessed the strength to look at the faces of the disappointed and grief-stricken and apologize. An apology wouldn't soothe neither their grieving, hollow souls, nor their mounting disapproval.

What would Peter think if he could see me now? I thought bitterly. Would he call me a murderer? A sister? A stranger? Just his name alone made my head want to explode from the pressure. How would I free him now? Stranded among the trees, I had no army, no technology, and certainly no strategy. How could I pick myself up and continue following this destructive path toward war when I had firsthand witnessed its consequences? An image of Peter flashed inside my mind, the broken boy's silhouette lingering in my consciousness, and I knew how I could, how I *would,* continue.

Exhaustion must've taken me over at some point during the night because the next thing I remember, Eric was gently shaking me awake, an urgent tone to his voice that made me spring up and accidentally smack my head into the vehicle's ceiling. The morning sun had yet to rise, so I was forced to squint to see clearly; upon further inspection, I saw that everyone else except for the two of us were still asleep. "What's going on?" I shout-whispered, straining my body as far as it would allow to try and stretch the stiffness out of my aching limbs.

A minute of intense silence followed my question until I saw Eric sigh in defeat. "I thought I heard something," he whispered back, his eyes still darting back and forth as he slowly started releasing the pent-up tension in his shoulders. "Must've been nothing." He attempted to smile to relax me, but it fell flat. "I guess I'm still afraid of the dark."

Eric and I are left alone once the door to my househut closes behind Mr. Woobi and Peter as they set off on their "evening walk," a daily tradition they had started after Eric's fifteenth birthday a few months previous, close to the time the elder and Eric began drifting apart. But the pair of us didn't complain; in actuality, I had grown a liking to spending time alone with the dark-haired boy. Eric and I sprawl out on the concrete floor, content with just gazing up at the gray ceiling and enjoying each other's company, when I spontaneously ask, "What's your biggest fear?"

Eric turns his face to look at me, and I do the same, not realizing how close we are until the tips of our noses brush together. I scoot just the tiniest bit backward after my stomach somersaults at our close proximity. "What's yours?" he retorts playfully.

I pretend to zip my lips shut and blink at him expectantly, making him burst into laughter. "Eye for an eye, Zelda," Eric says once we're done giggling. "I tell you mine, and you tell me yours. Fair?" After I nod in agreement, Eric adds, "You're not allowed to laugh, okay?"

"Oo, no promises there," I quip, grinning when his eyes widen slightly in betrayal. Eric moves to turn away from me, but I tug at his shoulder with a laugh and say, "I'm kidding. C'mon. Tell me."

Eric's eyes flit over my face, scanning every inch of my features until his inquisitive gaze becomes a soft, loving one that makes my heart pound so loudly, I'm sure he can hear it. "The dark," he finally admits, his voice suddenly an octave lower. "I'm scared of the dark."

I don't laugh. I can't. Not when Eric is staring at me in that way. It gets difficult to breathe; I break our eye contact and look up when I feel my face flush. "Oh," I squeak.

"And you?" he asks, but my brain takes a second longer than usual to compute his words. "Can't back out on me now, Zelda," he teases.

I don't hesitate this time. "Nothing," I announce proudly, loving the way the word echoes around my small househut. "I'm afraid of nothing. It was a trick question."

I turn my face again to look at his reaction and smile just as Eric's lips perk up. "I don't doubt it," he says, and little sparks sizzle through my bloodstream at the look he gives me.

The memory filled me with such intense gratitude for Eric's survival that I almost toppled over. *Eric almost died last night,* I thought, but the words didn't sink in until a second later. Eric almost *died.* I wished I could articulate the terror that thought evoked in me, or the extreme gratitude I felt for the opportunity to see him breathe, but I didn't have the vocabulary to eloquently convey these feelings to him. "How's your leg?" I settled on asking, motioning with my head in the direction of his wound.

Eric rotated his leg so I could see the slash in his calf from the bomb's shrapnel; although the darkness prevented me from seeing its full extent, I could see the outline of thick, black stitches holding his skin together. I almost gagged at the sight, but in the last second, I swallowed my disgust to avoid offending Eric. "Could be worse," he said with a shrug.

Yeah, I thought. *You could be dead.* But I chose to keep that particular thought to myself, instead opting to stutter, "Eric… I…"

"They're not dead, right, Zelda?" he asked suddenly, running his hands through his dark, thick hair. "Dave, Charles, and Eve aren't dead. Caleb wouldn't kill his family like that, right? Zelda, they're *my* family, too. Charles built me a family, and the last thing I said to him was 'okay, I guess that's settled.' I never once thanked him for raising me. And Dave, he really grew on me. He was my best friend." Eric plopped back down on the plush red cushion and leaned forward, as though someone had punched him directly in the stomach. "I was supposed to be the one to die last night," he confessed in the dark. "Not them. Never them. Me."

"Don't say that," I whispered forcefully as I took my seat next to him. "Never say that, Eric. You promised forever, remember? You're not supposed to die. I forbid it."

Eric picked up his hanging head to gaze at me tenderly, his irises wet with tears. "You forbid it?"

I nodded, and Eric abruptly wrapped me in a strong embrace, holding me so tightly that I momentarily feared I might combust. His body heat warming my skin felt exquisite, and as I listened to his heart beating, I could swear I knew not a sweeter sound. How privileged I was to hear the thump of Eric Stellenzer's heart for another day. My own heartbeat matched his—I could feel it—and I secretly hoped that when the time did come for me to go, the last sound the Earth allowed me to hear was Eric Stellenzer's steady, relentless, beating heart, with my head gently resting against his chest.

I hurt him. I couldn't stop hurting him, it seemed. I wanted to eradicate any and all his pain for him, just as I knew he wanted to do for me, but I believed his presence alone to be a strong enough painkiller. I just hoped I could provide the same kind of relief.

"I am so, so sorry, Eric," I whispered in the dark when I could think of nothing else to say. "You deserve so much better than this. Sometimes, I wish you hadn't met me, so you could live a happier life."

"Live a happier life?" Eric repeated, sounding incredulous. "Zelda, I could live a thousand lives in a thousand different places, but if you're not there, then they're worth nothing. Our situation right now is the worst I've ever seen. Our family could be dead, our home is burnt to the ground, but we're together, right now, in this life. And once we regain our strength, we're going to find Dave, Charles, and the others alive, because that's what you and I do. We solve problems together."

I slightly broke our embrace to observe his face, and even in the darkness of the early morning, I could see his kind, gentle eyes glow softly with adoration. An overwhelming urge to connect our lips surged through me so quickly, I shivered, but as I unconsciously inched my face closer to his, Eric swiftly tilted his chin up to plant a featherlight kiss to my forehead. "We'll see them again soon," he muttered against my skin. "I refuse to believe they're dead. They can't be dead. And then you can reunite with Dave, and everything will be how it's supposed to be."

Dave's name alone made me desperately hope he was alive, because I genuinely couldn't fathom a world where I didn't get to say to him, at least once, that I loved him. I believed I loved him. How could I not? David Woobi was selfless, compassionate, and the purest definition of *good,* and I knew as cruel as the universe could be, it would never dare take such goodness away from those who needed it most. I needed Dave's goodness around me, someone to hold me accountable, someone to keep me grounded in my own goodness, too. Peter's innocence. Eric's kindness. Mr. Woobi's knowledge. Dave's goodness. These are the things I knew I could never lose.

So, I nodded and found my voice to mumble, "Okay."

Eric pressed a kiss to my forehead one last time, as though savoring the feel of my skin against his lips. "Okay," he responded wistfully.

"You two are so disgusting," said a deeper female voice that made the two of us immediately spring apart. I scanned the compartment to see Sasha sitting upright, smirking slyly when she saw how uncomfortable Eric and I had gotten. "Oh no! Don't get all shy now. I heard pretty much everything. You forbade him for dying, which is kind of impossible, but to each their own, I guess. Eric's life wouldn't matter without you for reasons I really don't get; I mean, Eric, you're undeniably attractive. You could do so much better, honey. Oh, and who's Dave?"

"None of your business," I answered sternly. For once, I was grateful for the darkness preventing us from seeing each other clearly; otherwise, I knew Sasha would've pointed out the red splotches on my face.

Sasha shrugged. "That's fair. I didn't care enough to know, anyway."

I opened my mouth to say something when a strange, loud scratching sound from outside our car interrupted me. Eric jumped in his seat when the noise repeated itself and said, "That's what I heard earlier."

We heard it for a third time, a sound that imitated someone scraping metal against the metal of our vehicle, and I bristled at the intrusive noise.

"Is everyone from the Society this paranoid? It's obviously nothing," stated Sasha, but as she said so, I watched her slip a handgun out of her pocket.

Tick. Tick. Tick. Another noise invaded our small space, this time sounding like some sort of audible countdown, and the three of us listened intently for many seconds before Sasha's eyes widened and she commanded, "We need to get out of the car and run. Now."

"What?" questioned Eric.

"Now!" she screamed while forcefully shoving Lucy awake. "Everyone needs to get out of this car and sprint as far away as possible!"

Sasha's urgent shouts woke Will, Harmony, and Jannet, who scrambled to open the compartment's doors and jump down to the grass. I waited until those three and Lucy had evacuated before looking at Sasha expectantly, but she only scowled and yelled, "What the hell are you doing, Jadestone?! Jump! Go!"

"You go ahead," I insisted. "I'll be right behind you."

Sasha followed my gaze to Eric, who struggled just to put weight on his injured leg, and she rolled her eyes before she shouted, "I got one side, you got the other," and slid underneath one of Eric's arms, allowing him to put half of his weight on her.

I immediately followed her lead with Eric's other side, and together, we managed to direct Eric out of the car. He started hopping on one foot away from the vehicle, but that didn't last long after I heard Sasha vehemently demand, "Eric, sweetie, speed up a little. Damn, at this rate, we'll all be dead."

Eric hissed through his teeth as he stretched out his injured leg and used his toes as a way to propel his body forward, and with that strategy, we finally reached where the others had stopped, perhaps 250 yards away from the vehicle. We watched the vehicle for several more moments, just waiting for something to happen, and then:

BAM!

The car exploded in one large, fiery eruption, millions of fragmented pieces slicing through the air as smoke rapidly polluted the indigo sky above. The seven of us watched in shock, jaws hung open as we could do nothing but sit and stare at our mobile shelter engulfed in flames. At first, we were silent, but then Lucy let out a relieved, stunned laugh, Will copying her with Harmony, Jannet, Sasha, and Eric not far behind. Will came up to hug me while laughing, and Eric followed suit, instigating a group hug between the seven shocked, traumatized souls with truly no place to go. Even Sasha participated in the embrace.

"I'm scared," Will sighed, and I tugged him tighter against my body.

"You're safe, Will," I assured. "I got you. We got you."

And for a singular second, I almost believed my words. In our unifying hug, we were safe. We had each other now. Maybe that could one day be enough to satisfy us.

But the moment faded as quickly as it had come. Suddenly, someone ripped Will from my grasp, and I looked up to see the younger boy in the chokehold of a man, scraggly-looking and filthy down to his bones, as another man who looked about the same way held the barrel of a handgun against Will's temple. The first man, with clothes almost black with dirt and flies buzzing around his head, caught sight of me and smiled evilly. "You dropped your gun."

Out of the corner of my eye, I saw Sasha pat her pockets, and I vaguely heard her mutter a curse word.

The second man pressed the gun further into Will's skin as he cracked a grimace that let me see his rotting, yellow teeth. "Tell me who you are right now, or I will kill this boy here. You hear me? Tell me the truth! Are you Zelda Jadestone?"

I took one look at Will, shaking and so helpless, and nodded slowly. "I am."

The man holding Will smiled even wider. "Perfect. Abe, you know what to do."

I saw Abe smile, remove something from his pant pocket—another gun, perhaps—and aim it at my thigh. And then my vision went black.

CHAPTER 13

I awoke to a cloud of disorientation. *Zelda,* my mother murmurs as she works her nimble fingers through my messy, early-morning hair to wake me. *Where am I?* I thought. A thick haze blanketed my consciousness, and for a few fleeting minutes, my brain convinced me that I could be home. *Zelda?* my dad calls from the kitchen wafting delicious smells of roasted chicken and steamed broccoli. *No,* I thought. I didn't have a home. These sensations weren't real. *Zelda,* Peter babbles on the floor beside my mother's feet, the sounds of a crackling fireplace filling me with a false sense of security. The visualizations felt so genuine, I could almost taste the chicken, could almost hear the chirping birds outside our living room window, could almost see the blurry faces of my parents. My body swayed in disbelief, and I so badly wanted to be swept away by the sensations. I wanted to drown in these distorted, fuzzy memories, regardless of their authenticity.

But they weren't my reality. The caress, although incredibly soothing, was not my mother's, but instead, Jannet's as she tried to wake me slowly from my induced slumber. The smell was indeed food, but it was not prepared by my father and certainly not for me to eat. The fire, real as could be in a small furnace in the corner of this space in which I had found myself, was not meant to comfort me, but to block out the cold from the outside. I should have known better; my family is dead. That reality would never be mine.

I finally forced my eyes to open and survey my real surroundings once dreams of my dead family fully faded from my consciousness. It seemed like we were in a decrepit version of a Societan househut; the entirety of the house consisted of a small room apart from a tiny attached bathroom. There were rusting appliances next to a deep sink over to my left, with two small beds missing their sheets over to the right. The lighting was a harsh yellow-orange color that made the two men sitting and eating at an old, rounded table look even more disgusting than they already did. Exposed piping ran throughout the house, and as I attempted to sit up, I noticed that my hands had been chained behind me to one of the pipes. The house reeked of dust and mold like they hadn't cleaned the place in years, and it made me nauseous as I couldn't help but inhale the stench.

Will.

Just as his name appeared in my mind, reminding me of yet another person I had failed, I heard the murmur of my name to the right of me, and I turned my head to see the younger boy alive. His face was covered in sweat and streaked with dirt, looking up at me in terror with his hands also tied behind him to a different pipe. Upon further inspection, I saw Eric, Sasha, Jannet, Harmony, and Lucy all tied to pipes as well. Something like a gasp of relief escaped my lips at the sight of them before I cleared my throat and asked the strange men: "What do you want from me?"

The man I remembered as Abe seemed startled when I spoke, and he smashed his sandwich down on the table. He slowly rose from his chair and stalked over to where we sat, careful not to show any emotion on his face. He stopped walking about five feet away from where my legs were. "You have cameras?" he asked Harmony, to which she nodded with petrified fear etched on her striking features.

I was furious that he was purposely ignoring me, the person they were clearly after, and questioned, "Why should that matter?"

"Zelda," Eric hissed under his breath in warning, but I pretended not to hear him.

"Why should that matter?" The sound of the other man in the room mocking me sliced the silence and brought everyone's attention to him as he crouched mere inches from my face. He seemed to permanently sport a smirk, like he knew my darkest secrets. "What does matter to you, Zelda Jadestone?" He reached his hand out to grasp my face and squeeze my cheeks, tilting my face from side-to-side and inspecting it with that disgusting smile of his. His breath smelled fishy and horrible, and I fought the desire to spit in his face just so I didn't have to inhale his stench anymore.

"Get your hands off me," I growled as threateningly as I could.

He only chuckled lightly in amusement before pushing me away and standing back up. The way he twisted gave me the opportunity to see the Society's emblem drawn sloppily onto his left jacket arm. "Those people who died last night don't matter to Zelda Jadestone," he taunted, smiling even wider when he saw the effect his words had on me.

In reaction to his words, the hairs on the back of my neck stood to attention like the soldiers who had fallen with my name still stuck in their throats.

The man seemed pleased with my reaction. "Your fault, Zelda Jadestone. All of it is your fault."

"Stop," ordered Eric. "It's Caleb's fault, not Zelda's. He is the reason for this violence and anger. He took people's loved ones from them, erased their memories, and just murdered over a thousand innocent people, and you are here angry at Zelda for some reason we don't even know?" Eric looked appalled at the men before him. "That's sick."

Abe raised his eyebrows and seemed to deeply ponder Eric's statement while the other man's eyes twinkled in twisted amusement. "Why don't we let the girl with the words speak for herself?" the other man jeered. "Did she finally run out of things to say, or can she not talk because it's not written down for her first?"

I glared at our kidnapper. "I won't ever run out of things to say. Believe me."

"People like you never do," he said. We stared at each other for what seemed like hours, no one daring to move in fear of raising the tension in the room. "Abe, cut her loose," he commanded his comrade, the grin on his face beginning to really terrify me. The other man, Abe, leaned over to slice the ropes off Eric's wrists, but he was quickly stopped when the first man barked, "No, not him, you idiot. Just her."

Every muscle in my body tightened when Abe cut me loose and forcefully hauled me to my feet by my wrists. The other man immediately shoved me up against the wall, but as my back slammed against the concrete, I reversed our positions just as quickly, my forearm dangerously pressing into his throat as I kept him in place by stepping on both of his feet. My naturally tall height gave me an advantage over this shorter man, but despite his disadvantaged position, his grin grew, and he whispered so that only I could hear: "Be careful there, Zelda Jadestone. You don't want to get yourself into too much trouble now, do you?"

"Trouble seems to find me regardless of what I do." I shrugged before growling, "Let us go."

But he only laughed. He laughed until he coughed and sputtered, desperate for air that my arm prevented from reaching his lungs. His reaction only spurred on my rage until I saw his face turning purple from the lack of oxygen; it was only then that I loosened my hold just enough for him to breathe. I found tears in his eyes from laughing so hard as he composed himself long enough to cough, "You think you've won!" before dissolving into another laughing fit. I effectively pressed my arm that much harder into his windpipe, watching as his eyes began to roll to the back of his head, his laughter still ringing loudly in my ears, his eyes still bearing into mine...

"Get away from Kane!" screeched Abe.

BAM!

The popping sound of a gunshot made me jump away in terror before I was pushed back into a wall and a pair of cold, filthy hands wrapped around my throat. My hands flew up to my neck to try and pry the hands off me, but his grip felt like iron. "It's not fun to be powerless, huh, Zelda Jadestone?" taunted the man called Kane. When I didn't respond, he shook me in place a bit. "Now you know how it feels!" he screamed in my face. "People like *you* running the world without knowing what you're doing!"

"Like you do?" I managed to pant, but that earned me more pressure on my esophagus until I couldn't breathe at all. My brain pulsated against my skull, my eyes felt like they would pop out of my head at any given time, my lungs burnt. In my peripheral vision, I noticed Sasha lying on her back with her feet up against a kitchen drawer, working with the tips of her shoes to get the drawer to open, and I hoped she'd get there before I died from asphyxiation.

Kane's face bloomed bright red with rage as he shouted, "You don't know what it's like to suffer! You and the rest of your kind kill, lie, and cheat people. Don't act like you don't because I know what you do!" He grinned at my purpling lips and lowered his voice until only I could hear him. "Everyone is looking for you. No one knows if you're dead or alive, but oh, you're very much alive. What are you doing, Zelda Jadestone? Getting ready to kill some more people?" He pressed harder into my windpipe. "You're a murderer, just like the rest of those politicians."

I couldn't utter a word, and Kane laughed at my pathetic sputtering. "You're a political pawn," he accused. "You just let those bastards in the government use you. Do you not think for yourself, girl-with-the-words? Are words all you have to offer this world?"

"Excuse me, sir," interrupted Harmony politely. "Who are you?" Lucy looked over to Harmony in shock when the latter spoke.

Kane pushed against my throat one last time before he switched to grip my shoulders. "Abe and I are Societan supporters," he answered Harmony while I gasped air back into my lungs.

"I thought all Societan sympathizers chose to live inside the Society after the war ended," Harmony responded. "Why are you and your friend out here?"

Kane scowled. "We're Federalist soldiers," the man grumbled, and I turned my head in disgust when a speck of spit flew onto my nose. "Let's just say we didn't always agree with the cause."

"And now you do?" questioned Harmony, sounding skeptical. She knitted her black eyebrows together in confusion.

"Hello?! How is any of this relevant?" interrupted Eric suddenly. "What do you want with Zelda?"

"We don't wish to harm you or Abe," supplied Jannet gently, and both Will and Lucy nodded vigorously in agreement. "Please, let us go. We will leave you to live in peace."

Kane barked a short laugh, and upon feeling my struggle to escape his grip, he renewed strangling me, tough, calloused hands locked around my throat. "'Harm us?' 'Live in peace?' The moment this girl"—he shook my neck, and I wheezed—"showed up, there's been the opposite of peace. Now, because of her, people won't shut up about freeing the Society I fought to make a reality. They want to destroy the progress I fought for. I killed to make the Society happen, and you politicians think you can just change that?"

I coughed on the saliva sitting uncomfortably in my back of my mouth when I tried to respond, and Kane snickered at my pitiful state before declaring, "You don't learn that there are actions to your consequences, do you, Zelda Jadestone? None of you ever learn. How could you? You don't know what it's like to live like this. I followed every command. Listened to every order. And now, look at me. Your kind turned their backs on me! I live in a shack. I have no power. I have no voice. I don't care what the media says; this is not a democracy. People like me have never had a voice, not even when these states were united. But do you know who has power, Zelda Jadestone?"

"Me," I rasped, wincing when the word ripped my throat on its way out.

Kane grinned and released my throat again, expertly angling his short-yet-strong body so I couldn't escape his renewed grip on my shoulders. "You have the power to end this war before it begins, and that is exactly what you will do for me. You will give a speech to end the war, and these pretty women here will broadcast it for the whole state to see. No war means I still win."

"I have a brother to think about," I retorted after my throat quit throbbing. "I don't matter when he's involved. I won't say one word for you."

Kane relinquished his grip and took several steps away from me. "Did you ever stop to think about all the brothers you've already killed? All the brothers you will kill in the future if someone doesn't stop this?"

I lowered my gaze at the mention of the innocent people I had unintentionally slaughtered. "Of course," I muttered. Tears pricked the back of my eyes, but I refused to let them fall; I was sick of crying. "I never meant for any of this to happen," I professed. "I never meant for people to die because of me. I never meant for anyone to get hurt. I just want Peter back. My baby brother, I just want him home." My voice broke with emotion during that last sentence. "I just want Peter safe from Caleb's Society. That's all. I don't want *any* of this. I know it's my fault."

It took a while for Kane to say anything in return. "Well, will you look at that? Zelda Jadestone has a weakness after all." He cackled after what felt like an eternity of silence. "You want your brother back, but do you know what I want?" I shook my head, and he grinned in evil satisfaction. "I want to see you, Cody Dassian, and all those other useless politicians crash and burn. After this speech that you *will* give, I'll kill you, Zelda Jadestone. You'll die—"

BAM!

Kane collapsed to the ground with a horrendously agonizing cry, grasping at his shoulder and hissing through the teeth he had left. After the initial shock wore off, I looked over to find Abe with the same gun he had used to harm his friend aimed at his own temple, his hand shaking tremendously as he whispered, "Please. I want to forget."

No one spoke. No one moved. No one dared to do anything in fear of antagonizing him into doing something irreversible.

Except for me.

Impulsively, I jumped over to him and gripped his wrists hard in my hands until I saw his own beginning to turn white from the lack of blood. My fingers crawled up the hand holding the gun until they locked around the handle of it. Abe's eyes darted from looking straight ahead at the wall to staring at me suspiciously, but instead of looking away, I held his painful gaze. "You don't want to forget," I told him while searching his face for any sign of emotion besides fear.

"I made mistakes I want to forget," he murmured under his breath so only I could hear him. I felt him struggle the tiniest bit against my hold on his hands but not enough to break free.

"Sometimes, I want to forget, too," I confessed, which I saw kindled his curiosity. "Sometimes, I wish I could start again and make smarter choices, so I don't have to feel this constant weight on my chest. I don't know what will happen because of the decisions I've made, good or bad. But I do know that it's impossible to go back, so the only thing to do now is look forward and have some hope that things will get better."

I could see the gears in his head turning, trying to figure out what to make of me and my words. "You're not scared?" he asked, his eyes shut closed as he tried to process everything.

"No, I am. I'm terrified. Sometimes, that fear starts to overwhelm me, but then I think about seeing my brother again, safe and away from Caleb, and I can start to see that light again. The light that tells me that one day, I'll get to him. Then, hopefully, it'll be worth it. All of it will be worth it."

"I don't have a brother to see," Abe whispered. "Not anymore."

"But you have a life," I countered. "And that is worth everything."

Abe looked around the room apprehensively with glassy and haunted eyes, a somewhat wild look to them that strongly reminded me of Mr. Woobi. A single tear escaped his left eye when he muttered, "I'm their soldier. I've killed people."

"So have I."

"People I should've loved," Abe elaborated.

"Me too."

He tightened his grip on the gun and inched his pointer finger that much closer to the trigger. "You don't want to forget that?"

My heart rate sped up at his actions, but for his sake, I tried to keep my voice level. "I want to reverse the damage I've done," I declared loudly through trembling lips and salty eyes. "But I don't want to forget them. I can't." I hardened my voice for my final sentence: "I won't."

At first, nothing changed. Abe still aimed the gun at his skull, his eyes filled to the brim with deep sadness and immense fear. I saw his lips moving, but no sound came out of them. One of my hands still grasped the handle of the gun while the other gripped his lowered wrist. I was terrified. Terrified I hadn't done enough. Terrified I had said too much and pushed him over the edge. Terrified I had somehow made things worse. But then, after several minutes, Abe tossed the gun to the cement floor, turned to me, and mouthed, "I won't, either."

Giving him a hug was much too forward, and words were no longer needed. I opted to smile at him, and I twisted around to search for the gun he had thrown. I found it in Kane's hands, the barrel trained to my torso, hatred blazing in his eyes as he growled, "Abe, she's a fraud." He stayed sitting on the floor, blood trickling from the bullet wound to his shoulder. I detected no trace of a smile on Kane's face now, just pure malice.

Abe froze in place. "I don't think so," he responded. "I don't think she's one of them anymore." With that, he took careful strides over to stand in front of me, blocking my body from the bullet sure to come. I tried to push him aside, but he weighed much more than I could push. "She gets it, Kane. It's okay. She understands."

I became frantic, pulling on his arm and shouting at him to move when Kane didn't lower his weapon, but Abe refused to budge, regardless of how hard I tugged. "Is that so?" Kane sneered.

"Yeah. She gets it."

Sasha had finally wiggled the kitchen drawer open, and she powerfully kicked it off its tracks, its metal contents loudly clanging against the cement floor. But I didn't dare pay attention to her as I yanked Abe's arm. "Abe, please, *please,* move."

"Kane," Abe tried to reason. "She's not one of them. She's one of us."

"Abe, I'm begging you, please—"

"Kane, it's okay. Zelda understands."

Kane smirked. "You worthless bastard."

BAM!

I screamed. Kane laughed. Abe fell.

Dead.

Incomprehensible sounds made their way out of my mouth as I lunged for Kane, arms flailing until they wrapped around his hand and yanked the weapon out of it. After I had him trapped underneath me, my hands—which had discarded the gun by throwing it across the room—went to grip his throat like they had done earlier. I screamed and screamed, but again, Kane laughed. He laughed until tears streamed down his face. He laughed even as my fingers completely closed off his pathway for oxygen. He laughed until his eyes rolled to the back of his head. One-by-one, I slowly peeled my fingers away from his esophagus, and although he lay unconscious and could no longer cackle, I still heard it.

The pressure behind my eyeballs from unshed tears felt almost unbearable, but still, I could not cry. My face remained dry as I shrieked, fisting my hands into my hair until my eyes made contact with Abe's limp body. I crawled over to him as fast as I could, screeching, "He's going to die! He'll die; someone, hurry, he's dying! Help! He's going to die!"

Eric spoke up next, his voice low and cautious as he demanded, "Zelda, look at me." I slightly turned to see him standing, and I briefly wondered how until I saw Sasha with a sharp knife in her hands, cutting away the ropes around everyone's wrists. I looked to Eric for some explanation, some help, but all he did was soften his voice to say, "He's gone."

My lower lip trembled as the weight of his words hit me full force. "But-but... he promised he wouldn't forget. He told me. He... he..." I watched as blood spilled from Abe's chest, and unthinkable pain encased me when I whispered, "He's... dead."

"We have to leave," proclaimed Sasha. "The other dude is going to wake up soon. We can't be here when he does."

I shook my head. "I can't leave Abe here. I can't do it. I can't..."

"Zelda." Jannet's voice this time. "You must."

"No!" I screamed at her, a fresh, new wave of pain hitting my chest.

I didn't have a choice. Sasha announced she knew a place she would be willing to take us, but just as we followed her out the door, I realized I couldn't leave Abe like that, not when he deserved so much more than to lay at the feet of his murderer. I bent down, picked every wildflower in sight until I had formed a lovely bouquet in my hands, and sprinted into the house to place the bouquet on Abe's chest and shut his eyelids to make it appear as though he were only sleeping. I wanted to stay with him longer, maybe utter an apology for failing him, too, but when Kane started to stir, I galloped over to the rest of the group.

No one commented on what I had done, nor did I want them to. We walked in complete silence until I heard sniffling and Will broke down. He sat on the grass and sobbed into his hands, mumbling incoherent words I could only grasp in pieces: "didn't deserve to die" and "scared of death." I wanted to reach out to him but feared I would lose whatever sanity I had left, so I sucked in the pain and didn't utter a word.

Surprisingly, Eric was next. He fell to his knees and although he didn't make a sound, the tears that stained his face were all too loud. Lucy and Harmony followed him, their gulps for air along with the sound of them crying almost too much to endure. Jannet imitated Eric in that tears escaped her, but silently. Sasha pursed her lips together at the sight of them and harshly stated, "We have to keep going." I didn't appreciate her tone at all, but because my silence was the only thing holding me together, I didn't argue. It took a few minutes, but finally, everyone composed themselves enough to start our journey once again. Will insisted he and I hold hands, and I didn't mind. His sweaty palm against my clammy, cold one gave me some strength.

"That was nice," he told me a few minutes later, after he had found his voice again. "What you did for that man. That was the right thing to do."

I grunted, not fully trusting myself to speak just yet.

"Did you mean what you said to him earlier?" he asked. "Do you seriously want to forget everything sometimes and just start over?"

Again, words failed me, so I nodded and picked up my pace a little bit as if trying to outrun his questions.

His next question came out as a whisper: "Did you really kill people like you said?"

This one, I could not answer. Faces of those I had unintentionally killed swam before my eyes and made me dizzy—so dizzy that I had to stop walking just to recompose myself.

Will didn't press the subject. "You know, sometimes, I want to go back in time, too," he told me to steer the one-sided conversation away from the topic of death. "So I can see my family one more time, tell them goodbye, maybe even save them—"

"Will."

"Yeah?"

"Stop talking."

He did.

We walked in silence for about half an hour until Sasha turned around to face all of us. "You're probably wondering where we're going," she announced, and everyone nodded in agreement. "Those guys drove us out near the Society. I've seen them around before. We're about a two-day walk from the Redding village right now."

"You know them?" Lucy asked timidly. I hadn't realized how squeaky and high-pitched her voice sounded until then, and that combined with her short, thin stature made her appear childlike. I saw goosebumps on her exposed arms, and I wished I had a jacket with which to drape over her bony shoulders.

Sasha tilted her head toward Lucy and gave her a disbelieving look. "Yeah, they're my best pals, Luce." She whacked Lucy on the arm. "Of course, I don't know them. We just occupy the same territory. I've seen them foraging for food once or twice."

"What?" said Eric. "What do you mean, 'occupy the same territory'?"

Sasha placed her two hands over her heart dramatically and responded, "Oh Eric, you sweet little thing. So many freedom fighters live in these woods, you wouldn't believe."

"Freedom fighters?" Jannet repeated.

"Yes, Grandma. Freedom fighters," Sasha remarked defensively. Eric opened his mouth to express his disapproval of the way she addressed Jannet, but Sasha beat him to it, adding, "Sorry, Jannet. Yes, freedom fighters. People who hate Dassian's government but would rather die than live in a Society. We live out here." She gestured around her. "I just happen to live right next to the river, maybe two miles or so away. I'm leading you to the river, and then we can follow it until we reach my camp."

"No," I croaked. "I can't go back there."

"If we follow the river, it lowers the chance of getting lost." Sasha looked directly at me then, and I thought I saw the slightest trace of sympathy in her face before she hardened her expression again. "I think we want to avoid getting lost right now, with everyone looking for you and stuff. Those two aren't the only ones out to kill you, Jadestone. You're hated around here. We need to go somewhere safe."

I shook my head in opposition. "I can't go near the Society right now. Not after last night."

Sasha crossed her arms. "I'm trying to help us. This is our only option. Once we reach my camp, we can figure it out from there, but it's too dangerous here right now."

"I think we need help," stated Harmony a bit too loudly, inserting her voice to force us to listen. "We cannot do this alone. We need to find some way back to Neweryork."

"Wait, alone?" Eric questioned, turning his attention to Sasha. "You live in this forest alone?"

"No!" Sasha snapped immediately, as though offended by the question, but as Eric began to apologize, her face fell, and I thought I saw tears ghosting her eyelashes. She sniffled, dragged her hand roughly under her nose, and declared, "Well, I didn't. I do now, I guess."

"Sasha," I repeated, *and my mind flashed back to an image of her holding a lifeless body and screaming in repulsion. The memory made me grimace.* "I'm so sorry for your fr—"

"Don't," growled Sasha. "Don't apologize for Melanie when she means nothing to you."

"Melanie," I said as I painfully recalled the memory. "You used to live out here with a girl named Melanie?"

Sasha gritted her teeth, shut her eyes tightly, and hissed, "That is *none* of your damn business."

I respectfully chose not to push the subject further.

"Sasha, do you have internet access at your, um… home?" asked Lucy after our silence stretched a bit too long.

Sasha sniffled once again before blinking hard twice and quirking up an accusing eyebrow. "Who the hell do you think I am, Luce? Yeah, I have internet. There's no such thing as living totally off the grid anymore."

"We can connect once we get to the camp and send a distress signal out," said Harmony to Lucy. "Then we can all go home once they come to collect us."

Sasha huffed and said, "Look, Jadestone, if you really are going back to Neweryork, I won't follow you. I'm not cut out for that kind of lifestyle. I'm willing to bring you to my place, but after that, you're on your own."

I nodded in understanding. "Don't think I didn't see what you did with the kitchen drawer," I told her. "You saved us in there. You're a strong woman, Sasha. It'll be a shame to lose you."

"Yeah, you're badass," blurted Will, and everyone chimed in their agreement.

At our proclamations, a hint of a proud smile played on Sasha's lips before it disappeared so quickly, I thought I might've imagined it. "Someone had to save your sorry asses," she commented, but she made sure to hold my gaze when she added, "Thank you." I believed she meant it, too.

"I'll go with you to Neweryork," stated Will as he squeezed my fingers with his.

I ruffled the hair on the top of his head and gave him a tight-lipped smile. "Good, because I won't let you go otherwise." He grinned up at me at that.

The rev of an engine reverberated around the trees then, and a jolt of panic shot up my spine when Sasha announced that the sound was Kane's truck on his way to parole the forest looking for us. "Our best bet is to go into the river," she said, and finally, I relented. We walked until we reached the brink of the riverbank, where we found barely a stream running where there was once a raging river, reduced to nothing for the Uniforms to use as their hideout. Sasha slid down the gorge first, followed by Eric, Lucy, Harmony, Jannet, then Will, and I brought up the rear. My feet landed in wet sand, and the squelch of the granules underneath my shoes reminded me of the sound of Uniforms running up the ravine to murder hundreds. I resumed holding Will's hand for comfort; if he sensed my unease, he didn't show it, only clung to me more tightly.

After just a few minutes, Will's boredom kicked in, and he decided to play a little game he had conceived as we ambled behind everyone else. He would kick a pebble into the tiny stream to our left, then I would, and whoever kicked the stone the farthest "won." It was quite a simple thing, something small and stupid, but although he claimed to be bored, I had an inkling that he played it to trick himself into thinking that danger didn't lurk behind us. Truthfully, it worked quite well for that purpose; I soon got lost in the game, pretending to be annoyed every time Will's pebble went farther than mine and he would cheer and pump a fist into the air in celebration. Laughter still came so easily to him, even then. It amazed me.

The silly game consumed me so much that I failed to notice how much larger the stream had grown, to the point where water now licked our heels. Waves were suddenly present, and the water covered the entire width of the ravine. I finally noticed when my foot was fully submerged in water, and I stopped mid-kick to examine how that could possibly be. No natural water replenishes itself that fast. Will looked at me strangely and asked what was wrong, but I dismissed him as I tried to think. And then it hit me:

"No," Mr. Woobi exclaimed, pointing to a certain point in the water where the current seemed to be strongest. "See how the water gushes like that?" We all nodded, and he continued, "That's a pipe feeding this river. This is all man-made to keep us in, and the others out. It wraps around the Society completely, all 360 degrees of it. Caleb built it as a precaution. It's controlled by Caleb."

Controlled by Caleb.

He knew we were here. And he was about to swallow us whole.

As not to frighten Will, I picked up the pebble and threw it into the water, rushing over to Sasha immediately afterward with his fake-angry whines of "That's cheating!" ringing in my ears. I tapped her on the shoulder, the water now covering my ankles, and declared, "We're going to drown if we don't get out of this river. Now."

She kept walking and rolled her eyes at my statement. "No, we're not. The water is rising a little bit. Big deal. This happens a few times a year. It takes days for the river to slowly go back to normal after drying up."

I pulled on her arm until she was forced to stop. "I'm serious. This isn't normal. Caleb has control of this river through pipes, and he obviously knows we're here. He wants me dead, Sasha. He's going to drown us. We have to get out." The water started to swirl around the middle of my calves by then.

Sasha cursed under her breath. "Okay, yeah. Let's get out. I hope everyone knows how to swim."

But just as I shouted the order for everyone to start climbing up the gorge, Will's horrific scream pierced my ears. I twisted around in a panic to see a ten-foot wave coming at us at a speed I knew would be impossible to outrun. Will rushed to my side, and we had just intertwined our fingers together when the wave crashed into us with remarkable strength.

I fought hard to keep my grip on Will, but the water tore us apart. The force with which the wave slammed into me knocked all the breath out of my lungs, my mouth falling open uselessly, instantly filling with water. The power of the current prevented me from opening my eyes, and my limbs flailed as I tried to fight the water, but the more I fought, the more strength the river sucked out of my already-fragile body. The current dragged me down, kicking me until I almost lost consciousness, and a part of me wished I would, just to stop the assault.

The water was winning. With each passing second, I felt myself growing weaker until eventually, I gave up. This was how I would atone for my sins: killing my coworkers, abandoning Peter, driving thousands to die for me, not rescuing those left on the battlefield, leaving the Woobis to burn in a fire, not saving Abe in time. *All my fault.* I deserved to drown.

The faces of those I had failed entered my consciousness like a last montage, and I welcomed it, accepting that this might be the last time I would ever see them. I'd savor the feeling of grief for as long as I could, because as long as I felt *something,* I remained alive.

Dave. Mr. Woobi. Eve. They reopened the wound I kept ignoring, but in the water, I chose to finally bleed, to finally accept the weight of their deaths, and it crashed into me harder than any wave ever could.

Allyson. Marley. Sharlee. I hadn't known them long, but I had taken their lives. How sorry I was to know that they'd never see the sun rise again. My only hope was that I could repay my debt to them by depriving myself of the same scene. I just wished the water would make my death quick. The three of them frowned in my images of them, disappointed at my thoughts and current state. *How pathetic,* their faces said. I agreed.

Jannet. Lucy. Harmony. I hoped they'd make it home without me, and I hoped they'd find it within their hearts to forgive me for what I had dragged them into. I only wanted them to find peace after what we had experienced together.

Eric. Will. Sasha. They screamed at me to fight, if not for them, then for myself, but how could I face them again knowing what I had done? I had condemned their lives, reduced them to bodies flipping in a raging river. I had poisoned them, ruined them, in essence, killed them. How could I live with that guilt?

But then, a light. Peter. And he didn't demand a sacrifice. He didn't require a cleansed conscience. He didn't frown when he saw me; he smiled. And that was all I needed.

When my toes grazed the sand at the bottom of the river, I bent my knees and launched upward with the last of my strength, hoping that somehow, that would be enough to propel my face to the top. It was. My mouth breached the surface of the river just long enough to inhale air, and that gave me the momentum needed to tread water. Waves repeatedly splashed into my eyes, and it proved to be an annoyance as I tried to survey everyone else's location.

After many moments of searching, I spotted mostly everyone congregated around one large, protruding rock close to the riverbank, large enough to use for leverage to push oneself out of the water. Sasha clung to one side of the rock with one hand, the other occupied with pulling Jannet out of the surging waves. Eric was positioned right next to her, helping Lucy with her footing so she could make the jump to safe, dry land. Harmony was already out of the river, and although she seemed to be bleeding profusely, she leaned over the side, ready to catch Lucy whenever the latter made the leap. The only one missing was Will, which terrified me more than my own brush with death did.

Eric caught sight of me and almost dropped Lucy back into the water in surprise. He shouted at me to swim to him, and I kicked as hard as I could to reach the rock until I eventually grabbed onto its edges as the water yanked my bottom half. Lucy jumped into Harmony's arms, and the two of them helped pull Jannet, then Sasha, then Eric, and lastly me out of the river. "Where's Will?!" I yelled above the sound of rushing water after I caught my breath. But no one could answer. No one knew.

"ZELDA!"

It was him. It was Will. He sounded so afraid.

I readied myself to jump back into the water and swim after him, but Eric caught my upper arm just as I was set to dive back in. I screamed at him to let me go, kicking and slapping him in an attempt for him to release me so I could swim after Will, but he refused to lighten his grip. I heard him shouting, "I'm sorry, I'm so sorry, it's too dangerous, I can't let you," but his justifications didn't matter; I only focused on where Will went and how I could possibly save him.

I heard Will scream my name again, and I finally caught sight of him in the center of the river, complete and absolute terror on his little face. I knew I needed to jump in and rescue him, but Eric refused to give in to my demands.

Sasha ran to a nearby tree and stood on the tips of her toes to snap a large branch off the trunk, sprinting back to the riverbank as quickly as her legs could carry her. She tried reaching over the side toward Will, but upon discovering that her arms were too short to make any sort of difference, she enlisted Jannet's help in forming a human chain. Lucy quickly joined them after checking Harmony's pulse, and together, they got as far as the edge of the rock we had used to push ourselves out, Sasha stretching out the branch as far as her body allowed. The three of them encouraged Will to swim to them, to please kick toward the rock, to grab onto the branch, but he was too far away to reach them. I screeched at Eric to let me plunge into the water, but his grip on my arm only tightened.

Sasha, Jannet, and Lucy almost fell back into the river on several occasions trying to rescue him, but when he rushed past the branch, hands outstretched in a last-ditch effort to hold on, I knew there was nothing anyone could do. I had failed him.

We watched from the riverbank as the fifteen-year-old boy struggled to break free from the water, watched as one final, mighty wave crashed over his head, and we watched as his small, broken body floated away.

Dead.

CHAPTER 14

I was trapped in a world not even Eric could pull me from for three days following Will's death. No amount of pain I had felt up until that moment could have prepared me for the devastation of knowing that he was *dead*. When innocent people were slaughtered, at least they were strangers. When the village burnt, at least I didn't see any bodies, so I held onto hope that maybe, Dave, Mr. Woobi, Eve, and the rest might still be alive.

But I had no hope for Will. I had watched him die. He would never teach me more games to play when we grew bored, never accompany me to Neweryork, never grow older and experience life, real life, the kind of life that made pain worth it. Will was never coming back. And it was my fault.

I could have saved him, was the only thought that infiltrated my mind throughout that three-day period. I should have put more effort into looking for him before deciding to save myself from that rushing river. I should have fought harder to get away from Eric and jump to Will's aid. I should have done so many different things so he could be with me, alive, instead of submerged in murky river water, dead. Except I didn't. I didn't do any of these things. Will had died because even after everything, I was still afraid to die. Nothing could erase my fear.

Sasha, Jannet, Eric, and Lucy had to drag Harmony and me to Sasha's home—two tents with a small fire pit in between them—because we physically could not carry ourselves. Sasha designated the larger, spacious tent for Jannet, Lucy, Harmony, and herself to use, and she left the smaller one for Eric and me. Despite there being two beds to sleep on, I spent those three days curled in one corner of the tent, refusing to move. Eric tried to coax me to eat the food Jannet prepared over the fire pit, but I wouldn't take the nutrition. Jannet tried to help me walk, or at least stand, for the sake of my muscles, but I believed I deserved to feel my body ache if Will couldn't feel at all. Lucy tried to get me to talk, but I declined even squeaking a sound in front of her.

Zelda, my coworkers call, reminders that their deaths were for not.

Zelda, the Woobis reprimand. All four of them: Mr. Woobi, Eve, Caleb, and Dave. All four are disappointed in the woman I had become.

Zelda, Will's young voice joins the orchestra, so inharmonious with the others.

They yelled, they whispered, they preached. Their voices twisted into screams of pain, transformed into cries for help, changed into shouts of anger. They got louder each passing day until I was sure I was drowning in my grief. I wrapped my fingers around large locks of hair, pulling on my roots to knock them out of my head. I screamed to try and overpower them. Nothing worked. I would never evade the sounds of the dead.

On the fourth day after Will's death, early in the morning before anyone else awoke, I unfolded myself from the corner and quietly exited my tent, careful not to disturb Eric on my way out. The cold, crisp, fresh air stung my nostrils after days of inhaling stale air trapped in polyester, but I relished smelling the natural scent of the forest trees. Caleb hadn't drained the river, so the roar of the water as it churned, gurgled, and spat made my fingers curl into a fist in revulsion. The morning sun breached the horizon and flooded the forest with golden light that the tree trunks shattered, but I sort of enjoyed the way the beams scattered. Goosebumps lined my limbs from the cold air, my stomach howled for some sustenance, my eyes burned from the sudden sunlight, but I welcomed the discomfort freely. If Will couldn't feel pain, then I would feel it for him.

I found a sheathed knife by Sasha's fire pit—possibly the same one she used to cut our friends and herself free—and pocketed it carefully after observing the sharpness of the blade as an added form of protection. I crept out of Sasha's camp in the general direction of the village, determined to get far enough away that they wouldn't come after me, but I didn't make it far before I heard Eric's concerned voice calling out to me above the cry of the river.

I turned to face him, but I immediately wished I hadn't. In the sunlight, I could clearly see the damage I had done: the fragile, pleading nature of his eyes, the hunched curve in his long spine, the filthy coating on his skin of dried river water, sand, and mud. His dark, fluffy hair looked almost gray from the dust and dirt, and his wounded leg looked red, irritated, and swollen. I suddenly saw the argument behind Caleb's memory loss method because in that instance, I wanted nothing more than to forget that Eric Stellenzer ever looked this broken.

Eric asked me where I was headed, but when I didn't have an answer, he slumped against the trunk of a tree, ran his hands down the sides of his face, and begged me to come back in such a soft, tormented tone that I couldn't decipher if he was talking to me directly.

"I want to see the village," I rasped, my throat sore.

Eric picked his head up, nodded, and said he'd accompany me there once he asked Sasha if we could borrow her personal truck. I had neglected to notice the vehicle parked twenty-five yards or so away from the tents, but I felt thankful I wouldn't have to walk. Once Eric received permission from Sasha, who promptly reported she would not be joining us, he and I climbed into the truck, set the coordinates, and sped through the trees in complete silence.

It took over an hour to reach the ruins of what once was the village. When we arrived, Eric allowed me time to roam alone, insisting that if I needed anything, he'd be waiting for me back in the truck; he claimed seeing the village this way wouldn't be good for him, and I understood. I closed the door behind me quickly to stop the putrid stench from infiltrating the vehicle; although the fire had long since snuffed out, the stench of something burning was still quite strong—strong enough to make my eyes water and my mouth clamp shut so as not to taste the smoke.

Ashes were everywhere. They covered the ground, caking my shoes until they went from a light brown to a deep black. Whole building foundations were suffocated in ashes. I kicked up ash with each step I took, and I could smell the burnt scent that they carried. On numerous occasions, I found myself biting my tongue to keep from vomiting. Although I refused to listen to it, my subconscious knew it wasn't just wood that had perished in that fire.

One building remained standing, and although ash coated its exterior, it appeared structurally sound, which seemed incredibly odd given that the rest of the village had been completely obliterated by Caleb's firebombs. I decided to explore it despite the obvious dangers and pushed the doors open, only to recognize the white, speckled tiles as the hospital's flooring. The roof had countless holes in it, large and small alike, allowing for only broken sunlight to shine through the hospital. Shattered glass, torn fabric, ash, and mangled pieces of metal littered the tile floor.

I almost fell when something underneath my foot rolled and caused me to lose my balance temporarily. I bent down to observe the object, and I gasped when I recognized it as the golden bullet one of the Twelve Soldiers had gifted me; it must've fallen out of my pocket sometime before I left to follow Eric. I picked it up and twirled it through my fingers, examining the dents along its surface until I noticed ashes had wiped off onto my hand. Ashes that once might have been a living human being.

I collapsed onto my hands and knees and crawled underneath the twisted metal frame of a bed to hide from the voices that had resumed calling my name. My breathing accelerated tenfold to match my pounding heart rate as I dragged my knees upward to tuck them close to my midsection. The action caused the knife I had stolen to dig itself into my stomach, and I wrapped my hand around the bullet, clamping down hard enough to make my palm ache. I screamed into the floor, the sound bouncing off the walls and echoing around the gigantic room so loudly I was sure my head would combust, but at least it was noise after so many days trapped in silence.

I broke. After days of keeping them locked away, I finally allowed for tears to gush from my eyes and soak my face. My screams stopped when I ran out of air, that horrific hiccup-gulping sound replacing my screeches. I cried for Will. I cried for the people I lost when Caleb burnt the village down. I cried for the people I couldn't save out on the battlefield. I cried for Abe. I cried for Peter. I cried for Will again.

But I think the one person I really cried for was myself.

How could I have let this happen? I knew that if it hadn't been for my appearance in the village, the buildings and its people would still be standing, untouched by such tragedy. How come I couldn't seem to make a correct decision, even when I had the best intentions? All I wanted was

Peter's safety, but why did that have to cost other human lives? How could Caleb openly annihilate this many people, people he likely knew from his childhood, innocent people I thought he'd never harm? I hated him; more accurately, I hated who he was making me become. I wasn't a murderer. I wasn't a politician. I wasn't a leader in any sense, yet here I sat, lying in the ashes of the ones I swore to protect. I was a fraud, a fictitious version of who the public believed me to be, a perfectly concocted liar set to spew violence. I hated Caleb, yes, but there was no one I hated more than myself.

I'm not sure how long I stayed like that, but eventually, I heard a soothing call of my name, a sensation of familiar noise that delighted my eardrums, the sound of sunset and sweet regret. But no. That couldn't have been him. I could recognize that voice even if its owner stood a mile away, but it just wasn't possible. Yet I heard it again: "Zelda?" An expectant, gentle voice that sounded too close, too clear, too real to be in my head.

I stood up cautiously, disbelievingly, and walked out of the hospital to see him standing in the heart of the village, where we had once danced. I eyed the man before me with the curiosity of a newborn, my eyes traveling from his feet, to his torso, and finally, *finally,* landing on his eyes. The same electric-blue I will never forget. And when I felt my heart expanding, pounding so loudly I was sure he could hear it, I saw the same smile, too. I saw the same boy.

I took careful steps toward him until we were almost pressed up against each other, his breath tickling my face. I lightly touched his arm to make sure he was real, the action causing him to involuntarily shiver. "Dave?" I muttered under my breath, almost to myself.

The world buzzed with electricity as the both of us didn't move another inch, simply stared at the other in awe. Everything seemed slightly out of focus when an emotion I knew quite well began taking hold of me, seizing my body until I had to lean against a tree for support. *Longing.* I had missed him, more than I think my mind could handle, and in that very moment when he smiled sweetly and whispered, "Hi, sweetheart," I finally gifted myself the freedom to feel what I hadn't realized had been pent up inside me, waiting to be uncovered all the time we had been apart.

I flung myself at him, wrapping my arms around his neck, my face buried in the cradle between his neck and collarbone. He stumbled at the initial contact, but quickly regained his balance and returned my ferocity with an equally powerful hug of his own. There were so many things I wanted to say to him, so many questions I had for him, but I had no more words left in me. Dave began twirling us around, his laughter filling the charged air around us. "I've missed you," whispered Dave into my ear, his voice airy and desperate.

After Dave loosened his hold, I pulled away from our embrace to take in his face. He looked older, somehow, not the way I remembered him looking when we met. I ran my fingers through his blond hair to feel its soft texture, but his hair felt stiff and gelled. My action made him shudder again as he picked up my fingers and kissed each one of them. "I missed you, too," I whispered back to him, leaning so our foreheads touched and our lips were close, so close. "I missed you so much."

"Glad to know it's not one-sided," he joked with a grin, and just his smile, his beautiful smile, was enough to push me until I simply couldn't stand the lack of contact anymore and pressed our lips together. Dave's hands flew to cup my face sweetly for a moment before he gripped the base of my neck to deepen the kiss, and although I questioned his sudden roughness, the whimper that left Dave's mouth in between kisses erased any coherent thought from my mind.

All too soon, Dave hummed and yanked his mouth away from mine as though someone had grabbed the back of his head and pulled him. "Zelda?" he asked, attempting to respectfully put some distance between our bodies.

His voice startled me, but I still didn't let go of his torso. I made a sound in the back of my throat to indicate I was listening.

"They said they're on their way. C'mon, we need to leave before they get here."

I tilted my face just barely to see his. I hadn't noticed he had a little black box sitting in his ear. "Who's they?" I asked almost sleepily.

Dave cleared his throat, ready to answer, but he never got the chance, because just then, what felt like a hundred people emerged from the forest, most carrying cameras while others shouted orders at the cameramen. "We found her!" I kept hearing from different people in the mob closing in around me. That blinking red light that I hated was everywhere—above me, beside me, even below me as I punched one camera that got too close to my face down to the ground. The people in business suits and dresses, the cameramen, and the reporters trampled on a mass grave to get closer to me, talking excitedly like they had just found their favorite childhood toy. How dare they walk where people died? How dare they treat it as though innocent men, women, and children didn't die right where they were standing? How dare they shove a camera in my face during such an intimate, private moment in my life?

I wrestled out of Dave's embrace, anger obvious in my tone when I asked, "You knew they were here?"

He couldn't hold my fiery gaze for too long. "I'm so sorry. This was the only way they'd let me see you. I worked out an agreement to let them film if I got to be the first one to see you. Sweetheart, I couldn't wait. Once they told us this morning that someone had sent a distress signal saying you were on the way here, I couldn't stop myself." He repeated his apologies again, but I didn't care to hear any of it.

"Zelda Jadestone!" someone shouted above Dave's explanation. An orange-haired woman stepped beside me, standing so close to my frame that one could have mistaken us for being old friends. "How does it feel to stand in the ruins of your home?" she asked with a sadistic smile on her face.

"Zelda Jadestone!" called someone else. "What are your thoughts on the Society's teachings after seeing this destruction? Is there anything you want to say to Caleb Woobi personally? What are your thoughts on the Societan Massacre that happened just a few days ago?"

"Zelda Jadestone!" bellowed another. "Is it true you were held hostage by Societan supporters? Can you tell the camera here what that was like? Is it true you saved someone from suicide?"

"Zelda Jadestone, can you confirm the death of fifteen-year-old William Finnley?"

"Zelda Jadestone, what really happened by the Northeastern Society?"

"Zelda Jadestone, what do you believe should be the next steps following these tragedies?"

"Zelda Jadestone!" they yelled.

"Zelda Jadestone!" they shouted.

"Zelda Jadestone!" they screamed.

So finally, I screamed back.

"Leave me alone!" I shrieked at them, covering my ears to block out their questions as I pushed past them, Dave hot on my heels. The reporters chased after me, so I broke into a full sprint, not really paying attention to my destination. I just knew I had to leave.

I caught sight of Eric standing beside Sasha's parked truck just beyond the line of trees and sprinted in his direction, relieved when I saw him scramble back into the truck to start its ignition. I had just about collided with the door of the vehicle, almost in the clear, when I ran straight into one of Cody Dassian's secret servicemen. He was a burly, tall, square-shaped man, clearly trained in combat, and he picked me up to throw me over his shoulder. Eric flew out of the truck to reach us, and he punched the man straight in the stomach, demanding the serviceman let me go. Eric's impulsive action only served to alert other guards, who quickly swarmed us by the dozens and had Eric's arms behind his back in no time. Dave joined us soon after, insisting the servicemen relinquish their grips, but the ex-Uniform was swatted away as if nothing but an annoying insect. I fought, too, punching the man who carried me in the back as hard as I could. He didn't even flinch.

The guard carried me over to a plane that looked almost identical to the ones the Uniforms used in the Society and dumped me in a seat, Eric dropped unceremoniously into the one next to me with Dave taking the one beside him. As the door to the plane began to lift to close, my eyes traveled around the space to find Sasha, Jannet, Lucy, and Harmony in the seats across from Dave, Eric, and me. Something about their presences put me slightly at ease. "You're here," I panted, my gaze solely on Sasha as I remembered her saying she wouldn't join me to Neweryork. "You came with me."

Sasha sighed and rolled her eyes, but I knew her well enough by then to see that she looked somewhat relieved. "Yeah, well, I couldn't let you go back without seeing my face one more time." She lowered her head to stare at the floor. "And... for Will, you know? I'm doing it for him. Don't think I actually like you or anything."

"Wouldn't dream of it," I told her. I could swear I saw her smirk.

Lucy spoke up next: "I'm sorry, Zelda."

"We didn't know that many reporters would show up when we sent out the distress signal," added Harmony. "I swear."

"Dude, I thought you... when Zelda said the village had..." Eric stammered as he twisted his body to look at Dave. He shoved the blond-haired boy in his seat. "You scared me!"

"Me too," said Dave. "I thought you were—"

"Dead," interrupted Eric.

"Dead," finished Dave.

The boys stared at each other in silence for a moment before Eric proclaimed, "You can't do that again, man," through an exhale, running a hand down his face. "I mean it."

"Me?!" repeated Dave in feigned anger. "You were the one who went to the Society! *You* can't do that again!"

"I'm sorry to interrupt this love fest going on right now, but who the hell are you?" asked Sasha while eyeing Dave with distaste.

Dave corrected his posture and smiled as if realizing others also occupied the plane with him, Eric, and me. "Hi," he greeted. "I'm David Mon…"

"Woobi," Eric supplied softly.

"David Woobi," he carefully restated. "But please, call me Dave."

Sasha crossed her legs and whistled. "*You're* the Dave they were talking about? Like David, Caleb's son?" She glanced at me. "You're really connected, huh, Jadestone?"

"Zelda, again, I'm so sorry about those people," Lucy said, leaning over to get me to look at her. "If I had known filming you would cause all this…"

"Lucy and Harmony were secretly filming you during and after the battle near the Society. They sent a distress signal this morning after you and Eric left to visit the village," elaborated Jannet. "They collected us first and then flew to get you. They failed to mention anything about cameras."

"So, what's it like being the son of a serial killer?" Sasha asked Dave excitedly, resting her chin on her palms.

Sasha asked many more inappropriate questions after that, and Dave answered to the best of his ability while Eric chimed in occasionally. Lucy and Harmony tripped over numerous apologies, and Jannet tried to fill in their blanks as they explained their story. The chaos created a cacophony as they all chattered over one another, the small compartment filled with pointless sound I wished would quiet. My ears rang with the reporters' past questions, with Will's voice, with the meaningless conversations carried out in front of me, but I didn't dare disrupt their small moment of respite. Eric, Dave, Sasha, Jannet, Lucy, Harmony: they deserved time to talk about nothing for a while. I didn't disturb them for that reason, choosing to observe their friendly-yet-disorganized exchanges from afar. It warmed my heart when Sasha got both Dave and Eric to laugh at a comment she made, and although I would've wanted to sit and process in peace, I was glad to hear their loud laughter once again. It had been too long since any of us found humor in anything.

The second the plane landed, the seven of us were greeted by President Dassian's displeased secretary, who immediately made a grab for my arm to tug me away from the others. I despised leaving them, and I fervently opposed it until Dave assured they were only going to the nearby hospital just a few blocks down for inspection. I relented after recalling Eric's shrapnel wound—loosely held together by hideous, black stitches—Sasha's forehead gash, Harmony's arm injury from the river, Lucy's excessive fatigue, and Jannet's weakness. The sight of these people I now considered friends walking away tempted me more than once to run after them, but Dave squeezed my hand and said, "You'll see them soon, sweetheart, I promise. Right after this meeting with President Dassian, you can see them, okay? Deal?"

His touch brought on a rush of gratitude, and I leaned against Dave for support when it struck me how lucky we were to still be alive. "Deal," I muttered. Dave insisted I visited Dassian's office while he followed the others to the hospital to watch over them. I followed his suggestion reluctantly, walking behind Dassian's secretary as we exited the helipad to wait beside the elevator doors. I vaguely heard murmurs from inside the elevator as it rose to meet us, and I thought I heard someone familiar shouting, "No," but I couldn't quite place the voice. The doors slid open then, and out stepped a short, hunched over older man with a head of wispy, wild, salty white hair and frosty blue, vacant eyes. He leaned heavily on a cane in his right hand, and when our gazes met, I saw something in his face, past his white-rimmed glasses, wrinkles, and age spots… scars, all shaped into an S, the Society's symbol. Only one man I knew had those markings, and I found his name on my tongue: "Charles Woobi."

He seemed startled that I had used his full name. "Zelda Jadestone," he said back as if this were a game, but I wasn't amused in the slightest.

"I thought you were dead." It came out much harsher than I intended, but I didn't apologize.

"The thought is mutual."

There were still so many questions whirling in my head, so many things left unsaid, so many people I wanted to ask about, but I couldn't stop myself from blurting, "How are you alive?"

He dropped his gaze. "I'm not living, Zelda Ellyn. Merely surviving."

I understood. His words caused me to break our distance and wrap my arms around him, letting him envelop me in the familiarity of his arms, despite my taller height. He stunk of ash and grief. "Where's Eve?" I asked him, lowering my head so that it rested against his shoulder.

Mr. Woobi brought a hand up to cradle the back of my head, but I noticed how he stiffened in our embrace. "You saw David earlier, yes?" After I voiced my answer, he said, "Don't worry about anyone else. Look at me, please." I pulled away to stare into his eyes, cloudy, hazed-over, and distant, the way they were when his past overtook him. "I made you a promise that day we left the Society, didn't I? You made me promise you that we would go back for Peter Adrian Jadestone under any circumstance." He lifted his head higher into the air, so I couldn't misplace his intentions. "I am prepared to keep that promise now, dear girl. I am ready. It's time you're repaid for all you have done."

I scowled at him and backed out of our embrace, a gross feeling of shame crawling all over my body. An image of Will flashed through my mind then. It was *my* fault he was gone—I knew that—and just thinking about him made me want to run. "All I've done is cause destruction and death. The gift of having Peter back is not the kind of punishment I deserve."

The elder's expression softened at my words, and he placed a calloused hand on my shoulder. "You've seen enough punishment to last a lifetime, Zelda Ellyn."

"I could have saved all of them by the Society, Mr. Woobi. I could've stopped the village fire if I had just stayed away."

He said nothing, but I didn't need a verbal response; a deep understanding passed between the both of us. Mr. Woobi nodded in the direction of Dassian's secretary and instructed, "Go and do what they tell you. Peter will be your peace, Zelda Ellyn, I promise you that much. It'll all be over soon."

Just as the secretary's nails dug themselves into my forearm, I turned back to him. "It won't ever truly be over, will it, Mr. Woobi?"

"No, my dear," he answered honestly. "No, it won't."

"And things will never be the same, will they? I'll never go back to being the girl I was before."

"Zelda Ellyn," Mr. Woobi proclaimed after sympathy swept over his face. "It takes someone brave to pick up a gun and fire, but it takes someone braver to put down her weapon and fight with her words instead. You won't ever be the same girl again. That part is true. But you'll be stronger. You *are* stronger. I am so proud of you, my dear. More than I think you understand." He gripped my shoulders to give me one firm shake. "Go show the world what real strength looks like."

The elder guided me into the elevator that took me one level down from the roof to President Dassian's spacious, ostentatious office, where the president himself greeted me as he did the first time we met—with a nasally, ugly laugh and a fake grin on his round, flushed face. He kissed both my cheeks in greeting and commanded I sit at one end of his conference table; the second I did so, his eyes narrowed, his smile turned into a deeply rooted frown, and he barked, "What were you thinking, Zelda?"

I took the golden bullet out of my pocket and started twirling it through my fingers. "I had to save Eric Stellenzer. I wasn't thinking of anything else but that." From my sitting position, the knife dug itself into my stomach, so I pulled it out of my pocket secretly and sat on it.

The president mumbled something under his breath before running a hand over his forehead in annoyance. "You disappeared," he stated. "Do you know how many people thought you had died? There were no survivors after the massacre, Zelda, which means no one could testify to your existence. What's worse: you could have died! The cause would have been lost if Lucy Catray and Harmony Holland hadn't decided to film all your little adventures, and Allyson Killians wasn't a wizard at reporting. Zelda Jadestone, I'm going to ask again: what would make you jeopardize all we've worked so hard to build together?"

"Allyson Killians is alive?"

President Dassian sighed and rubbed his forehead some more, clearly frustrated with me. "Yes, she's alive. Now please, Zelda, answer me. Why didn't you contact my people right away? Why did you stay out there when you knew it was dangerous?"

I leaned forward in my seat as my mind began to reel from all this new information. "How many others survived the fire? Can you tell me some of their names? Where are they now?" *They could be alive.* It didn't matter what state I would find them in; I only needed to see the people who looked to me so blindly, who took me in so lovingly, who I had considered family.

"Insta-Aid handles survivors of a disaster; I certainly do not," Dassian said with a hint of disgust in his voice. "That does not matter right now. What do matter are your foolish actions over the past six days and their impact on this coming war. You must understand that these actions cannot be allowed. You blatantly disobeyed orders to travel to Neweryork. Then, once the battle was lost, you fled into the woods where absolutely no one could track you down. You stupidly get yourself kidnapped by Societan supporters, no less, and then you almost drown in a raging river. Do you not see how ridiculously reckless that is? It's like you have no regard for your safety and well-being, or, for that matter, the well-being of this state."

"But you got some good footage, didn't you?" I sneered. "Lucy and Harmony filmed me unknowingly through all of it, so you got good, raw footage of me to broadcast to the public for your war. C'mon, Mr. President. I may be young, but I have seen enough for you to know by now that I am not stupid. You're upset with me because I didn't check with you before doing what I did, and I could have died at an inconvenient time for you in some of these situations. You want to talk about the well-being of this state, Mr. President? Fine. Then tell me why you agreed to send untrained civilians to the Society to get slaughtered."

President Dassian knitted his thick, coarse, black eyebrows. "Excuse me?"

"I watched people die." President Dassian looked stunned, but I persisted: "I watched the only home I have ever known burn to the ground. I watched people I cared about get broken by the beginnings of a war I don't even want to fight. Did you really expect me to come running back to you after witnessing all that? Did you honestly think I would want to return to the city, making speeches on a subject that has killed thousands? Did you seriously believe I would be *okay* after that? I wish I knew what you were thinking when you heard the news, but I can almost guarantee your thoughts weren't what the public would want to hear."

The president flared his nostrils. "What are you insinuating?"

"What do you think of what happened?" I bit back.

Dassian crossed his arms. "It's a tragedy. Caleb Woobi murdered thousands in a couple of hours. We were completely unprepared, but those people did not die in vain. This is a stepping stone to something bigger. This provides us with an incredibly unique opportunity to use this sorrow to turn public opinion. Tragedy has a humorous way of convincing people to want to fight."

"We were *not* 'unprepared,'" I bellowed. "Caleb's Uniforms were already waiting in the gorge when we got there. Caleb's bomber planes must've already been in the air when we got there, too, because not once did the boundary vanish to let the planes leave. You're telling me you don't have the Society surveilled? You didn't see the boundary disintegrate before the troops arrived? Am I supposed to believe this was some unfortunate accident? I don't buy it."

"Caleb Woobi hacked into our surveillance system and shut it down hours beforehand. We had no way of knowing," explained Dassian.

"And that didn't set off any alarms?" My rage threatened to destroy me, so I took a deep breath before spitting, "You're a coward, Mr. President. You're a fraud, you're a liar, and you're a coward. Now if you'll excuse me, I'm going to see the people who survived a fire that you, in part, caused." I got out of my chair defiantly and slipped the knife back in my pocket as I marched over to the elevator doors.

President Dassian scurried and slammed his hand over the elevator button before I had a chance to press it. "You will sit back down in that chair *right now*," he ordered me menacingly. "Although this war cannot be stopped—the momentum is much too strong now—I can most certainly charge your brother with high treason for appearing in Caleb's cyberattacks. I'm guessing, after fighting this hard to get him back, you don't want that, do you, Zelda Jadestone?"

He had won. Any mention of Peter was enough for me to walk shamefully back to my chair and sit down, glaring at the man making his way back to his own seat as I retorted, "Peter isn't the enemy."

President Dassian shook his head. "Of course, he isn't. Caleb Woobi is, and if you pull another stunt like you did this time, you will be, too. I don't want you—"

"You don't want me, what? You don't want me not telling you my every move? You don't want me doing something that isn't scripted or pre-planned? You don't want me ruining your show? Mr. President, if I am to help you—"

"If?!" he yelled, interrupting me as he bolted out of his seat and slammed his hands down onto the table. "What is this talk of 'if'? You came here demanding *I* help *you* to free your brother. Is that not what I have been trying to do this entire time? Is that not your final goal? Is that not why we are speaking right now? I have kept up my end of the deal, darling. Now it's time you keep up yours."

I stood up as well and placed one hand over my heart, feigning a shocked and hurt look on my face. "Oh, I'm sorry, I didn't realize our deal incorporated sending innocent people with no previous military experience to their deaths and burning an entire village down!" My words came out as sharp as the knife in my pocket.

"I did not burn that village down!" he shouted.

"Yet the blood of those people still stains your hands!" I yelled. "How can you live with yourself?"

He pulled out a handkerchief from his pocket to wipe the sweat off his brow. "We have to cooperate if you are to free your little brother and the rest of the people trapped in that Society," he stated, breathing heavily through his nostrils in an effort to control his temper. "You will stay here, on the 152nd floor, which was originally designed for state diplomats to stay, but no matter. I will give you and your friends these apartments, and you will occupy them for the foreseeable future while you carry out your end of our deal. There will be guards stationed at your door as a safety precaution."

"So, I'm a prisoner."

President Dassian shook his head at my words. "You're not a prisoner anymore, Zelda Jadestone. Those days in the Society are over now. You're free, and soon, so your brother will be. So *everyone* will be. Once we win this, there will be peace. I promise you."

He took my immediate reticence as an opportunity to speak again. "You will make a speech regarding the massacre in a couple of days, and then, we will begin to launch full-blown cyberattacks against the Society with you as our shining star. Zelda, I know the pain you must be experiencing right now is terrible and draining, but I urge you to look past it and fight for what this world really needs more of: freedom. You can give others hope. You can inspire. You can change the narrative. All you need is a little bravery to step up and do it." He smiled at me and stuck out his hand for me to shake. "So, I will ask you: are we on the same page?"

"What do I get out of all this?" I asked, still unsure.

"Your brother back home with you, where he belongs."

"And you, President Dassian? What do *you* get out of all this?"

His smile almost blinded me with how white his teeth were. "I get the wonderful satisfaction of knowing my citizens have their loved ones back home. You'll find we often land on the right side of history."

"Because you've rewritten the narrative, Mr. President. History doesn't equal truth."

Dassian rolled his eyes at my statement. "Enough talk, Zelda Jadestone. Can we agree?"

I couldn't trust him, not after the events outside the Society, the village fire, *Will*. How could I openly conspire with a murderer? How could I work with a man who didn't care about any of the people I had watched suffer? How could I honor their sacrifices in that way? I couldn't. I wouldn't.

Dassian sensed my unease and lowered his outstretched hand. "You don't have to like me, darling, but even you must recognize that I am the lesser of two evils. I did not send my army to kill innocent people, nor did I drop bombs on any unarmed civilization. *Caleb Woobi* did those things, Zelda Jadestone, not me. Will our cause profit off this tragedy? Of course. But no one has more to gain from these unspeakable horrors than Caleb. Let me show you something."

The president directed my attention to the large monitor positioned in the corner of his office, wedged between the two walls. At first, the screen remained black, but once Dassian pressed a button on his remote, the television erupted into the ear-splitting sounds of gunfire, screaming, and my name, over and over again. The video was too dark to make out anything specific, but that didn't matter; one only needed to hear the sounds of the dying as they screeched to know the meaning. The chaotic scene was overwhelming, and I almost yelled for Dassian to turn it off before that portion of the video ended with a lasting image of the village engulfed in flames before it faded to shadows, the same shadows Caleb used to conceal his true identity.

"Citizens of Neweryork and its surrounding regions," addressed Caleb from his place hidden in the dark. "When will you see that you are all nothing but groomed sheep for slaughter? What will it take to make you see the consequences of following the girl with intent to kill? I have no desire to harm you. I want to leave you be, our two societies coexisting in peaceful disregard for the other's existence, yet you continue to meddle in my affairs, and for why? I do not wish to punish you, but I will. I already have. And where was your savior, Zelda Jadestone? Where was she while your people stained my grass red? Where was she when that peaceful village collapsed in ash? Where was she when you needed her to guide you, since you are incapable of leading yourselves? Wake up, my sheep. She is not your God. She is not your savior. She will not and cannot save you from this hellfire. But I am, and I can." The leader of the Society grinned. "I can easily make your pain vanish. I can stop attacking you. I can let you live if you stop this meaningless quest to kill me, if you stop attempting to tarnish my life's work, if you let this Zelda Jadestone go. I can assure you she will destroy you before you ever reach my door."

He receded from the screen, allowing for another image to take his place. In a stark white room knelt Peter, his dark eyes so bloodshot that it took me several seconds to recognize him. His hands were handcuffed in front of him, and his once-rosy skin looked gray, stained by two lines of tears that dripped down his cheeks. "Zelda," he gasped. "Please." Videos of bodies strewn through the grass, ashes of obliterated buildings, the rage of the river water lingered on the screen, and Peter exhaled a final word: "Enough."

The video cut dead, and I fell to my knees.

President Dassian walked to stand beside me and pat my back. "He's the enemy, darling," he said. "Not me. Look at what he's doing to your brother, your little brother. Together, we can stop him. We can kill him. We will. You just need to put some faith in me. I know what it looks like, but I promise you, this is all for the right cause. Focus your energy on someone who deserves to die for his crimes, Zelda Jadestone. You will soon discover that man is not me."

The flames inside of me flickered from the image of seeing my brother in pain, and I found myself rising to shake hands with a man I did not trust. "We can't fail," I told him. "Caleb can't win. Peter can't die."

"We won't fail, darling," President Dassian guaranteed me with an optimistic smile. "We have you."

Two guards came to escort me out of President Dassian's office, into the elevator, and to my new living quarters after my conversation with him was over. Both were burly, strong men with guns slung across their shoulders and badges on their chests, but only one grinned the second he saw me. His short red hair reminded me quite a bit of Sharlee Davidson's coloring, but his smile and the twinkle in his blue-green eyes were something all his own. He introduced himself as Gunther Mefedee, second-in-command in the security department, a title in which he took great pride. Multiple different patterns covered all four of his limbs, but when asked why he had so many "skin paintings," as I called them, he shook in violent laughter for what seemed like forever.

"They're tats," he tried to explain to me, still chuckling, but the other one was quick to shut down his laughter, reprimanding him for not staying vigilant.

My other guard's tone wasn't as amicable. After he introduced himself as LeRoy Thompson—head of security and assigned as my personal bodyguard for the foreseeable future—he remained quiet, but I took his silence as an opportunity to observe his features. His ebony skin tone was much richer in color than Sasha's sepia-brown coloring. He buzzed his coarse, kinky, black hair on the sides of his skull, leaving it just a little longer on top, but not by much. His wider-set nose fit his square face well, and I didn't think I had ever met an individual with as sharp of a jawline as his. His shiny, dark eyes stared down at me almost accusingly, like I had offended him somehow. If I had possessed any energy left, I would've stared right back.

We arrived on floor 152 and walked down the hall, passing numerous doors along the way before arriving at a door that had my name blinking at me on a screen. Gunther put his badge up to the screen to unlock the door and smiled down at me when he opened it to let me in. "If you need anything, Miss Jadestone, we'll be right outside," he said sweetly. I thanked him graciously and tried to tell him he didn't have to call me "Miss Jadestone," that I was just Zelda, but LeRoy had already closed the door behind him before I had a chance to get the words out.

My room was beautiful in that modern sense, even though I considered it my personal prison cell. Spacious and with a great view of the city from the common area and the bedroom, I felt a bit out of place in such a strange, luxurious setting. There were too many gadgets, too much furniture, too many *things* that I simply didn't need or want.

I sat on the couch and curled up with a pillow on my lap, closing my eyes to try and ignore the ache I felt opening again in my chest. *What have you done?* accused that nagging voice in my head. *You're about to condemn thousands more to die.* I knew the voice was right, but all I could see behind my eyelids was Peter's face shifting from peaceful to agonizing every time I blinked, and it gave me the courage I needed to disregard the little voice. I thought of Will and what he would have thought about these new circumstances, but that was too deep of a wound, so I scampered off the couch and ran into the bedroom, as if trying to escape my own thoughts.

Connected to the large bedroom was a bathroom that I walked in just to look around. I found myself staring at my reflection in the gigantic mirror that covered the entire wall, tilting my head slightly and making strange faces just to affirm the reflection was mine. I remembered not recognizing the lost girl in the mirror ages ago, back in the Society, but as I looked now, I did not recognize this girl either. My hair was tangled more than it had ever been before, and I brought my fingers up to try and detangle the knots at the ends. Gigantic purple bruises covered my neck from Kane's iron grip around my throat four days before, and another bruise had developed on my right bicep from Eric's hold on me when I had tried to dive after Will. I lifted my filthy shirt to see a slash across my stomach from when the knife scraped it in the village. My nails were raw and throbbing from chewing them off. My skin looked pale and almost yellow, with dark blue and purple circles underneath both my bleary, tired eyes. *Who am I?* I asked myself as I pinched my cheeks to bring back some color. I wasn't the same girl who used to sneak out of her househut every Wednesday night to meet with Dave. I wasn't the same girl who loved to hear Charles Woobi tell his many tales of life beyond what she knew. I wasn't *me*.

That thought terrified me, so I rushed to climb into the bed and hide under the multiple different purple, gray, and white blankets. It was dark and warm underneath all the different layers, but eventually, I had to peek my head out to get a good intake of air. Shadows scared me, and I could feel my heart beating through my skin. *Inhale. Exhale. Repeat,* I thought over and over like a mantra, but it didn't work. Nothing relieved my fears.

I heard shouting coming from right outside my main door, and I removed the blankets from my body to investigate. I opened the door to see Sasha with her hands on her hips, arguing with LeRoy and Gunther to allow her to do something. A large white bandage covered the gash across her forehead, and its brightness stood out against her dark skin. She scowled when she saw me staring at her curiously. "Are you going to help me or not, Jadestone?" she asked with an annoyed tone to her voice.

"I don't know what you're trying to do, exactly," I answered back honestly.

She rolled her eyes and turned her attention back to LeRoy and Gunther. "Let me in. She and I have been through a lot together, haven't we, Zelda? We almost died together several times when your organization failed to protect her and your own citizens." She lifted her eyebrow challengingly at them both and smirked when LeRoy frowned. "Zelda, can you please tell these two idiots that we're friends? They won't believe me, obviously."

"We're friends," I found myself saying, immediately squinting at Sasha inquisitively the moment those words left my mouth.

Gunther eyed me up and down before putting on a smile. "You can go in," he told Sasha, stepping out of the way to make room for her to enter my apartment.

LeRoy still wasn't convinced, and he blocked the entrance with his leg to stop her from going in. His eyes narrowed at her muscular frame accusingly. "I don't think so," he snarled. "President's orders: no one without security clearance goes into this apartment."

Sasha laughed and raised a hand to push against LeRoy's chest. "Oh, that's cute. You think I need permission from a man to do something!"

LeRoy looked as though he was seconds away from arresting her when I assured him that I had invited her to visit. My words put him at ease somewhat, and after consideration, he relented and allowed Sasha entry.

Sasha cackled louder, sidestepped LeRoy's blockade, and winked at him. "See, boys? Not so hard." She bolted the door before my guards could respond and went to sit on my couch leisurely.

I scurried over to go join her, copying her position as I tucked my legs underneath me. "What are you doing here? Where are the others?"

"Eric, Jannet, and that Dave guy are on this same floor with you and me," she said. "Lucy and Harmony went off to their own apartments somewhere in this city." She scowled at the mention of them. "Traitors."

"I didn't know they had anything to betray," I said.

Sasha gave me a disbelieving look. "We had a pretty good troop going, I thought. Eric is one of the only decent guys I've ever met. Jannet is like our wise grandmother. Lucy and Harmony are clueless but likable enough, and

Will felt like he could've been my annoying younger brother. We could have lived out in the forest forever, just the seven of us."

"Will's dead," I told her.

"Like I don't know that?" she snapped.

"I wish he wasn't."

Sasha eyed me with what I read as sympathy before she softened her voice to mutter, "Me too."

I lowered my head in shame. "I'm sorry I didn't do more to save Will," I exhaled, untangling my legs from underneath me to draw them up toward my stomach. My knife uncomfortably poked my skin. "I'm sorry for bringing you here. I know it's not what you wanted."

Sasha didn't respond for a long time; I could feel her eyes traveling over my body for what felt like eons before she finally said, "You're different than I thought you were, you know that? We actually matter to you." Sasha made a disgruntled noise at the back of her throat. "Oh, gross. Don't make me start caring about you now, Jadestone. You'd have to kill me."

The corners of my mouth perked up. "Noted."

We traded identical amused smirks before descending into a comfortable quiet, both of us content with getting lost in our own respective thoughts for a while. By the time I glanced her way again, Sasha had fallen asleep in the corner of the couch. Not wishing to leave her alone, I retreated into my bedroom to take the extra blankets from my bed and drape them across her sleeping form. I withdrew into the other side of the couch, slumping into the armrest for comfort, and tried to concentrate on anything other than the knife slowly digging itself further into my side, a harsh reminder of the burden I now carried.

CHAPTER 15

The sunshine brightly streaming through my lavishly large windows woke me the next morning; I had to squint and blink several times to adjust to the change in lighting. I surveyed my living area to find Sasha in the kitchen smirking at me with two mugs of some steaming brown liquid in her hands. She crossed the room and handed me a cup as she proceeded to sit down next to me on the couch. The drink actually smelled quite good, but the moment I took a sip to taste it, I wrinkled my nose and stuck out my tongue in disgust as I set it down onto the table gently so as not to offend her.

Sasha raised an eyebrow at my reaction. "Not into coffee, huh?" she teased as she watched me wipe remaining drops of the stuff from my upper lip. "You *are* stranger than I thought. People live off this stuff, you know." To prove her point, she took a huge gulp and smiled when she swallowed.

"It's a bit bitter for my liking," I replied.

Sasha didn't get a chance to finish her coffee before someone knocked on my door once, not bothering to wait for a response before she entered with a flourish, her long, straight, blonde hair swishing effortlessly behind her. She stepped into the living room with a commanding presence, her checkered, asymmetrical, watermelon pink miniskirt hugging her narrow hips so tightly, I wondered if she had enough room to breathe. Her once-brown eyes were now a bright fuchsia, the same color as her three-inch heels. She grinned once she stood in the middle of the room, her dazzlingly white teeth distracting me as she greeted, "Zelda Jadestone! Miss me?"

"Allyson?" I asked disbelievingly, watching as Gunther, LeRoy, Eric, Dave, Mr. Woobi, Jannet, Lucy, Harmony, and a bunch of other people I didn't recognize trailed in behind her. I pinched the back of my hand to confirm I wasn't hallucinating. Out of the corner of my eye, I saw Sasha grip her mug tighter, as if preparing for someone to confiscate it.

"Hey there, gorgeous!" Allyson squealed. She clasped her hands together, the tips of her fingers covered by thick, acrylic, neon pink nails, and wiggled her perfectly sculpted eyebrows. "Ready to get to work?"

"Uh..." I observed the flurry of activity happening around me: the unknown people twisting my kitchen island bar stools around to face us; Lucy, Jannet, and Harmony sitting in said stools with their eyes closed; Dave and Eric talking quietly amongst each other; Mr. Woobi staring blankly at the wall in front of him. My head spun from the sudden stimuli. "What..."

"Knew Magazine has requested another cover shoot with you and your little band of buddies here," Allyson elaborated. "We're here to get you ready." Allyson turned her head to talk to the girl standing beside her: "Make sure they're dressed and prepped in two hours maximum; we need to leave by eleven." The action reminded me of how Allyson would interact with Marley, her cheery intern and my self-proclaimed "biggest fan," but when I asked about the whereabouts of the heavier-set, strawberry blonde girl, Allyson's smile slipped off her face. "She's taking some time off," Allyson said.

"Her older sister died in the village fire or something," explained another random person in the room, preoccupied with tracing the outline of Harmony's eyes in black pencil. "Or was it her older brother? I don't remember."

"You don't remember which of her family members died in a fire?" repeated Eric incredulously. Dave muttered something I couldn't hear in Eric's ear, and Eric nodded in agreement. The two boys traded disapproving looks.

Allyson shrugged, her upper body constrained by a ribbed, long-sleeved, white shirt neatly tucked into her skirt. "She'll be back soon enough. She can't afford the unpaid days off. That's enough about Marley; Zelda, you and your friend on the couch need to get ready to go. Cover shoot is in less than three hours."

Sasha scoffed and scooted farther into the cushions. "Yeah, no, that's not happening. Have fun with that, but count me out."

Allyson stepped closer to the couch until she towered over Sasha and me, her manufactured-sweet perfume wafting over us and making my nose hairs tingle as I fought back a sneeze. "Anyone associated with Zelda Jadestone is required to stand behind her on this cover to show their support for her mission. That includes Charles and David Woobi, Eric Stellenzer, and the people she saved after the Societan Massacre. The only exceptions are William Finnley and Eve Redding for obvious reasons."

Mr. Woobi swayed on his feet, suddenly pale, at the mention of his wife, and Dave swiftly lowered his head to cough into the crook of his arm, a clear distraction for the silence that now encompassed the room. "What?" I inquired upon seeing everyone's reactions, watching as Mr. Woobi leaned against the closest wall and Eric wrapped an arm around Dave's shoulder in solidarity. "Why is Eve an exception? Where is she?"

"Dea—"

"Gone," Mr. Woobi interrupted Allyson from his place against the wall, his eyes betraying his torment. "The flames got to her before I could."

The news punched me in the gut, and I struggled to find a response adequate enough to utter to the man whose heart had ripped in half. I could see the years on his face, his grief hidden in the wrinkles around his mouth, eyes, and forehead, his pain written so clearly in his icy irises that I hated myself for overlooking before. Although Eve and I had our differences, I respected her strength and admired her composure in the face of adversity, especially alone, with her husband, son, and grandchild locked away somewhere she couldn't touch for fourteen years. I knew she loved her family, loved that little village she commanded, loved me, even, and grief struck me deeply.

"Wait, so Caleb killed his mom?" Sasha questioned, and her question brewed a new kind of rage within me.

Caleb dropped incendiary bombs not only on innocent men, women, and children, but on his own mother. Caleb didn't care who perished so long as Mr. Woobi or I died with them. Caleb robbed his mother of the chance to ever see her family whole again, and that alone was enough to make me rise to my feet and declare, "I'll do the photoshoot. I'll do the speech. Whatever it takes. Caleb cannot keep killing."

"Me too," Sasha resounded, standing up beside me. "Let's get this piece of sh—"

"That… that disgusting vulture," Lucy interrupted awkwardly, delicate hands on her hips.

"Good one, Luce," Sasha remarked.

Lucy didn't pick up on Sasha's sarcasm as the former smiled at the supposed compliment.

I made sure Mr. Woobi saw the sincerity in my gaze when I added, "For Eve."

"For Eve!" the rest of the room echoed. And we began.

I allowed the strangers in the room, who finally introduced themselves as the makeup, hair, and fashion teams, to "beautify" me in whichever way they saw fit, my mind too preoccupied with my anguish to care. Once I agreed to cooperate, they hurriedly ushered the men into my bedroom area to prep them for the photoshoot individually, and instructed me to lay on the couch to laser the hair off my legs and underneath my arms. The procedure was quick and painless, but when asked about its purpose, the hair team gazed at me sympathetically and said, "It's about time you're polished up, sweetie." They tried to do the same procedure on Sasha, but she refused so harshly that they dared not argue.

I felt naked and bald, uncomfortable with the new sensation of my pants rubbing my skin, but I continued to put faith in their process nonetheless. The hair team applied direct heat to my hair next, straightening it and angularly cutting the dead ends so it framed my slim, long face beautifully, the way Harmony's hair naturally fell. They pulled Lucy's mousy brown hair out of its usual low, messy ponytail to gently curl it around the edges of her face, giving it beautiful waves that made her already-innocent appearance that much more youthful. The team plaited Jannet's long, salted black hair into two front pieces to give her a mature-yet-maternal look, and the way the braids framed her face made her square jawline that much sharper. Sasha advised against them messing with her hair too much, so the hair team chose to only coil her hair to tighten her curls, accentuating the bigness of her gorgeous natural locks. Once the hair team finished, Sasha's afro looked like a black, springy, cloud-like halo around her head; when I pointed this out, she fluffed the bottom of it near the nape of her neck and quipped, "You *wish* your hair did this, Jadestone."

"I do," I told her sincerely. "It looks pretty."

Sasha bit the inside of her cheek to keep from smiling.

The fashion team dressed us five women in traditional, army-green camouflage that cinched our waists. The stiff fabric combined with our homogeneity reminded me strikingly of Uniforms back in the Society, but I chose to keep the observed similarity to myself.

The makeup team applied our makeup the same way as well: dark powder applied to our eyelids, a rim of black pencil in the outlines of our eyes, flesh-colored liquid covering our skin for everyone but Jannet, whose tanned, sun-kissed skin they left alone in favor of emphasizing her age. I didn't enjoy the weighted feeling of the liquid and powder on my bare face, but again, I didn't argue.

Once the team applied some sticky, glossy, clear substance to our lips, they announced that we were ready and ordered the men to emerge from my bedroom suite. I had my back turned when they eventually reentered the common area, but once I turned around, the five of them, all dressed in various outfits, stopped in their tracks to stare at me in shock.

Eric's eyes widened, and his Adam's apple bobbed as he attempted to swallow. "Wow," he exhaled almost to himself, bringing a hand up to rub the back of his reddened neck just as his cheeks began to glow pink. His hair, matted with blood and dirt just a few days before, had been blow-dried to appear fluffy and soft, a combination that made me flex my fingers to squash the urge to run them through it. The black boots he wore accentuated his already-tall height. The color of his stiff buttoned-up jacket and pants matched my jumpsuit, and the green emphasized the green of his eyes, still as gentle and beautiful as ever.

Eric took my breath away, but I scrambled enough air together to respond, "Wow yourself. Looks like you became a Uniform after all."

Eric and I are walking Peter to school on the way to the Career Building when a squadron of eighty or so Uniforms marches by in perfect formation. We slow to a halt to watch them walk past, enraptured in awe at their precision, but right as Peter opens his mouth to say something, Eric jokes, "I wonder if I would look any good in one of those stiff suits."

I throw my head back and laugh. "Oh yeah," I tease. "Real good."

Eric turns to smile at me, shoves his hands into the pockets of his gray sweatpants, and shakes his head as if to swish his hair, despite his recent serious haircut a few days after his fourteenth birthday. "Well, in that case, where do I sign up to be a Uniform?"

I drop my jaw in mock surprise. "You wouldn't."

"Would I look good as a Uniform?" Peter asks sheepishly, his tone barely above a whisper, but I'm too busy gazing at Eric to notice his small voice.

Eric shrugs as we resume our walk, Peter now trailing behind us. "You never know. One of these days, maybe I will, Zelda. Then maybe you'd miss me."

"Hm," I hum through pursed lips. "Maybe."

Eric smiles wider and replies, "I'll take 'maybe,'" before twisting to start walking backward. "Peter!" he calls out, stretching out his hand for my ten-year-old brother to take. "C'mon, bud, walk a little faster. We don't want you to be late."

Eric grinned in surprise at my joke, and although they dusted his face in the tiniest layer of makeup, I could see the crinkles around his eyes when he chuckled breathily. "Well," he breathed, "do I look good at least?" When I nodded, he dropped his gaze, blushed a deeper red, almost the color of the Uniforms' boots, and said, "Zelda, you look—"

"Stunning," Dave finished, and I tore my gaze away from the dark-haired boy to observe the ex-Uniform in a customary black business suit, the same one his grandfather wore beside him and one that looked eerily similar to suits Caleb wore. His golden-blond hair had been clipped into a military style cut akin to how it looked in the Society, but the darkness under his electric-blue eyes was new, as was the heavy makeup they used to try and conceal it. "You look stunning, sweetheart."

"You don't look too bad yourself," I retorted, tongue in cheek as I noticed the way his arm and shoulder muscles filled out his suit jacket.

He crossed the room to quickly peck my lips, and the entire room swooned apart from Sasha, LeRoy, and Eric, who gagged, rolled his eyes, and looked away, respectively.

"You do look nice, Miss," remarked Gunther in his navy-blue slacks and shirt, a bulky bulletproof vest wrapped around his abdomen, an outfit identical to LeRoy's. "All you girls clean up nice." We barely had time to thank him before Allyson instructed us to get into the vehicles awaiting us downstairs.

I slowed my pace to match Mr. Woobi's at the back of the group as we all filed out the door. "I'm sorry about Eve," I said. "I admired her a lot."

Mr. Woobi leaned so heavily on his cane as he walked, I was afraid he would snap it in two. He didn't reply to my sentiments, only snorted in response, and the two of us spent the entire ride to Knew Magazine's headquarters in silence, content with listening to the idle chatter around us. I noticed Dave didn't participate in the conversation much either, instead choosing to sit up straight and bounce his leg repeatedly. I placed my hand on his bouncing knee to calm him, and although he smiled in gratitude, my touch did nothing to stop his anxious tick.

We arrived at Knew Magazine's headquarters fifteen minutes late, but the interviewer who stood outside to greet us didn't look irked in the slightest, his once-platinum blond hair now a deep maroon, still gelled as three spikes on the top of his skull. I recognized him instantly as the man who had interviewed me before, Vincent, and despite our less-than-enjoyable first encounter, I was always grateful to see a familiar face.

He approached me first, cupping my face in his manicured hands and air-kissing both of my cheeks to avoid ruining my makeup. "Zelda Jadestone, looking as powerful as ever," he announced. "Please, take your seats. Let's get this show on the road."

We all took our respective assigned seats across from Vincent, two rows of five chairs each, with Gunther, LeRoy, Jannet, Harmony, and Lucy in the back row and Mr. Woobi, Sasha, Eric, Dave, and me in the front. The cameras around us focused on my face, and as I felt their pressing stares, I took the golden bullet out of my pocket to play with it between my fingers to keep myself occupied. Before we began, Vincent introduced himself to everyone and instructed them on the interview process, but before anyone could ask any questions, he motioned for the cameras to begin rolling.

The first half of the interview was relatively standard. Vincent asked predictable questions regarding the Societan Massacre to the six of us who witnessed it: "How shocked were you when the Uniforms opened fire? How surprised were you when Zelda Jadestone emerged from one of the trucks? How brave was Zelda to save you from the senseless killing?" To Mr. Woobi and Dave, he asked expected questions about the village fire: "How terrible was it to witness that? How unprepared was the tiny, unarmed village for such a brutal attack? How crazy is it that Caleb burned his old home, especially after watching it burn once before?" We answered his questions to the best of our abilities; when one of us got misty-eyed or choked up, another would swoop in and respond. We were all getting through it fairly well until about halfway through, when Vincent stated, "Let me also express my condolences for that little boy, Will is his name? Yeah, my sources say he was a fifteen-year-old named William Finnley. So tragic watching him drown. And so unexpected! What a twist ending."

Vincent stopped his rambling to give one of us the opportunity to interject, but I couldn't form words from the constriction of my chest at the mention of Will. I vaguely heard Sasha spit, "Back up. What do you mean, you watched?" but her accusatory, angry voice was muffled by the sudden water in my ears. The river swallowed me whole again, swirling water causing my body to sway in my seat, despite my efforts to stay still, and I felt nauseous at the memory of Will's body sinking in the water. Eric swallowed hard beside me, but I didn't dare look at him, afraid of what I'd see in his face if I did.

"It was broadcasted on the nightly news a couple days after it happened," Vincent explained. "We saw everything Zelda did: the Societan Massacre, the Redding village burning, the men in the hut, and Will's death. Lucy Catray and Harmony Holland, what made you decide to pick up your cameras and film these moments?"

Eric, Sasha, and I twisted in our seats to glare at Lucy and Harmony, who respectively shrunk in her chair, and adjusted her posture to sit up straighter. "The public has the right to know," answered Harmony evenly. "It was our duty to film what happened to inform the public how cruel Caleb Woobi really is. I mean, look at what he did to those people outside the Northeastern Society, that little village, and gosh, that poor little boy. They deserved to see the truth."

Sasha turned back around, scoffed in her seat, and muttered, "Entitled brat."

Eric grumbled in agreement, but I bit my lip to keep from saying anything.

"You saw how beautifully Zelda handled those moments," Lucy added. "She's a natural, humble leader who made the best decisions she could in those situations. She's honest. We felt the people should get the chance to see that side of her."

These moments, these memories, these intimate pieces of my consciousness had been ripped from my cognitive grasp in an instant, stolen to hand to the masses for inspection, stripping me of whatever freedom I had scavenged. *And for why?* How could anyone watch those moments and see a strong leader? I only saw a girl too caught up in her own selfishness to realize the extent to which she scorched the people around her, the ones who loved her so dearly, those who so blindly died for her. How could anyone not think me a fraud? How could any of these viewers sit and observe the death of such a young, innocent, perfect soul like Will and not consider me a murderer? None of my actions had been fruitful: the mission to the Society failed spectacularly; the village burned to nothing but ash; Abe ended up dead regardless of my efforts; Will barely got to live another twenty-four hours before the river took him, too. I didn't save anyone. I didn't accomplish anything. I didn't rescue Peter. How could anyone paint me as anything less than a failure?

"Zelda," Vincent said, interrupting my thoughts. "We saw footage of you and Will playing some game by the river right before he died; it seemed you two were getting close. Do you have anything to say about his death?"

My vision blurred to become kaleidoscopic from unshed tears, and I sucked in an inhale sharply to keep from sobbing. Other than Peter, there was no one I failed more enormously than Will. How naïve I was to promise something as fickle as safety when Caleb would stop at nothing to destroy me. How stupid I was to think that saving Will from that battlefield would benefit him in the end; anyone who came close to me ended up hurt, it seemed. How hopeful I was to believe that one day soon, Will would get to meet Peter, and the two boys could be my little brothers.

Upon seeing my reaction, Eric promptly instructed Vincent to move on, and Vincent eyed me sympathetically for a second before following Eric's orders and turning to the two Woobis to inquire, "And you two, how are you handling Eve Woobi's death?"

"Next question," Mr. Woobi asserted.

"She was your wife of thirty-seven years, Charles, and you have nothing to say?"

"Next question," Mr. Woobi repeated, louder this time.

"David, what about you? How are you handling the death of your paternal grandmother?" When Dave didn't immediately make a sound, Vincent leaned forward and prompted again, "How do you feel?"

I turned my head to watch Dave's eyes shut tightly, his posture rigid and tense. He shook his head, a clear indication to forgo the question, but that small movement wasn't enough to stop Vincent from exclaiming, "I can see that this is difficult for you. It must be especially difficult knowing that your own father coordinated the attack. Can you speak to that?" When Dave still refused to utter a word, Vincent leaned forward in his seat and added, "Talking to the son of the dictator is such a great opportunity, Mr. Woobi. I—"

"Don't call me that, please," interjected Dave through clenched teeth. "That's what people call my grandfather. I'm just Dave."

"Well then," Vincent cooed. "What does 'just Dave' think about his father blowing up the village?"

The ex-Uniform sat quietly for a moment, his eyes bouncing from the interviewer, to the cameras, to Mr. Woobi, until his gaze finally landed on me, where he lingered for several seconds before proclaiming, "I think someone needs to help him realize what he's done."

Vincent smirked. "And who do you believe that 'someone' is?"

Dave didn't hesitate in his answer this time: "My girlfriend, Zelda Jadestone. She's the person to lead this war against my father, so he comes to terms with what he's done."

Vincent looked to everyone else. "Does everyone agree? Is Zelda Jadestone capable of taking down Caleb Woobi?"

"I hated her at first," declared Sasha suddenly. "I didn't think we needed to fight a war, but now, after watching this Leader Caleb guy purposefully try to drown us, murder so many people, murder Melanie, my girlf... my..." Sasha cleared her throat and swallowed hard. "He deserves for Zelda to take him down, and she can do it, too."

"I agree that Zelda can defeat Caleb," Jannet chimed in. "I'm a retired doctor from the Second Civil War. I've seen many things, but I have never seen a young woman as fearless as Zelda. She is everything Caleb is not."

"Zelda's strong," Lucy added. "All those moments we filmed were real; she didn't know we were filming any of that through the cameras on our clothes. That's really her saving people on the battlefield, talking someone out of suicide, and trying to jump in after that little boy. She cares about her family, but she cares about us, too. She has the strongest, bravest heart. I admire her and her cause so much."

"Once we breach the Northeastern Society, Zelda will kill Caleb Woobi," proclaimed Harmony. "She won't let these deaths we witnessed be in vain, right, Zelda?"

Everyone trained their gazes to me next; the cameras' lenses narrowed to focus on my face, eager for an answer, *the* answer, the resounding "yes" I knew they all anticipated. Who was I to let them down? After everything I had put Eric, Sasha, Jannet, Harmony, and Lucy through, they deserved to hear me say I would kill their perceived enemy. Will and the others who perished deserved to know that I would stop at nothing to extract revenge in their honor. Peter deserved to feel the hatred in my words when I voiced my agreement. Yet I still found it extremely difficult not to pay explicit attention to the way Mr. Woobi uncomfortably shuffled in his seat, or the way Dave began bouncing his knee beside me, or the way my voice wobbled when I declared, "Of course, I will."

Vincent frowned. "Can you say that one more time? I don't think our microphones caught that."

The hairs on the back of my neck rose when Dave's sudden accelerated breathing floated over my skin, but then again, I didn't sympathize with the man who ordered Uniforms to kill innocent, untrained people, who heartlessly set fire to a village full of men, women, and children, who killed a child without hesitation. I couldn't. Caleb Woobi *did* deserve to die. Didn't he? His death would be his last penance for his many, many sins. I would make sure of it. So, when Vincent prompted me again, I had no hesitation, no wobble to my voice, no regret in saying, "Of course, I'll kill him," loud enough for the microphones to carry it to the Society itself.

After Vincent wrapped up the interview, he directed us to another room, where yet another person ordered us to assemble into a staggered pyramid formation with me positioned as the central focal point. The cameramen instructed us to "look disgruntled," and on the note in which we left the interview, it wasn't difficult to channel that anger onto my face, dark eyebrows knitted over my dark eyes, jaw clenched, arms crossed in front of me. The rest of the group promptly followed suit until the cameramen claimed they captured the perfect "power shot." They released us on the basis that the magazine would be published within the week.

Only Dave, LeRoy, and Gunther were in the vehicle with me on the way back to President Dassian's building; I snuggled up next to Dave the second we stepped into the car, and he crowned my forehead with a kiss, lingering there for longer than usual. Dave sat unusually quiet and still, and as I replayed his strange behavior since our reunion, I couldn't help but blurt, "What happened to you?" halfway through the trip. I broke the hold his lips had on my head as I twisted to see his face, so much older than when I had first laid eyes on him, and my pointer finger traced a path along the newfound wrinkles on his forehead, which he crinkled at my touch.

"You don't want to know," he barked, already turning back to the window, his sudden change in attitude frightening me somewhat.

"Yes, I do."

"No, you don't," he tried to reason with me.

"Yes, yes I really do."

"No."

"Yes! Dave—"

"Just tell her," sighed LeRoy, his chin resting on the palm of his hand as he eyed the two of us with distaste. "There's only so much you can keep from Zelda Jadestone."

I raised my chin and huffed triumphantly.

Dave looked incredibly agitated, but I didn't press for information during the first few minutes of his silence, waiting until he wanted to tell me. After it seemed he was fully prepared to not speak at all, he unexpectedly shouted, "I watched people die, okay?! Not just people either, Zelda, but women! Children! The elderly! I watched them all *burn!*"

At his outburst and in order to hide my horror, I tried placing a soothing hand to his shoulder, but he moved away as if my touch scorched his skin.

"Don't touch me, please," he whimpered, and I noticed how his blue eyes, usually so clear and piercing, glazed over, and how his breathing changed from an even rhythm to unsteady intakes of breath followed by trembling exhales, just as it did when Vincent brought up Caleb. "You really want to know what happened that night, Zelda?" he demanded with a fury in his voice akin to when he discovered his lineage.

I could only nod in reply.

"No one was prepared for it," he began. "When Charles came running into the house yelling about some incendiary bombs and that the village was on fire, I laughed. *Laughed.* I was so worried about Eric, Blake, and you that I completely ignored what was actually going on. It wasn't until I smelled the smoke that I finally followed Charles out of the house. So many people were…" He sounded distant as he relived the experience in his head. "They were going to die, Zelda. Everyone was going to die. Charles tried pulling me away into the forest to safety, but I couldn't leave everyone else, not in the condition they were in. I had to run back to them."

I vaguely heard Gunther suck in a breath, as though preparing himself for the rest of it. Out of the corner of my eye, I noticed the way LeRoy leaned toward Dave inquisitively.

Dave tried composing himself, but he failed at doing so; a tear slid down his cheek against his will, although he refused to wipe it away, letting it continue its journey down to his neck. "So I did," he said through a shaky exhale. "I went back for the rest. I tried to save them all, Zelda. I really did." He turned sharply and gripped me by the shoulders. "Believe me!" he screamed. "I tried to save all of them!" When I assured him that I did, that I did believe him, I expected him to relax, but my voice seemed to set him on edge that much more. "I saw Sharlee there," he whispered now, slowly releasing his grasp on me. "She wasn't crying like the other children, though. She seemed… shocked. Confused, just like I was. I picked her up and carried her in my arms, but Zelda, she was coughing so much. Her face was black with soot, Zelda. She kept asking me where her mom was, where her dad was, but I didn't know, I didn't know. I still don't know."

I shrieked in surprise when he twisted to punch the velvet back of his seat, the action causing the entire vehicle to shake. "People were hurting, Zelda. Lots of people. I told them to follow me, that I knew a way out, but I lied. I didn't know a way out. I didn't even know a way *in*. I didn't know anything. I was just trying to save their lives, to save Sharlee, to find you… I couldn't breathe, there was so much smoke."

Once again, I tried placing a hand on him, but he scooted away from me. "They followed the sound of my voice. They heard me and started to pick up and follow me. Some were burnt, some weren't. Some were crying, some weren't. All of them were coughing, though. Just like Sharlee. Everyone coughed. I couldn't see anymore, I couldn't hear anything except for the roar of the fire, I couldn't *feel*. That terrified me, the fact that I couldn't feel. I wanted to die, I think. I don't remember. When I saw Charles again, I fell. I couldn't move anymore, Zelda. Everything felt so heavy. My heart, my legs, my head."

"He yelled at me to stand up and keep going," Dave continued. "So that's what I did. I kept going. I didn't look back at the others, I only ran with Sharlee in my arms, running until I didn't see the fire anymore, but I still haven't run far enough to escape that. I still see it, even now. I still smell the burning. I can still hear the… the screaming." He loosely tapped the side of his head. "All up here, I see it." He turned slowly to face me, a piece of my heart ripping out of my body when he croaked, "But I didn't see you."

"Emergency people from the city arrived, and then, Charles and I realized Eve wasn't with us," Dave gasped, stocky shoulders hunched over. "We learned later she went back to save some people and died trying to help an old friend. She told me when you and I first got there that the population of the village was two thousand or so. Two thousand people, Zelda, and only five hundred survived. I could have saved more than that. I could've done so much more for them. I could have…"

I shushed him gently and decided to cuddle up next to him, my head resting on his shoulder; although initially he sucked in a breath and tensed up, he eventually tilted into my embrace. "You did all you could," I whispered softly, so as not to upset him. "You went back for them instead of running away. You didn't back down from returning to help them. So many more people would be dead if it weren't for you, Dave. The entire village, even."

"But I—"

"She's right," stated LeRoy while wiping away a tear that must've fallen at some point during Dave's speech. "You saved so many lives that night. Five hundred is better than none, and they have you to thank for that. That's a lot of people, 'Just Dave.' You saved that village, whether you want to believe it or not." Gunther nodded in agreement, clearly not trusting himself to speak.

Five hundred, I kept repeating to myself for the rest of the trip. *Five hundred out of two thousand.* Dave and I embraced each other before Gunther and LeRoy led me back up to my room, where all I could do was picture those two thousand dancing around the bonfire the night following our arrival, their smiles illuminated by the beautiful, golden glow of the lights in those jars and the bonfire that burned in front of them. All of them joyous, all of them carefree, none of them ever expecting such an attack in their lives. And now, seventy-five percent of them, dead.

Crawling into my bed, I hid underneath the heavy blankets, shaking with my knees drawn up underneath my body as the images blurred together in my head. Sharlee. Dave. Fire. People yelling. People screaming. Fire. Coughing, bleeding, burning. Fire. All there, for me to picture. Gunther's soft request for me to come out from under my sheets didn't register until a few moments after he said it, but still, my answer would remain the same: "Go away. I want to be left alone."

Zelda, the villagers exclaim, elated by my arrival into their simple lives.

Zelda, the villagers scream, looking for a way to escape these flames I caused.

Zelda, Dave reprimands disapprovingly, hot tears streaming down his face as he struggles to face his new reality. *Two thousand people, Zelda, and only five hundred survived.*

"I don't think it's a good idea to be alone right now, Miss," Gunther pleaded after I tried to dismiss him. "Please come into the living room for me while I whip up something for you to eat, okay? Miss?" When I didn't respond, still too stunned to process his words, my guard gently peeled the blankets from my body. "Come now, Miss Jadestone," he begged, softening his teal eyes and extending an inked hand in my direction. "Please, follow me."

I collapsed onto my couch and buried my head under a pillow after Gunther persuaded me to leave my bed, but the voices followed me regardless of where I went:

Zelda, my coworkers coo, old reminders of the destruction I cause.

Zelda, Sasha's Melanie calls out joyously, moments before she loses her life in my arms.

Zelda, Peter cries for me. His young, soft voice always rings louder than the others' do.

Gunther prepared a beautiful meal of grilled chicken, steamed broccoli, and mashed potatoes, but I didn't touch any of it, too trapped by the voices bouncing inside my brain to move. The sheathed knife inside my pocket poked my thigh, a tangible souvenir of the pain, but I refused to rearrange my contorted posture, again intent on having the knife dig itself into my skin until I bruised. I only lifted my body into a sitting position when I felt the couch dip beside me. I looked over to see Dave planted on the other side of the couch, his blond eyebrows knitted tightly against his eyes, so much so that I couldn't make out their brilliant blue hue right away.

"LeRoy and Gunther let me in," Dave hurriedly offered as an explanation when I didn't say anything right away.

"Okay," I responded, confusion laced heavily through my tone. I drew my knees up to my chest, and the new position allowed the knife in my pocket to stab me even more directly in the stomach.

Dave swallowed his words, opening and closing his mouth a few times before he finally gathered the courage to ask, "Did you mean what you said earlier?"

"Of course, Dave. The village fire wasn't your fault—"

"No," Dave interrupted, his voice thick. "What you said before that, about killing my father. Did you mean that?"

Did I? I thought I meant the words when they left my mouth during the interview, but I looked at Dave now—quiet in the moonlight, awaiting my reply, silvery tears threatening to leave his dulled-blue eyes, back hunched over—and I suddenly couldn't find the strength I had before to tell him that I would. But how could I even contemplate the mere idea of keeping Caleb alive after all he had done? Leader Caleb Woobi of the Society had ordered his Uniforms to open fire on unsuspecting targets, had incinerated the village, had murdered even his own mother; how could I let him live? Didn't he deserve to rot in a grave no one would visit? Didn't he deserve to receive the same fate he so graciously handed to others? Didn't he deserve to be robbed of ever seeing the sun again, just as Will, Eve, Melanie, Abe, Nelly, Alvin, Anna, Jack, and the others were?

But regardless, Caleb was Dave's father. My Dave, who had already sacrificed and suffered so much. Who was I to decide life or death, anyway?

"Zelda?" Dave squawked when I took too long to answer, and I broke my reverie to see the ex-Uniform rocking back and forth so slowly, the motion was almost unperceivable. "You can tell me the truth. Do you want to kill him? Because if you do, Zelda, if you do want to kill my dad, that's fine." He clenched his fists once resting on the tops of his knees so tightly, his knuckles turned white. "But you have to let me talk to him first, deal? I have to talk to him."

I shook my head. "Dave, no. That's—"

"Please don't tell me it's a bad idea," Dave interjected. "Like it or not, he's my father. I am the son of a murderer." The sentence made him jump to his feet and begin pacing around the coffee table. "For as long as I can remember—which isn't that long, by the way—I have tried to find myself, only to find out that I am the grandson of two legends, one of them now dead, the son of a mother I don't remember, and the son of a *murderer*. I have tried so hard not to let these things define me, but then I realized, what else does? I'm not a Uniform. I'm not a war hero. I'm nothing. Nothing at all, Zelda."

Dave stopped his pacing for a second to run his hands through his short, neatly clipped, golden-blond hair. "But I don't want to be nothing. I don't want to be remembered as your boyfriend, or the son of Caleb Woobi, or just as the boy who sat there and did nothing when everyone else went to fight because my grandparents locked me in their house. I want people to remember me for *me*, not for my girlfriend, father, or grandfather, but what else am I? I spent years as a Uniform, but that's not who I am. I thought I was a Monsella, but that's not true either. And I am definitely not a Woobi. What else does that leave me with, Zelda? It leaves me with nothing but a dead grandmother, a dead mother, a grieving grandfather, and a murderous father. This is why I have to talk to him. I have to figure out who I am with him as my father. I have to make sense of this war inside my head."

He dropped to his knees directly in front of me then, and the moonlight streaming through my enormous windows illuminated the cracks in his once-youthful face. "But then I look at you, and I see what I hope is my future," he professed, lowering his head so his forehead rested on my knees. "I look at you and see who I want to be, not the man I am right now. I look at you, Zelda, and I want to give everything I am to you, but there's nothing to me to give away."

"Don't do this," I warned, placing my hands on the sides of his head to lift his gaze. "Don't destroy yourself over all these things that are out of your control. You are Caleb's son, but he does not have to be your father. You aren't bound by your last name. You're right. You were never Uniform number 125, you were never a Monsella, and you still are not a Woobi. But you know what you are, Dave? You are good. You define good. Everything you are is good."

"Sometimes everything you are isn't enough," Dave muttered brokenly.

"Good is *always* enough," I countered fiercely.

Dave raised a skeptical eyebrow. "To whom?"

"To me."

I leaned down to connect our lips together, and Dave reciprocated immediately, tugging me off the couch by the back of my knees to sit on his lap. Again, I took notice of how much rougher he kissed me, almost as if searching for something in the space between our lips, but I didn't stop him, choosing to match his enthusiasm until salt infiltrated my mouth from the tears streaming down the ex-Uniform's face. I tore away from the hold his lips had to gently kiss the tears from his face, and as I did so, he gasped, "I'm so tired. I just want to be happy, Zelda."

The sentence resonated a little too closely, but I didn't wish to dwell on my sorrows any longer. "Just wait," I whispered as I moved my lips to his ear. "One day, we'll be happy. You promised that we'd live long enough to forget what this pain feels like. Let's stick to that promise."

My words soothed him enough to let him crack a small smile as he mumbled, "Deal," against my lips, and as I watched him sleep beside me that night hours later, I made my own separate promise to speak to his father for him, so Caleb knew the irreversible damage he had caused his family.

CHAPTER 16

The next morning, Allyson burst through my bedroom door with my guards on her heels, ordering her to slow down as she dramatically collapsed at the foot of my bed. I drew my feet close to my body before she had the chance to squash them, but Dave wasn't so lucky; he rocketed upright, visibly startled, when her head hit his thigh. Allyson shrieked when he moved, citing that she didn't know he slept here, and I would've laughed at their equally shocked expressions if LeRoy hadn't said, "Killians, tell her and be done with it. Your scheduled visitation time is short."

Allyson hopped off the bed while I praised her relatively simple outfit: sage-green tank top tucked neatly into a pair of dark-wash jeans, blonde hair tied into a high ponytail, a matching green bandana acting as a loose headband. Her subdued appearance threw me off more than her unsolicited grand entrance. "Tell me what?" I inquired.

Dave yawned, stretched his arms, and rubbed the sleep out of his eyes. "Hm? What's going on?"

"I made pancakes for you and Mr. David," Gunther announced brightly, but his grin quickly diminished when LeRoy shot him a glare.

"Now, Killians," barked LeRoy.

"It's speech day!" Allyson borderline yelled as she threw her hands over her head. "C'mon, Zelda, get up. We have a bit of a long drive ahead of us, and I have a surprise for you when we get there."

I groaned from the back of my throat and flipped over to hide my head beneath the pillow. "Get where?" I asked, my voice muffled.

"The village," rasped Mr. Woobi, who must've quietly walked into my room after I had buried my face into the mattress. "They want you to make this speech in the place where it happened."

"No," I tried to state forcefully, but my voice cracked halfway through as memories of the village and its people crashed into my consciousness. "No. I can't go back there." My heart jumped in panic, and I attempted grasping Dave's hand in support, but he had already curled his hands into fists, his muscles taut and tense. I looked around the room for an ally, but no one had the courage to make direct eye contact with me, not even Gunther. *I cannot go back,* kept repeating in my head, making me that much more frantic, to the point where I pounced out of bed to grab Mr. Woobi and beg, "Help me, please. I can't go back. I can't. Tell her no for me. I can't..."

Mr. Woobi tugged my body into an embrace that took me several moments to reciprocate. The older man reeked like he hadn't showered in a month or more. Still, his arms felt the same they always had, and I found myself falling into his false sense of security as he whispered in my ear: "I don't want to go back either, Zelda Ellyn."

"Then why?"

"Because this is for Peter, my dear girl," he said. "This is for the people we couldn't save, and for the one person we still can."

Peter. Of course. I'd do anything for Peter, even make a speech in the ruins of a town I once considered home. If this speech brought me closer to him, saved Peter from even just a minute of pain, I'd do it as many times as they wanted. I tried to keep that in mind when Allyson dressed me in black lace, when Sasha scowled at me as we loaded into the vehicle to leave, and when Mr. Woobi couldn't bring himself to look me in the eyes.

When we arrived at the village's remnants over an hour later, I saw an agglomeration of people over by where the houses were, walking slowly around the ruins as if in a trance; an entire group of reporters, about three dozen or so, all with cameras in their hands and talking excitedly to themselves; and a gathering of people in seats, looking solemn as their eyes refused to travel anywhere but straight ahead at the newly-constructed stage. "Why here?" I pestered Allyson as she swiped her hands over my shoulders, pretending to rid them of dust. "Why here, in this place, where they all died?"

Allyson smiled at me pitifully and gave the shoulders of my dress once last sweep. "Because it's powerful," she answered before she grinned and added, "Remember that surprise I had for you? Well look, Zelda, here it is!"

She turned my body around, and I almost slammed into a larger-built, redheaded girl standing right behind me. I recognized the face instantly. "Marley?"

Marlena Heist, Allyson's intern who tragically lost one of her older siblings in the village fire, blushed furiously when I called her name, the rosy color almost perfectly matching the little flowers dotting her black, long-sleeved shirt. "You remember me?" she asked, and her words were enough for me to wrap my arms around her in a warm embrace.

"Of course, I remember you," I said after pulling away. "I thought Allyson said you were taking some time off."

Marley lowered her gaze to the ground when her bright green eyes filled with tears. "Yeah," she responded quietly before clearing her throat. "Yeah, I did. But my family needs this money, especially now, and Zelda…" She smiled despite the tears in her eyes. "Caleb Woobi killed my older sister. I think it's time we fight back, so no one else dies because of him. I came back for you because I believe in you. You can stop this. You can kill him."

She gave me one last, short hug before returning to sit with her remaining family, and I pondered her parting words: "I don't get to see my sister again, but you will see your brother, and that's enough to give me hope. You'll see Peter again, Zelda. You just have to get through this first."

Marley was right. I had promised myself that I would see Peter again, regardless of the cost.

I only had to get through this.

Harmony and Lucy took their seats behind the main camera situated center stage, and although the pair instructed that the pre-written words would appear in the camera lens for me to read, their words of encouragement were not enough to distract me from letting my eyes wander to the people in the crowd. The men and women with their own personal cameras all stood the instant I walked on stage, the flashes from their machinery causing little colored specks to fly up into my vision. The people observing the ruins gathered around the ones with cameras, talking quietly amongst themselves. Those sitting in chairs stared hauntingly at my body on their stage, their burns, bruises, scrapes, gashes, and the like proudly on display for my viewing… the survivors. *Why are they here?* I asked myself. *What is the purpose of having them sit through this?* I wished to personally apologize, but before I could, Harmony started counting down from five.

"Five." *Inhale.*

"Four." *Calm down, Zelda.*

"Three." *Exhale.*

"Two." *You need to do this, Zelda.*

"One." *For Peter.*

The main camera's red light blinked on, and the words Allyson had written began appearing on the lens.

"Good afternoon," I addressed my audience, my eyes bouncing from the words I read to the people watching me. "We are gathered together to celebrate the lives of the ones we lost in the Northeastern Societan Massacre. Each and every life lost is a tragedy in and of itself, which is why we come together to remember the people Caleb Woobi stole from us: mothers, fathers, daughters, sons. Teachers, doctors, farmers. Family and friends, *our* family and friends. Precious lives Caleb Woobi ruthlessly murdered."

The words tasted forced and sounded insincere to my own ears; I stole a glance at the survivors and saw their eyes brimming with angry tears, jaws clenched as they tried to contain their hatred. My own eyes filled with hot tears, the words fading into silence the instant I locked eyes with the familiar face of the woman who vouched for me to stay in the village, all that time ago.

I couldn't do this. Not to them. Not to the people who fought every day just to stay alive. Not to the people who had welcomed me so openly.

I cleared my throat and sidestepped away from the main camera's gaze, so I faced the people who deserved to know what I truly felt. Big, bolded letters materialized in the lens—READ THE WORDS—but I shook my head. "No," I announced to no one in particular, and I suddenly took a lunge forward to knock the camera off its podium.

My impulsive action sent the ones who brought their own cameras into a frenzy, but I refused to allow their obnoxious shouting to distract me from speaking clearly to the people who deserved my words most.

"I'm sorry I couldn't save them," I said, nodding to each survivor with whom I made eye contact, feeling relieved when I saw a few of their faces soften. The sound of my voice quieted the rest of the people, their own eyes staring at me in awe, anger, and in some cases, admiration.

"I know I could have," I told the survivors. "I know that if I had just stayed away from the village, from all of you, I wouldn't have caused this. Everyone you love would still be alive. I'm so, so sorry."

I pressed on despite the sudden stinging tears that pricked my eyes and coated my throat. "I saw what happened that night. I saw your fathers, brothers, mothers, and sisters die right beside the boundary that separates the Society and us. I saw them all fight for what they believed in, and nothing can ever erase that memory." I sniffled and nodded through my next words: "I tried saving a few, though, like this one boy, William Finnley. Will was full of life, practically bursting with it, and he reminded me so much of my own little brother but... he died, too."

My body shook violently from mentioning Will, and a small, anguished squeak left my mouth. Some of the people standing in the back lowered their cameras, their own little red lights turning off as they watched me live and not through a screen.

"It's my fault that little boy is dead," I spoke through heavy sobs, my words almost indistinguishable. "It's my fault your loved ones are dead. It's my fault my own brother is trapped inside that Society, tortured by Caleb."

Peter. Oh, Peter. How I begged the universe to help him forgive me when he eventually discovered the truth behind my sins here. I hoped he was worth the cost of other people's lives.

"I know you are missing someone monumental in your lives," I continued after swallowing the lump in my throat. "I know you are angry because of it. I know you feel some sort of pain, no matter how hard you might try to ignore it. I can see it whenever I look into your eyes. I hear it in your cries for war. But most of all, I can feel it, because I feel the exact same thing."

"My little brother is the reason I fight to return to the Society," I explained. "I'm angry because he isn't with me, because Caleb is hurting him, because I had a chance to protect him and I couldn't. I miss him with everything that I am. I'm in pain every second he's not around me, just as I know you are without your own loved ones. I want you to know that I understand you. I understand your anger. I understand your loss. I understand your pain. But above that, I understand now that a different fire started that night, not one that destroys, but one that inspires. A fire we will carry with us to the end."

Zelda, the massacred gently hiss my name.

I sank to my knees, letting the survivors cast their final judgments as I begged the voices *please, not again.*

Everyone in the crowd, from the cameramen to the survivors, assessed my words in silence. No one smiled, no one clapped, no one dared to move until the survivors stood to their feet some minutes later. I expected harsh words, something heavy hurled at my head, even, but instead, they all looked to one another, nodded in agreement, and began to sing:

"I stand here tonight.
So afraid. So alone.
But you're there, in the light.
You won't leave me on my own.
It's so dark. It's so dark.
The whole world has turned black.
But you, you've made your mark.
Please tell me you'll be back.
Hold me tight tonight.
Right before you go,

Tell me everything will be alright.
We never did fit the status quo.
Tell me you'll miss me.
Tell me you need me.
Tell me you love me so.
I know I'll miss you.
I know I need you.
I know I love you so.
I know you love me.
I know I love you.
Tell me…
What I already know."

My eyelids fluttered as I blinked away the tears pooled in my eyes from their lullaby, the same serenade their children sang the night Dave and I first appeared outside their home. In the times I most needed them, words failed me; I knew nothing I could articulate would reach the level of gratitude I felt toward these people, these simple, kindhearted people, these people I considered my found family. I wished to give them something as meaningful as the song they gifted me—perhaps my bloodied, beating heart would suffice, but even that didn't feel worthy—but could think of nothing that would even come close to equating to what I had taken.

Just as Allyson stepped up to usher me off the stage, one man stepped forward from the crowd of survivors, taking off his hat and placing it above his heart before speaking.

"I remember when you and David Woobi first came to us," said the man unevenly, clearly uncomfortable as his eyes darted back and forth between me and the cameras that had turned to him. "You told us that you have to realize the bubble you live in, and that anyone can pop it as long as they're willing to try. Back then, I didn't understand what you meant. I still can't fully get it, since I didn't live the way you did in the Society. But I think I understand what you're trying to say. Everyone in the village thought we were invincible but look at us now. I know you blame yourself, but we are realizing that some of it was our fault, too. We lived in our own little bubble, too. And I think we're going to learn from all our mistakes to build something better."

Another man stepped up and added, "Yeah. I remember when that footage of you with those two homeless men came out, and you said that you knew you can't go back in time and fix all of your mistakes, so the best thing you can do now is look forward and hope that things will get better. There's no need to hope now, Zelda Jadestone. Things *will* get better. We'll make sure of it. For your brother, for my boy, Sammy, for everyone."

I watched, speechless, as a woman a few rows behind the men stepped forward as well and projected, "Caleb Woobi took everything from me, Zelda Jadestone. Now it's our turn to take everything from him."

Caleb Woobi. The name alone made the air quiver in fear, but the crowd refused to cower. They stole the name and internalized it, chanting, "Kill Caleb," until the mantra caused them to erupt and merge into one cohesive, moving mass that resembled the flicker of the flames that almost killed them. The cameras didn't know on which aspect to focus: the survivors' organized chaos, my scramble from the stage, or the way they engulfed me the moment my foot hit the scorched grass.

The survivors grabbed at my ankles, at my torso, at my arms, trying to pull me down with them, their angry screams of war and an end to Caleb Woobi overpowering my senses until my head throbbed and my limbs felt heavy. I could see nothing but their furious faces the more they enclosed around me.

"He's a liar!" they screeched, drowning out my yelps for help.

"He's a murderer!" they yelled until someone shouted to burn the Society down, and then their voices all joined in a chorus of agreement as they all screamed, "Burn him!"

The shouting in the back became gunshots and explosions, the survivors' angry faces transformed into the ones of the deceased, and the scene around me turned into the night outside of the boundary, when I watched the slaughter unfold. I became frantic in my search for someone familiar, but they pressed in closer, suffocating me with their cries for a war I did not want to fight.

War, Mr. Woobi had called it once, so long ago back in the Society.

I saw the blood. I saw the bodies. I saw the agony in their eyes.

I was back on the battlefield.

Dropping to my knees and crawling out of the madness presented itself as the only option, but I couldn't move from the assault of sound on my brain.

Caleb, this crowd chanted. *Kill Caleb.*

Zelda, the victims chant inside my head, their last words before bullets bite their brains.

Caleb, the cameramen joined in, already reporting live from the scene down at the Redding village.

Zelda, Will yells, a wasted breath before the water swallows him.

Caleb, the survivors screamed, wanting nothing more than to see his blood staining the ashes they stood on.

Zelda, Peter whimpers, a final prayer before execution.

The sounds didn't stop, repeating over and over until the two names melded together to become one ugly roar.

The second I felt a hand on my shoulder, I twisted around and pleaded for its owner to help me, the terror lining my pupils turning to relief when I recognized the figure as Sasha. She gripped my wrist roughly and dragged me behind her, visibly agitated with my actions; her touch was a slap of reality, exactly what I needed, and I sprinted with her out of the crowd and over to the edge of the forest, where the scorched trees met the destroyed village and the untouched greenery. Sasha scanned me worriedly, but she had no time to articulate her concern before Eric came stumbling toward us from the mob. Mr. Woobi wobbled not far behind him, leaning heavily on his cane.

Dave, Jannet, Gunther, LeRoy, Lucy, and Harmony spilled out of the crowd next, all breathing just as heavily as Sasha and me. We remained silent, content with finding solace in each other's presences, before Mr. Woobi declared, "Enough of this. Zelda Ellyn, this needs to end one way or another."

The others wordlessly agreed, and I knew what I had to do.

President Dassian quickly looked up from his paperwork, alarmed, when the booming sound of his heavy doors slamming against each other reverberated throughout his office space an hour or so later. "I need to speak to Caleb Woobi," I proclaimed. "Directly. Now. Please."

The president eyed me suspiciously, clearly apprehensive about my request as he slowly set his papers back down on the desk. "I don't think that's the wisest idea, darling. Why would you want to do such a thing?"

"Caleb is not someone we have the luxury to ignore anymore," I retorted. "After seeing firsthand the destruction he's caused, I need to see him face-to-face."

No more than ten minutes later, President Dassian's secretary told us we were receiving a return signal from the Society, which meant we'd be able to see Caleb in a few seconds. My heart pounded loudly in my ears, the sound of it almost drowning out the concerns streaming from President Dassian's mouth, and it stopped beating altogether when the leader of the Society's face materialized on screen.

Caleb chose not to hide in darkness this time, allowing me to observe the changes in his appearance since our last real encounter the day I left the Society. His wispy, blond hair looked plastered to his head a little too neatly—too much grease, perhaps—and his oval face seemed noticeably slimmer than before, his cheekbones high and prominent. I instantly recognized the gleam in his dark brown eyes as the same as when I left, though, as was his excited, borderline giddy smile when he taunted, "I wondered when you would gather the courage to speak with me directly, Zelda Jadestone. How I've missed you."

His natural voice—smooth and calm, even without the programming to disguise it—shot shivers up my spine. "Can't say I feel the same," I said while crossing my arms across my chest from the sudden chill.

His smile grew to a grin when he remarked, "You don't look well. What has happened to the once-fearless girl who stood up for my father not so long ago? Where has she gone?"

"You killed her."

At my words, Caleb leaned forward close enough to where I could see the individual hairs above his thin lips. "No, I don't think so," he responded. "I don't believe I've had the pleasure of destroying her quite yet. But I will."

Despite only interacting through the monitor, the sight of this man made my insides churn, a hot sensation of perceived hatred. "You lied to me," I said, curling my fingers into my palms and pressing hard enough to draw blood. "You said you don't take pleasure in killing things that are alive, but you've murdered so many people, Caleb. Why?"

"Oh, Zelda Jadestone," Caleb tutted, clicking his tongue against the roof of his mouth condescendingly. "I did not kill anyone. That was all you."

"No. You killed Will," I accused, and just that statement was enough to spark my nerves into tiny capillaries of flame. My skin felt hot, and I could feel the warmth visibly spreading to my face. "All those people in the village, in that battle by the Society, you killed them, too. What about them, Caleb? What made them different enough for you to murder them under your so-called policy that you don't kill those who are alive?"

Rage brewed inside my bones, causing me to snatch the caramel-colored drink President Dassian held and throw it at the monitor Caleb appeared on, watching as the glass shattered into multiple pieces and the liquid splattered his face. "You killed them!" I screeched, picking up yet another object—a remote, this time—and slamming it against the monitor in an attempt to break him. "You monster, you murdered them! Yes, you did! You killed Will! You killed... you... I hate you!"

A third glass object smashed against Caleb's projected face as my fury grew stronger, but the screen was too strong; nothing would shatter it. Nothing would shatter *him,* the one man I wanted nothing more than to destroy. President Dassian reached for me to try and intervene, but I furiously shoved him away.

"You don't mean that," Caleb spoke softly, his eyes shiny with an emotion I could not place as he watched me search for another thing to throw. "When will you learn that only you are responsible for the consequences of your actions?"

A sound bordering both a scream and a sob escaped my mouth as I half-heartedly hurled the knife I kept hidden in my pocket at him, watching it blurrily through unfallen tears as it uselessly bounced off the monitor and clattered onto the floor. I wanted nothing more than to drop to the floor, curl into a ball, and scream until my noise overpowered Caleb's voice, but I refused to fall. Caleb had ruined me, completely corrupted my core from the inside out, rotted me until I was nothing but a melting shell of my former self, but I would not give him the satisfaction of knowing.

"Let me tell you something," Caleb informed. "Look at where we are now. You have inspired so many people to die for you, Zelda Jadestone. You have started so many fires. You wield so much power over the ones who follow you. I am convinced if you stood on the busiest street corner in that filthy city and shot someone, they would *still* find a way to praise you. They think they know you, Zelda Jadestone. They don't. Only I do. You are an eighteen-year-old girl oh, so desperate for her brother in my possession. You are a naïve, ignorant child making adult decisions for the first time in her life. You are nothing, Zelda Jadestone, nothing compared to me. All these people, all this glory and grandeur, they're just temporary crutches. You'll still be broken when they inevitably go away."

"Like you?" I bit back, gripping onto this anger to ignore the stabbing sensation in my chest. "You broke the moment you decided to turn your back on your family, Caleb."

Caleb scoffed and leaned back in his large leather chair, attempting to appear nonchalant, yet I noticed the way his eyebrows furrowed at my words.

"Will you finally feel powerful when I 'inevitably' lose to you?" I asked him, taking careful and calculated steps toward the camera above the monitor so he could see my sincerity. "Will that lust for revenge fill the empty void Juniper Monsella, Dave, your own father left in your heart? Because I don't think it will. Let me tell *you* something now, Caleb. I think you're an empty shell of a man grasping at straws of success you didn't even earn. I pity you."

Rage blazed behind his pupils. "Don't ever mention Juniper Monsella again," he barked, "or Peter won't live to see another day."

"Are you scared, Caleb Woobi?" I pressed on, refusing to relent despite the very real threats to my little brother's life. "Are you scared of the way she made you feel? Are you scared of what she would think of the man you have become?" I understood now. No amount of glass could ever touch him. No amount of screaming could ever deter him. No. Juniper

Monsella would always be Caleb Woobi's weakness. *This* was how I would break him.

"I'm not afraid of anything." Caleb's wobbling voice gave his emotions away, but he cleared his throat to disguise his hurt.

I raised a challenging eyebrow. "Really?"

"Yes."

It was my turn to smile. "In that case, Caleb, your mother is dead."

In an instant, Caleb's façade crumbled, and I watched satisfactorily as he searched for an escape, his mouth agape. *Good.* I wanted to steal the breath from his lungs and step on his trachea before he could inhale again, just long enough for him to know I owned every aspect of his life. I wanted him floundering for a pulse, my hand wrapped around his arteries, trapping his blood, controlling his every heartbeat. I wanted Caleb's blood on my hands, if only to feel it go cold.

"How... what? That isn't... I made sure... no, Zelda... I..." His struggle for coherency soothed me, and I watched the leader of the Society crack with a cold, hard stare.

"Eve lived in the village *you* burned," I sneered. "Your own mother died saving the people you wanted to kill. She protected her home, her family, and she died the same way your wife did."

Caleb leaned over, clutching his stomach, and I licked my lips to hide my grin. "Are you scared now, Caleb?"

"No," Caleb muttered, but he couldn't find it in himself to return my gaze.

"You should be," I growled, the venom in my voice enough to lift Caleb's head and direct his full attention back to me. "You should be afraid of yourself and what you are capable of when you let your anger guide your actions. And you should be very, very afraid of me. I am not under your control anymore, Caleb. I am not a brainwashed Societan citizen. I am not going to leave Peter with you. You're right. These people adore me, and if you think I won't exploit their loyalty, you're wrong. I *will* come back to the Society. I will free Peter. And I will happily watch you die in the process. You underestimate me, Caleb Woobi, but that ends today. I'm coming to kill you."

I expected Caleb to fear the power behind my words, but my speech sparked renewed light into his unbelievably dark eyes, and he wiped his mouth before he grinned. "Brave words from the child in charge. Watch out; I may not have to destroy you at all. You'll be begging to die by the time this is done. Get ready, Zelda Jadestone. I am prepared to watch you burn yourself to ashes."

And the screen faded from white, to gray, to black.

CHAPTER 17

I spent the monotonous week that followed my conversation with Caleb in relative solitude, save for my interactions with the guards every time they entered the apartment to check on me. Any time the opportunity arose, Gunther cooked extravagantly gorgeous meals for the three of us, and we ate them on the couch, rehashing our experiences of the day. I never contributed much to the conversation—I rarely ventured outside my apartment, too consumed by my grief to leave my bed—but I enjoyed hearing LeRoy and Gunther playfully bicker about who stood guard outside my door best. *What a boring job,* I thought as they talked one night. *Watching over a girl who does nothing but pace inside her room.* I voiced this thought after finishing my steak, but it was LeRoy who disputed it, saying, "It's our job, Jadestone. We're happy to do it."

I raised my eyebrows in surprise. "Happy? To watch *me*? I thought you hated me."

LeRoy stuffed more roasted carrots into his mouth to avoid answering me, but from the elated look Gunther gave him, I knew the big, burly man had warmed up to me somewhat, maybe had even started caring for me in some capacity. I developed a soft spot for them as the week went by, and soon, their constant vigilance became comforting rather than irritating. I even enjoyed listening to their conversations outside my door late at night, after they thought I had fallen asleep, in which they would ask each other questions to get to know the other better. I never listened for too long, of course, to respect their privacy; Gunther's lingering smile when he flipped pancakes in the mornings told me enough.

Exactly a week after my speech at the village, Mr. Woobi knocked on my door thrice during our routine dinner. LeRoy, agitated, went to send him away before the older man barged into my apartment, closely followed by Sasha, Eric, Dave, Jannet, Lucy, and Harmony.

"Oh, look who it is!" Sasha declared with her arms raised for dramatic effect. "I haven't seen you in so long, Zelda, I was beginning to forget what your face looks like." She scanned my face with her liquid amber eyes, the corners of her mouth perking up as she quipped, "Still ugly. That's good to know."

I giggled and would've retorted something equally snarky if Dave hadn't swooped down to kiss me full on the mouth. His sudden rush of affection stole the breath from my lungs, and I could only muster a breathless, "Hi," in greeting.

"Hi," Dave replied with a smile as he settled down beside me, but I couldn't unsee the dullness in his eyes.

"Would you please leave us to converse for a few minutes, Major Mefedee and Lieutenant Thompson?" Mr. Woobi asked spontaneously, looking to me for reinforcement of his command.

Only I didn't. I couldn't. If we were to converse about something, our little troop wouldn't have been complete without the two tall, broad men who only wanted to see me safe. "Wait," I called out to my guards before they could close the door. "I think you should stay with us."

Mr. Woobi shot me a disbelieving look. "Zelda Ellyn, I don't think that's the wisest idea."

Sasha pretended to gag as she declared, "This is the most testosterone I've been around in a long, *long* time." She turned to Eric to ask, "How'd you handle being the only man until blondie came along?"

"I don't mind being surrounded by strong women," Eric replied with a nonchalant shrug.

"Wait a minute. Who are you calling 'blondie'?" Dave asked, and the four of us chortled until Mr. Woobi demanded our attention once Gunther and LeRoy had settled into their places on the floor.

The elder ran out of patience to lighten his tone, so his tone became insistent when he asked for our consideration again. I scowled when I turned to face him. "Right, then," stated Mr. Woobi while clapping his hands together once he had our full attention. "I suppose I owe you all an explanation as to why we're gathered in Zelda's living room tonight."

The nine of us nodded.

Mr. Woobi faced me fully so I could absorb his next words: "We're so close to getting in the Society again, Zelda Ellyn. We only need to perfect our technology to pop the boundary and train the troops for battle, and then we'll be in. But I know Cody won't let us go."

All the hope that had been building up inside me at his words deflated. I narrowed my eyes at the elder as I growled, "What do you mean, they won't *let* us? I'm seeing Peter the second that electric boundary is down. No one is getting in my way of that."

Sasha whooped in agreement, and I vaguely heard Lucy and Harmony echo her excitement.

"You are too precious of an asset to risk sending straight into the line of fire again," Mr. Woobi retorted calmly. "Look at how Cody reacted when you went off on your own to save Eric. Cody was not happy because he could have lost his greatest ally. He's not going to make the same mistake again. Cody and Allyson are not going to risk it."

"I want to see them try and stop me," I snarled.

"Oh, they'll stop you," interjected LeRoy. "That's why we were hired."

"I thought you were hired for my protection," I conjectured.

"Protection from yourself, Miss," Gunther elaborated. "We're supposed to watch you just as much as we're supposed to watch the people around you."

"Oh," I squeaked.

"Don't worry," Gunther reassured. "We trust you now."

LeRoy laughed humorlessly at his comrade's declaration but chose not to comment further.

Gunther's statement put me at ease somewhat, and I promised that I trusted them in return before training my attention back to Mr. Woobi. "What's your point, Mr. Woobi?"

"I want you to go back and find Peter," answered Mr. Woobi. "I want to go back and see my son again. I'm telling you this now, so we can devise a plan to do so before it becomes too late."

"What do you think we should do, then?" inquired Lucy from the corner of the couch.

Mr. Woobi eyed my guards with disdain. "Are you sure you trust these men, Zelda? Place your faith in the wrong people, and all your work will be for nothing. You won't see Peter until they make your reunion one big show that marks the end of this war."

"That isn't going to happen," I proclaimed intensely. "Answer Lucy's question. What are you suggesting we do about it, Mr. Woobi? Run away?"

Mr. Woobi cast his icy eyes down to the coffee table, drawing mindless shapes on the glass before nodding.

"You're crazy," declared Harmony with her arms crossed in front of her.

"Why?" asked Sasha simultaneously.

"Oh, my goodness," Lucy yelped with a hand over her mouth.

"When can we go?" I asked with them.

LeRoy whistled in surprise. "Oh yeah, I am definitely glad I decided to stay to watch this train wreck. Count me in."

Eric, Dave, and Gunther exchanged apprehensive looks.

Jannet looked like she wanted to laugh at our different reactions, but one glance at Mr. Woobi, and she quickly thought better of it.

The older man rubbed his forehead as he questioned LeRoy borderline accusingly: "That's it? You're joining us just like that?"

"I hate this place," stated LeRoy like his answer should have been obvious, and as he spoke, I saw the boredom in his dark eyes I had neglected to notice before, his usual silence a secret scream for excitement, his yawns throughout the day a signal of his tiredness toward his present situation. "I don't trust President Dassian or the media. Never have. I've wasted too much of my life working for people I don't trust. I'll go wherever I'm needed."

Dave bit the nail of his thumb and assessed the entire situation before he spoke up. "I agree with Charles," he finally said. "We need to leave if Zelda wants to see Peter, and I want to speak to my father. They're going to execute him for burn…" He sharply inhaled. "Burning down the village," he finished slowly. "I have to speak with him before that happens."

"As do I," Mr. Woobi chimed in solemnly.

Sasha stood up abruptly and waved her fist in the air, shouting, "Well then, what are we sitting here for? Let's sneak out tonight! We can steal a vehicle from downstairs." She hopped on the balls of her feet impatiently, furrowing her dark eyebrows when none of us budged from either the couch or the floor. "Are you all a bunch of snails? I said let's go!"

"I have a good idea, everyone!" Harmony exclaimed, matching Sasha's excitement. "Let's do the exact opposite of what Sasha just said."

"It's a lot more complicated than just leaving the building, Sasha," I said after Sasha finished glaring at Harmony.

"We need the technology to pop the boundary and enter the Society," added Jannet.

"Not to mention, us gathering in Zelda's room and then missing the morning after would be suspicious, to say the least," said Eric. "Dassian's people would find us in no time."

"Think of the survivors of the village fire and the family members of the people who died at the Societan Massacre. They're just starting to trust Zelda again after what happened to them that day. How will it look if she picked up everything and left them? She needs to build relationships with them, so maybe they could help her in the future. The public would get so sick of her if she left *again*, and we can't have both sides against us. We need all the support we can get if we're going to win this," reasoned Dave.

Sasha plopped back on the couch in defeat as she groaned in frustration. "Well, if you don't like my plan, then what's yours?"

Mr. Woobi explained that everyone had specific parts to play in this elaborate scheme if we were to pull it off. To secure weapons for our protection, Eric would feign an interest in artillery—believable, since his job in the Society consisted of creating different weapons for the Uniforms—and over time, slowly start stealing weapons from their warehouse for our use.

Jannet and Mr. Woobi would request to go walking around Dassian's building before bed every night, and as they did so, they would mark the location of each camera they came across. Sasha would fake a passion for architecture—a thought that made me almost explode into laughter—and learn the ins and outs of the building, so she could move or disable the cameras Jannet and Mr. Woobi identified for her at a later date.

LeRoy, Gunther, and I would continue with our press tour: talking to survivors, interviewing with magazines, conforming to Allyson's demands. Lucy and Harmony would accompany us on these "business trips," as Mr. Woobi called them, to ensure Allyson didn't get suspicious of my sudden cooperation. Dave was free to do as he pleased, which I could tell disheartened him. We were expected to continue this charade until the perfect opportunity arose for us to escape. Mr. Woobi didn't know when or how this opportunity would present itself, but he felt confident it would. We were expected to put our faith in his hope.

LeRoy shook his head in disagreement after Mr. Woobi explained his plan. "President Dassian will hunt us down the second we leave this building. Zelda is too important to this upcoming war to let her escape a second time."

"I have thought of a solution to stop Cody from chasing after us," declared Mr. Woobi. "We bring Allyson. Zelda could persuade her to follow us when the opportunity to leave arrives."

I twisted to look at him bitterly at the mere mention of another camera crew following me against my will, specifically when I would be reunited with my brother. "What? Absolutely not."

"Zelda, listen to me," Mr. Woobi tried to reason. "If Cody doesn't get any footage of you during the most important time of the war, he's going to come after you, and he will not stop until you're back here, right where we started. We need to give him something, *anything,* that will satisfy him and the public enough for us to continue our own journey. He'll be less inclined and too swamped in work to act on us leaving. You must see the logic in that, dear girl."

I did, and I told him so, however reluctantly. "But I have to know when they're filming," I compromised. "No surprises, okay?"

Mr. Woobi was all too happy to oblige.

"Hold on," said LeRoy again with two hands raised to still us. "We need a plan for inside the Society, too. Otherwise, we'd walk in blind."

"That's so true," Harmony stated with a curt nod.

Sasha rolled her eyes when Harmony spoke. "Harmony, do you ever, I don't know, say anything useful?"

Harmony's black hair swished effortlessly behind her shoulder as she swiftly turned her head to give Sasha a pointed look. "Sasha, do you ever, I don't know, say anything nice?" she snapped back.

"Girls, please," reprimanded Jannet. "Lieutenant Thompson makes an excellent point. If we are to go through with this plan, we need to be prepared."

"Any ideas, then?" Eric asked the group.

We grew quiet until Mr. Woobi shook his head. "Not at this moment," he confessed. "Not to worry. I'll think of a plan before the opportunity presents itself."

"How long until we can leave, then?" asked Sasha while twirling a piece of her hair around her finger.

"Months, I'd say," responded Mr. Woobi. Everyone but Sasha nodded their heads in silent agreement.

She groaned again and covered her eyes with her hands. "Months?" she whined. "You've got to be *joking*."

"Can't we cut it down to weeks, at least?" I inquired, feeling the same gnawing sense of urgency as Sasha. "Peter won't last that much longer. I can only imagine what Caleb might be doing to him today, never mind months from now."

No one dared look me in the eyes after I had mentioned Peter, except for the elder who convinced my brother to leave me years before. Pity coated Mr. Woobi's voice as he said, "I'm sorry, Zelda Ellyn, but I can think of no other way."

The ten of us looked around the room at each other, evaluating our loyalty to this plan and by extension, this family, fear and excitement emanating from our bodies. The silence almost became deafening before Eric shrugged, raised his fist above the coffee table, and said, "For Peter, right?"

We all shifted so we could place our fists above the coffee table in solidarity, and together, we yelled, "For Peter!"

For Peter. Always for Peter.

CHAPTER 18

The months that followed went by strangely, some crawling by to the point where I thought I would tear my hair out, yet others, I would blink, and they would be over. I spent my afternoons visiting various parts of the city and conversing with the people there about the war. It was tiresome, draining work, seeing people whose lives had been changed forever because of Caleb's wrongdoings and being forced to communicate with them, hearing their problems that somehow always became mine, too. Naturally, I wasn't alone when I did this; Allyson, Marley, Harmony, Lucy, Gunther, and LeRoy accompanied me to every place we traveled, and unexpectedly, the six of us grew close as a result of these "business trips."

As per Gunther's suggestion, we spent the travel time to and from these locations asking each other sometimes personal, oftentimes utterly ridiculous questions, and I treasured the answers, as they gave me a small window into my companions' distinct personalities. During these "question sessions"—so lovingly named by Lucy—I learned Allyson's parents weren't wealthy during her childhood, but as her career in media grew, she was able to provide for them financially, a feat in which she took immense pride; her favorite color was a fiery, bright orange; and she'd rather die than live under the control of the Society. I valued Allyson's rare vulnerable moments, and more than once, I found similarities between us that I didn't know if I appreciated.

I learned Marley didn't live in the city after all, but in an upper-class suburb just outside the metropolis with only her parents, since she was the youngest out of her family of six; she chose to take a gap year before professional journalism school to focus on gaining "real-world experience," a decision she didn't make lightly, since her entire high school class went to professional school directly after graduation; and she found difficulty in navigating her grief over her older sister, since their age difference resulted in time spent apart. I could sympathize with the last one.

I learned Harmony had once been a high-profile model for fashion magazines before the industry almost killed her, although she didn't elaborate on how; she had impulsively married a man she met seventy-two hours before the ceremony, their marriage lasting about seventy-two hours after that; and she refused to eat any meat, even poultry. While staying at Sasha's tent near the river after Will's death, she ate only canned vegetables because of her dietary preferences, and she wasn't sure how she had managed to survive on canned peas alone.

I learned Lucy owned a cat—a furry, four-legged, orange creature the size of a small desk lamp—and called it "Linus," citing an old cartoon from a century before our time as the inspiration behind its name; she was most afraid of failure; and she had developed quite a strong liking for Eric, claiming he was "everything she looked for in a partner." When Allyson,

Harmony, and Marley concurred with Lucy that Eric was indeed "perfect boyfriend material," I squirmed in my seat; the mere idea of Eric being romantically interested in any of the four girls made my stomach churn..

I learned Gunther attended professional school for cooking, which didn't surprise me in the slightest; he promised to cover every inch of his body in skin paintings, or tattoos, except for his face; and he almost landed himself in prison for the attempted murder of his sister's abuser-turned-killer, but escaped jail time in exchange for this job as a government security guard because of his clean record before that impulsive, poor decision. The last one caught me off guard, but I valued his honesty more than anything else, and I knew he appreciated my nonjudgmental gaze more than he let on.

I learned LeRoy's favorite season was summer because he loved the feeling of the hot sun on his bare back when he visited a special place called "the beach;" he utterly despised skin paintings, but "surprisingly didn't despise Officer Gunther;" and one day, he wanted to save a life, even though he feared death most. When I asked about "the beach," LeRoy unexpectedly promised he'd take me one day, maybe once this madness died down, so I could see its wonder firsthand; I accepted his invitation enthusiastically.

And I learned I loved them fiercely. Whenever one of them would laugh, or we'd share a comforting glance after a particularly difficult trip, or they'd simply greet me good morning, my heart throbbed with that same feeling of over-protectiveness that would wash over me whenever I thought of Peter, that overpowering urge to keep them safe at any cost. I knew I had developed this same feeling for my coworkers back in the Society, and I desperately wished these new friends wouldn't be handed the same fate as my last makeshift family. I didn't think I could handle another massacre.

After my interviews, speeches, and general appearances aired on the screens, Caleb always retaliated with propaganda of his own, showing the violence from the Societan Massacre and the destruction from the village fire before ending on the same note: Peter, chained or in a fetal position, begging for my help. The sight of Peter in such tremendous pain used to make me cower, but once we devised the plan, I channeled that pain into fury, fury I utilized when giving my speeches. Caleb and I were caught in a vicious, bloody cycle, one antagonizing the other, neither of us willing to surrender. I couldn't wait for the day I finally took his life.

When I returned to Dassian's building from these business trips, I typically spent my evenings with Eric, Dave, or both. Dave, I discovered, had landed himself a job at The Refugee Center of Neweryork helping the village fire survivors, and I didn't wish to disturb his important work. On the days he didn't work late, we mostly cuddled up on my couch in silence, since Dave didn't enjoy talking about his work at the Refugee Center. Even when his nineteenth birthday rolled around, December 19, Dave refused to let me do anything special for him, although that particular night, Eric, Mr. Woobi, and Gunther prepared him a small, special meal I could tell he secretly appreciated. I didn't mind Dave's sudden introversion so much, content with just soaking in the feelings his mere presence evoked in me. The quiet moments when I'd peacefully rest my head on his shoulder while we watched some silly television show together helped solidify the comfort we found in each other.

Eric, on the other hand, would try to come up with different activities for us to do, from roaming the stairwells and exploring the building to lounging in my room talking about nonsense while absentmindedly playing a board game, all of which were equally enjoyable. I admired Eric's efforts in trying to distract me from our reality, and on many occasions, it worked; although, I believe that might've had to do more with the sweet way his face would soften in the stolen moments he thought I couldn't see him observing me than with the actual activities themselves.

My favorite evenings were the ones the three of us spent together. Dave and Eric's combined energy created the best kind of chaos, and somehow, we always found mindless ways to keep ourselves occupied. When Dave came home early from work in a good mood, we three would ask Mr. Woobi to explain games he played in his youth; hide-and-seek around my apartment quickly became our collective favorite, although watching the boys compete in "dance battles" against each other in my living room was a close second for me. Eric particularly enjoyed having Gunther give us cooking lessons, which often resulted in more ingredients on the floor than in the pots and pans once the four of us inevitably dissolved into having amicable food fights. Dave preferred calmer activities, like following along to Jannet's gentle instructions as she taught us how to paint, despite not being exceptionally good at the detail-oriented tasks. Truthfully, I didn't care what we did. I needed the carefree pandemonium to distract me from the horrors of our reality, and the boys' presences worked quite well for that purpose.

On the rare days neither Eric nor Dave was with me, I became anxious and frightened, which oftentimes led to me never leaving my room. The weight of everything—from the village to Will, from my coworkers to Peter, from my responsibility to my grief—would press up against my chest until I ran into a corner of my room to escape it. Days like these caused Gunther to worry as he tried to coax me out of my haze, but we both knew there was really nothing he could do. I was far beyond any point of repair.

Sasha visited every night. Before dinner, she would knock on my door and ask to join me in a not-so-polite manner; by the third time she had done this, LeRoy decided she was safe enough to just let in my room without an explanation. I always wondered that myself—why she was there when she made it explicitly clear all that time ago that she despised me—but I never had the heart to question her. We would contently eat our dinner either just us and my guards or with whomever happened to still be in my apartment by then: Dave, Eric, or both. Sasha and Eric bonded particularly closely over the course of these months, I noticed; she taught him the concept of "pranking" someone, and the two of them got into plenty of mischief trying to make the other laugh. Over time, she fully warmed up to Dave as well, and more than once, I was the victim of those three's jokes; I guess my surprised face after opening a carton of dyed-blue milk was funny enough to warrant the three of them on the floor, close to the verge of tears from laughing so hard. I would've been more annoyed by their antics if I didn't adore the sound of their laughter.

On the nights Dave didn't stay over, Sasha would get comfortable on my couch after dinner, ready to fall asleep right there, despite having her own apartment just down the hall. Her actions never bothered me, though—I secretly loved the company, especially once the sun set for the night—and I would always drape one of the many blankets from my bed over her body after she fell asleep. When asked what Sasha did on her "off nights," as she called them, she explained that she'd sleep on Lucy's couch at the latter's apartment a few blocks away. I didn't ask why she needed the company to sleep comfortably; I understood.

Falling asleep for me proved the worst simply because I couldn't. I lay in my bed thinking about everything I had done, and in those early morning hours when there was truly no one, I would hear the echoes of the dead calling to me softly—*Zelda, Zelda, Zelda*—until the sun rose again. By the time I dragged myself out of bed, Sasha or Dave would be gone, and I would eat breakfast with Gunther and LeRoy before starting my day over again.

My days were exhilarating, to say the least.

Three months had passed since the day we devised the plan to run away, and it was now January, which meant the weather required me to wear a green jacket Allyson purchased for me everywhere I went, along with a lilac scarf wrapped tightly around my neck. The tan boots that went up to my knees were the most bothersome part of the outfit, but when the small white crystals people called "snow" started to fall from the lint gray sky like it had in December, I was secretly grateful for the traction the bulky shoes provided.

One day in mid-January, immediately following my morning press rounds in the outskirts of the city, President Dassian called me up to his office via intercom. When the elevator doors slid open to reveal his office, I found the short, stout man staring at his glass table, watching an overwhelming number of blue dots surround red dots on a grid similar to the city's grid, but as seconds ticked away, the red dots quickly grew, and after about five seconds, the red ones had completely overpowered the blue ones. I awkwardly cleared my throat to announce my arrival, not wishing to disturb him.

He waved me over and pointed to the paused grid projected onto the table. "Blue dots represent the number of anti-war demonstrations over the last year. The red dots represent the number of pro-war demonstrations," Dassian described. "As you can see here, when we first began, those pro-war rally numbers were quite small compared to now."

"Impossible," I said, shaking my head despite the data presented in front of me. "When I first came here, everyone wanted the war. I only met a few who didn't or were at least wary of it. I think your statistics are reversed."

President Dassian chuckled and resumed the slideshow. "You only paid attention to the people with the loudest voices. You heard their voices above all the others who were, perhaps, too afraid to speak up. Loudest does not always equal largest. But now, as you can see, right after the Societan Massacre, things began to shift." The red dots began overpowering the blue ones on the screen then. "People began changing their minds about you, Zelda. They began to see the war differently."

I chose to ignore the way those words constricted my throat with guilt. "How much longer, then, until we have readied troops and technology?" I asked, cautiously trying to avoid hope from creeping into my voice.

"Not for another few weeks, at least." At my defeated expression, the president crossed his arms and twitched his big, puffy nose to push his thick black glasses back up. "I remember a time when you demanded we not start a war, and now look at you, wondering when we can send our people out to fight. I'm wondering what caused this change in you, darling."

I copied his posture. "Caleb Woobi burned my home to the ground," I declared convincingly. "It has become my personal mission to make sure he burns, too."

President Dassian reached out to graze my arm, and it took everything within me not to cringe at his touch. "That's my girl," he said with a bright, sadistic smile that I tried eagerly to match. "Time to get Peter back, eh?"

Gunther informed me once I reached my room some minutes later that Eric had left to go to the WeaponsCore Corporation headquarters and learn about the status of their updated artillery while Dave, unsurprisingly, had gone to work with the survivors. Since it had been a couple of days since I had last seen Dave, I made the decision to go and surprise him at the Refugee Center before returning to my room for my routine dinner with Sasha.

I'm not sure what I expected from The Refugee Center of Neweryork, but it certainly wasn't a single large warehouse with nothing but tiny makeshift beds scattered around, a few baskets of nonperishable food items, and portable toilets set up in the back. I spotted Dave's blond hair and broad frame in the farthest corner of the warehouse, close to the row of sinks, standing right next to a bed surrounded by men and women in laboratory coats resembling my work attire in the Society. He seemed to be talking to someone in the bed, and as I crept closer to the scene, I saw Sharlee

Davidson, the little girl from the village with the bouncing red curls who had first discovered Dave and me. Only it wasn't her. It couldn't have been her.

This little girl smiled up at whom I presumed to be her doctors, talking energetically with Dave as she practically bounced in her seat with excitement. One man in a laboratory coat was fitting what looked like a lower arm to the scarred, red roundness that cut her right elbow off from what should have been the rest of her right arm. *But that isn't possible,* I kept telling myself as I watched this unfold. *This isn't real. This can't be happening.* The room spun, and I grasped the headboard of one of the nearby beds to steady myself. I had to leave.

But something stopped me, something that had to do with the little girl right in front of David Woobi. I couldn't seem to take my eyes off her little body, watching her smile grow to a grin when the doctors clapped and praised her for something she must have done right. I watched as she tried to wiggle her now-mechanical fingers to match the real ones on her other hand but failed in doing so, and I watched as tears pooled in those big brown eyes of hers. Dave acted quickly to sit beside her on the bed and place her on his lap, murmuring words I could not hear from where I stood. But I did hear her sobs, her cries of wishing things were different, her pleas for her parents to be with her. I wondered why they weren't by their young daughter's side at a time like this. *Especially at a time like this.*

The doctors excused themselves, telling Dave they'd return shortly, and I watched them leave through a back door before turning my attention again to Dave and Sharlee. She was still crying against his chest, her little hands—one flesh, another flesh-colored but what I now knew to be mechanical—wrapped loosely around his torso as he rubbed her back in soothing circles. He suddenly pulled away from her and asked, "Do you want to play a game, Sharlee? Do you remember the game I taught you?" He stuck both of his arms out in front of him and beeped like a machine, frowning when he saw she wasn't playing along. "What's the matter, sweetheart?"

Her little face scrunched up impossibly tight, tears leaving her eyes like a thunderstorm's raindrops. "I can't move my fingers, Dave," she sobbed. "I don't like this!" She attempted to pull the fake arm off her elbow, but Dave jumped into action and stopped her immediately with a look resembling both horror and helplessness.

"I know you don't like it. I know. But you have to wear it so you can get used to it. That's what the doctors told you, right? They said it's going to take some time, but you'll get used to it, and then you'll be fine."

"Wrong. I don't like the doctors, Dave. Just like I don't like *this*." She pointed to her prosthetic angrily.

"Sharlee..." He tried to reason, sighing deeply and clenching his jaw. "The doctors are only trying to help you. Dr. Placee and Dr. Phoboto are so nice, remember? They're only trying to help you. We are *all* trying to help you, but you have to let us."

Her face twisted into a scowl, and she semi-turned away from him. "I don't want help. I wish I had my arm back, Dave. I wish Mommy and Daddy were here. I wish I was back home. I don't like it in this place. When can I go back home?"

"Soon," Dave lied. "But for now, let's try moving your superhuman arm again, okay? Want to try again, Sharlee?" When Sharlee shook her head in protest and looked at that part of herself in disgust, Dave switched gears, a smile appearing on his face as he exclaimed, "Okay then, tell you what. Let's play a game. You know so many, don't you?"

Again, Sharlee pressed her lips together and shook her small head in opposition.

"Do you want to hear a story, then? I have lots of those."

Her silence screamed no.

For a moment, I thought Dave would combust from his frustration, but he miraculously kept his temper in check.

Sharlee wiped away the tears on her face and studied him intently for a few moments, much to Dave's delight, before asking, "Why do you smile if you're not happy, Dave?" Her intellectual brown eyes blinked at him questioningly, and I had to slap my hand over my mouth to contain my gasp of surprise.

He sighed again at the question before laying her down and bringing the tattered blanket to cover all but her petite oval face. "Sometimes, you have to smile for other people in order to make them happy," he tried to explain to her.

She closed her eyes, but I could tell she struggled to grasp that sentence when her little eyebrows knitted in confusion. "Don't you have to be happy before you can give your happiness away?"

"I wish it were that simple, sweetheart, but let's not talk about that now, okay? Go to sleep now, you need your rest." Dave stood up, but Sharlee grabbed the back of his neck to drag him back down for one more comment.

"Do you miss the before?" She didn't have to elaborate on what "the before" implied; we both knew what she meant.

He leaned forward to kiss her forehead. "More and more with each passing second, Sharlee."

"Is that why you're sad all the time now?" she asked.

"It's part of it," he told her honestly as he readjusted the blanket to tuck under her body. "Lots of things make me sad now, but that's okay. I have you."

"I get sad sometimes, too," she confessed, propping up on her natural elbow. "I miss Mommy and Daddy, or my arm, and then I get sad. When are they coming back, Dave?"

I heard him suck in what sounded like tears before telling her: "Not for a while, but don't worry, you'll see them again. They will always be with you. Never forget that."

She settled back down, satisfied with his answer. "And you will always be with me, right? Promise?"

He smiled at her sweetly. "Right. I promise, Sharlee."

She grinned at him before stating, "You don't have to be sad anymore."

Dave drew his head back in surprise. "What makes you say that?"

The little girl turned her head slightly so that she and I could lock eyes, and she pointed at me with a huge smile brightening her face. "Because I see Zelda right behind you."

Dave turned swiftly on his heel to stare me down, his blond eyebrows crunched together in either leftover frustration, confusion, or anger, I couldn't distinguish which. I chose to ignore his sour look, however, and went walking over to the little girl, my face lighting up when she widened her smile as I drew nearer. "Hi, Sharlee," I greeted warmly, stretching my hands out so she could hug me if she wished.

"Hi, Zelda," she chirped, equally cheery as she reciprocated my hug. "What are you doing here?"

"Well, I had to surprise my absolute favorite seven-year-old, didn't I?" I teased as I came closer to sit beside Dave on her bed, tapping her lightly on the nose in the process.

She feigned a scowl and proclaimed, "I'm not seven anymore. I'm eight!"

"Eight! You're such a big girl now!" I leaned close to her so we could rub noses, which made her giggle adorably.

Dave stood up abruptly and announced, "It's better if we give Sharlee some time to rest now, Zelda. We can see her later." He leaned down once more and kissed her hard on her hairline before saying, "I'll be back soon, okay?" to which Sharlee nodded sleepily.

I bid Sharlee a heartfelt farewell, and by the time I had said my goodbyes, Dave was already out of the gigantic warehouse, waiting on the street corner for Dassian's personal transportation service to take us back to his building. I resorted to sprinting toward the vehicle when I saw him beginning to close the door on me. "Why did you do that?" I asked.

"Do what?" he replied innocently, staring intensely at his fingernails.

"Don't play dumb with me," I snapped, watching the effect my words had on him as he shrunk a bit in his seat. "I think I have the right to know why you were so standoffish toward me just now. I also think we need to talk about Sharlee."

The vehicle door opened just in time for him to avoid my questions, but I caught him by the arm before he had the chance to enter the lobby of the building. "Why did you hide her from me?" I questioned, not bothering to make room for the heavy foot traffic. I knew my face attracted onlookers, but my confusion prevented me from moving away from the middle of the sidewalk.

"I didn't want you to know," Dave answered while he lowered his head in shame. "I didn't want you to think she was… an invalid, or something. I'm sorry."

"Why in the world would I think that?!" I yelled. "She's the same Sharlee I've always known, just now without her right lower arm, and that's fine. Nothing about her has changed, except for maybe her physical appearance. And where are her parents, David?"

"Don't call me that, please."

I pretended not to hear his quiet request. "Shouldn't her parents be with her during this time? What could be so much more important to them that they had to leave their daughter in that disgusting—"

"They're dead, Zelda."

"They're dead! Wow! Isn't that… wait, what?" My eyes widened as I met Dave's heated stare with shock. "No," I declared with finality. "No, they can't be. No. Dave, Sharlee needs her parents. They can't be dead." I brought my hands up to my mouth. "No, no, no." I refused to believe it. There was no way Sharlee was an orphan. *No.* She couldn't end up in my situation. She couldn't end up like me. *She couldn't be me.*

"I found out when we were brought to Neweryork, and they did a count on who was alive. Mr. and Mrs. Davidson weren't on that list." Dave's voice trembled. "I think I remember seeing them run back to save more people. They died as heroes." *Just like Alina and Owen Jadestone. Just like my parents. Dead heroes.*

"Who's going to take care of her?" I asked slowly, almost trance-like. "She needs her mom, her dad, her brother, too… Why aren't they here when she needs them?"

"Sharlee doesn't have a brother, Zelda," Dave reminded quietly, but I didn't listen.

"Where's her mom to hold her? Her dad to guide her? Her brother to support her? Why did they have to be so selfless?" The questions ricocheted off the surrounding skyscrapers and smacked me in the chest, painful pangs serving as reminders of what I had lost. "She needs her family, Dave."

The ex-Uniform eyed me with concern. "I'm taking care of her now, Zelda. It's okay."

"No!" I yelled. The knife I always carried grew heavy in my pocket. "She needs her *family,* Dave." I pictured a little orphan girl growing up, raised by someone who pitied her, wondering what she had done wrong to make the universe punish her in this way, and I wanted to save Sharlee from that fate. *Sharlee couldn't be me.*

I slammed my hands down on the cold, shiny exterior of the building, not satisfied with the feeling violence gave me. "Why can't she just have a family?" I tried to shout, but the question came out as a whisper, words not spoken loudly enough for anyone around to hear.

I didn't know what to do with myself. I looked around for some place to escape, but the people passing by made it impossible to think straight, forcing me to sink down onto the crowded pavement for some kind of privacy. The position caused the knife to stab me in the thigh.

Sharlee would go the rest of her life without her mother and father. Eventually, the sound of their voices would fade from her memory, and as time passed, she'd forget she ever missed them the way she did now. She'd forget what it felt like to have them near her, as I had. Alina and Owen Jadestone's memory died when I forgot them, and I carried my guilt everywhere, strapped to my body like the knife in my pocket. Sharlee couldn't turn into me. *She couldn't.*

Zelda, my parents instruct me to do better, but how can I please the people I don't remember?

Zelda, Sharlee squeals happily, but all too soon, her cries become ones of anguish.

Zelda, Peter scolds, and I want to tell him I know. I'm aware. I understand the depth of my failures in keeping this family, *our* family, intact.

I hadn't realized my descent into panic until Dave grabbed me by the waist and held me against him even as I tried to break free of his grasp, screaming my throat raw, the shrieks echoing through the lobby Dave had yanked us into. He tried to shush me gently, whisper sweet things in my ear, rock my body back and forth soothingly; nothing worked. Spots swam before my dry, closed eyes, little sparks from the fire behind my eyelids. *Fire.* I heard the fire, its roaring and spitting making it seem almost human. Peter's whimpers for help soon joined in the symphony until I was a perfect hyperventilating mess, my arms stretched out in front of me, grasping for something I could never reach.

Gunther and LeRoy rushed out of the emergency stairwell minutes later, and between them and Dave, they led me back into the elevator, toward my room, and placed me down on my bed, where I stayed shriveled and distant, dead to reality and stuck inside my own head. I stayed in that position until Mr. Woobi entered my room and sat at the foot of my bed, not saying a word until I growled, "What do you want?"

"Nothing," he answered honestly with a shrug. "My grandson and your guards called me over here to, as they say, 'talk sense into you.'" He tilted his head. "You and I both know that won't work, will it, Zelda Ellyn?"

"I miss my family," I whimpered like a small child.

The older man scooted closer to me so he could stroke my hair, the action involuntarily making my eyelids droopy. "I know you do, dear girl," he said.

"My parents would be so disappointed in me," I confessed.

"No, Zelda Ellyn," Mr. Woobi rebutted. "On the contrary. Owen and Alina would be so proud of you. Their daughter grew up to become such a strong, selfless, courageous, and kind young woman. What is there not to be proud of?"

"I left their son alone in the Society. People have died because of me. I'm not a hero like they were."

"You love your brother more than anything else in the world; your actions prove your love for him. And you are not responsible for anyone else's actions but your own. Your parents would be more than proud of you, dear girl. You were their joy, and you still are. Soon, once everything is in place, we will go save Peter. I promise you, Zelda Ellyn, you will have a family again." He brought my chin up to hold his loving gaze. "I promise you."

Mr. Woobi left sometime after that. Gunther, LeRoy, and Dave decided it was best for me to be alone for the night, so I sat swathed in silence, body covered entirely by the heavy blankets on my bed, until Sasha entered my room sometime after the sunset. She didn't ask for permission to crawl into the bed and lie beside me, and we didn't speak until she asked, "What happened, Zelda?" When I refused to answer, Sasha didn't press the subject, instead choosing to ask, "What is he like?"

I flipped over to look at her inquisitively. "Who?"

"Peter."

I flipped back over; the pillow muffled my reply: "I don't want to answer that."

"Why not?" she inquired in a voice so soft and gentle, I had to pinch myself to make sure I wasn't dreaming. "I'm going to be seeing him soon, right? Might as well know what the boy is like now, so it's not awkward later."

It took me a few minutes to say anything back, but when I did, it was one-worded: "Selfless."

"Seems to be a family trait," she commented. "What else?"

"Generous."

I heard the smile in her voice when she said, "What a nice quality no one has nowadays. What else, Zelda?"

And as I flipped on my side for the last time to face her, I told Sasha everything that night. I told her how he used to laugh at everything when he was a toddler, regardless of how stupid or insignificant the joke. I told her about all of his favorite things growing up: the color red, the planes Uniforms flew, the crackling sound of our leftover food scraps in the incinerator, my raspy voice when I woke him up for school in the mornings, mathematics class, Eric's laugh after he told a joke, Mr. Woobi's stories from our past. I told her about his least favorite things, too: whenever anyone cried, raised voices, the color gray because it was "too boring," the emotionless expressions of the Uniforms we'd walk past, the executions we were forced to attend.

    I told her how, when he knew Eric and I were bored, Peter would reenact these elaborate, intricate, nonsensical stories that only the mind of a then-eight-year-old could create. I told her how he was always afraid to sleep in the dark, even though he didn't have any reason to be afraid of anything in the Society, save for the consequences that came with breaking the law. I told her how carefully he watched over Mr. Woobi, always offering to walk him back to his househut when it was time for the elder to leave ours. I told her about the time Eric threw him into Province Two's fountain as a birthday celebration when Peter turned ten, and how we sprinted back to our househut after being chased by Uniforms. I told her how cuddly he was, how he would love to snuggle against my side at night because to him, I felt safe. I told her that out of the two of us, he was *better*, in every sense of the word; he was the best person I knew.

    Sasha listened to me as I ranted about his eye color, how sometimes his brown eyes could appear lighter or darker depending on his mood, and how long his eyelashes were. She listened to me talk about how funny and quick-on-his-feet he was, how smart and intuitive he was, how great of a listener he was. She listened to me as I described how nimble his fingers were, how quickly he could create beautifully intricate paper objects I'd put on display in the center of our dining table, how his fingers never trembled when he spent hours making said small objects on the weekends. She listened to me ramble about our history: how we grew up together, how he left me to collect information for Mr. Woobi, how we reunited in the end, only for him to leave again so I could escape the Society alive. She listened as I listed all the reasons I loved him, from the simplest of things, like the way his brown hair curled when he grew it out, to the most abstract of concepts, like the way my heart settled perfectly in my chest when he smiled at me.

And when I was finally finished, she didn't laugh, or tease, but instead took my hand and said sincerely, "He sounds wonderful, Zelda."

I agreed showing the tiniest of smiles.

Just as I thought she had fallen asleep given the fact that it was well past midnight by then, she muttered, "Melanie was smart, too."

Melanie. The girl who had collapsed in my arms during the Societan Massacre, the same one who once lived with Sasha on the edge of the river, her dead girlfriend.

Sasha began by telling me about how they met, both orphans who had escaped the Redding village orphanage at a young age—she guessed around thirteen—because of the mistreatment and abandonment they faced there. She explained the story of how they hopped onto a cargo truck, stole the tents that would later become their home, and walked for days out into the forest until they found a secluded, "perfect" spot right by the river with an "amazing" view of the Society. She told me they would spend hours hunting together; most of the time their laughter scared off the animals, but neither of them cared, since Melanie usually went back to the village once a month for supplies and food anyway. She told me Melanie would always dream about rescuing her older sister from the Society when they first met, but as time passed, Melanie talked less and less of her biological past, and more of her future with Sasha.

She told me Melanie never complained about their simple life in the woods, but Sasha knew she had a very soft, feminine taste in clothes, so to appease her, Sasha would bring her back floral, "girly" dresses when it was her turn to go to the village to restock on stolen supplies. She told me how after she would surprise her with these gifts, they'd have "dance parties" outside their tents, in which the two of them would jump, swing, and kick to music Sasha blasted from her personal screen. She told me Melanie loved sugary things, so they ate dessert almost every night, when they could afford it. She told me Melanie was the epitome of sunshine, and Sasha was convinced her long—too long, in Sasha's opinion—blonde hair caught the sunlight in each strand, her eyes the color of a clear, blue summer sky. She told me Melanie would call Sasha "her moon," a reflection of the sun, her perfect complement.

She told me everything changed when my appearance in the village went viral. She told me I was all Melanie could talk about because I gave her hope again that she could free her sister, and my words were the reason Melanie volunteered excitedly to go to the Society, even though Sasha had warned her against the idea. She told me they both died that night.

"Do you still feel dead?" I asked once she had finished speaking.

"Ask me that when we leave this place. Then I'll know for sure," she replied.

I clung to that answer long after she fell asleep, hoping that one day soon, we'd both be able to relish the feeling of being alive without thinking it's a punishment for the ones who are not.

For Peter, I thought as sleep claimed me that night. *But, for Melanie, too.*

Just as Mr. Woobi said before.

For the people we couldn't save, and for the one we still could.

CHAPTER 19

"Happy birthday, Zelda!"

My eyes burned as Eric ripped back my bedroom curtains to reveal the harsh sunlight, and I groaned while flipping over onto my stomach to hide my face from my visitors. *Happy birthday.* As much as I dreaded acknowledging it, twenty days had passed since the day I visited Dave at the Refugee Center, and it was now February 7, my nineteenth birthday, the first birthday I recalled spending outside of the Society.

I struggled accepting that only a year before, I had spent the day walking around the Society with Eric after we were excused from our jobs, happily ambling down the concrete streets as we reminisced about memories from childhood. Eric had grabbed his dinner from his househut to join me in mine, and after I had finished crying about Peter's absence on my special day, Eric produced a mug from behind his back. It was a standard, bland little thing, nothing but white ceramic, and I was about to ask why he brought random dishware from his househut when he turned it on its head to reveal small, barely noticeable, silver etchings on the bottom: "Z+E," sloppily carved in Eric's messy handwriting.

Gift-giving was a nonexistent practice in the Society—we had nothing to give, since Caleb only provided us with the bare necessities—but Eric explained he felt it essential to give me something, even something as insignificant as a mug for my water in the mornings, on my eighteenth birthday, if he couldn't give me the gift of my brother back. I didn't use any other cup after that until our quick flee from the Society forced me to leave it behind.

On my nineteenth birthday, exactly one year later, Eric and Sasha jumped on me and shook me awake excitedly, happily singing a simple "birthday tune" Jannet had taught them minutes before. Gunther and Dave tried coaxing me up with promises of sweet desserts, and Lucy and Harmony arrived bearing huge shopping bags of "gifts they thought I'd appreciate." Despite all the excitement, I only left my bed after Mr. Woobi leaned close to my ear to whisper, "I have news regarding our plan. Our opportunity may be upon us."

Everyone but LeRoy stayed for breakfast that day, the sound of our shared laughter floating through the apartment as we swapped stories from our time before the impending war. Gunther cooked a delicious meal of something he called "Belgian waffles" that the nine of us dove into like ravenous animals, and afterward, Lucy and Harmony placed one of the twelve shopping bags at my feet for me to open. I did so nervously, having never opened any sort of gift bag before, and slowly, I pulled out a gray t-shirt and pant set that matched my mandatory Societan attire almost perfectly. Lucy clapped excitedly despite my perplexed reaction and rationalized, "If we're going back to the Society, we should all look the part, right?"

Harmony pointed to the other bags in the corner of the living room and added, "We got everyone a pair. This outfit is sold in, like, every retailer now, ever since you went viral months ago."

The attire reminded me strongly of my dead coworkers, of their blood on my shirt after Uniforms gunned them down in front of me seconds after my friends had saved my life, of their own gray outfits stained a dark, rich red as the blood trickled onto the gray cement. I glanced at Eric, and judging by his sudden paleness, I knew his thoughts matched mine. Dave's scrunched face displayed clear discomfort, the outfit probably a stark reminder of the citizens he was forced to publicly execute during his time as a Uniform. I didn't wish to alarm our newfound friends, however, so I swallowed my malaise, feigned a gracious smile, and thanked them as sincerely as I could for their thoughtful present. At the very least, I knew it would aid in camouflage when we inevitably raided the Society, and for that, I genuinely felt grateful.

Mr. Woobi cleared his throat to quiet our chitchat after the gift exchange, claiming he had information that could heavily impact our plan to escape. Once we settled down, he explained that last night during his nightly walks with Jannet, they overheard one of the men on the president's committee talking about some huge announcement being made on "her birthday."

"I have to talk to Dassian," I replied sternly before my hopes rose too high. "I have to make sure all of it is true before we make any rash decisions."

Everyone agreed excitedly, and about an hour or so later, Gunther pressed the elevator button to take us to President Dassian's office. As we sped up toward the 200th floor, LeRoy interrupted our silence by saying, "Happy birthday, Zelda Jadestone," with the smallest trace of a smile on his face, a rarity I hardly got the privilege to see.

I thanked him sincerely and offered to give him a piece of the sweet dessert Gunther had baked the night before when we got back to my room, but he politely declined, cocked an eyebrow, and jested, "I'm hurt I wasn't invited to the festivities this morning."

"You said you had errands to run," muttered Gunther under his breath half-angrily, unable to pick up the heavy sarcasm laced through LeRoy's voice. LeRoy and I exchanged knowing, friendly glances at his expense.

President Dassian was waiting for me right outside the elevator doors with a gigantic, utterly ridiculous grin and a pathetic piece of paper with the words "Happy Birthday, Zelda Jadestone!" scribbled sloppily as a clear afterthought. I would have laughed at its sheer absurdity if Dassian hadn't jogged back toward his table after handing me the birthday paper, pulled out papers from behind his back, and waved them up in the air triumphantly.

I scanned the documents quickly once he had handed them to me, grasping words such as "declaration," "war," and "Caleb" to try and piece together the bulk of it. "What are these, President Dassian?" I asked without taking my eyes off the papers.

He snatched them from my hands with a flourish, his mouth stretching into a grin even further than I had ever thought possible. "These, Zelda Jadestone, are the official documents for the formal declaration of war against Caleb Woobi's Society. These are your tickets to Peter, darling. These are everyone's tickets to freedom. Congress passed my request early this morning."

"Our troops are ready, then?" I asked.

"Trained by the finest computers around," the president declared proudly as he lifted his chin to keep his glasses from falling down his red, bulb-shaped nose.

I wanted to ask him how he expected computers to properly and fully train human beings for something as entirely, uniquely human as war, but I held my tongue for appearance's sake. "And the technology? It's perfected?" I settled on asking.

He ran over to his table and projected an image of guns in all sizes and styles with a bolded, black symbol on the handle of them. When asked about it, he said that was our "war symbol," a symbol under which the state could unite. "The Electric Zelda," his team of digital art creators named it, saying it perfectly blended a bolt of lightning and the first letter of my name.

When asked to describe the technology, Dassian explained the scientists working for WeaponsCore discovered the Society's boundary radiated incredibly strong energy waves capable of mass destruction if provoked, which clarified why nothing living could ever penetrate the Society's borders without instantaneous disintegration. "It was near impossible," he read from WeaponsCore's official statement. "But everyone in the lab refuses to believe in the impossible, so we uncovered a way to contain and counteract that energy with our own weapons." Dassian went on to read that they developed a gun that shot not bullets, but energy, a different kind of energy that would coat the Society's bubble in an invisible reflective shield of sorts. The reflective shield would trap the waves emitted from the boundary and force them to bounce back toward itself. The shield, in turn, would contain the waves until the pressure became too much, and the boundary would pop from all the built-up energy, essentially attacking itself.

"Shoot it directly at the boundary, and it will begin to pop like a bubble," Dassian read, "but shoot it at a human being, and it will turn them to dust. Signed, the WeaponsCore Corporation."

I thought of absolutely nothing to say in return, my gaze still transfixed on the powerful weapons displayed in front of us, so before the silence turned uncomfortable, Dassian said, "I will be making an official speech declaring war on Caleb Woobi and the Northeastern Society in a few minutes. Then, darling, you and your little band of friends will attend the gala I'm hosting later tonight. I'll see to it that you are properly dressed for the festivities."

I despised the idea of celebrating the marked beginning of an event sure to kill thousands more, of mindlessly chitchatting with politicians who didn't seem to care whether those individuals lived or died, of pretending to be entertained while Caleb tortured my brother, but I agreed to attend nevertheless. A distraction might have been exactly what the ten of us needed.

Before I left his office, Dassian stuck his sweaty hand out for me to shake. "After months of hard work and dedication, this is the moment we have been anxiously awaiting," he stated. "You will be reunited with your little brother, thousands of people will get the freedom they deserve, and Caleb Woobi will finally crash and burn. It's been an honor working with you, Zelda Jadestone. Without you, I never would have gathered the support for this war. You truly inspire us all."

An eerie feeling enveloped me then, almost as if President Dassian's farewell was meant to be our final one, but not wishing to draw attention to my suspicions, I chose to smile, shake his hand firmly, and reply, "Thank you, Mr. President. I look forward to seeing you at the gala."

"Hm," he hummed, placing a hand on the small of my back to guide me toward the elevator, not saying anything else until I stepped inside. "I'm sure you are," he sneered, but before I could speculate on his strange behavior, Dassian stepped back to press a button on the wall that promptly closed the elevator doors in my face.

My friends were all gathered around my couch, so engrossed in the screen in front of them that they didn't hear Gunther, LeRoy, and me walk into my apartment some minutes later. I took a seat beside Dave on the couch, a tad squished between him and Mr. Woobi, and told my guards to join us on the floor, which they did all too happily.

Together, we watched as Allyson introduced the audience to what they'd be hearing in the coming minutes, stating the president had an announcement that would affect the entire state, and it was prudent that every citizen tune into the broadcast. When Dassian appeared on the screen, he sat behind his clear table, dressed in a military-metal decorated, army-green jacket, his unkempt hair gelled down to look neat and authoritative.

"Good afternoon to all citizens of this great state of Neweryork," President Dassian addressed the nation, captivating all of us with his powerful voice and strong words. "Today, February 7, 2125, we celebrate the birth of Zelda Jadestone, the courageous young woman who fought for her own freedom and has dedicated her life to fighting for the freedom of our loved ones. We celebrate her and how her resilience has impacted our lives since the day she arrived at the village Caleb Woobi mercilessly destroyed. She has singlehandedly inspired this state to fight for access to basic human rights for those in need of them most. But more than that, ladies and gentlemen of this fair state, we celebrate the strength she has implanted in all of us over these last few months. The strength we needed as we faced terrible, horrific tragedies such as the Societan Massacre and the Redding village fire. The strength we will all need as we plunge into this state's civil war."

I could almost hear the gasps around the city as Dassian nodded his head in affirmation. "Today, on February 7, 2125, at this very hour, we formally declare war on Caleb Woobi and the Northeastern Society, effective immediately. We declare war on his warped ideologies and barbaric policies. We declare war on his senseless acts of violence against innocent human life and his selfish disregard for those victimized by his power. We declare war, citizens of this great state! We declare war, I say! We refuse to be stifled by Caleb Woobi's regime. We refuse to cower in the face of his evil wrongdoings committed against our people. We refuse to bow down to a senseless dictator who shows no remorse over the crimes he continues to commit. Through her inspiring words and heroic actions, Zelda Jadestone has provided us an inferno that will burn Caleb Woobi to the ground, just as he did to our families fighting for the freedom of their loved ones. Follow her, follow *me*, and we will prevail in crushing Caleb Woobi into nothing but ash."

Everyone held their breath as we awaited the president's next line like fish on the hook, waiting to be reeled in toward our deaths. President Dassian seemed so convincing, so genuine, so real and *raw*. Only I knew better. I spotted the way his eyes moved, indicating he was simply reciting sentences fed to him through the camera's lens. It both terrified and angered me that he could mindlessly spew life-changing, monumental, incredibly powerful words with such persuasive authority. Even Caleb chose his own words. What an actor Cody Dassian was. What a good actor indeed. I wished to never be like him.

The president continued: "Today, on February 7, 2125, we come together as a united state to stand up against injustice. Today, we mark the end of the cycle of imbalance, torture, and inequality Caleb Woobi established fifteen years ago. Today, let us be a shining example that equal opportunity and integrity will always prevail in the face of evil."

"This war is our chance to finally hold Caleb Woobi accountable for his crimes. This war will grant us the opportunity to extract revenge on the man who stole our people, our land, and our freedoms. This war will provide a better life for everyone: the people trapped inside the Northeastern Society and those outside who have suffered for far too long without the ones they love most. This declaration is long overdue. Caleb Woobi's actions have been excused for too long. Our system has failed helping these innocent, helpless people sooner, but because of Zelda Jadestone's brave decision to escape her impoverished, appalling life in that prison of a Society, she has sparked the fire we have needed for years."

"I have seen this fire spread rapidly over the course of these few months," President Dassian said, and I couldn't help but draw similarities between the next part of his speech and my improvised speech at the village's ruins almost four months prior. "I saw this fire in the survivors of the Redding village fire when they so beautifully serenaded Zelda Jadestone after her speech. I have heard these flames on these very streets as you rioted, protested, and marched for human rights. I have felt this heat when Zelda speaks about her poor, sixteen-year-old little brother Peter Jadestone, currently being tortured to the brink of death by Caleb Woobi. It is this, my people, this fire I see, that has convinced me that we are ready for a war. We declare a war, my people. We declare a war. We declare a war in the names of our loved ones, and in the name of freedom. Thank you."

The screen flashed the same emblem on the handles of the weapons I saw earlier: a tilted, skinny, red "Z" lingering over computerized flames, surrounded by nothing but darkness.

None of us said a single word after Mr. Woobi powered off the monitor, each too stunned by Dassian's speech to speak, until Jannet asked what had occurred between Dassian and me when I visited his office earlier in the morning. I explained to everyone what had transpired, and once I had finished, Mr. Woobi pursed his lips, nodded, and exclaimed, "Tonight's the night, Zelda Ellyn. Tonight, we leave."

Sasha whooped excitedly as Eric, Dave, and I exchanged equally giddy looks at Mr. Woobi's announcement, but LeRoy didn't appear convinced. "How so?" he asked with his arms crossed. "We are expected to attend the president's gala tonight."

"Gross," Sasha stated as she bounced in place on the couch. "No thanks. We can sneak out before then."

"No," Mr. Woobi refuted sternly. "We will be going to that gala. It would be too suspicious if we didn't show."

"So, what are you thinking, Mr. Woobi?" I asked.

The plan proved complicated, intricate, and risky. Just as the older man stated before, we would attend Dassian's gala as planned, dressing up and playing our parts spectacularly so as not to raise doubt about our loyalty. Mr. Woobi and Jannet had walked every inch of the building over the last three months to mark the security cameras' locations, and sometime before the gala, Sasha, LeRoy, and Gunther were expected to disable the cameras on our floor, the ballroom floor, and the lobby via their connections with the building's security team to ensure no one could pinpoint our disappearance.

Once Mr. Woobi signaled our individual, unique times to quietly exit the party, we would change into the outfit Lucy and Harmony had purchased and wait for the others in the lobby. When Mr. Woobi signaled me, I would approach Allyson and Marley, instruct them to join us, and unite with the rest of the group outside, where we would all pile into our shared vehicle to drive to the WeaponsCore warehouse. Eric cut in to announce that over the duration of these couple of months, the corporation had granted him access into their building, so we would use Eric's access code to steal some of their perfected weapons to use in disintegrating the boundary once we arrived outside of the Society. If anyone were to suspect any ill intent during these next crucial hours, our plan would be ruined, so we were required to remain extremely vigilant.

When asked about the plan once we breached the Society, Mr. Woobi turned to Dave. "You trust this Uniform friend of yours, Blake Yandle, correct?"

Dave nodded, albeit stunned. "Of course, I do. Why?"

"Do I have your word, David?" Mr. Woobi pressed.

"I promise," Dave assured. At the mention of Blake, Dave started bouncing his leg rapidly.

"Why are you asking about Blake?" I asked.

Mr. Woobi explained he had devised two separate courses of action, since we had discussed two different reasons for re-entering the Society. The first group would accompany me to find Peter; after receiving Dave's vow that he trusted Blake Yandle, Mr. Woobi elaborated that the plan to rescue Peter was contingent on Blake's total cooperation. Dave would tell us Blake's Uniform apartment number, and we'd go to the Uniform sector of the Society to convince Blake to take us to the Jail, where Peter was most likely being kept. With Blake's help, we'd be able to stay relatively under the radar, and he could cover us until we escaped with Peter. The invitation to leave would be extended to Blake as well, of course.

The second group would follow Mr. Woobi and Dave to find Caleb. With Dave's knowledge from his time as a high-ranking Uniform, they'd sneak around until they reached Caleb's building. Dave described a special access code Uniforms could type into the elevator that would take them straight to Caleb's office, and Mr. Woobi's team would use that to reach Caleb and avoid Uniforms. Dave and Mr. Woobi would then somehow convince Caleb to leave with them—how could Caleb resist the begging of his own son?—and they'd meet us at Sasha's old camp she used to share with Melanie at sunrise, where we'd reconvene and formulate another plan to go back to the city.

After much debate, we ultimately decided two teams of six would enter the Society and conduct the separate plans. Gunther, Allyson, Marley, Harmony, Jannet, and I would consist of one team, with Dave, Mr. Woobi, Eric, Sasha, LeRoy, and Lucy on the other. Dave put up quite a fight to stay with me, but we concluded that besides the need for Dave to be in the other group, the two of us together would pose as an extra danger, as would Mr. Woobi and I together; we three were Caleb's largest targets.

If anything went wrong during this phase of the plan, we'd be jailed, tortured, and most likely executed, so exercising stealth was crucial.

"What about Sharlee?" Dave inquired frantically once Mr. Woobi finished explaining the entire plan. "I can't leave her without telling her where I'm going."

"You must, David," Mr. Woobi replied. "Telling anyone outside of this room compromises our entire mission."

"She'll think I abandoned her," Dave argued.

"Which means she'll be extra excited to see you when you get back," commented Eric with a consoling clap on Dave's shoulder.

"She can come with us," Dave proclaimed, but I shook my head vigorously.

"No," I countered harshly, memories of Will hitting my conscious harder than the wave that inevitably took his life did when it slammed into my body all those months ago. "We're not bringing a child into this. Not after Will."

"You'll see her soon, bud," promised Eric, his gaze softening as Dave turned to him for reassurance. "In the meantime, she has plenty of doctors and therapists to keep her company. No worries."

Dave eyed the room skeptically, his fists clenched at his sides as he said, "We can't stay in the Society long then."

"Ew," said Sasha, not bothering to look up as she picked the dirt from under her nails. "Who would want to?"

Dave shot her an exasperated glare. "I'm serious. We free Peter, talk to Caleb, and come back. Deal?" He looked to me then, electric-blue eyes simmering with desperation.

I made sure to hold his gaze as I answered, "Deal. In and out," and before anyone could dispute further, I declared, "This is it. Tonight, we rescue Peter."

"For Peter," chimed Eric, rising to his feet.

"For Peter!" the room echoed, standing up as well.

For Peter, I thought as Allyson and Marley entered my apartment an hour or so later, their faces bright and merry as Allyson congratulated me on the war announcement. *This was all for Peter.* I hoped that sufficed in appeasing my aching conscience.

After a catering service served the twelve of us lunch, Allyson and Marley's team of expert stylists dressed all of us according to our personal fashion preferences and body types, and five hours later, we strutted into the second-floor ballroom of Dassian's building together. I wrapped my arm around Dave's bicep for support, since my high-heeled, ruby-studded shoes and the longer train on my skin-tight, fiery red dress prevented me from walking normally. I had already tripped over the extra material gathered around my feet more times than I could count, so when Dave suggested he escort me into the gala, I all too quickly accepted his offer.

As we walked into pulsating, blaring music, multicolored spotlights, and thunderous applause, Dave leaned his head close to mine to whisper, "You look beautiful, by the way."

I didn't feel beautiful. The straps that held up my dress were much too thin for my liking, the cut much too low, the fit of the dress much too tight. The makeup around my eyes resembled embers in the dark, red sparkles and orange glitter against a black background, and the liquid makeup on my face felt much too heavy for my taste. Yet when I had glimpsed into the mirror in my bathroom right before we exited my apartment, I knew I looked powerful. I looked dangerous. I looked set ablaze by the fury that had fueled this fire the day I left the Society. A flame personified. Perhaps the smoldering anger in my eyes made me beautiful, too.

I accepted the compliment regardless, appraised his own outfit—a bright blue suit, complete with a darker blue tie—and teased, "You look beautiful, too."

Someone walked by with a tray full of bubbly, golden champagne in skinny, tall glasses, and Dave quickly grabbed two for the both of us. Bodies filled the entirety of this room, people of all shapes and sizes swaying and conversing loudly over the throbbing, electronic beat of the music, and my palms grew sweaty from the claustrophobic atmosphere.

Dave raised his champagne flute and yelled above the noise: "To being beautiful."

We clinked our glasses together and took a sip, but the fizziness of the tart drink made me shyly spit it back into my flute, much to Dave's amusement. He asked to dance once we had found a standing table to place our glasses, and after I agreed wholeheartedly, he swept me up in his arms and rocked our bodies to the music, a gentle movement compared to the others around us who jumped in place. We reviewed their dance moves and scored them accordingly, a fun game that rendered me laughing over his shoulder in mere minutes, and we only stopped when the music switched to a softer melody. As we swayed in time with one another, Dave intertwined his fingers in mine, strategically placed my hand on his shoulder, placed his mouth near my ear, and muttered, "Are you sure you're okay with all this?"

I knew what he meant. "This is my chance to reach Peter," I reasoned. "Of course, I'm okay with it. I'm okay with anything that will help me get to him."

He nodded and moved so our foreheads collided, his lips mere inches from mine. "I'm sorry I've been so distant," he whispered, yet when I opened my mouth to protest, he pressed his pointer finger to my lips to quiet me. "Hear me out. The fire changed me; I know that. I know you know that, too. I wish I could be the way I was before, but with Sharlee, and everything that happened, I don't..." He inhaled sharply, betraying the tears that infiltrated his beautiful blue eyes. "I don't know if I'll ever be the same man again. I'm so sorry for that, Zelda."

I cupped his oval, symmetrical face in my hands and closed the distance between our bodies, sealing my lips to his and allowing for that numbing, tingling, electric feeling he gave me to drum out all other senses, if only for a few moments. "Let's get through this first," I sighed against his now red-stained lips. "Once this is all over, we can heal together. Deal?"

"Deal," he murmured, and we danced for a few moments more before a flash alerted us to someone secretly attempting to snap a picture of the two of us together. The act intruded on our privacy; we smiled and played it off anyway to save face, but after that invasion, we chose to go our separate ways and meet sometime later.

I scanned the energized, heterogeneous crowd for a familiar face, relieved when I spotted Sasha several yards away in a stunning, one-shoulder, emerald-green dress she chose from Allyson's collection. The satin fabric bunched up right at her waist to accentuate her curves, and a left slit ran up to her mid-thigh, making the dress appear much shorter than it was. She was conversing with Lucy, her polar opposite, with the latter's floor-length, pastel yellow dress with delicate flowers embroidered in the tulle material. The pair of them smiled in pity when I cautiously wobbled in their direction, and Lucy eventually lent me her hand to guide me over to stand beside her.

"You look like a baby learning to walk for the first time, Jadestone," Sasha joked with a hand on her waist, and I scowled as Lucy covered her mouth to suppress her loud giggle.

"Zelda, have you seen Eric?" Lucy asked timidly, wringing her delicate, small hands in front of her petite body.

"Hm?" The idea of Lucy actively searching for Eric rubbed me the wrong way, like a bad itch under the surface of my skin, but I tried to ignore my sudden discomfort. "Oh, um, no, I haven't. I'm sorry." Indeed, I hadn't seen him since we all entered the ballroom and split up, and I searched the crowd for any sign of him with no success.

Another tray of champagne passed by, so the three of us each grabbed a flute and simultaneously pretended to take a sip to blend in with the crowd. The music amped up once again, the multicolored lights flashing in time with the beat, the crowd hopping to the nonsensical melody like their lives depended on it. As I observed the strange scene, I tried to dissect what exact moment in my life had led me here, to this ballroom, with these people, listening to music that assaulted my eardrums with each pulse from the speakers. Harmony joined Sasha, Lucy, and me shortly after, her long-sleeved, cobalt blue, sequined dress hugging her narrow hips perfectly. She nodded in greeting, snatched the champagne glass from my hand, and swallowed its contents in one gulp, smirking devilishly when I looked up at her in surprise. "What?" she questioned, licking the remaining champagne droplets from her lips. "We can't have a little fun while we're here?"

"That dress looks gorgeous on you," complimented Lucy sweetly in response.

"Thank you, lovely," replied Harmony, running her hands down the front of her dress to smooth the material. "I wanted to honor Will with the sequined wave patterns."

My stomach lurched into my throat as the memory of Will's tragic death knocked into me, and I clutched my abdomen as bile threatened to spill from my mouth. I quickly excused myself from the group to bunch up the train of my dress in my hand and rush out of the ballroom, so focused in my intent that I neglected to notice someone calling after me as I raced toward the closest wall to lean against and stabilize my heavy breathing. Black dots swam into my vision as my heart pounded in time with the pulsing music, and I shut my eyes to alleviate this rush of panic before I heard a distinct male voice call my name.

"Zelda! Hey, are you okay?" Eric asked once he found me against the wall, and I opened my eyes to see him standing over me worriedly, his black suit and skinny black tie beautifully complimenting his extremely dark, fluffed-up hair.

His familiar, kind-hearted, green eyes diffused the anxiety clacking inside my chest like a bomb, and I heaved a heavy sigh before pushing the hair from my face and apologizing. "What are you doing out here?" I asked to distract us from my sudden panic attack. "Lucy's looking for you." I tried to smile as the words left my lips, but it probably appeared as more of a grimace on my face.

Eric shrugged and shoved his hands into his pant pockets. "Not really in the mood right now," he answered. "I'll find her later."

He leaned his back against the wall and propped up a foot; the stance accentuated his tall height, and I couldn't help but sweep my eyes over his lean figure. "You look nice, Eric," I complimented. "I've never seen you dressed up before. You look good." I assessed his look one more time and added, "Really good."

Eric's face softened as he dropped his foot back to the floor and brought a hand up to rub the back of his neck. "You look nice, too, Zelda. More than nice. You look…" His Adam's apple bobbled as he swallowed hard. "I don't think I have the words to explain it. Beautiful as always."

My cheeks bloomed red at his flattery, and that tug between us threatened to yank me into his arms, little sparks sizzling inside my body from the center outward. I melted under his tender gaze, and a different kind of nervousness swept over me, an emotion only Eric could elicit. I cleared my throat awkwardly to break the sudden tension between our bodies. "Well, I'm going back inside," I declared a bit too loudly. "Join us when you're ready."

As I turned to leave, Eric called me back. "Zelda?"

"Yeah?"

Eric shifted his weight from one foot to another as he confessed, "I can't stop thinking about him. Will. He should be with us tonight, and I can't stop thinking about where he is instead."

I readied myself to jump back into the water and swim after him, but Eric caught my upper arm just as I was set to dive back in. I screamed at him to let me go, kicking and slapping him in an attempt for him to release me so that I could swim after Will, but he refused to lighten his grip.

"Do you blame yourself?" I asked suddenly, the feeling of Eric's hands gripping my upper arm ghosting along my skin.

Eric's lowered gaze was my answer.

I hadn't given myself the chance to evaluate Eric's complicity in Will's death, not until I saw the guilt hidden in his green irises, and a disgusting, itchy feeling crawled into my pores like a particularly terrible infection. I scratched my upper arm until red welts appeared to try and rid myself of the irritation.

Eric blinked away tears as he croaked, "He haunts me."

"He haunts me, too." They all did. Will, Eve, Abe, Melanie, my coworkers from the Society, the people from the village, those murdered near the Society, the Uniforms Blake Yandle killed to protect me, the ones who fought to free Mr. Woobi after my speech, Jack Garrole: they all lived inside my skull, ghosts drifting across my consciousness any moment my brain tried to rest, constant reminders of the pain I could inflict. Their blood stained my hands, a permanent red pigment on my skin no number of showers could ever wash away. Their last breaths stole my own in the moments I woke up gasping. Their lost lives made mine duller. Yet every time Caleb showed a clip of Peter in pain during one of his propaganda videos, I could ignore the guilt I carried, if only for a moment, because my little brother needed me. Peter needed me to rescue him as much as I needed him to save me from the shame infiltrating my soul. Peter needed a family, *his* family, and I needed mine. I would deal with the dead bodies resting on my mind, waiting for their chance to be buried, once I rescued Peter from Caleb's harm.

"The Uniform I killed in the Society, and now Will. I'm going to carry these deaths forever," Eric muttered.

"Maybe we can carry them together," I suggested softly, a reference to his words the first night we spent outside the Society, all that time ago.

"Yeah, maybe we can," Eric agreed, a sad sort of smile forming on his face.

I wished to embrace him, but just as I stepped closer to do so, Gunther and LeRoy seemingly materialized beside me, requesting our presences back inside the ballroom, claiming President Dassian was set to make a speech in the upcoming minutes. As my guards escorted us inside, I almost commented on their color coordination—LeRoy's maroon tie matched perfectly with Gunther's maroon velvet suit jacket—but I chose to keep the observation to myself to avoid unintentionally embarrassing them. I instead complimented LeRoy's tweed suit and how wonderful the texture looked against his dark skin tone; I earned a bashful, "Thank you, Zelda," in response, which I took happily.

The four of us joined Dave, Sasha, Lucy, Harmony, and now Jannet, who looked beautiful in her simple tan pantsuit, standing in the closest corner to the main doors. We exchanged compliments for one another's outfits until President Dassian was introduced onto the stage at the front of the room. The short, round man waved to the cheering crowd adoringly as he approached the podium, his smile much too big for his plump, small face. "Good evening," he greeted, his booming voice ringing through the speakers and effectively quieting the crowd. "Is everyone having a good night so far?"

The crowd yelled happily in response, including the nine of us for appearance's sake.

Dassian's grin grew at the crowd's excited cheers; how it was even humanly possible for a man's smile to be that large, I didn't know. "What a day," Dassian exclaimed breathlessly. "We declared war today!"

The crowd yelled once more in delight.

"We declared war today," Dassian restated. His face looked flaming red under the harsh white spotlight. "We declared war against Caleb Woobi today." He paused to sigh, as though he had just lifted three hundred pounds, and placed his hands on his hips. "Feels good, doesn't it?" At the crowd's hollers, he said, "Yeah, it feels good! Every single person in this room deserves to celebrate this amazing success tonight. Everyone here has worked for months, most even years, to make this dream become a reality, and here we are, celebrating the start of the downfall of a violent oppressor we have let rule for too long. You should all be so proud of yourselves. This night belongs to you."

The crowd broke out into deafening applause, although Eric fervently refused to clap with the rest of us.

"I wish I could shake every single hand in this room," Dassian said. "You all deserve to know the impact your actions have on this war. The media specialists, news anchors, journalists, and social media managers: you are the collective voice of the people we serve. You turned their whispers into war cries, and do you know what the people want, ladies and gentlemen? They want to destroy Caleb Woobi just as much as we do."

The crowd screamed enthusiastically.

"I also want to extend special recognition to the special interest group representatives in attendance tonight," Dassian continued, "notably, the lobbyists from the Neweryork Republic Association, Save the Survivors Foundation, Redding Relief Fund, and the WeaponsCore Corporation. Without your steadfast dedication, unwavering loyalty, and devoted service to this state, we would not be going to war against this Society today, and I most certainly would not have been elected president years ago!"

Dassian's comment elicited rumbling laughter from the crowd while Dave, Eric, Sasha, and I traded equally confused glances. LeRoy rolled his eyes and huffed in annoyance.

"I am honored to have been elected into this position," Dassian said, one hand over his heart. "Ever since the Federation won the Second American Civil War fifteen years ago, I have fought against the terms signed in the Washington Peace Accords. It is unfair for innocent individuals to sign away their freedoms and live under the tyranny of a dictator. Every person has the right to life, liberty, and the pursuit of happiness, as stated by the founders of the old United States of America almost three hundred and fifty years ago. Caleb has denied these people access to their human rights for too long. The Washington Peace Accords have failed these people we swore to protect. Today, we end this injustice. I am forever humbled to be your president during this historic moment. Know I will do my very best to lead us into this war with strength to ensure a prosperous future for all."

I scrunched up my nose at the mention of the Washington Peace Accords, a treaty I had never heard of until then; I promised myself to ask Mr. Woobi about its significance when the opportunity arose. The crowd chanted Dassian's name to show its support, and I reluctantly joined, wincing each time I participated.

The president raised his hands to quiet the crowd. "I have one last person to thank," he said with a laugh. "She just so happens to be the birthday girl, too. I would like to personally invite Zelda Jadestone to join me on the stage. Zelda, darling, come on up here!"

Mortification overcame me as Gunther led me to the stairs on the side of the stage, the roar of applause and shouts of my name enough to cripple me on their own, regardless of my inability to walk in these heels. The crowd refused to settle down as Dassian made a big show out of embracing me, kissing both my cheeks sloppily and shaking my hand firmly. His dark, beady eyes looked shiny under these bright white lights, and when we got close, I saw the sweat lining his forehead. *Good,* I jeered in my head as he asked the crowd to settle down once more. I reveled in the satisfaction that I could make these supposed leaders, Caleb included, nervous enough to perspire. Dassian grew uneasy in the presence of my fame and purported power. As he should. I could mobilize this crowd—or any crowd, for that matter—more effectively than he ever could.

Once the people quieted down, Dassian said, "I think we can all agree when I say Zelda Jadestone has changed our lives. I know she has changed mine for the better. This young woman miraculously escaped an impossible situation, and instead of hiding, she chose to raise awareness for those still trapped. She hasn't acted selfishly; she has acted selflessly for the sake of the ones she was forced to leave behind."

Dassian paused to chuckle. "I remember the first day I met Miss Zelda Jadestone. Only hours before, she had witnessed her brother being tortured on Caleb's first public broadcast, and she immediately wanted to devise a plan of action for rescuing him from the Society. I knew the second she left my office that day that we had found someone special. Without Zelda Jadestone, this war wouldn't be possible. In these past months, Zelda Jadestone has garnered unprecedented support. Let us give her the praise she deserves."

Dassian stepped back to turn toward me and begin the applause, and the people erupted into high-pitched whistles and chants of my name once more. I pretended to enjoy the admiration, pressing my palms together and smiling sweetly in gratitude, and I only faltered when I caught Mr. Woobi's piercing gaze among the invigorated crowd, closer to the stage where I could analyze him thoroughly.

The multicolored lights highlighted the Society's symbol carved into the elder's expressionless face, his body frozen despite the flurry of activity around him. I remembered a time, not that long ago, when he sat on display on a different kind of stage—limbs strapped down to a metal chair, form unmoving, demeanor calm despite the direness of his situation—and I thought that maybe, this was my own execution, too, just a different kind.

As the crowd continued to cheer for me, I counted down from ten, just as Caleb had done before Mr. Woobi's scheduled killing.

Ten. I scanned Mr. Woobi's form for any sign of struggle or strife—for any sort of emotion at all, truthfully—but he stood impeccably still, leaning only slightly on the cane in his right hand.

Nine. My heartbeat increased to where I heard my blood rushing in my ears, but I remained steadfast and standing, refusing to let this Woobi man best me.

Eight. Mr. Woobi adjusted the white-rimmed glasses on his face, and for a second, I thought I saw tears in his light blue eyes, but he blinked before I could confirm my suspicion.

Seven. Dassian stepped off the stage; blaring music resumed; the crowd went back to dancing beside Mr. Woobi; but neither of us paid attention to the external stimuli.

Six. The elder started to crack under the weight of my stare. His body trembled, and his grip on the handle of his cane tightened when he lurched forward to increase his lean on the walking aid. The purple tie he wore swished with his jerky body movements.

Five. I curled my fingers into my palms for some sort of physical relief from the buzzing in my bones.

Four. Mr. Woobi mouthed something to me from his place in the crowd, four words I didn't know I needed to hear until my father figure uttered them: *I still love you.* He didn't have to elaborate. Even after the death of his wife, Charles Woobi was still capable of feeling love. Despite my heavy involvement in our present situation, despite my actions indirectly causing Eve's death, he could still love me. Regardless of his forever grief, he chose to love, and he chose to continue to love me.

Three. I knew my response: *I forgive you.* For what, I wasn't necessarily sure. Perhaps I forgave him for exploiting Peter's innocence and coercing him into becoming a Uniform five years before. Perhaps I forgave him for allowing a man like Caleb Woobi to be born into this world, for raising him into existence, for not seeing the warning signs he might have exhibited as a young man. Perhaps I forgave him for putting me in this horrific position in the first place. Perhaps all three; it didn't matter. I forgave him for it anyway, as I knew I always would. Mr. Woobi raised me, provided me a familial structure in my childhood, took it upon himself to care for Eric, Peter, and me when we weren't his blood family. I would love him forever, regardless of his actions.

Two. We exchanged small, knowing smiles, and I wanted nothing more than to embrace him with Peter by my side, a broken family now whole.

One. "Ten o'clock," Mr. Woobi mouthed. His words confused me before I spotted Jannet weaving her way through the crowd, headed discretely toward the doors to make her exit, and all at once, I understood.

Ten o'clock. I would secretly leave this ballroom at ten o'clock to escape to the Society and rescue Peter. I only had an hour more to wait.

I grinned at the revelation, and Mr. Woobi winked before disappearing among the squished, dancing, almost formless bodies.

I joined the remaining members of my group in their designated spots in the corner immediately after, and judging from the giddy looks on their faces, I knew Mr. Woobi had informed them of their individual scheduled times as well. As the eight of us danced to the rhythm of the music, Dave wrapped me up in his arms and strategically placed his lips by my ear in a way that looked like just a normal embrace. "One of us leaves every six minutes," Dave informed me, spinning us around in a slow circle so as not to raise suspicion from the random onlookers around us. "First, Jannet left, then it will be Harmony, Lucy, Mr. Woobi, Sasha, Eric, Gunther, LeRoy, me, and then, you'll go talk to Allyson and leave with her and Marley at ten. Got it?"

I nodded, and he kissed my temple lightly before resuming our regular dancing. Gunther and LeRoy sweetly danced together beside us, and Eric kindly alternated between the three girls to keep them entertained. We developed genuine smiles once we allowed the music to control our funky, unnatural movements, and twenty minutes later, when only my guards, Sasha, Eric, Dave, and I remained, we laughed loudly when Eric sent Sasha spinning under his arm. Once Sasha exited, Eric joined my embrace with Dave, the three of us slinging our arms around each other and pretending to know the lyrics to the songs blasting through the speakers. When his time came, Eric sneakily snatched me from Dave's arms, tipped me almost to the floor, and jokingly did the same to Dave before maneuvering through the crowd and slinking out the main ballroom doors.

9:36. LeRoy gazed into Gunther's turquoise eyes so devotedly, I thought the two might share a kiss, but the former only nodded, took an awkward, stiff step out of their tight embrace, and rushed out of the ballroom. Six minutes later, Gunther followed suit, but he made sure to say goodbye to us before he did so.

9:48. Dave kissed me sweetly, lingered for a moment when we pulled away, and promised he'd meet me in the lobby before leaving me alone.

9:54. Despite the jumble of thoughts in my brain, I took off my heels and pushed through the crowd on my hunt for Allyson.

I noticed Allyson's silk, rusty orange romper first when I found her standing by the refreshments, leaning her elbow casually against the bar as she idly chatted with a few associates. My face attracted immediate attention, of course, and in seconds, everyone standing in the vicinity screamed either my name or a variation of "happy birthday." The commotion caught Allyson's attention, and she lavishly threw her sleek blonde hair to one side when she turned to look at the source of the fuss, her face splitting into a grin when we locked eyes. "Zelda Jadestone, everybody!" she yelled, and although her announcement of my presence wasn't needed, it did prompt those around us to burst into an animated round of applause.

I waved awkwardly. "We need to talk," I stated in a low voice after I got close enough, my eyes traveling around the table to find almost every pair of eyes staring at me in awe. "Privately, please," I added.

Allyson seemed to want to protest, but one look at my serious expression, and she led me over to the opposite corner of the ballroom from where my friends and I had danced, a corner without as much activity. "I'm here to ask a favor," I started off by saying. "A big one, actually."

She smiled at me sweetly, the kind of fake smile I instantly wanted to slap off her heavily powdered face. "You name it, gorgeous. I'll make sure it gets done."

I lowered my voice that much more before asking, "Can you and Marley meet me in the lobby of this building in five minutes with your recording equipment packed and ready to go?"

"Why?" Allyson eyed me, perplexed. "What are you planning?"

I held my breath for a second, two seconds, three seconds as I scanned Allyson's face for anything that would stop me from divulging our plan to her, but when I only saw genuine confusion, I exhaled and whispered, "Running away, Allyson. We're running away to the Society, but to pull it off, I need you and Marley to meet in the lobby in…" I glanced at the huge clock in the center of the ballroom. "Four minutes, okay?"

Her face slacked, and she sputtered, "Wha… what? *What?* I'm sorry, I think I heard you wrong. You're doing *what*? Zelda, you're ordered to stay in this city unless we need to do press runs. Isn't it breaking the law to go against the president's personal request?" She curled her upper lip in disgust. "I have a good mind right now to turn you in for treason."

"No!" I pounced on her, gripping her shoulders tightly. "You can't do that."

She crossed her arms defiantly, arching a flawlessly shaped eyebrow. "Why not?"

"Because I cannot live without Peter anymore, Allyson!" I screeched. My shriek attracted some attention, but I couldn't have cared less in that moment. "I cannot live without Peter for a second longer. I cannot live with the knowledge that he's stuck in the Society's Jail, being tortured by Caleb for some retaliation video against me. I cannot live not knowing if he's dead every time it takes Caleb a few extra days to release a video. I have lived through months of people ordering me around, instructing me on what to say, how to say it, when and how to act, and I am done being a media puppet for you and President Dassian. I am going to save my brother, destroy Caleb myself, and live a life without all of this." I ushered to our surroundings and spat, "*That's* why not."

Allyson narrowed her eyes at me, silently assessing my words to see if they held any meaning to her. "If you think anything you said makes me want to help you, Zelda, you're wrong," she stated. "You insulted me, you insulted our president… gosh, you insulted just about everyone who lives in my city. Why would I want to do anything for you now? You know, for a public hero, you really aren't any good at making friends." She lifted her nose up triumphantly, and I physically restrained myself from punching her in the face.

"You need me," I snarled, taking a step closer to her until I had her back against the wall. "Without me, the momentum for this war burns out. You need my words. I can leave with or without you, and I will, but I know Dassian would hunt me down if he didn't get some footage of me, which is where you and Marley come in. Allyson, you need me much more than I need you. If you care about your war, you'll follow me."

I knew from the way her mouth twitched that she knew she had no other choice than to listen to my instructions. "You're just as manipulative as Caleb Woobi," she growled as an insult, but I smiled as though it were a compliment.

"You're just as much of a coward as Cody Dassian," I snapped back. "Now please inform Marley, gather your belongings, and join us in the lobby. We're meeting at ten."

And without so much as a second glance behind me, I shoved my way through the crowd, stormed out of the ballroom, and sauntered into the emergency stairwell to meet the rest of the group.

I was a couple minutes late when I appeared in the first-floor lobby, and the nine people waiting for me rocketed to their feet when they saw my figure emerge from the staircase. Harmony threw me a bag containing my wardrobe change—the gray shirt, gray sweatpants, and gray shoes that imitated my mandatory Societan citizen attire—and ordered me to change as quickly as humanly possible; everyone else had already changed while waiting and promised they'd wait for Allyson and Marley while I did so.

I sprinted to the nearest restroom, slipped out of my revealing, tight, uncomfortable dress, and scrubbed my face with the hand soap by the sink to take my heavy makeup off. Once all my makeup washed down the drain, I stashed my dress in the trashcan and threw the Societan clothes onto my body, almost not noticing the clinking noise inside my pant pocket as I did so. Slowly, I reached inside my right pocket to feel my personal items: the golden bullet the Twelve Soldiers gifted me and the knife I had stolen from Sasha's home by the river after Will's death, along with a handwritten note wrapped around the handle of the knife: "Thought you might want these. Signed, Jannet."

I made a mental note to thank her when I could and ran out of the restroom to be greeted by Allyson crying and Marley looking incredibly flustered. To calm her jittery nerves, I complimented Marley's rose-colored, short, A-line dress, specifically the flowers at the bottom of the tulle overlaying the silk, and my sincere praise seemed to put the girl at ease.

Once those two changed into the clothes Harmony handed to them, the twelve of us slipped outside in a straight line, Mr. Woobi in front. Different shapes in varying colors appeared in my line of vision from all the lights sparkling from the city's skyscrapers and screens, and as I heard my name floating through the busy streets, I decided to tuck my chin down to my chest and lower my gaze to follow the shoes in front of me. We all loaded into the large vehicle Mr. Woobi chose quickly, with LeRoy as our volunteer driver.

"I'm going to put this thing on manual, so they can't track us through the GPS," shouted LeRoy from the front of the rectangular vehicle, a pane of glass separating the seating area from the driver's chair. The eleven people in the passenger's compartment voiced our agreement, and in under two seconds, we sped through the night toward the WeaponsCore warehouse. I vaguely recall Allyson asking who this vehicle belonged to, only to pucker her lips in disapproval when Mr. Woobi replied he had stolen it for its size.

When we arrived at the warehouse, Allyson and Marley insisted on staying inside the vehicle, and none of us complained, promising we'd be back as soon as possible. Once we reached the warehouse entrance from the parking lot, we were surprised to find absolutely no security guards standing outside, although no one chose to question it. Eric typed his access code, 73887, and we crept inside carefully, waiting until Eric flipped on the lights to reveal a warehouse full of shelves stocked with every gun type, shape, and size imaginable. I picked a small handgun, confirming it had the "Electric Zelda" symbol Dassian had shown me earlier that morning to verify it was a model with the newest technology. Everyone else chose relatively the same size weapon, some a bit larger.

When we filed into the car, Allyson looked around in confusion. "I thought there were people guarding this place at all times." Her jaw dropped when she saw the weapons in our hands, and I watched as tears pooled in her eyes. "You killed them?!" she gasped in horror, bringing a manicured hand up to her mouth.

Sasha almost laughed, but she kept her composure long enough to snap, "No, you idiot. Of course, we didn't kill them, but I'm about to kill you if you don't stop that ugly look on your face and toughen up. This is a war, Killians. Act like it."

"I am!" Allyson shrieked as one tear, then another, and then another fell from her eyes. She desperately tried to stop them by flapping her hands like some kind of bird.

"It *is* weird that there was no one there," Eric said, choosing to ignore Allyson as she wept freely onto Harmony's bony shoulder. "Usually, there are at least two men guarding the entrance when I'm here, and that's during the day."

"Let's be happy there was no one working tonight, Eric," I retorted rather forcefully, not wishing to dwell on my skepticism regarding how well we had executed our plan. We had encountered not a single flaw, which did seem odd. Regardless, I felt grateful for how smoothly it went. I took the golden bullet out of my pocket to rub it anxiously, thanking Jannet as I did so for placing both the bullet and the knife in my pocket.

"You do not own much," she explained. "I figured you would want those two items during this time, especially after having them for so long. They must bring you some peace. Maybe they are your good luck charms."

I chuckled. "If they are, then I am particularly grateful you brought them."

The older woman gave me a tight-lipped smile, and I realized I had forgotten to thank her for something much more significant than a few souvenirs. "Jannet?"

"Yes, Zelda?"

"Thank you," I said, having to pause to clear my throat before continuing, "for saving Eric's life the night of the massacre. I don't think I ever recognized you for that. Truly, thank you."

Dave's head snapped to the side to look at Eric in surprise, and the latter lowered his head bashfully.

"I was doing my job, Zelda." Jannet smoothly dismissed my compliment. "I was taught how to stitch a wound many years ago. I should be the one thanking you for saving *my* life that night. Medical school doesn't teach bravery."

I leaned across the vehicle to squeeze Jannet's leathery hand briefly, and I wished I could adequately articulate my gratitude for her presence in our little family as well. She didn't say much; out of everyone in the group, she spoke the least, and because of the large age difference, I often thought of her as an outsider, watching the rest of our interactions from afar. Yet every time she did choose to speak, I knew she had a vast amount of knowledge and life experience waiting to be shared. At the very least, I was glad she and Mr. Woobi had bonded during their nightly walks around Dassian's building, but I promised myself in that vehicle that I would make a point to get to know her more once we got the chance.

No one spoke much during the two-and-a-half-hour drive to the Society, either choosing to gaze out the window or fall asleep. I snuggled into Dave's arm wrapped around my shoulder, periodically placing a kiss on his square jaw; although my actions caused his lips to quirk upward, the way he bounced his knee reminded me constantly of the weight on his heart. I tried to sleep, but the idea that I could be reunited with Peter in less than twelve hours kept me awake and restless.

It was well past midnight by the time the vehicle rolled to a stop outside the Society's boundary, and although the ones who weren't present for the Societan Massacre hopped out of the vehicle without issue, the rest of us hesitated.

Being back at the place where such a deeply painful event occurred triggered something deep inside me to snap, and I froze in deep terror as memories from that night kept lapping at my consciousness like the waves at the river's edge. I saw Uniforms slaughter innocent people. I met Will. Eric almost died. I wanted to run—run out of this vehicle, run away from these memories, run from this ache I couldn't heal—but my body refused to move, regardless of how intensely my mind commanded my legs to operate.

Zelda, the almost-dead had cried. My name was the last word they ever uttered.

Zelda, the massacred cry now, still as awed and inspired as before.

Zelda. I know, trust me. I failed those people. I know.

Eric eventually helped Jannet, Harmony, and Lucy out of the vehicle, and although he tried to reach me, my ears only heard static. My eyes darted to Sasha, and I saw her bite her bottom lip so hard, she drew blood.

"Melanie," she murmured, and that was all it took for me to understand.

My hand found hers in the dark, and I wove our fingers together for support. "I'm here," I told her once my lips awoke from this panic-induced paralysis. "I'm here for you."

Sasha snatched her hand back so fiercely, I momentarily feared she might punch me. She harshly wiped a single tear from her cheek instead. "You don't get it, Jadestone. I don't need your help," she argued. "I can do this on my own."

"No one can mourn alone," I declared fiercely as I took her hand again and forced my body to move, if not for my sake, then for hers. "C'mon, we can do this."

With great effort, I managed to get the two of us out of the vehicle, our feet crunching the grass below as we walked over to where Mr. Woobi had gathered the rest of our group. The elder reminded everyone of their placements on which teams, explained the beginning of the plan once more—the twelve of us would pop a hole in the boundary just big enough to walk through and immediately split up—and granted us five minutes for departing words, claiming we wouldn't have time to do so once we were inside.

Dave immediately squashed me in a hug and lectured me on safety. "Zelda, please be careful," he implored. "I don't know what I'd do if something happened to you. Remember, go straight to Blake's apartment—"

"Straight there," I repeated. "Got it."

"Fifth floor. Walk straight until you can't anymore, then take a left and follow the hallway until you are forced to take a right. He's the left door at the end of the hall. Take the stairs; all the Uniforms use the elevators. Blake never works the overnight shift, so he should be in his apartment when you get there. And remember, Zelda—"

"Straight, left, right, left door at the end. It's okay, Dave. I'll be fine."

Dave couldn't seem to stop his nervous rambling, despite my best efforts to soothe him. "Avoid Uniforms, Zelda, please. This mission should be in and out, like you said. Blake will help you; I know it. Make sure you stay in the househuts' shadows as much as you can. Avoid windows. Gosh, please, be safe. I—"

I kissed him full on the mouth, not letting him go until we both were forced to inhale through our mouths. "Just come back to me," I whispered, resting my forehead against his own. "And I'll do the same. Deal?"

"Deal," he promised. "I'll see you at sunrise."

I kissed him one last time to seal that deal, too.

Mr. Woobi approached me next. "I'll see you in a few hours, then," he proclaimed with a nervous smirk.

"And if you don't?" I inquired.

"Then take care of that brother of yours for me."

"I meant if I die, Mr. Woobi."

The older man wobbled up to me to squeeze my hand. "You won't."

I didn't have the heart to protest.

After saying his goodbyes to Jannet, Eric rushed over to me, stopping just a few feet away. "I'm sure Lucy is happy about the team selection," I joked after some silence.

Eric managed to puff out a laugh, opened his mouth as though he was about to retort something snarky, but instantly thought better of it. Instead, he took steps toward me to close the awkward distance between us, tugging me toward his chest and squeezing my frame so hard, I almost suffocated. "You die, I die," he declared, and I nodded in understanding.

"I forbade you from dying, remember?" I told him, wrapping my arms around his torso.

"I remember. If you forbid it, then I won't," he promised. "I promised forever."

"And I, always," I murmured back, and I swear he smiled as he rested his cheek against the top of my head.

Sasha and I didn't let go of each other until Mr. Woobi yelled at her to fall in line beside him, and even then, it took both LeRoy, who smiled as a goodbye, and Lucy, who cried when we parted, to pry Sasha off me. "Don't do anything stupid!" I called out as she retreated.

She turned back long enough to wink and yell, "No promises!"

"We better get going," Gunther announced, and I agreed.

The six of us—Allyson, Marley, Gunther, Jannet, Harmony, and I—took a few steps closer to the boundary, the familiar hum of energy radiating from it bringing me back to almost half a year prior, when Mr. Woobi, Dave, Eric, and I stepped outside its borders for the first time. "On three!" I shouted.

Inhale. "One!" The roar from our weapons caused Marley to jump, and even I grew nervous from the light beaming inside the barrels and the heat intensifying on the handle.

Exhale. "Two!" My heart beat furiously inside my chest, yearning to reach Peter.

Repeat. "Three!" Peter. Peter.

For Peter.

We took aim at the boundary simultaneously, and we pulled the triggers. Together.

CHAPTER 20

BAM! After thirty minutes of consistent firepower aimed at the boundary, the beige bubble finally began to degenerate with a loud pop, and my team of six hurriedly bowed our heads to walk through the short entry we had created, the second team bringing up the rear. As the boundary crackled during its reformation behind us, a deafening siren rang around the Society, no doubt alerting Caleb of his broken boundary. With a curt nod to the others, I ordered my squadron to follow me to the Uniform building, a place I hadn't visited since Dave and I broke into the database ten months prior.

As we slinked in the househuts' shadows, I was surprised to see that nothing had changed since my departure almost half a year ago. The brown, one-story, boxy househuts in which the citizens resided looked untouched, that sickly, dim yellow light the streetlamps emitted still bathing their boring exteriors. As we snuck through Province One, I noticed my old province's swirling, stair-like sculpture still standing as though nothing had changed, and its presence reminded me of the Wednesday nights Dave and I illegally spent sitting on its peak, talking to learn more about one another. Simpler times then, and we didn't even know it; how could we? How could we have predicted what would happen to us? Just a year before, Dave refused to arrest me for saving Mr. Woobi from a brutal punishment. How little I knew of how significant that golden-blond, blue-eyed Uniform would become in my life. How little I knew of how drastically my life would change in one year. I briefly wondered if given the knowledge I possessed now, would my younger self still make the choices she did? But I didn't wish to dwell on that thought for too long.

Once we arrived outside my pristine househut—strange, given the fact that Uniforms had blasted my door to pieces the day I left—I slowed my stride to quickly peer inside through its sole window. My old househut looked much cleaner than when I left it half a year ago. Along with the new door, the Society had replaced all my furniture and arranged them in their original positions, down to Peter's small bed against the wall, perpendicular to mine. I wanted to check the cabinet for the birthday gift Eric gave me, but when I heard the pounding of the Uniforms' boots on the cement intensify, I waved for my friends to follow me and increased our already-quick pace. As we moved, I hoped those on the other team successfully evaded the Uniforms now teeming the streets.

So many Uniforms had accumulated by then that we were forced to decelerate to avoid detection. Allyson and Marley weren't necessarily born for sneaking around the Society, so on many occasions, Jannet, Gunther, Harmony, or I had to physically cover the girls' mouths to keep them from speaking, much to my chagrin. I knew once we lost the protection of the househuts outside of Province One, the risk of our mission would increase dramatically, and I told my group so as we crouched behind the last househut at the edge of the province, watching as Uniforms poured out of the Uniform building, headed for where we had broken the boundary. That apartment-style building and the Uniform Academy behind it were the only complexes in the Uniform sector of the Society; the rest was empty cement, a wide courtyard of sorts. Because of this, there were no places to hide, so I explained our best bet was to wait until the Uniforms stopped exiting the building, and when the opportunity arose, we'd make a dash for the lobby. If I remembered correctly, the closet Dave and I had hidden in when I attempted to become a Uniform was just around the corner from the entrance, and the door to the stairwell wasn't too far beyond that.

"I don't like this," Allyson grumbled. I noticed the subtle, blinking red light on the collar of her gray shirt, a hidden camera intended to film me, and although I hated being filmed, I didn't draw attention to it; footage of me was part of our agreement.

"Me neither," Marley muttered under her breath, lower lip protruded as she pouted.

"Get a grip, ladies, please," Harmony whispered sharply. "This is for Peter, right?"

I nodded when Harmony looked to me for encouragement. Of course, this was for Peter. I still had trouble believing that I would get to see him so soon after many months apart—many years apart, really. Our reunion last time had been short-lived. I wondered what he would be like now after enduring Caleb's torture, but truthfully, I didn't care what condition we found him in, so long as he was alive and conscious. Peter would be Peter, regardless of whatever trauma he suffered. He'd be thrilled to see me, just as I was to see him. *Right?*

The six of us sat behind this househut and waited a long time, possibly an hour or more, for the commotion by the Uniform building to settle, and as we did so, I observed my team with great affection. The burly man who started simply as my security guard had become one of my closest companions; despite Gunther's intimidating stature and sheer size, he remained gentle and kind, much more a lover than a fighter. Harmony, despite her oblivious, clueless tendencies, had nothing but the best intentions, and I admired her dedication to whatever she poured her heart into, whether that be her modeling career, her position on the camera crew for NewerNews, or this friend group she stumbled into. Jannet offered a maternal presence my life had lacked before her appearance. Marley's bubbly personality never failed to make me smile; I found it amusing that both she and Sasha were seventeen years old, since their personalities, hobbies, and passions were so different. Allyson, as annoying as I sometimes found her stubbornness, pushed me to do better. How lucky I was to have these loyal people as my friends. I couldn't wait for Peter to finally meet them.

When the opportunity presented itself, I signaled my team to follow closely behind me, and we sprinted into the Uniform building's lobby, swung around the corner, and rushed into the stairwell, shutting the door behind us gently to lessen the noise. Déjà vu swept over me as we crept up the steps, but instead of continuing to the fourteenth floor to reach the database like Dave and I had done, we paused at the landing for the fifth floor. I relayed Dave's instructions to my group—walk straight, turn left, follow the hallway, turn right, last door on the left—and we slid out of the stairwell slowly, careful to step lightly as we inched our way down the hall one foot at a time. After checking the next hallway multiple times, we turned left and continued our painfully slow trek. Thankfully, neither Allyson nor Marley uttered a single word during this process; if anyone so much as sneezed, our mission would be compromised, so I was grateful they had the forethought to shut up.

We turned the last corner and were halfway to Blake's door when the sound of voices encroached from a nearby hallway. Jannet scrambled to cover Allyson's mouth when the latter audibly gasped, but I didn't pay them any attention, instead choosing to wave my friends to stick close to my side as we hurriedly tip-toed to Blake's door.

I knocked as softly as I could on the smooth wood, to no avail. The voices grew closer, and I calculated in a matter of two minutes, we'd be trapped. My brain spun as I attempted to think of a solution before Harmony harshly shoved me out of her way, picking a bobby pin out of her black hair gathered in a sloppy bun on the top of her head. She squatted until she was eye-level with the scanner Blake would presumably use to scan his finger for entry, analyzing the mechanism with amazing scrutiny. The voices sounded close enough to be in the hallway before this one by then. Just as I opened my mouth to hurry her, Harmony slid the bobby pin into the space between the scanner and the door, and she wiggled the little metal stick around until something inside the device clicked, the scanner's blue light dimmed, and the door slid open with ease.

We didn't waste any time hurrying into Blake's apartment. Once we all piled in and Gunther had manually slid the door closed, we turned to stare at Harmony in amazed shock, who eyed us in confusion. "What?" she asked, crossing her arms in front of her chest.

"Where did you learn how to do that?" Allyson inquired.

Harmony shrugged. "Granddad's a handyman. He taught me a bunch of weird tricks like that when I was little. The metal bobby pin trips the wire if you get it in the right spot." She raised her small chin proudly. "I'm not as useless as Sasha likes to think."

Her last comment made Jannet snicker.

"I thought handymen went extinct, like, fifty years ago," said Allyson with a hint of superiority to her voice. "Machines do that kind of work now."

"Maybe here they do, but before the Second Civil War, I grew up in Boston," replied Harmony defensively.

Allyson's face contorted like her nose caught the scent of something rotten. "That explains it. Bostonians are so stuck in tradition that you forget to modernize with the rest of us."

"I moved to Neweryork to pursue modeling pretty much right after puberty," Harmony replied with just as much disgust in her tone. "When the Second Civil War ended, I got trapped in this state because of the closed borders. Trust me, I wouldn't be here if I had the choice."

"Bless those closed borders," Allyson mumbled sarcastically as she turned her back to Harmony.

I turned on the overhead lights to both survey our new surroundings and to silently signal Harmony and Allyson to end their petty bickering, especially since I had no clue what they were arguing about. Blake didn't appear to be home, but I couldn't imagine why; if I had an apartment as wickedly beautiful as this one, I didn't think I would ever leave. White marble tile floors ran throughout the apartment, sleek-but-unwelcoming gray leather sofa and loveseat duo in the spacious living room that led to a rather large balcony overlooking the Uniform sector. The kitchen was small—there was no need for one, since food appeared cooked in the kitchen window—but still beautiful with gray slate countertops. I didn't dare venture past the common area, but I guessed his bedroom and bathroom were just as nice. It surprised me that even a lower-ranked Uniform like Blake would get to experience such luxury, but then again, Caleb had to entice people to leave their families somehow. Allyson commented on her surprise that the Society wasn't a "completely disgusting pit," and although I usually took offense to those comments about my past home, in this circumstance, I had to agree. In comparison to my househut, Uniforms lived like royalty.

We had just finished exploring the common area when the familiar sound of the Uniforms' boots filled the hallway outside and stopped right outside the door. I waved my arms to signal everyone to crouch behind the sofa just in case; I knew our position wouldn't matter if Uniforms other than Blake were to enter, but the action seemed to help put Allyson and Marley more at ease, so I indulged.

"545537, there's light coming from inside," said a harsh voice I knew could only belong to a Uniform. *545537.* I recognized that number. I squinted in an effort to remember to whom that number belonged, but my mind blanked.

"That's strange. You think she's hiding in here?" replied a hopeful, distinctly male voice that sounded extremely familiar. He placed much more emotion in his tone, and it drove me mad that I couldn't place a face to the number.

I heard a whacking sound from the other side of the door. "Don't be stupid. Why would she come to a Uniform's apartment?"

The mysteriously familiar one said, "That's fair. She's somewhere in the Society, though, right?"

"The alarms went off for a reason, 545537."

"Yeah, what a dunce," Harmony whispered. I shushed her quietly in response.

"Well, I'll see you during the next shift," the familiar one announced. "Take care of yourself, 43468."

We heard footsteps indicating that the other Uniform retreated to his own apartment, and we waited with bated breath as the familiar one tried to enter the apartment with no success. Harmony giggled into her palm when the Uniform cursed the scanner, but she quickly stopped when he manually pushed the door open, entered the foyer, and slid the door closed once again, leaning toward the locking system to search for a reason behind its failure.

Before he could investigate further, I impulsively hopped up onto my feet and greeted, "Hi."

The Uniform seemingly jumped out of his skin as he turned around with a loud, terrified shriek. "Oh my f—"

I placed my hands out in the surrender motion. "Don't freak out," I implored. My gaze traveled over the Uniform, analyzing his jet-black hair and narrow, dark eyes, his pasty, pale skin and sunken features that told me he hadn't slept in weeks... I recognized him. 545537. The same Uniform who had murdered nine of his own so I could escape my workspace, the same one who helped me heal the gunshot wound to my shoulder, the same one who promised to watch over Peter. Dave's close friend from Uniform Academy: Blake Yandle. I released an exhale when he dropped his defensive stance to gaze at me in shock, mouth agape.

"Zelda? Is that you?" Blake shout-whispered in awe, his arms swinging loosely at his sides.

I ran to hug him, wrapping my arms around his bony body and refusing to let go despite Allyson's appalled gasp. I tried to keep Dave's words from months ago in mind—that Blake didn't kill those Uniforms maliciously; he only acted in self-defense—as I told Blake how relieved I felt to see him again, smiling widely to show my sincerity.

Blake grinned back and lowered his hands from my waist down to my hips. Heat rose into my cheeks, and I cautiously stepped out of his embrace. "You... you're here," he stumbled through a toothy smile. "You're here! How are you here? Why? How did you know this was my apartment? I have so many questions."

His bewildered expression made me want to laugh, but I refrained from doing so. "It's hard to explain," I answered honestly.

"It's so nice seeing your face again, after so much time," he told me seriously, trying to take a step toward me again; I retreated and awkwardly giggled. "I thought about you every day since you left. How's your shoulder?"

I swung my arm in circles. "Healed, thanks to you. Here, let me introduce you to my friends." I instructed the rest of my team to crawl out of hiding, and they did so reluctantly, going over to shake hands with the Uniform and introduce themselves as if the action pained them. Once everyone became acquainted, I asked, "Blake, where's Peter? Is he okay?"

"Peter?" the Uniform questioned. He cocked his head to the side in confusion.

"Peter Jadestone, my brother. Uniform number 73235. You promised you'd try to protect him with your life."

Blake's angular eyes widened in remembrance, but he swiftly dropped his gaze down to the floor. "Oh. Peter. I tried stopping them, Zelda, honestly, but—"

Trepidation crept into my voice when I cautiously asked, "But what?"

"Leader Caleb wanted him in a special cell in the Jail. Even I don't have access to it."

"Do you know where this 'special cell' is?" I asked as I dug my fingernails into his forearms. "Can you bring me there?"

"I've been looking for Dave for months, too," Blake continued, either ignoring my questions or talking too much to hear me. "I think they took him with Peter. I can't find him anywhere, Zelda, and believe me, I've looked. I—"

"Blake, focus," I ordered harshly. "Do you know where Peter is?"

"I mean, yeah, I know where the cell is, but Zelda, Dave is miss—"

"Take us to him," I pleaded, motioning behind me to the rest of my troop. "Take us to Peter. We'll figure out how to rescue him, and then you can leave the Society with us. It's a lot to process, I know, but there are people outside that can help us, help *you*. You just need to take me to Peter."

Blake eyed me in perplexity. "Are you listening to me? I said Dave is missing. He's been missing for months. I think Leader Caleb took him to the Jail. I thought you cared about him. Why aren't you—"

"Dave's fine," I snapped to shorten his unnecessary rambling. I found it slightly ironic that both he and Dave exhibited that quirk. "Dave's with me. He escaped with me months ago."

The Uniform stumbled backward, any color left in his face now drained as he asked, "What are you talking about?"

"Yeah," I confirmed nonchalantly, turning back to look at the rest of my squadron, although they seemed only focused on Blake and his reaction to the news. I followed their gazes and twisted around to see Blake gripping the corner of his kitchen island, doubled over and exhaling unsteadily.

"You told me he was here," Blake muttered disbelievingly.

I sighed and bounced on the balls of my feet anxiously. "Blake, c'mon. We can deal with this later. Please, can you take me to this special cell in the Jail? I'll find a way in. I just need you to get us in there safely. Dave said we could trust you to help us."

Blake picked his head up to glare at me, and the betrayal lining his pupils unsettled my stomach. "You lied to me."

I stole a glance at Gunther, and the two of us silently agreed to start taking cautious steps toward the door, the four other women quickly collecting their weapons and following our lead. Thankfully, opening the door this time wasn't as difficult. "Blake, no. I didn't lie. Dave is safe, I promise."

"You lied to me!" Blake roared, and before I could blink, the Uniform lunged for me, hands outstretched to coil around my throat.

I pushed off the wall with one hand to dodge his grip, and Gunther rammed his large fist into Blake's diaphragm, effectively slamming the wind out of the Uniform's lungs. Blake collapsed on impact, giving the six of us precious seconds we took full advantage of as we sprinted down the hallway, twisting and turning our way through the building's maze to rush into the stairwell.

"What now, Zelda?" Jannet asked as we raced down the steps, Blake not too far behind.

What now? Our entire plan had been dependent on Blake's collaboration, but we were far from getting that now. Forcefully breaking into the Jail and rescuing Peter ourselves looked like the only option we had left, and I told them so, foolishly promising that everything would be fine, so long as they stuck by me.

We burst from the Uniform building's lobby some minutes later, and our sudden presence shocked every Uniform in the vicinity. As they called my name as a signal for reinforcements, I nodded toward my loyal group, and we galloped toward the Main Square together.

Blake dashed out of the building, catching up to me and trying to pin me to the ground. I spun around and elbowed him straight in the face the second he put his hands on my torso, watching carelessly as he fell and cupped the area around his injured eye. Gunther agreed to cover me as I grabbed the gun from my pant pocket and shot at random, refusing to look where the energy bullets went in fear of witnessing my collateral damage.

As we sprinted, I noticed a group of four others running in the same general direction, and upon further inspection, I recognized the others as Dave, Eric, LeRoy, and Sasha. Stupidly, I screamed Dave's name to grab his attention, and he identified me instantly, instructing the rest of his group to integrate with mine as we ran toward the same section of the Society.

"Mr. Woobi? Lucy?" I inquired when Dave came up beside me.

"Captured," he explained breathlessly. "Too slow."

Damn, I thought. *Nothing about this night is going according to plan.* I wanted to rescue Mr. Woobi and Lucy, too, but the adrenaline pumping inside my body persuaded me not to care until later.

The Uniforms we rushed past paused when they saw us, their human shock getting in the way of their robotic duties for a few moments before they began firing at our zigzagging, sprinting forms. Blake hollered my name hatefully, still chasing after me. The chaos around us dizzied me, and I wished for some kind of respite when:

BOOM!

A massive explosion rocked the entire Society and sent me falling to my knees. I looked up hesitantly toward the sky; instead of beige, I saw the beautiful colors of dawn—muted pinks and magnificent purples reflected against navy blue clouds—and I knew the entire boundary had popped for the second time in its history.

For a moment, everything went still, and I genuinely feared my senses had died until thousands of shouts simultaneously echoed from the edges of the Society. The Uniforms paused to look to each other in utter confusion and panic, but I knew who they were. *Dassian's troops.*

The streets of the Society shook from the invasion of thousands of men and women into Societan territory, the screeches of gunfire, yelps of pride, and screams of pain mixing together in a hideously glorious way I knew no other species could emulate. Despite the increasing anxiety I felt building up in my chest, I pushed up from the ground and forced myself to keep running, faster and faster...

Zelda, my coworkers shout. They died here, in this Society. How did I not see their collective sacrifice coming?

I ran not just to reach Peter, not just to escape the Uniforms, but to outrun the gut-wrenching sound of my own name repeated inside my head.

Zelda, those slaughtered in the Massacre bellow. They died right outside the now-nonexistent border. Whose side was I on, truly: the one who killed, or the one who placed them in the position to be killed?

I tripped on my own feet, stumbling down to my knees once more and struggling to rise. My breath changed to uneven, ragged pants that I tried my best to contain but failed at doing so. I hyperventilated, and the lack of adequate oxygen to my brain made my body swim in lightheadedness.

Zelda, Will squeaks. He drowned in the waters surrounding my old home. Why didn't I?

Tears sprang into my eyes and blurred my vision, distorting my surroundings despite my best efforts to blink them away. I screamed. I punched. I kicked. Nothing worked. I couldn't escape these ghosts holding me hostage. Explosions. Gunshots. Fire. Terror. Grief. Anger. All in my head, yet another war I had to win.

Uniforms surrounded me. They pinned my arms behind my back much to my screeches of pain and fury; it did fill me with a strange sense of pride to know that it took five fully trained Uniforms to pin me down completely. I screamed for Dave, for Eric, for *anyone* to help me, but more and more Uniforms appeared and captured the rest of my friends when they all turned back to rescue me. When the Uniforms shoved me close to Dave for a split second, I pressed a quick kiss to his lips in fear it would be our last.

My spontaneous action made Blake drop to his knees and scream, "You used me!"

"Blake!" I whined, using the last of my strength to try and reach him at the sound of his voice. "Please, help me! Help *us!* Blake!"

But the Uniform I thought I could trust didn't move from his kneeling position on the pavement. He watched as I helplessly squirmed against the hold the Uniforms had on my arms, twisting around foolishly to try and break their grasp. I begged for Blake to help me in any way he could, but his dark eyes filled with boiling hatred, his harsh gaze fixated only on my desperate body trying to escape. I managed once to break free and went sprinting in his direction, but Uniforms tackled me to the floor right in front of him, my chin colliding forcefully with the concrete. "Blake, please…"

Blake stood up then, and a rush of relief went through my body. He stopped in front of me, his blood-red boots eye-level, and I heard him tell the Uniforms to bring me to my feet. Just as I opened my mouth to thank Blake for helping me, his hand connected with my cheek and sent my head spinning to the right, complete confusion clouding my judgment.

"I'll kill you," Blake threatened menacingly, slapping me again for good measure. He stepped back when I tried to make a grab for him, and he grinned when I struggled. "I'll kill you, Zelda Jadestone. I swear I will."

My cheeks burned from the blood rushing to them, and as I felt my left one beginning to throb, I shouted, "What did I do to you?!"

"You took what was mine," he growled, but before I could ask for an elaboration, he nodded at the Uniforms to take me away.

At first, I believed the Uniforms were leading all of us to the Jail, but as we drew closer to the Main Square, I noticed my captors began to separate me from the rest of my group. Dread filled my limbs when I saw the tall, black iron gate that protected Leader Caleb's building looming over my head. I yanked against the Uniforms' grips on my arms, dragged my feet, and twisted to dislodge their hold. My friends attempted to break free from their own Uniform jailors to save me, but they were much too slow, much too weak, and much too late.

Blake entered the code—5864737—to open the gigantic iron gates guarding the largest building in the Society, a structure that looked eerily similar to Dassian's, complete with a flagpole flying the Society's emblem to its right.

The Uniforms shoved me into the elevator, entered yet another code to take me directly to the fifteenth floor, and shut the doors in my face, trapping me inside the metal box until it opened again to reveal my new prison.

Stumbling into his office, I found the man himself looking out of the large, floor-to-ceiling windows at the destruction taking place below with his arms crossed in front of his lanky body, blond eyebrows furrowed in concentration as he turned to face me at the sound of the elevator doors creaking open.

We locked eyes, fire on fire, and I found the words I needed to say to him: "Caleb Woobi."

The leader of the Society nodded his head, never once breaking our gaze. "Zelda Jadestone."

"I brought my war."

"So you did." And then he smiled.

AUTHOR'S NOTE

In 1985, Sharbat Gula unintentionally became one of the most recognizable faces in the world when photographer Steve McCurry's portrait was plastered onto the front cover of *National Geographic*. Many revere the photo as one of the most beautiful, honest portrayals of the horrors faced by Afghani and Pakistani refugees during the Soviet war to this day. But it's a lie. Gula wasn't furious or scared of the war, but rather of the photographer himself as he took her out of her school and forced her to pose for his picture. Gula is nothing more than a child manipulated to satisfy the Western world's lust for tragedy. Westerners have this insatiable urge to claim we know how to heal the victims of catastrophe to feed our superiority complex. Zelda Ellyn Jadestone finds herself in a similar predicament; she is reduced to a newly roasted pig for the public's consumption, and boy, do they eat her story up.

This story is not inspired by Gula's—in fact, I only learned of Gula's story very recently, and I developed Zelda's story years ago—but I couldn't help but draw similarities after I read about Gula's struggles. Unfortunately, these two narratives are not uncommon. We see the same situation in this current political climate; politicians and media stations on both ends choose victims and exploit those misfortunes to further their respective agendas. Same deal, different packaging.

I hope you, as the reader of this novel, take a moment to pause and realize that although Zelda Ellyn Jadestone is fictitious, her story is all too real. Think of the children you put on your posters. As Zelda fans the flames, I hope this novel sparks a fire in you, too. Thank you.

ACKNOWLEDGEMENTS

I want to begin by thanking my immediate family: Averie, Ryan, Mom, and Dad. I could not have been blessed with a better group of individuals to call my sister, brother, mother, and father. You have put up with so much regarding my dedication to this series, from talking your ears off to locking myself up in my room for days at a time when "inspiration struck." Without your unwavering support, I do not think I would have been able to dedicate myself fully to this project, and for that, I owe you everything. I love you all.

Abigail Baxter, thank you once again for your steadfast support. I can feel your encouragement halfway across the country at any given time, and I thank God every day for that. You are the Dave to my Eric, the Sasha to my Zelda, the Lucy to my Harmony; basically, you are the shorter one in our inseparable duo. I love you to the edge of the universe and back again.

Thank you to my two strong, fiercely loyal grandmothers. I can always count on you to cheer on every single one of my endeavors, and for that, I am extremely grateful. I feel your love every day, and I hope I reciprocate that love.

Thank you to Aunt Lori and Uncle Grant, my personal comedians and the champions of Iowa merchandise and Emalie support. I do not know a way to thank you for the way you love me so unreservedly. This is my attempt: thank you, truly. I love you (and Archie, too, of course).

Thank you to the ones I have found in Iowa: Kayla Van Langen, Caitlyn Frahm, Ryleigh Collum, Julee Baker, and beyond. You have welcomed me with open arms and have embraced this series wholeheartedly, and I do not think I can repay you for how your support has helped heal my heart.

Thank you to you, the reader, for trusting me with your time. I sincerely hope this story has not disappointed. I will see you in the next, and final, one.

Thank you, Zelda Ellyn Jadestone. You are not real—I know that—but over the course of your creation and development, you have inspired me, have changed me, have naturally shaped me to become a better person. I am not even entirely sure how, either, but thank you anyway.

Thank you, Gramps. As always, the series is dedicated in your honor. I will continue to try and make you proud with each word I write, each step I take, and each sentence I utter. I miss you during milestones like these, but I know you are waiting for me somewhere in the stars, walker at the ready for me to sit on as we amble down Heaven's sidewalk together. We don't have to go fast this time, I promise. When I see you again, I want to walk slowly, the way you used to when you were here, so I can catch you up on things. I will have lots to tell you, I'm sure.

Lastly, thank you to Grandpa. You had lots of other names, too—Captain Bob, Grandpa Gaga, G'pa—but to me, you were simply Grandpa. You were simply my grandfather. You were the man who first taught me how to shift gears in a car. You were the man who read *Horrid Henry* books to me in silly voices that never failed to make me laugh. You were the man who took me to the Coral Gables Public Library and let me roam the dusty shelves for hours on end. You were the man who gave me the names "Zelda" and "Mr. Woobi" to use in this strange story I spontaneously created in the seventh grade. You were the man I read the beginnings of this story to at the dinner table. And I hope I am the granddaughter who publishes books you would be proud of (you never got to read them in action, but Zelda and Mr. Woobi didn't turn out all that bad, I'd say). I know I am the granddaughter who loves you and will continue to honor you in whichever way I can. Mark my words.